THE
PAINTED KISS

THE
PAINTED KISS

Elizabeth Hickey

WASHINGTON SQUARE PRESS
New York   London   Toronto   Sydney

WASHINGTON SQUARE PRESS
1230 Avenue of the Americas
New York, NY 10020

Copyright © 2005 by Elizabeth Hickey

ISBN-13: 978-0-7434-9260-7
ISBN-10:   0-7434-9260-9
ISBN-13: 978-0-7434-9261-4 (Pbk)
ISBN-10:   0-7434-9261-7 (Pbk)

First Washington Square Press trade paperback edition March 2006

10 9 8 7 6 5 4 3 2 1

WASHINGTON SQUARE PRESS and colophon are
registered trademarks of Simon & Schuster, Inc.

For information regarding special discounts for bulk purchases,
please contact Simon & Schuster Special Sales at 1-800-456-6798
or business@simonandschuster.com

Manufactured in the United States of America

FOR JONATHAN

Acknowledgments

Each of the following people has contributed immeasurably to the writing of this book: Catherine Drayton, Greer Hendricks, Rosemary Ahern, Suzanne O'Neill, Michael Albin, Pierce and Alexis Selwood, Jim and Anne Hickey, and, of course, my husband, Jonathan Selwood.

One

When I left Vienna, I took one thing: a thick leather portfolio with a silver buckle. I departed quickly and had to leave many things behind. A rosewood cabinet Koloman Moser made for me. Twelve place settings of Wiener Werkstätte silver, designed by Hoffmann. My costume collection. One of Fortuny's famous Delphos gowns. A pale yellow bias-cut satin gown by Madame Vionnet. Paul Poiret's sapphire blue harem pants and jeweled slippers. And the paintings. The most precious of all, they were too large and unwieldy to be taken on the train. And once I realized that the paintings could not travel, bringing yards of fabric, or a hatpin, or newspaper clippings and fashion magazines seemed ridiculous. What was I going to do, make a shrine of the remnants of my old life while the bolts of it sat in the closet of an abandoned apartment?

My niece Helene made the lists of things we'd need and packed up suitcases and went shopping for twine and woolen stockings and camphor liniment. I told myself that she needed to keep busy, that I was doing her a favor by letting her get everything ready, but that was just a lie I invented, an excuse for my empty-eyed catatonia. I couldn't have helped her because if I did I would have had to admit that we were actually going.

I stepped on the train as if I were going across town to deliver

[1]

the portfolio to a gallery, and this second lie was the only thing that kept me from throwing myself onto the tracks. I was afraid I would die without seeing the city again.

"Since when are you so histrionic?" my niece said. She's my sister Helene's child, and her namesake, but sometimes she reminds me more of my other sister, the practical one, Pauline. "You're getting to be like Grandmama," she said. "We're not going far, and for all we know the war will be over in six months." She handed me a hard roll with a thick slab of butter in the middle.

The train was packed with sweaty children wearing coats on top of jackets on top of sweaters and women carrying lumpy bundles of teakettles and soup pots and knives wrapped in linens. The women were thin and grim, their faces gray. Though their outer layer of clothing was presumably their best, nearly all of the skirts were stained and frayed, and the children's jackets were patched with scraps that did not match and coarse dark thread that only accentuated their pitiable condition.

We rolled slowly through the city, past the suburbs and the outlying towns, stopping frequently to load more and more of these families onto the train. Each time I thought the train could hold no more, but then at each station I saw the crowd and knew that we would make room for them. They piled onto the luggage racks; they stacked like bowls on each other's laps.

We passed barren hills where grapes once grew. We passed muddy fields where hundreds of people camped, cobbling together whatever shelter they could from pieces of tin and newspaper. We passed the Army barracks. Trucks full of soldiers crowded the roads.

I gave my roll to a chap-cheeked child on the floor next to me. She put the whole thing in her mouth and seemed to swallow it without chewing. Her mother's fervent gratitude shamed me.

Five hours later our train arrived at our station, two stops east of Salzburg, and deposited us in our exile. I can't pretend that we are here for the summer: the clouds are gunmetal gray and the lake is icy cold. The birches are naked and shivering. Up in the mountains it is snowing.

I have been lonely for my things. I have so much time on my hands.

I keep the leather case inside a Biedermeier cabinet in my bedroom. My father loved Biedermeier the way he loved a well-made pipe. It stands there, so crafted and finished and correct, a reproach for all that I'm not.

Sometimes in the afternoons, when the path to the lake is too muddy even for me and the thunder rolls through the valley like mortar shells, or perhaps it's the mortar shells rolling through the valley like thunder, I can't really tell them apart, I take the portfolio out of the cabinet and lay it on the bed. The thick hide is scuffed and scraped and smells of the fiacres that used to line up beside St. Stephen's. It looks out of place on the lacy eiderdown that's been mine since I was a little girl. I look at it for a minute, run my hand over it as if it were a doe I've killed, then I undo the buckle and upend the case so that all of the drawings inside fall onto the bed. One hundred and twelve of them, to be precise. I sit there on the bed next to the pile and pick them up sheet by sheet. I make smaller piles, subsets, arranging them according to pose, model, date. I grade them on how much I like them and put my favorites on top.

All of them are different: some of them are drawn with charcoal and some with graphite pencil and some with colorful oil crayons. Some are the size of my palm and others are folded many times to fit inside the leather case. Some are on thick heavy paper with a nubby finish, while others are on thin slick paper that slides through my fingers and onto the floor. Some of the drawings are already dull and brittle and break in my hands like rotted lace.

Yet they are all the same, too, because they are all of women in various stages of undress. They are quick, casual, a few lines, without contour or shading, tossed off in a minute or two. Weightless women, empty, like figures in a child's coloring book. Here is a woman astride the arm of a divan, twisting her torso in a languorous stretch. Here is a woman wearing a high-collared dress and boots, reaching underneath layers of petticoats to touch herself through a gaping hole in her knickers. Here is another, a woman with a direct gaze wearing garters and stockings and a blouse. Here is a drawing of a woman lying on her back with her legs thrown to the side, her buttocks dominating the page as her foreshortened shoulders and head barely register as a mark.

I know all of their names, these women. There is Alma, and Maria, and Mizzi, and Adele. Some of them I knew well and some of them I passed coming in and out of the studio and some of them I never saw, but I have thought of them and heard of them so much through the years that I feel intimate with each one of them. I know their lives.

When I said the drawings were all the same, I wasn't being strictly accurate. One is different. This one is of a man embracing a woman, who turns her face toward the viewer with an expression of simple bliss. I keep that one at the bottom because it hurts too much to look at it.

This was all I could bring from Vienna, Gustav's drawings. He never thought much of them or took them seriously as art, they were preparatory, exploratory, they were plans, blueprints, mistakes. But now they may be the only things of his to survive, and I must curate them for lack of something more important or finished. I must scrutinize them and draw parallels between them and place them in a historical context for someone, someone in the future who might be interested. In the meantime they are mine, and I am alone with them, and I look at them to keep them alive.

I find my way to the bureau by touch and I light the oil lamp. I walk over to the dressing table and sit before the mirror. My hair is white but still thick and wavy. My features are not as sharp as they once were. An artist would overlook some folds in my chin and neck so as not to hurt my feelings. But my eyes are as piercing as they were when I was twelve. I pull the combs out of my hair, ivory combs that were once my mother's, that my father bought her in Venice, and let it fall to my shoulders. Crone hair, Helene calls it. She thinks that women of a certain age should crop their hair very close, like Gertrude Stein. She tells me this as she plays with her dark fat braid, touched with the faintest frost. I think when she is seventy she will feel differently, but I just tell her that when I am dead she can do with me what she likes.

The bristles of my silver-backed brush are yellowed and soft with age and their shallow nudging has no effect whatsoever on my hair and its tangles. I reach into the drawer and pull out a pair of scissors.

I could gouge my thigh cutting a hole in my modest under-things. The skin of my thigh is tissue-thin. It wouldn't take much to finish me off, a little puncture wound that gets infected, a little blood poisoning. Or I could slice the cotton fabric like I was open-ing a box. The cutout would fall to the floor like a paper snowflake. I could move back to the bed and open my legs, pulling the skirt of my dress over my hips. I could put my hand in the hole I've cut and rub my fingers up and down. I could arrange myself into the poses in the portfolio. If I did, perhaps Gustav would appear, in the red caftan I made for him, looking like John the Baptist. I would model for him in a way I never did in life, and he would draw me the way he drew the others.

But I don't do any of those things and Gustav doesn't appear. Instead I put the scissors back in the drawer, blow out the lamp, and crawl into bed. Perhaps in sleep I can return to Vienna, to the studio. Perhaps in dreams the drawings next to the bed will become more than dull scraps of paper.

RECLINING NUDE, 1888

It is a very cold afternoon in the studio, but the transoms must be cranked open to keep the turpentine and other chemicals from poisoning the air. Gerta, with bones as light as straw and pale flesh like paraffin, stands with her wrists crossed in front of her breasts, waiting for instructions.

Gustav doesn't see her nakedness. She hardly registers as a woman to him. He sees a taxing problem of light and dark, of geometry, of volume.

"Could you cup your breast? The left, not the right. Good. Now could you lie down on the pallet? Open your legs. Turn that knee inward. All right."

Gerta does these things without comment, with the patient boredom of women who make money from their bodies. He draws her over and over, knuckles and knees, elbows and stomach. She does two-minute poses and thirty-minute poses. Gustav turns the pages on his drawing pad again and again.

It is early afternoon but it is already twilight and he works feverishly to beat the encroaching darkness. When he can work no more he tells her enough. Her flesh is goose-pimpled and sickly pale, he notices. The flesh under her toenails is purple. She has become a woman again, more than a visual exercise and also somehow less. He climbs the ladder and closes the transoms. She pulls on her chemise, her stockings. She buttons her dress and ties her boots. It all seems like such a wasted effort to him.

Would you like to stay? he asks. She nods.

There is a bed in the corner and he leads her over to it. While he undresses she waits, her head propped on one narrow hand. He sits on the bed next to her and unbuttons and unfastens and unties until she is naked again. Then he draws his palm across her skin as if his hand were a brush.

TWO

O n my twelfth birthday I went with my father and my two sisters, Pauline and Helene, to watch an imperial procession.

For the Viennese, an imperial procession was the most important event in the calendar. It was more important than Easter and Christmas put together, and the Viennese were in general very devout. It was as if God himself had chosen to come to Vienna and ride around town on the back of a horse. For me, as a child, to be able to witness such a spectacle was the most wonderful thing I could imagine.

We stepped into the street from our apartment building to the clangor of the noon bells at St. Ann's, on the corner. Faintly, like an echo, we could hear the bells at St. Stephen's, a mile away. They were pounding out the same Bach melody. We all turned to look up to the third-floor window where Mother was standing. She would not come with us, no matter how much we begged. She had no use for pageantry, she said.

Our building was so new it still smelled of cedar and whitewash. It was yellow stucco with stone Sirens gaping grotesquely from the cornices. It sat between the older, smaller buildings on either side like an oversize cat playing with two feeble gray mice.

We had moved there the year before, from a shabbier place a few blocks away. The ceilings were so tall that Papa could not touch them while standing on a stepladder. Plaster cupids on the moldings draped skeins of grapes. There was a tile stove in every room.

We waved good-bye to our mother and she waved back, but I knew she wasn't seeing us. She wasn't even hearing the bells. She was staring across the roofs of buildings toward the river and humming an aria she was composing to see if it worked. The acoustics in our new apartment were stunning and her full-size concert grand piano was the one thing we owned that looked like it fit.

Across the street the tobacconist was pulling his shutters closed, leaving early so that he could join in the festivities. My father ran over to buy a packet of tobacco. He bought a Turkish kind that came in translucent red-striped paper. He would smoke it at home, later, after we went to bed.

"Need anything, Georg?" Father asked as he examined the man's selection of pipes.

"It's a holiday, Mr. Flöge," answered Georg with a grin. "Why don't you worry about it tomorrow? Enjoy the day."

He gave each of us a plug of toffee and said he would see us later. Father was still writing things down in a little notebook. He told the tobacconist he'd send someone over in the morning.

My father owned a factory that made meerschaum pipes. He employed sixteen men in a small warehouse on the river. Since I was old enough to walk it had been a special treat to visit him there, and to watch the artisans at work. Many times I had watched a man pull a block of meerschaum from a tub of water. The quarried stone was soft and white as cheese. The man would carve into it with his knife, always knowing in advance exactly where to cut. He could dig from the mineral a horse, or a bull, or a plump-faced man, just like a sculptor. The men had different specialties: kings, caricatures of politicians, animals.

After the bowls of the pipes were carved they were fitted to their stems and fired in a kiln. Then they were polished and waxed. The apprentices did these things. When the pipes were finished they were light and smooth as eggshells, but stronger than porcelain. Flöge Meerschaum was embossed on each one in tiny gold letters. They were very popular and Father said that the emperor himself had one.

He never tired of telling us how lucky we were. His father had been a poor blacksmith and had died of tuberculosis before we were born, while we lived in a six-room apartment in Vienna, the most beautiful, cosmopolitan city in the world.

The medieval cobbled streets and marzipan-colored buildings were magical, and the dimly-lit shops selling sheet music or crystal goblets were enchanted, but I didn't know it yet. It was just the place I lived. I believed that all other cities, all other towns, must be similar.

But that day was different. We joined the crowds streaming like rainwater from the narrow alleys to the wide avenues and finally to the Ring, the road that had been built just decades before to replace the old medieval fortifications. It encircled the old town like a necklace, passing the emperor's palace and the government buildings and the new art museum. All kinds of people were on their way to watch the procession. The factories were closed. It was a school holiday. Even the university students were excused from classes.

Carts and carriages that were stopped by the throngs clogged the streets and the drivers cracked their whips against their wheels and shouted for people to move, but no one seemed really angry. Children were running into the streets with apples for the lathered horses.

The day was bright and hot. As we got closer to the Ring the shady streets where moss grew on the roofs gave way to wider, tree-less avenues where the monumental stone buildings offered little shade. I felt the pavement through the soles of my boots. Pauline remarked that we should have brought parasols. All of the ladies had them. They threatened to decapitate those near them with every step.

"Little girls don't carry parasols," snapped our father. "What's next? Low-cut evening dresses and beaux?" He gripped me tightly by one hand and my sister Helene by the other, as if someone might snatch us if he relaxed his grip for even a moment. If he could've carried Pauline on his back I'm sure he would have, but as it was she was ordered to hold on to my other hand. It made navigating through the crowds a complicated waltz.

Pauline looked as if she was going to remind him that Mother had been seventeen when she married, not much older than she was now, but she knew it was futile and so she bit her lip hard instead. I saw the drop of carnelian blood in the center of her lower lip. Father was overwhelmed with anxiety at the thought of steering three girls safely toward marriage, and his solution seemed to be to deny that we had grown up at all. Even Pauline had to wear the high lace collar of a little girl, though she had just turned seventeen. The challenge was not to scratch at it or squirm uncomfortably. Mother said it was good practice. She said that lace collars were nothing to corsets.

Across from the opera house we passed a silk tent. Shadows moved behind it. We could only guess at who was there and what was happening. Nobility were gathering there, sitting on velvet cushions and eating oysters. Their footmen filled their crystal glasses with cider. People milled nearby and waited to see who would alight from the carriages that kept arriving. We watched a thin man with a monocle and a variegated sash escort a plump woman in a turban into the tent.

In the crowd, boys sold commemorative newspapers and confetti, old men sold sausages with sweet mustard, old women sold roses. My father bought four blood-red ones from a woman in a gold bonnet for us to toss when the emperor passed. Some people around us held bouquets wrapped in paper. The street smelled of frying meat and horse manure.

It became increasingly crowded, and the throngs moved more and more slowly. I wished I were still young enough for my father to lift me on his shoulders. I was small for my age and there were people crowding me in front and on either side. I couldn't see the avenue where the procession would soon be.

"Don't worry," said Pauline. "When we get to the steps we'll be up high. Then we'll be able to see."

Next to me, Helene was worrying her neck through her lace collar and I could see red scratches like streaks of paint on her skin. I poked her; if Father saw we'd all be in trouble. Pauline showed us smugly how she didn't move her neck at all, turning her whole body when she wanted to look at something.

"What's wrong with you?" said Father, catching sight of her. "You look like a chicken."

Pauline didn't answer. "Why do you look so comfortable?" she said irritably to me. "You haven't squirmed all morning."

When Pauline had turned away I showed Helene my secret. Underneath my collar I had pinned a pilfered linen dinner napkin. It was practically invisible, and I could turn my head in comfort.

We looked almost like twins with our curly red hair, but Helene was nearly three years older than I. Sometimes she thought of things first, and sometimes I did, but we always shared our discoveries. We formed a strategic alliance against our proper older sister, our rule-bound father, and our mercurial mother. In sartorial matters, Pauline was our most dangerous adversary. It wasn't just the lace collars. It was the enormous hair ribbons ruthlessly attached to our scalps with pins. It was the vigorous scrubbing of our chapped hands with freezing-cold water. It was the precise calculation of how long each of our steps should be, and the angle at which we should hold the prayer book in church. She watched us all of the time, and when she couldn't, Father did. Our mother could leap to our defense or come down on us hardest of all, and we never knew which it would be. But Helene I could always depend on.

"How did you get it?" she whispered to me.

I told her about the elastic band I'd placed around my thigh so that I could hide the napkin under my skirt.

"You're crazy," she said admiringly. "What if you'd been caught?"

She couldn't figure out when I could have found the opportunity to hide my napkin at one of our formal, silent, and endless dinners. I sat with Father on one side and Pauline on the other. My hands, since they held the glass and the knife, fork and spoon, were always being watched. I might spill something, or hold my knife in a bar-baric way, or take bites that were too big, and these errors must be quickly and harshly corrected. I suspected that since there was little conversation, it gave Father and Pauline a way to pass the time.

I reminded her that Mother had had a coughing fit at dinner the Thursday before last, and said that I had taken the opportunity when Father was pounding her on the back and Pauline was up getting water for her to drop my fork.

"What are you two giggling about?" Father asked, not very kindly.

We said nothing, trying not to look at one another. Sometimes that alone could set us off again. I felt that my face was pink and hot, and my lungs were full of unexploded laughter. Beside me I felt Helene shaking.

"Well, compose yourselves," Father said, and when he spoke in that tone all of the merriment inside of us died.

A balding man in spectacles passing us checked the fob on his coat and announced to no one in particular, "They should be here in twenty-six minutes."

We passed a woman selling ices from a painted cart.

"Would you girls like an ice?" Father asked. We were stunned. Normally we were not allowed to eat sweets, and certainly not from a street vendor.

Pauline looked doubtful. "Really, Papa? Are you sure it's all right?" Helene and I held our breath and squeezed the other's hand tightly.

"It's Emilie's birthday, after all," he said. When he smiled, which wasn't often, his ruddy face was briefly handsome. He gave the money to Pauline. "Don't be shy. Go right up to her."

The woman called out to the crowd: "Hurry! Get an ice before they melt! It's getting warmer by the minute!"

We stood in line in back of a woman carrying a green parrot in a wire cage and watched the ice woman shaving ice for the cus-tomers ahead of us. Her arms were very tanned and she wore a red apron embroidered with fruit: lemons and pears and pineapples.

Off to the side, a little girl in a white dress and expensive boots was screaming. Though she looked to be about ten, I noted with envy that her parasol was made of pink lace and that the embroidery on her dress was like nothing I'd ever seen. I think it was her clothes that made me watch her so carefully. That, and the scene she was making. I'd never seen a little girl throw a fit in public. No one I knew would have dared.

"Adele," a man said, "you know we don't eat things sold on the street." He was her father; he was large and lumpy and had a dark mustache. This only made her scream louder. Helene and I exchanged looks.

Her father was embarrassed. Next to him, her stylishly dressed mother tapped her foot.

"Shame on you!" her father said. "People will think you don't love the emperor."

"I hate the emperor," the little girl said. "I hate the emperor." She said it a little louder this time. The people next to them pretended not to listen.

"I hate the emperor," she shouted. Her mother took her by the shoulders and looked into her eyes for a long time. Then the mother shrugged. "Buy the girl an ice."

Her father wouldn't let her go to the cart with him. So I watched her standing off to the side while he got into line. Her eyes gleamed like emeralds.

Then it was our turn. The woman shaved some ice into paper cups and asked us what flavor we wanted. There were three kinds: strawberry, cherry, and lemon. We decided to get one of each. She poured the syrup from three different watering cans onto our ice. Pauline handed her a coin, which she put in a leather belt at her waist. Then she wiped her face in her apron and went on to the next.

We waited, licking our ices, to see what the girl would do. When it was her father's turn he fumbled in his pocket for the money. The woman in the apron teased him but he didn't smile. He held the ice awkwardly, as if it were a small animal. When he returned to the girl he handed the paper cone to her without looking at her. If he had looked at her he would have seen that Adele held the cone without tasting it until it melted down her arm and dried into a sticky poultice. The sleeve of her beautiful embroidered dress was stained sickly pink.

When we got back to our father he was talking to a man we didn't know. The man was wearing a threadbare sack suit and a pink daisy in his buttonhole. We had never seen a man wearing anything like that. He was not tall, but broad-shouldered and strong-looking. He was tan like the woman selling ices. He was carrying a leather case in one hand and what looked like a toolbox in the other.

We hung back shyly.

"He's not wearing a hat," whispered Pauline.

"Maybe he's a Gypsy," said Helene.

"Here are my daughters," our father said. "Girls, come and meet Mr. Klimt."

"How do you do, Mr. Klimt." We curtsied as we had been taught, trying not to spill our ices. As I bobbed my head I could see that the man was laughing at us.

"I feel like an old man, or a prince," he said. "Everyone calls me Gustav. And no one ever curtsies."

"Mr. Klimt is a painter," Father said, as if that would explain it all: the suit, the flower, the tan, the laugh, everything.

"I'm on my way to set up an easel near the art museum. My brother is already over there. It's good publicity. And sometimes people pay us a little to make a drawing, which doesn't hurt." He winked at us. None of us knew what to do. Could we eat what was left of our ices, or was that rude? Helene tried to quietly sip the juice in the bottom of her cup, but Pauline kicked her.

He said he had some ideas about a new style of pipe. It had a smaller bowl with some complicated combination of walnut veneer and gold filigree. My father listened and seemed interested. He thought Klimt should come by the factory sometime and show him the drawings.

Then Father said we had to hurry on, and shook his hand. Klimt bowed and was gone, moving through the crowd, but he turned around once and smiled at us.

We walked on, toward the Rathaus. I was quiet, thinking about the man. New people did not appear very often in our closely chaperoned, narrowly circumscribed lives.

I wanted to watch Klimt draw. I knew Papa would never agree; we only had a few minutes to make it to our place.

"Papa, there's Anna Vogel," I said. "Can I go over and say hello?"

"Where?" said Helene, scanning the crowd for our school friend. I pinched her.

"Quickly," he said. "Be on the steps in ten minutes." I tried not to run.

A small knot of people was gathered behind Klimt and a thin boy with a smock tied on over his suit. That must be his brother, I thought. They were unfolding what looked like wooden music stands and clipping paper to them. I stood behind, peering into the spaces between men's elbows, trying to get closer.

An old woman passed carrying two pheasants tied around her neck with string. Impulsively, Klimt called out to her and motioned to the birds. Money changed hands and Klimt wound up with one of them. The woman bowed her thanks and chattered in a language I didn't understand. I thought it was Polish.

Klimt shook his head and backed away, but she followed him, waving the second bird by its floppy neck. Finally he relented and gave her the money. He draped them over his easel.

Then, haltingly, Klimt asked the woman in her language if he could sketch her. At first she said no quite adamantly, but the crowd around her started to clap and cheer. Men pushed her toward the empty circle around the easel. Klimt smiled and beckoned. Finally, laughing, she agreed.

Despite the warm weather, the woman wore so many wool sweaters that she resembled a ball of yarn with feet. She was like a doll with a dried apple for a head and silk floss for hair. I looked at her, and then at the paper, then back again, watching as a line appeared here, then there, trying to see as Mr. Klimt saw her. It was impossible. There was a dark triangle, then a haystack of crossed lines, a few ovals, and she was there. How had he done that?

When Klimt gave her the drawing he had done she giggled like a child and gave him a small cloth pouch filled with hazelnuts.

Slowly I worked my way through the tightly woven crowd until I was standing right behind the thin brother. Dimly I realized that I had better return to my father and my sisters, and that I would be in trouble when I appeared, but it didn't matter. I had to get closer.

By some silent sign they had agreed and were both sketching two shop girls who were standing with their arms around each other, talking about bonnet trimmings. Yellow silk flowers or lace with delft blue ribbons, which would be nicest? Look at the rich lady with the hummingbird in her hat. How wonderful to be able to afford such things! The brother used a pencil, I noticed, while Klimt was holding a thick piece of black chalk in his fist like a fish he'd just pulled from a lake. He worked quickly and turned the page of his pad over when he'd finished. I barely had time to examine them before they were gone.

When they saw the artists looking at them the two girls blushed and ran away. I could see the last rough sketch that Klimt had made, and there was no doubt as to whom it was. In a moment he had captured their self-conscious slouching, their excited eyes, the way they leaned into one another.

Then two university students stumbled by and asked to have their portraits done for a few shillings. The brother said no. "We choose our subjects," he said. "They don't choose us." The crowd laughed at the drunken boys, who looked surprised, as if it had never occurred to them that anyone might find them less than worthy subjects. As it slowly dawned on one of them that he was being rejected, his face flushed with anger.

"Look here, you," he said, poking the brother in the chest and nearly knocking his easel over.

Then Klimt stepped in front of his brother, into the path of the student's fists. "Speak for yourself," he said. "Personally I would be honored to sketch these gentlemen." For a moment the brother looked as if he might hit Klimt, but then he smiled and shrugged and went back to his easel.

The students leaned against one another and affected postures of great wisdom. Their gowns were too long and trailed in the dust. Klimt, in a few curving strokes, managed to delineate their extreme youth, their skinniness like starving dogs, their drunken eyes. He and his brother both ripped the papers from their easels and presented them to the students, who were pleased beyond all sense, the argument forgotten. They dumped their pockets for them. They showed the sketches to anyone who would look at them. Then they folded them into tiny squares and walked away. I winced when they folded the papers. The magical drawings looked like trash folded up like that. The students would probably forget about them in ten minutes and carelessly lose them. Klimt didn't seem to notice the rough treatment of his drawings. He was counting the money.

Next to him his brother had begun to sketch a Hungarian couple in the brightly embroidered national costume. Klimt came and stood in front of him, blocking his view. People had begun to drift away, but I couldn't move.

"We're artists, not street beggars," Klimt's brother hissed angrily.

"Where did we get this charcoal?" Klimt said calmly. "And this paper?"

"From school," said the brother sullenly.

"We took the paper out of the garbage pail and wiped it clean. We got the charcoal off the floor. With this money we can actually buy some supplies."

The brother clearly did not like to admit that Klimt was right.

"We have enough to get a piece of cake at the café," said Klimt, in a way that told me that this was his brother's weak point. Then they both laughed.

"How much did we get?" asked the brother.

"Stupid kids, they gave me ten shillings for a drawing I wouldn't wipe my ass with."

My head spun. The artists were so poor that they pulled paper out of trash bins and used them. They had almost caused a brawl. Their language was vulgar and frightening. I was repelled, and yet fascinated. I had never met anyone like them.

Suddenly the only thing I wanted in the world was for Gustav Klimt to draw me. I had no money, but I thought if I got in his line of sight maybe I could do something interesting to attract attention. Then someone shouted that the carriages had been spotted and everyone rushed to the street. I ran to the steps of the Rathaus. Helene's red hair stood out like a beacon, and when I saw it I slowed to a walk and slipped into place beside her.

"Where were you?" hissed Father. I tried not to breathe too fast or hard and give myself away.

"I'm sorry," I said.

"After all I've indulged you today," he said. "You ought to be ashamed."

"There he is!" said Helene.

I forgot that Father was angry and jumped up and down in an effort to see better. Pauline craned her neck in a distinctly unladylike way. Even Father was straining and waving.

The emperor rode on horseback, and he looked very brave and strong. The epaulets on his coat and his hands on his knees remained perfectly still as the horse trotted past. A corps of soldiers encircled him.

"What does he look like?" asked Pauline, though she'd seen his picture a hundred times.

"Like a sad walrus," I shouted. I was elated; I had caught the emperor's eye, and he had smiled at me.

Pauline looked shocked. Helene giggled. "That's no way to talk about the emperor," said Father.

"When have you even seen a walrus?" asked Pauline.

"A zoological book. At school." I tried to explain how his upturned mustache made him look as though he were smiling, though his eyes were sad. I tried to explain how he had smiled at me.

"He is not smiling at you," Father said. "You aren't anyone. He is smiling at Vienna."

The soldiers that followed the emperor on foot had horsetail tassels on their helmets and marched in a formation like a flock of geese, kicking up dust and pounding out a tune with their footfalls. Their commander shouted commands, and they raised their rifles and shot into the air. The crowd cheered.

The carriage behind the soldiers came into my view then. It was filigreed like a page of music. The grand horses pulling it had garlands around their necks and pink and yellow ribbons braided into their white manes.

"What do you see?" Pauline cried impatiently.

"She's got her veil on inside the carriage," I said. "She's not even looking at the crowd."

"She" was the empress, of course, the one we had really come to see. It looked as if we would be disappointed. We were resigned though; she hadn't been seen in public in five or six years.

Then the window of the carriage was pushed open, just a little. A glove appeared and gripped the gilt whorls that framed the window. Not just any glove, either. A glove of the softest kid, dyed black and trimmed with what I now know was maribou. The hand reached out toward the crowd, tentatively touching the air, not quite waving. A sleeve—the most delicate lace sleeve shot with golden threads—dangled from the glove, blowing a little in the breeze, and that was all. The carriage passed and was gone.

Three

At breakfast the next day Papa read us an article in the newspaper about the Klimt brothers. They'd been hired to paint the murals for the new theater that was being built not far from where we lived. Papa said it was a very prestigious commission for such young artists.

There was so much more I wanted to know: what were they going to paint? How did they paint the ceiling? What kind of paint did they have? Was it like the paint on the walls of our apartment? But Papa brushed my questions aside.

"I'm late," he said. "And so are you."

We went to a convent school next to St. Ann's church. Everyone there was very nice to us in a pitying sort of way because we were Protestant, which meant in practice that when the Host came by in chapel we had to cross our hands across our chests into an X. It always felt to me that we were pronouncing ourselves excommunicated. In principle it meant that we were going to hell. Why they bothered to educate us if this were true the Sisters never said. Mother told us not to listen to them when they talked to us that way.

The stone interior of St. Ann's, where we said Mass, was stained with age and the air inside was sweet and murky with incense. Candles hung from wrought iron cages like instruments of medieval torture. White-robed figures glided by with censers lighting and extinguishing candles. Christ was dying everywhere and with much suffering: on the stained-glass windows he performed the stations of the cross bleeding and crying and falling again and again, on the frescoed ceiling he wore the crown of thorns. On the tapestries that covered the cold walls he was wrapped in a shroud, he was lying in the tomb. Father told us not to look at it, it was barbaric and blasphemous, but it was hard neither to look nor listen. Next I thought they would tell me to hold my nose so as not to inhale the sandalwood and myrrh as it wafted through the air.

The school was housed in the nearby convent that was nearly as old as the church. The flue was clogged with centuries of soot and our eyes were often stinging red when we came home. The nuns were the only ones who would teach girls Latin and mathematics and philosophy, and that's why we went there. Father was afraid that his business would collapse and we wouldn't be able to support ourselves. He didn't say why it would collapse; there were things out there, invisible malignant hands, trying to pull him down. At least that's what it seemed like to me, listening to him talk. Mother had been pulled out of school when her own mother died and never got over it. You will be educated, she said darkly, no matter what happens. So in their different ways, united only by a sense of doom and helplessness, they encouraged our educations.

In the mornings the three of us walked to school together. We walked home again for lunch. After school we would sometimes invite friends to our apartment. More often the three of us would entertain ourselves. On Saturdays we might walk in the park, or listen as our mother played the piano.

She had wanted to be a pianist, and her teacher thought she had talent. Instead, she did what she was supposed to and got married. My father loved to hear her play, but he had no idea that pounding out Strauss tunes for him at home did not satisfy her. Intermittently she tried to be a good bourgeois wife and mother, but most of the time she forgot. She was too abstracted, lost in compositions that could only be played for us.

That was my entire world. I had no contact with the musicians who played at the Opera, or the men who taught at the University, or anyone, really, outside my family and my schoolmates. Occasionally I went to the market with Mother and looked longingly at the girls who came in from the country with their families to sell cheese, or sturgeon, or rabbits. They stood outside in all weathers, calling to people as they passed, flirting with customers, making change, wrapping things into parcels and tying them with string. It seemed so much better than my own life. Their hands were red and chapped, but they were doing something useful. And they were free, at least freer than I was.

When I was supposed to be doing my homework I drew in one of my school notebooks. I drew little girls with curly hair and giant eyes. Their heads were always too big for their bodies. I drew dancers arabesquing but couldn't figure out how the neck melted into the back. My dancers all had jutting shoulder blades like fish fins. I attempted to draw Helene while she slept and only succeeded in terrifying her when I threw my slate and the paper it held across the room in disgust. I had more luck drawing clothes than the people who wore them. I drew the empress's beautiful glove, and tried to recreate her dress, even though I had only seen the sleeve. I thought the dress must be brocade of a golden peach color. It would not have a princess collar, but would plunge from little cap sleeves adorned with skeins of pearls. Fastened to the shot-gold lace at her décolleté would be the largest ruby brooch anyone had ever seen. Of course such a dress would not provide much warmth, so I designed a white fox cape and matching hat. I was quite satisfied with the results.

Once I had drawn the dress, I was inspired to play drawing room. We gathered some of Mother's old evening dresses from a hall closet and supplemented them with various scarves, robes, tea towels, jewelry, whatever we could find. We were forbidden to touch any of it, of course, but Mother was in bed with a headache and wouldn't appear until supper, which was hours away.

When we were dressed Helene began choreographing a dance inspired by a famous troupe of dancing sisters. Every so often one of us ran to the bed and ate from a bag of chocolates we had smuggled into the house after school.

Our dancing quickly unraveled into quarreling. Helene had teased me about my clumsy dancing, which only made me clumsier, and I stepped on the hem of my dress and tore it. I believe I then hit her with my shoe. Pauline came between us and caught a heel in the eye, which made her scream. I ran away before I could be evicted from the game. So there I was, not dancing, pouting in the windowsill.

Helene tried to entice me back. She held out her arms to me and fluttered them in what was an annoyingly passable imitation of a sylph, though her gray silk taffeta robe was much too big and hung from her arms like laundry on a clothesline. Then she began to sing. Helene knew that when she sang she was nearly irresistible. She had a high, clear voice like a choirboy. Her bright hair curled around her face like a Raphael. But I was her sister, not an admiring teacher or a proud parent or a gushing parishioner. I ignored her. She finished a stanza and then, when she got no response, stopped.

"You're just being lazy," said Pauline, who was really too old to be playing this game but had done it to humor us. She was squeezed into a high-waisted pink organza evening dress and looked like an overstuffed pillow.

She didn't like our games much anyway. Pauline was practical like our father. She was the only one who could soothe Mother when she had one of her hysterical crying fits, and the only one who could make the noodle pudding with cinnamon and raisins the way that father liked it. I thought she was depressingly lacking in imagination.

I said nothing. I opened and closed the clasp on the rose-shaped brooch I was wearing on my sash. The jewels in the brooch were pasteboard, of course, but they looked remarkably like rubies and pink diamonds.

Helene shrugged at Pauline. They were used to my sulks. They returned to their dancing, which required a lot of intricate work with scarves. It was hard not to get them tangled up. In fact, the dance had to be interrupted frequently for untangling and arguments over who was to blame. I half-listened to them as I watched the people passing below.

Fortunately for me, the street on which we lived was a very busy one. There was always someone interesting passing by. I watched a woman with a velvet cloak pulled tight around her throat step into the apothecary. I recognized her as a well-known soprano. I wondered if something was wrong with her voice. When she came out a few minutes later she was reading the label on the back of a small bottle as she walked. She nearly collided with two doctors with leather satchels and worried expressions. I saw one of the drunken students that the artist Gustav Klimt had drawn. He no longer looked drunk, but his hair was very messy and he was quite pale and in a rush. He dashed past my building and out of sight.

Just as Helene was saying that Pauline looked like a goat and Pauline was about to cry because she did a little, with her close-set brown eyes and long face, I saw something I couldn't believe. Someone was at the door. It was a small man carrying a valise in one hand and a cane with a glittering handle in the other. He set the case down and rang our bell. Then he took off his hat to let the wind ruffle his hair, and he looked up, directly at me.

It was Gustav Klimt.

He smiled and bowed to me with a flourish of his hat. I nearly fell off the window seat in my haste to hide. Pauline and Helene stopped dancing.

"What?" Helene said.

"He's here," I said.

"Who?" said Pauline. She gasped when I told her.

I didn't tell them about the bow. I don't know why. It was something special that set me apart. "But what's he doing here?" said Helene.

No one ever came to our house except the doctor. It was puzzling why this artist we'd never heard of until a few weeks ago was now standing at our door. We waited, peering around the curtains. When the door opened and Gustav Klimt disappeared into the building, we crept into the hall and leaned over the banister, straining to hear.

Mother took him into the parlor, leaving the valise and the cane in the hall, a sure sign that he was staying awhile.

Then we ran up the stairs and into our room as fast as we could, because Mother had come out of the parlor and was coming up the stairs. We stripped off the evening dresses and hid them in the armoire. By the time she arrived we were in our regular clothes and arranged in a slightly breathless tableau: Helene and I looking out the window, Pauline reading at the desk.

She frowned at us and said, "It's no good trying to look innocent. Your faces are too pink." We weren't sure whether she meant that she knew about the dresses, or knew that we knew about Klimt, so we all tried to look chastened but not say anything to give ourselves away.

"What is it Mother?" asked Pauline, not very convincingly. "We heard the bell."

"Mr. Klimt is here." Our mother was fond of dramatic pauses. Helene couldn't wait.

"Why? Why is he here?"

"Your father has asked him to draw your portraits."

We stared at one another. Pauline looked horrified, but Helene looked as excited as I felt.

"Don't keep the poor man waiting down there," said Mother. "Straighten yourselves up, put on your school blouses, and come downstairs."

"Our school blouses?" said Helene.

"That's what your father wants."

I nearly cried. Our school blouses were thin white cotton, with a plain neck and a bib-like appendage hanging over the chest. The bib-like appendage was embroidered with cheap floss because we'd been forced to do it ourselves. Pauline's had turned out all right, but Helene's, and especially mine, were poorly done. It was like performing at a dancing recital in my nightgown. I might've tried to slip past my mother in something else, but then I heard Father come home early from the factory. He was going to chaperone the sittings.

When we were dressed we brushed our hair and sighed over our complexions.

"If I had known I would've done the honey milk bath," said Helene, who already glowed like a Madonna. I pinched her.

"Or the cucumber walnut scrub," said Pauline. "That's what the empress does when she's about to be photographed."

Pauline went first. While we waited Helene and I tried to imagine what was going on behind the closed parlor door. The wood was so heavy we couldn't hear anything, even when we stood right up against it. Helene, who was shy around people she didn't know, was afraid she'd have to talk to him. I thought it would be more awkward to sit there and not say anything.

We listened for the clock in the hall chiming on the quarter hours. Six passed before Pauline emerged. We scanned her face for a clue. She looked sleepy and dazed.

"Helene," Papa called. With a terrified look she disappeared behind the door.

I quizzed Pauline about her time in the parlor but all she would say was that it wasn't worth getting excited about. When I asked what Klimt was like, she shrugged. When I asked what they talked about, she said she didn't know. The clock chimed, then chimed again. At last it was my turn.

When I went in Father was sitting in the corner of the room reading the paper. The air around him was dim with smoke and smelled of leather and cinnamon. He smiled at me but then went back to his paper, leaving me standing nervously in the doorway. The painter was standing in the middle of the room in front of a spindly-looking easel.

"Was that in your valise?" I asked in surprise. I was so curious about all of his things that I forgot it was rude for a girl to be too curious or to ask too many questions.

Klimt laughed. "Handy, isn't it?" he said. "Let me show you." He laid his paper on the sofa and deftly folded the easel until it resembled a bundle of kindling. I remembered I had seen it before.

"Oh yes, you had one like that the day of the procession."

He smiled. "You remember." He held the bundle out for me to take. I saw when I got closer that he had patches of red in his beard.

The easel was surprisingly light. "Wouldn't it blow away?" I asked.

"Emilie," my father called, "stop badgering Mr. Klimt and do as you're told."

"It's all right," Klimt said to my father. "Open it up and see," he said to me. I unfolded the easel and saw that its three legs, splayed wide apart, made it more stable than it looked. He took the easel from my hands and moved it back to the middle of the room.

I stood while Klimt attached some paper to the easel with what looked like clothespins. I waited for him to tell me what to do. When he was finished with the paper he turned around but didn't say anything. He crossed his arms over his chest and stared at me. It made me very uncomfortable, but I tried not to squirm.

"Well," he said. I waited. The expression on his face was alarming in its intensity. I couldn't wait any longer. I rocked from one foot to the other and scratched my face, though it didn't itch.

"What should I do?" I asked. It was if I had woken him from a trance.

"Sit in the red chair, and be as still as you can. If I want you to move I'll move you." He spoke abruptly, almost rudely.

I sat the way I had been taught in my posture lessons. When Klimt turned to me he sighed. He came to stand just inches from me and frowned. His jacket smelled of cedar shavings, as if it had been stored for a long time.

"How would you sit if you could sit any way you wanted?"

No one had ever asked me such a question. It didn't matter to anyone what I wanted, only what they wanted. I looked at him blankly.

"I don't know, sir," I said.

"No idea?" he said.

"No, sir," I said.

"All right," he said. He looked tired all of a sudden. "Stay that way, if you like. Do me a favor though, and look straight at your father and don't move."

My father was not nearly as interesting as the artist and his drawing, so it was hard to keep looking at him. Klimt put a smock on over his jacket, which made him look like an apostle. He stood in front of the easel and chewed at the end of a pencil while he looked at me. It was hard not to fidget. I tried to smile prettily.

"Do you normally smile?" he asked.

"Not very much, sir," I said.

"Well, then, by all means don't smile now," he said. "Just a normal expression, please."

"How do I look, Papa?" I asked, wanting Klimt to hear me praised. Father set his paper aside and glanced over, but he barely seemed to see me. "Very fine," he said. He tried to think of the highest praise he could bestow. "You look like your mother," he said, which I knew wasn't true. My mother was beautiful. She had glossy chestnut hair and a soft, round face. My father, his task accomplished, lifted his paper again and immediately fell asleep.

Klimt didn't have any paint, only some chalks lined up on a piece of wax paper. A glass of water was next to them. I wanted to ask him what they were for, but I had remembered my manners. He saw me looking at them.

"I use the water to wet some of my lines," he said. "It creates a different effect, as you will see."

He was looking at me so closely that I blushed. I hoped he wouldn't notice, but I knew that was unlikely. No one had ever looked at me like that before. It made me want to crawl underneath the sofa.

"Do you always spy out of the window at visitors?" he said. I noticed that the tendons in his wrist as he drew were as taut as the mainstay of a sail.

"Excuse me?" I said, pretending I didn't know what he was talking about.

"When I rang the bell you were at the upstairs window."

"Was I?" I said. "I didn't see you." He stopped drawing a moment and grinned at me. Just then he reminded me of my friend Ulrike's older brother, who liked to pull our hair and punch our shoulders and trip us at every opportunity.

"What do you look at when you stare out of the window?"

"People," I said. "I like to look at what they are wearing, and the way they walk. Some people are fast and others sort of waddle, or hobble. I see some of the same people every day, and some days they look cheerful and other days not. Some days they're alone and some days they're with their families. It's interesting."

"So you haven't had all the personality trained out of you after all," he said. He went back to work.

"What do you want to be when you grow up?" he said next. He had figured out by now that I had trouble avoiding direct questions.

"An actress," I said. This time he didn't grin. He kept his eyes on his paper. "Have you been to see many plays?" he said.

I had to admit I hadn't.

"I don't go often, but I know a lot of actresses," he said. "Some of them model for me for extra money."

What I knew about actresses I had gleaned from the papers, and from watching the ones I recognized parade down the Mariahilferstrasse. They were always stylishly dressed, and carried themselves with such grace it was hard to imagine them needing extra money, though if their modeling involved what I was currently doing, it didn't seem so bad.

"They're not as glamorous as you think," he said as if he could read my mind. "They're all right. Poor, most of them. It's not an easy life, you know. You're much better off here with your parents."

That made me angry. How did he know what it was like with my parents? But I wasn't allowed to contradict an adult.

"Sometime I'll take you to the theater," he said. "You'll see."

Then he furrowed his brow and stopped drawing. He stepped back and looked at his paper for a minute, then went back. But he was still frowning. I wondered what I had done wrong. He put down his pencil and came over to where I was sitting.

"I don't like your hair this way," he said.

"This is how we wear it at school," I said.

"It's ugly," he said. Roughly I started to pull the bow out but he stopped me.

"Let me," he said. His hands moved toward my face and I saw that they were stained brown in places.

"No, thank you," I said. "I can do it myself."

"All right," he said. He backed away slowly. He went to the window and opened one of the casements. I struggled with the ribbon, yanking at it until tears sprung to my eyes, but Pauline had pinned it with ferocious thoroughness, and without a mirror I couldn't pull it loose.

Klimt came back.

"I promise I won't hurt you," he said. "Now, let me take your hair ribbon out." He was very gentle with the tangled parts.

"We must put it up properly," he said when he was finished. "Do you have a pair of combs?" It surprised me, that Klimt should be so familiar with a feminine accessory like a comb. Papa could never remember what they were called and referred to them as "hair contraptions." I looked over at my father but he was still snoring underneath his paper.

"Shall I go look for some?" I said. I went into the hall. No one was there. I heard mother in the kitchen, singing Verdi. I ran upstairs to her room and opened her jewelry box. Inside were strands of pearls and a diamond bracelet, a gold watch, as well as a variety of pins and combs. Mother had several plain tortoiseshell combs for everyday, and then there were the small cloisonné combs she had bought when she and Father went to Paris. Dare I borrow them? I conveniently decided that Father would like the portrait even more if he saw them.

Back in the parlor, I sat in the chair again and let Klimt put up my hair. When he was finished he stepped back to look at me and seemed pleased.

"It's much better this way because the line of your jaw will show more clearly."

That didn't make sense to me. I'd always been told that my jaw was too strong, unfeminine. I was told that I should camouflage it at all costs. Why was he going to play up my worst feature? I began to suspect that the drawing would not be what I hoped.

"Do they teach much drawing at your school?" he asked as he worked.

"A sketching teacher came for a while, but then he left to do military service and they didn't get another one."

"Did you like drawing?"

My foot was asleep and my neck was getting a crick in it, which is the only explanation I can offer for what I said next.

"Not very much," I said. "It bored me." Immediately I clapped my hands to my mouth in horror, completely forgetting that I was supposed to remain still. I looked over at my father. He was still asleep and could not have heard me. I waited for Klimt to scold me and threaten to tell my parents how insolent I was. But to my surprise, he laughed.

"Maybe it comes too easily for you. People like me, who have to work very hard just to be competent draftsmen, don't get bored with drawing."

I was afraid to open my mouth again, for fear something rude would come out.

"What did you draw that was so boring?" he asked.

"It was always the same still life," I said. "Two glass bottles, three apples, and a bunch of grapes."

"You can learn a lot about volume and light and shadow drawing apples and bottles, you know. And grapes! They're too difficult for beginners."

I fervently hoped that the subject could now be dropped.

"What do they teach at your school then, if not drawing?"

"History, German, mathematics."

"Sewing?" he asked, glancing at my blouse.

"Once a week," I said.

"Tell your teacher it should be every day," he said. He was laughing at me.

"I will, sir," I said as politely as I could.

We were quiet for a while. I heard the clock chime three, four, then five more times. I wondered why my drawing had taken the longest. Finally, he turned his page around. "What do you think?" he asked.

My twelve-year-old vanity immediately sustained a mortal wound, seeing myself through the artist's eyes. The drawing showed just my head and shoulders. There was my jaw, jutting like a rock formation on a mountainside. My mouth was grim and stern, like a general's. My eyes were glowing with light like rays of sun. How had he done that with just chalk? The little of my body that showed was indistinct, just a round white blouse shape with just a hint of a peach glow underneath to indicate flesh. He'd left the parlor out completely, the red chair, the wallpaper. For background he'd simply rubbed an apricot shade over the paper with the heel of his hand. I thought if this was what I looked like, I must be the ugliest girl in all of Vienna.

"Do you like it?" he said. He actually sounded worried about what I thought. I was too mortified to take his feelings into account. Only my strict training saved me.

"I think it's lovely," I said, but he knew I was lying.

* * *

Klimt woke up my father and sent me to fetch my mother to see the finished products. He leaned all three drawings up against the parlor wall and we all gathered around to look at them. Pauline was smiling and soft. He'd drawn the whole room in around her, and the drawing was bright and busy. Helene of course looked like an angel. There was even a corona around her head. I was the only one who looked like I could turn people to stone.

"They are wonderful," pronounced my mother. "I especially like Emilie's. You have really captured her personality."

Klimt caught my eye and winked. I looked away. I just wanted him to leave. Then my father asked Klimt to stay for dinner. To my despair he said he would be delighted.

As we walked into dinner Helene nudged me. "Do you like yours?" she whispered.

I stared at her incredulously.

"It does look like you," she said reluctantly. I wanted to cry.

"I like yours better than Pauline's," she said. "She's hardly even in it."

I had never seen anyone eat as much or as fast as he did. His hands were tanned, and wide, with thick flat thumbs like wooden spoons. They were clumsy with a knife and fork; it seemed incredible that I had just watched him wielding pencil and chalk with such skill. It was bad manners to draw attention to other people's bad manners, but I made sure that he could tell what I thought from the way I was looking at him.

He was telling my mother about some work he was doing for the imperial family.

"I'm going to do some murals for the empress's villa in Italy," he said. "Something lighthearted, colorful, not too difficult. I've never been to Italy so it will be a great chance for me to see Rome and Florence."

"How did you get the job?" Father wondered.

"The usual way," he said. "There was a general announcement at the Kunstlerhaus about it and I submitted a proposal. But I think it was the Burgtheater commission that got me the job. I've met a lot of important people. Everyone wants his portrait to be on the wall. Two or three judges and doctors and court officials come to my studio every day now."

I watched him drop a piece of boiled beef into his lap and smiled at him evilly.

"Did you meet the empress?" asked Pauline shyly. Papa glared at her but Klimt ignored him.

"I never saw her," he said. "No one sees her anymore, not even the emperor, you know." A piece of potato fell from his mouth back onto his plate. My mother coughed and asked if anyone wanted more cabbage.

"Emilie says she doesn't do any drawing at her school. I think that's a shame. Every girl should be able to sketch a little." He turned to Mother. "I imagine you are quite accomplished yourself."

My mother blushed. "Oh no, I have no talent at all. I can't imagine that the girls have any."

"Nonsense, you have a wonderful eye."

"Well, I did study drawing with Hans Lerner when I was in school."

"Hans Lerner, he's a legend. And for him to take you as a student, what an honor!" Helene kicked me under the table. Why was he flattering our mother so outrageously?

"And I went to Italy," she said. "Before I was married."

He sighed in rapture over her descriptions of the Fra Angelicos and the Tiepolos and the Masaccios she'd seen.

"Your girls should have the opportunity if they wish." I waited for Papa to say that it was his business to decide what opportunities we should have, but he didn't.

"Helene is musical," said my mother. "She has lessons every afternoon. I doubt she'd have time for more."

"What about the other two?" said Klimt.

"Pauline is scheduled to begin a special language course when she finishes school in the spring. But Emilie is free."

I looked at her beseechingly but she either didn't understand my look, or didn't care.

"I know she must be busy with her acting," said Klimt. "I see by her sash that she must have been practicing before I arrived." It was only then that I noticed the pink silk band tied around my waist, poking out from under my school blouse with the brooch still attached. I had missed it in my rush and we'd all been too preoccupied by the sittings and the dinner to notice. But now, thanks to Klimt, everyone in the family was staring at it.

"Emilie!" shrieked my mother, "go upstairs and take that off right now!"

I left the table, wishing I didn't have to go back, that I could crawl into bed and stay there until Klimt had gone. I tried to remember what the punishment was for borrowing Mother's things without asking. Was I to go without dinner for three days? Though this time it would be worse since I had embarrassed my parents in front of a guest. Would Father take out the strap? As I climbed the stairs I could hear my mother making excuses for me. "I know she's too old to play dress up, but she enjoys it so much, and it seems harmless." I pulled the clasp around my waist, unhooked it, and balled the sash up in my fist, wishing it was Klimt's face.

When I came back down, it had already been decided. Klimt was going to be my drawing teacher, and there wasn't anything I could do about it.

Four

The day of the first lesson I woke up before it was light. I tried to wake Helene, hoping her soothing voice would calm my nerves, but despite my vigorous prodding, she only frowned, and rolled onto her back, eyelids fluttering and hand dangling dramatically, as if she were a society queen with the vapors. She was obviously having a dream from which she didn't want to be taken. I threw off the covers, which Helene promptly grabbed. It was cold. The bones in my feet ached as I walked over to Pauline's bed. She was muttering in her sleep, explaining to her teacher why she was late and why she wasn't wearing shoes.

I went to the windowsill and pulled my cambric nightgown over my feet. Soon it would be time to bring our flannel nightgowns out, and our heavy goose-down comforters, stuffed by the farmer's wives in Attersee.

When I was in a temper, I often sent my thoughts to Attersee, a small town in the lake district several hours west of Vienna. My family had been spending summers there since before I was born. Mountains ringed the glacial lakes there and the hills were covered with wildflowers. It was impossible to think of it and be upset.

The air outside my window was foggy and dense. The apartment building across the street looked as if it were underwater. A few people were out; the man who sold newspapers on the corner came into view rolling a dolly loaded to the handle and slid its pile of Vienna *Times* onto the pavement. He pulled a knife out of his pocket and sliced the twine on the bundles and stacked them in his cart. Then he disappeared around the corner to do it again. Rolling, unloading, cutting, stacking.

The carts were just starting to arrive from the country with produce for the market. There was always a man in a wide-brimmed hat driving and a few children of various ages sitting on pumpkins in the back. They rattled and bounced like seeds in a gourd. Idly I wondered how early they had to wake up to get to Vienna at that hour. Most likely they were used to it. It might even be fun, to see the countryside in the half-light, clopping into the city when everyone there was still asleep.

The light paled. Soon shafts of sunlight would pierce the watery early morning and things would get stark and clear. Soon I would have to wash my face with cold water that would bring up the goose bumps on my arms. I would have to eat every bite of the coarse porridge mother said was the best thing for us, though I noticed that she ate pastry stuffed with raspberry or apple. I would have to listen to many admonitions to mind my manners and apply myself. I would have to put on my ugly felt hat and leave the house and walk past the newspaper man. I didn't want to think beyond that.

More than cannibals, more than inoculations, more than tripe, I feared being laughed at. What would the artist say when he saw my clumsy attempts at drawing? It was going to be so humiliating. My stomach cramped at the thought. Maybe I would be sick and not have to go.

Helene appeared next to me, wearing her coverlet over her head like the Virgin Mary. "It's too cold to sit there like that," she said. "Go back to bed."

I shook my head and turned back to the outside. One of the men with a cart was trading a bag of yellow apples for a newspaper. The children were throwing what appeared to be chestnuts at one another.

"Are you nervous?" she asked sympathetically.

"About what?" I said.

I had never had a lesson that wasn't given by a nun. Not that they didn't have their terrifying qualities: their stern, thin-lipped mouths; their ghostly costumes; their fondness for standing over your shoulder while you worked on an assignment until you were so flustered you couldn't even remember what subject you were doing. But a nun was a known quantity. I already knew what pleased them: tidy hair, clean hands, wide-open eyes, and a slight smile, but never a grin. I could fall asleep with my face arranged like that.

"When I had my first singing lesson I was terrified," said Helene. "I thought I would forget all of the notes. The night before I had a dream that I was a pigeon and could only make that horrible cooing sound. But then Mrs. Schraft was not so bad."

Mrs. Schraft was seventy and her wool coat always smelled like a sheepdog. She carried hazelnut candies wrapped in colored foil in her skirt pocket and liberally dispensed them to her students.

"I wish I was going to Mrs. Shraft."

Helene sat down, unfurled her headdress and wrapped me in it as well. We sat back to back, like caryatids.

"I wish I could go with you," she said.

I wished she could, too. It would take half of the attention off of me. Maybe afterward Papa would let us go to a café and we could order hot chocolate and laugh about it.

"You want to learn to draw?" I asked her.

"I want to see the studio. I wonder if anyone famous will come while you're there."

"I doubt it. I think he made all of that up."

Helene shook her head. She didn't understand why I didn't like Klimt. She thought he was interesting.

"What are you going to wear?" she said. I leaned forward and dumped her off of my back. I turned to glare at her.

"Why does it matter?"

"Don't you want to make a good impression?"

"I don't care if I make a good impression on Klimt."

"You'd better say Mr. Klimt," she said, shocked. "What if Mama and Papa heard you?"

Then I told her my secret plan: I was going to be polite, and quiet, but completely inept. Klimt wouldn't be able to complain about me, but I would frustrate him so much that he would give up, and return me to my family as unteachable. Then everything would go back to the way it was, and I wouldn't have to see him again.

"You're not the least bit curious?" she asked. "You're not the least bit interested in the studio, or the artists, or learning how to draw?"

"No," I said, but she knew me better than that.

"Maybe I'll let you borrow my new gray skirt," she said. "It would look nice with your pink blouse."

After breakfast my father took my arm and walked me briskly toward the east, toward the Naschmarkt.

"I thought the studio was in Leopoldstadt," I said.

My father was annoyed. He hated any evidence that we had failed to listen to our instructions. "We're not going to the studio," he said. "Whatever gave you that idea? We're going to their house, it's in Hietzing."

Hietzing was a long way away, in the countryside. It was where the summer palace was. I had never been there.

A man my father knew passed us, reading the newspaper as he walked. My father stood in front of him and the man nearly collided with him. The man folded up his newspaper and shook my father's hand.

At the corner was a cab stand. The horse-drawn carriages were lined up for a block, waiting. My father gave a wave that was more like a salute, and the driver nodded and hopped down to open the door. He was in his shirtsleeves, and underneath his oily mustache a cigar as fat as a snake was clamped between his teeth. The smoke was acrid, not sweet and spicy like the tobacco I was used to. I coughed without meaning to as he helped me into the compartment.

"Ever smoke a pipe?" asked my father. "Much healthier."

I curled into the corner of the carriage, trying not to breathe. Why did my father try to sell pipes to everyone he met?

The man's laugh was full of phlegm. "Don't worry about me. My wife'll kill me long before these things do." He wrapped a plaid blanket around me, rather too tightly.

We passed the dry goods stores, the florists, the churches, and bakeries that lined the busy street. There was a gaping hole where they were building the new theater, in between two somber stone apartment buildings. Men were standing in the muddy maw passing stone blocks to one another. We passed blocks of rowhouses with windowboxes cascading ivy and geraniums and impatiens.

His house! Whatever small appeal the morning had was now lost. A studio was mysterious, exotic, peopled with men with fevered eyes. A house had lace antimacassars pinned to the furniture.

My father pulled out his pipe and the leather pouch in which he kept his tobacco, maybe hoping that in the process of packing and lighting and smoking he would entice the driver with the aroma. I was turned away from him but I could tell he was ready to speak.

"You know, Emilie," he said, "this is a great honor for you."

I wanted to say that I had ridden in a carriage before, when Pauline had scarlet fever, but I didn't.

"Yes, Father," I said instead.

"And for our family," he continued. "I trust that you won't do anything to jeopardize our good opinion of you."

"No, Father."

"I expect to receive a full report on your performance from Mr. Klimt at the end of the lesson."

With a nod of his head, the interview was over. I was free to turn back to the window. We had passed the train station and things had started to change. A bareheaded man in a bright red vest was selling what looked like small pieces of paper.

"What is that man doing?" I asked my father. He explained that the man was a charlatan. He sold fortunes, the cheapest ones preprinted on a card, the more expensive ones written out after a consultation. The flowers in the florist's were limp and tinged with brown, like burned toast. A knife-sharpener pushed his cart. Three wizened old men with white beards were lurking outside a bakery, waiting for the day-old bread.

"Have you ever been to Klimt's house?" I asked nervously, forgetting to call him Mister, but my father didn't notice.

"Of course," he said. He, too, looked a little nervous. "Now that the boys are working they're doing fine. Their house is very serviceable."

It was a tiny cottage covered in creeping vines that were just starting to turn a brilliant red. The tiny panes of the casement windows gave the façade a medieval look. On one side was a brick tenement, on the other, a cannery. The neighborhood smelled of fish and sulfur from the nearby smelter.

My father opened the gate and hesitated there as I went through. He seemed uncertain whether or not to leave. He followed me up the steps and rang the bell. Then he took out his pocket watch and looked at its ivory face.

"It's quarter past nine," he said. "I'll be back at eleven." He handed the watch to me and I put it in the pocket of my coat. "I'll expect you to be ready." I didn't ask him how he would be there on time if he didn't have a watch. He was never late.

Holding the watch gave me courage when the door opened and Mrs. Klimt appeared. She was a tiny woman who had the wrinkled, tanned face and rough hands of someone who had worked outdoors for many years. Her gray hair was pinned in a haphazard knot on top of her head, and her apron was variegated with ancient stains that had not washed out.

"Come in," she said grimly. Her bright eyes took in my neatly combed hair, my coat, a gray-purple felt with a plum velveteen collar and trim. She pulled it from my shoulders and held it in her arms like an infant. I even saw her stroke it.

She led me into the dining room and sat me down at the table. Then she left with my coat. I was afraid she might squirrel it away somewhere and I'd only see it again on the back of some farmer's daughter at the Naschmarkt, but I had to give it to her. Later I realized that she admired a good coat the way an engineer might admire someone else's ingenious architectural plans. She knew the work that had gone into it, and appreciated it. All I knew then was that it was expensive.

I wondered what I was supposed to do. I had brought a pad of paper and a sheaf of pencils. The paper was cheap newsprint. I could see wood chips in it. I put a pencil to the paper but didn't know what I might want to draw. Of course, that was what teachers were for.

Mrs. Klimt returned with a dirty-looking smock.

"Put this on over your dress," she said. "Can't have that merino getting soiled, it's too good."

I put it on, wondering if the smock would dirty my dress more than the art lesson. It smelled faintly of clay, which wasn't unpleasant. Mrs. Klimt sat down next to me.

"Lovely day," I said politely. She said nothing, but continued to stare at me without speaking. Was I supposed to keep trying to make conversation, or not? I smiled at her, but she didn't smile back. In fact, the wrinkles between her eyebrows deepened, as if she were looking at something very far away.

There was nothing in the room to suggest that an art lesson was going to happen. It was an ordinary dining room, like ours, only shabbier. The carpet was worn to the backing and the soot-blackened windows turned the light sepia. The table was rather primitive-looking and several of the chairs had broken legs, including the one I was sitting in, but the red cotton cloth on the table was embroidered with yellow flowers, and the china cabinet was full.

When Klimt came in a few minutes later, he carried the by now familiar toolbox. Without so much as a look at me he set it on the table and began pulling out bits of chalk, stubs of pencils, erasers that looked like gobs of glue, some discolored sponges, and rags stiff with paint. They were as mysterious to me as Egyptian artifacts.

"Here's what we need," he said brightly, holding up a piece of charcoal he'd dug from the bottom of the box.

"I brought pencils," I said, showing him the brand-new tin case.

"It's too early for pencils," he said. "Charcoal first, then pencils."

Reluctantly I held out my hand for the gray shard. Why a piece of burned, compressed wood no bigger than my pinkie was a better tool than a pencil, I had no idea, but I had to obey him. As his hand touched mine I saw that there were calluses on the inside of his middle finger and on his thumb. Would I get them, too? The hands of young ladies were supposed to be very smooth and white. Every Saturday we bathed ours in buttermilk and scrubbed the freckles off with lemon juice.

"Don't worry," he said, "charcoal is hard enough to use, you'll see."

I looked down at my paper and said nothing.

He sat down across from me. "Now what's wrong?" he said. "And don't tell me everything's fine. You have a transparent face."

That was a horrifying statement, and I blushed and tried not to blush and blushed even more. "I wish we could go to your studio," I said. "This place doesn't seem very artistic."

Klimt laughed and pushed the front legs of his chair off of the floor, leaning back. "There's nothing magic about the studio, I promise. But if you like I'll take you there sometime if you'll stop frowning for a little while."

"The studio's no place for a young lady," said Mrs. Klimt, giving me a stern look.

"But won't we get your nice dining room all dirty?" I asked politely.

"As long as you are presentable when you go back to your mother, that's all I care about," said Mrs. Klimt. "I wouldn't want her upset with me." I wondered if she knew my mother. Did she know that my mother could forget who we were for weeks at a time?

I examined the charcoal in my hand. It was long and thin and incredibly light. It imprinted my fingers with a gray shadow.

"Are you ready?" asked Klimt.

"But where's the easel?" I asked in surprise.

"Today we'll sit at the table," said Klimt. He swept the red cloth aside. Mrs. Klimt took it up, folded it, and put it on her lap. Then he taped a sheet of paper to the table and pulled a brick out of the tool-box. I tried to guess what the brick might be for. To keep the paper from blowing away? To sharpen the chalk? He placed the brick in front of me and stood with his arms folded. I waited.

"Well," he said. He looked at me expectantly. The morning sun made his eyes blue and brilliant, too brilliant to look at directly. I looked at his beard instead.

"Well what?"

"Draw."

"I don't understand," I said. "What am I supposed to draw?"

He nodded toward the brick.

"Draw the brick?" I said incredulously.

"That's right," he said. "Draw the brick."

"But it's just . . . a brick." I knew I sounded like an idiot.

"And what is a brick?" he said. He sounded like he was teaching a very young child. Was this a joke? But he was waiting.

"I don't know, clay that's baked in an oven . . ."

"Stoneware is clay baked in an oven, too, but you wouldn't confuse a pitcher with this brick, now, would you?"

This wasn't how a drawing lesson was supposed to go. I should have been sketching a bowl of fruit, or some bottles, like we used to do in school with our art teacher. I didn't know how to respond. "No, sir," I said.

He laughed. "I know you think I'm insane," he said, "but this was my very first lesson in art school when I was eleven, and it will be yours. Try to give me a better definition. It won't hurt."

I took a deep breath. "A brick is a rectangular piece of clay that is fired in an oven and used as a building material."

"Excellent. Now forget everything we've just said and draw what you see."

I picked up the charcoal and drew a rectangle. I didn't even fill it in. It took ten seconds. I put the charcoal back down and placed my hands in my lap.

"Are you finished?" he said. I nodded.

"Interesting," he said thoughtfully. He picked up the paper and looked at it closely. "That's really what you saw?"

Why was he being so deliberately stupid? "Yes, sir," I said. "That's what I saw."

"All right." He smiled. "Your next assignment is to look at the brick for twenty minutes, and then draw it again."

"I have to look at it for twenty minutes?"

"I will time you. Begin."

I thought I would die of boredom. The brick sat there in front of me, dull and solid. I looked at it. Mrs. Klimt was still sitting next to me. She had not shown surprise or amusement at anything that had happened. She was staring into the kitchen, as if she were thinking about the pies she had in the oven. Probably she was. The tablecloth was still in her lap. Some of the flowers had missed stitches in them. Many of the flowers had black yarn outlining the petals. I looked at the shelf across from me, where a parlor ivy in a ceramic pot appeared to be slowly dying. Below it, two china shepherdesses glared at one another, vying for possession of a lone china sheep. Klimt sat in front of me, idly whistling and drawing. I looked at his paper. He was drawing the brick.

He felt me looking at him.

"You have ten more minutes," he said.

"Why are you drawing it?" I asked. "You're an artist already."

"Because an artist can always learn by looking, no matter how mundane the object."

His answer shamed me into looking at the thing I was supposed to be drawing.

It was red. A dark-orange red, like stewed tomatoes. Parts of it looked burned black, and parts of it looked charred to ash. It was pockmarked. There were grooves on one end of it. I picked it up.

Some brick dust crumbled onto the table. I looked at Klimt to see if this was all right, but he was not paying any attention to me. He was bent over his drawing with an eraser.

The corners of the brick weren't straight, as I had thought. They wobbled like my voice when I tried to sing. How to make the object three-dimensional? How to show texture?

I looked at the clock. Three more minutes.

"This is too hard," I said. My eyes were filled with tears of frustration. Surreptitiously I tried to wipe them away with my hands. Klimt looked up. He closed his sketchpad and put it on the floor.

"Now you're ready to be taught," he said. He turned his drawing around. It looked like a wedge of moldy cheese, yet there was no doubt that it was a brick, and there was no doubt it was the brick on the table in front of us. It was more detailed than a fingerprint.

"I can't do that," I said. The tears were in my throat, and I tried to cough them out.

"Of course you can't," he said. "At least not today. But if you keep looking, you will."

At the end of the lesson I had several pages of what was supposed to be the brick, but looked more like a set of bruises. When our time was up he put the charcoal back in the box and locked it. He pulled the papers off of the table and asked me if I'd like to keep them. I shook my head. I thought he would crumple them into a ball and throw them in the stove, but he folded them carefully. Take them, he said. You'll want to see these some day. You'll laugh about it, he said. I found that hard to believe, but I agreed. Then he directed me to the sink where I could wash up. When I looked at myself in the mirror I saw that I had streaks of charcoal under my eyes where I had tried to wipe my tears away. I looked like a grieving widow. And he had never said anything.

I met my father at the door. "Wait here," he said. "I need to speak to Mr. Klimt."

I was afraid for the first time. My drawings were very bad, in spite of the fact that I had tried. I thought that Klimt must be annoyed that he had made such a mistake. He was telling my father that it wouldn't work out after all. My father would be angry with me. He was going to tell me I was an embarrassment, that I had failed.

I sat in the carriage and waited for the inevitable. I hid myself under the blanket, but in spite of that I still shivered. Father came out to the carriage whistling "My Vienna," which was unlike him. He did not look at all angry, but I thought maybe his cheerfulness was for the benefit of the driver.

"Would you like to stop at Demel's on the way home? Don't they have a chocolate walnut torte that you like?"

What had Klimt said to him? I never found out.

I showed my drawings to Helene when I got home.

"What are they supposed to be?" she asked. I told her.

"No wonder he picked you," she said. "It's going to cost a fortune before you can draw." She brightened for a moment. "But you did these on purpose, right? So you wouldn't have to go anymore?" She saw my face. "Oh."

The next Saturday my father took me to Klimt's house. And the next, and the next. Every Saturday I sat at the table with the red cloth. At the second lesson I progressed to spheres drawn with the flat of the charcoal, for volume. I drew with my eyes closed. I drew without looking at the paper. I drew in loops and squiggles, in one unbroken line, in sharp crosshatchings. I drew things I would never have thought to draw: a book lying open on the table, a dead pigeon. At the end of the lesson Mrs. Klimt always brought out raisin scones in a woven basket, and poured coffee for Klimt, steamed milk for me. I tried to unobtrusively pick out the raisins.

Klimt was generally patient and cheerful, but several things I did made him crazy. For one thing, after the first lesson I refused to wear the smock. I didn't want to look ugly while I was drawing, I said. He reminded me that no one cared in the least what I looked like. Were Ingres's drawings rejected by the Beaux Arts because his hair was awry? Was Toulouse-Lautrec barred from painting because he was deformed? But I was obdurate. When I got home I shook the charcoal dust from my dresses and brushed my shoes and coat, but my sisters still took to calling me the scullery maid.

I held the charcoal wrong, he said. It wasn't a fistful of money, it was a skein of silk to be unwound. Held too tightly it would catch or snare. I said that if I held it too loosely I would drop it. He said held too tightly I would break it, that I was supposed to trust it. How can I trust it, I thought, when it gives me these horrible, ugly drawings? I drew better when I was a baby and I was allowed to scribble on the back of used wrapping paper. But I said nothing and tried to do as he asked.

But his main complaint was that I was too impatient, that I didn't take enough time to look. I wanted to be good, but I didn't want it enough to submit fully to the grueling apprenticeship. That was true. I was never patient. And at twelve it's hard to look at anything for long, except oneself.

One Saturday he met me at the door and said we were going to the Volksgarten.

I had ridden with my father in the carriage for half an hour to get to his house. It was more than a half hour back to the center of town. Why hadn't he made arrangements the week before? And how were we going to get there?

On the train, he said. Why were we going to the Volksgarten, I wanted to know. Was I going to draw flowers, or people, or the tempietto? I was to leave my sketchbook behind, he said. For an hour I was to do nothing but look. It seemed no different from looking out of the window, and was a welcome relief from the tedious exercises.

It was noisy on the train. We stood without speaking on the platform where the cars attached, as the train stopped and started. I concentrated on not losing my footing and accidentally bumping his sleeve.

We got off at the Karlsplatz. I had never been alone with him before and I had no idea what to say as we walked. I waited and looked down at my skirt, whipping itself into whitecaps in the wind. The speckled leaves under my feet were as soggy as bread dipped in milk. We had spent so many bright fall Saturdays sitting indoors, why had he decided that today was the day to go to the park? Was he exasperated by my poor performance? Was he tired of giving me lessons?

"There's the Kunstlerhaus," he said, finally, pointing at a grand building. "All the artists meet there, they post the calls for submissions on the wall there, we have lectures and shows."

"It's pretty," I said politely.

"Do you really think so?" he said, and stopped walking. "Or did you just say what you think I wanted to hear?" He turned me by the shoulders and faced me toward the building. I felt caught out.

"Of course it's not pretty," I said. "The bottom is too delicate for the top, or the top is too heavy for the bottom, and all those marble carvings are just vulgar."

He laughed. "That's my girl. You'll never offend me with the truth, remember that."

"Why is the artist's building so ugly?" I asked.

"Because of committees," he said. "A committee tries to appease everyone and ends up with the worst parts of all the ideas that are discussed. The Kunstlerhaus is full of committees. I'm on one myself, the Traveling Show committee. We try to bring the work of foreign artists like Pissarro or Turner or Burne-Jones here so people can see them. But the Finance committee wants to abolish the Traveling Show committee on the grounds that it costs too much, and absorb it into the general Exhibition committee. That's the latest controversy. Artists are horribly political."

"So you think it would be better if the Kunstlerhaus was a monarchy?" I asked pointedly. I don't know why I said that. I suppose I was showing off; we'd been studying political systems in school.

"Yes, with me as king," he said teasingly. "What's wrong with that?"

I shrugged, because I didn't really care who ran the Kunstler-haus, and paused to look in the window of a bakery we were passing, where a particularly delicious-looking caramel cake sat atop a crystal cake plate.

"You like sweets?" he said, watching me. "I'll see if mother won't bake something chocolate next time."

"With hazelnuts," I said. Then I felt guilty. "If it's not too expensive," I added.

"Are you a socialist?" he asked, returning to the subject of the Kunstlerhaus. "What would your father say?"

"I'm not anything," I said. "It just seems like everyone being able to express their opinion is better than one person telling everyone else what to do."

"You'd think having everyone's opinion would be a good thing, but most people don't have opinions worth taking into account. Especially when it comes to art."

I thought about my father and the cab driver with the pungent cigar, and decided that he was probably right.

We had arrived in the Volksgarten and Klimt led me to a bench and took an acrid handkerchief from his pocket and wiped the seat. The bench was small and even when dry the cold of it traveled up through my bones. I wanted to huddle against Klimt for warmth like a child, but I couldn't. I sat rigidly to keep myself from shivering. I could see my breath.

The air was thick and gray with cold rain that threatened to turn to ice. Everyone who passed wore an expression of concentration, a determination to endure the discomfort of the cold, thinking of the café or the fireplace that awaited him at his destination. Not one of the pedestrians with clenched teeth would be out if they had a choice. It was hard for me to concentrate on looking. My feet were going numb. Ten minutes passed, then twenty. Klimt didn't say anything. When I looked over at him he wore the same expression his mother did when she sat at the kitchen table.

"Do you torture all of your students this way?" I asked after thirty minutes. He startled, as if he'd forgotten I was there, and turned to me with a puzzled look.

"I don't have any other students," he said.

"I thought . . ." I stumbled for a diplomatic reply.

"That I must need the money badly to give lessons to you?" He seemed amused. "When we got the theater commission we got a lot of money. I tried to buy my mother another house, but she likes that one. She's used to it. My father made her move several times a year for twenty years, always promising the next house would be better, and always it was worse. Now she says she will never move again."

"What about you? You don't have anything," I said, thinking about the ill-fitting suit.

"Only paint," he said. "But I don't need anything else."

"Then why did you take me as a student?"

"Everyone needs a protégé."

"I'm not a protégé," I said. Surprise made me blunt. "I'm terrible."

"You're not as terrible as you think you are." It was as close to a compliment as he had ever given me, and I didn't know what to do with it. I looked quickly around for some visual to distract him. I found a woman with red hair leaning against a slick dark tree trunk. It elicited a lecture on contrast. As he talked I wondered about the woman. She wasn't much older than I and wasn't wearing a hat, which was a horrible faux pas in addition to being foolish, given the weather. She was pale and looked worried. Her hands moved constantly, smoothing her hair, adjusting her coat. Who was she waiting for?

As we walked back to the train station at the end of an hour, he told me that the cartoons for the theater were being exhibited at the Kunstlerhaus in a week's time. I should come, he said, and bring my parents or my sisters. There would be a reception. It was important for a student to see her teacher's work. Then you can decide if I am worth respecting, he said. I said I would try to come.

I told Helene. We decided we would not tell our parents, who surely would forbid us to go. We would make an excuse and go by ourselves. It wasn't far to walk; we could hurry back before anyone missed us. We said we were going to the coffee shop for *Schlagobers*. Pauline, thankfully, did not want to come. She thought we were going to ogle some handsome new waiter, which didn't interest her. She'd preferred to stay home with a book.

Our plan seemed brilliant until we were mounting the steps of the building, the one Klimt had forced me to admit was ugly. Ugly or not, it was intimidating to two young girls. Everyone else there seemed much older, sure of themselves. They looked as if they knew where they were going. We watched several groups swing open the brass doors and disappear before we took a deep breath and slipped inside.

The floor of the rotunda was mosaic tile and the ceiling was frescoed with angels. At a long table artists were pouring new wine, still bubbling and fermenting in the bottle, into cheap glasses. Lots of people Klimt had talked about, people who had modeled for him, were there, including Katherina Schratt and the crown prince. Or so Helene told me later. All I could see was the cartoons.

They were only long rolls of paper fixed to the wall, but they were filled with light, like crystal chandeliers. I stepped very close to look at the brushstrokes. The paint slid across the paper in rivers, and trickled down in rivulets. I thought I could tell which ones Klimt had done. It was hard to say how I knew. They were less careful, though not at all sloppy, just the opposite. The brush ran free like a virtuoso's bow.

Each scene was from the history of the theater, from a Greek amphitheater to a Viennese play from last season, but I didn't know that yet, because I was mesmerized in front of a scene from an Elizabethan production of Romeo and Juliet, all peacock blue and moss green velvet. I thought I recognized Mercutio.

I don't know how long I was standing there before Klimt saw me. He must have watched me for a while because he asked if I was all right. He introduced his brother Ernst to Helene and me.

Helene told Ernst politely how much she admired the cartoons. I, on the other hand, couldn't say anything.

"Don't you like them?" Klimt seemed worried.

Helene told him that dumb amazement had always been my usual response to something I loved. She told him about the first time I went to see the Lippizaners and estimated that I loved his cartoons at least as much, if not more than, the dancing white horses.

Did she have to betray me like that?

He brought me some wine. I didn't tell him I wasn't allowed to have it. "So you like them?" he said. I could only nod. My school-girl vocabulary seemed inadequate and I was suddenly intimidated by him. Men kept coming up to us and shaking Klimt's hand. They didn't even look at me, and I realized how insignificant I must be in his life. I thought that at his own reception he should leave me and go talk to the important people, and I decided it must be good manners that were keeping him.

"Where's Helene?" I said, to give him an excuse. "I must go and find her."

"She's a grown-up young lady," he said. "She can take care of herself. Let me show you the rest." He led me around the room, showing me the different panels, telling me who each person was, whispering bits of gossip so that no one else could hear, explaining why he had done things a certain way. I really did wonder what had happened to Helene but after a while I forgot to look for her.

"You like it?" he kept saying. "Are you sure?" He wanted to know why I liked it. When I said I thought it was beautiful he frowned. That was not the right answer. I tried to explain about the brush-strokes but he said any artist worth his smock could do that. I didn't know what else to say.

"It's no good," he said. "I've failed." I didn't understand his sudden gloom. I had never seen him this way. It seemed as if the party, which should have been the high point of the whole process, was in fact depressing to him. I couldn't convince him that the work was good.

A burly blond man approached us as we tackled the Greek section. "It's Moll," Klimt said. "I don't feel like talking to him right now." He pushed me toward the back of the room. I thought he was actually going to hide us behind the drapes, but Moll accosted us before he could.

I had heard Klimt talk about Moll. He had a powerful personality and liked to organize things, which made him a valuable comrade. I knew that Klimt liked him, but had doubts about him as an artist.

He clapped Klimt on the back, practically knocking him over. "Magnificent!" he said in a loud bass voice. "A triumph!"

"Spare me your bullshit, Moll," Klimt said. "You can say that to the reporters, but tell me what you really think."

"You've outdone Makart," said Moll. "It captures the Viennese spirit."

"I know," sighed Klimt. "That's the problem. It's tired and bourgeois." He sounded defeated. I wondered, if this was such a failure, what one of his successes would look like.

"You're worn out," said Moll, "and you've looked at it so much you can't see it any more. Come away from it and have a drink with me, that ought to help. There's something I want to discuss with you anyway."

Klimt gave me an apologetic smile as Moll led him away. I realized as they disappeared that he hadn't introduced me to Moll, and that Moll hadn't looked at me once.

I found Helene with a girl she knew, two years ahead of her in school, talking Schiller. On the way home she told me that Ernst had asked if she'd like to model for their next project, a Roman mural for an Esterházy palace outside of Budapest. She said she would if I could come, too. The sittings would be in the studio.

It was one thing to sneak away to attend an art opening in a public place, and quite another to go alone to an artist's studio. We would be risking everything, and we both knew it. Still, neither of us hesitated. We spent that night discussing how we could accomplish it without our parents finding out.

Now, when I thought of him, it was not as Klimt, but as Gustav. And I thought about him much more. It was as if I had cracked open his chest and seen his beating heart, and I could never look at him the same way again. I told myself that I admired his talent, that I thought he was a good teacher, that somehow over time he had become my friend. If occasionally a thought rose to the surface that there might be something more, I rigorously suppressed it.

Five

Kammer am Attersee
November 11, 1944

Today our neighbor Heitzmann came to the house with a basket full of vegetables: red onions, sweet onions, parsnips, small fat carrots with feathery heads cascading like a mermaid's hair. His wife had woven the basket from saplings soaked in water. The whole thing was as beautiful as a still life, and I nearly cried. They had some extra, he lied. If we didn't eat them, they would go to waste. He and his wife have seven children and it didn't rain much this summer, but we knew better than to refuse.

We've always known Heitzmann. He was a fat, red baby who grew into a chubby, ruddy boy who delivered eggs and milk to us from his father's dairy farm on the other side of the road. Now he is lean and tanned, but he still flushes easily in heat or embarrassment, and rocks back and forth on his hobnail boots in that way that I remember. He married a girl from St. Wolfgang whom he met at a harvest festival. That's the way of things around here.

He feels sorry for us, I know. My sisters and I were grand ladies to him once. Now I've had to write him for help and here I am, decrepit and alone. No family other than my niece. The modern, sophisticated life I lived in Vienna seems so far away now, and my money doesn't really do me any good under these circumstances.

We thanked him gratefully for the vegetables. All we ate last night were some potatoes we had found in the pantry, their shoots like little green snakes crawling across the floor. We roasted them but they still tasted mealy and bitter. Supplemented with crackers and coffee, they weren't much of a meal.

Helene asked him if his wife might like to earn some money baking bread for us. I could tell she felt a little guilty, paying someone for something we should be able to do ourselves, but neither of us has the energy or the inclination for baking. I listened as they settled on a price and a delivery schedule. He said he would send his son Hermann on Tuesdays and Saturdays with a loaf of rye and a loaf of wheat.

When he left I put on a jacket and went out to examine the place where our garden used to be. If we are going to stay here for a long time we will have to grow some vegetables for ourselves. We can't depend on Heitzmann forever; something could happen to him.

The flagstone path that leads from the front porch is overgrown and difficult to see. Lichen has spread colorfully over the stones and I stooped to examine the coralline ruffles and starbursts. There are shelf mushrooms growing at the base of the trees. I can't recall which ones are edible and which not. Perhaps there is a book in the library that will refresh my memory.

We had roses in the garden, and herbs: rosemary for bread and lavender for sachets. Sometimes one of us would become enthusiastic and try to grow various exotic things: cotton, indigo, mulberry trees. We hoped to have silk worms. We trained orchids and bonsai in the greenhouse. Once we even obtained a pineapple tree. But that was a long time ago. What I found was merely an indentation in the ground, matted with yellow grass, like a grave the year after the funeral. All around the opportunists were thriving, as they always do: Queen Anne's lace and goldenrod and thistle. The stone bench was still there, worn and pitted, and the sundial, its brass dial bent. In any case, there's not much sun this time of year.

It was quiet, as I remembered it being when I was a girl. Later city people in open-roofed automobiles would honk their horns and shout and wave, as they passed on their way to a picnic or a boating outing, but no one has any gasoline now and if anyone's going on picnics I don't know about it. Everyone's walking, or riding a bicycle. Occasionally a farm cart rattles past, or a cow bellows to another, but the loudest sounds are my own breath and my anxious fingers tapping against stone.

There are ghosts everywhere here, not the kind that fill the pages of sensationalist magazines or terrify schoolboy campfires, but the kind we use to simultaneously torment and comfort ourselves. Gustav is sitting on the bench next to me, drawing on my wrist with a charcoal pencil. He is calling to me from under the black cape of the unwieldy wooden camera he had back then. Stand still, he says, though he knows I know what to do. My mother is reading letters out loud from under one of the larch trees. Pauline is spraying the rose leaves with a red pepper mixture while Helene practices her vocal scales. My father is standing quietly in the woods beyond, observing birds and marking down his observations in a red leather journal.

Worst of all is the ghost of myself, weak with longing as I'm drawn upon, swelled with pride as I model my own designs, teasing my mother about her proper accent, digging slugs in the garden, running to give my father a kiss, and scaring all the birds away.

At the end of the garden is the greenhouse that Gustav used as a studio when he stayed with us. Some of the glass panes are broken. All of them are opaque with grime. Maybe Heitzmann could give the place a thorough washing. I'm afraid to go inside. It's like a jar you find in the back of the icebox. You can no longer remember what's inside, and you know it can't be anything good. However, it must be faced. Waiting will not get rid of it.

I circle a few times, ripping the seeds from some wheatlike grasses as I go. It burns my hand in a satisfying way. The door sticks, of course. I lean on it and step inside. It's damp and cool, like a potato cellar. My eyes are slow to adjust to the close dimness. Then my heart stops for a moment.

There are three people standing on the other side of the room. Thin, wasted people: refugees? Ghosts? They are looking out toward the back of the studio, toward the woods. They are standing at attention, in some sort of formation, like soldiers. They don't seem to notice me. I start to back out, trying to catch my breath.

Then with a blink I see that they are easels, skeletal and wooden. My heart resumes pumping and I have a laugh at myself. I used to be braver.

Some chipmunks and squirrels have clearly made their home in the corners, dragging in leaves and grass for their dens. There's an old table that used to be my grandmother's. It began in the kitchen, then moved to the porch, and finally, when even my father admitted it was too scratched and marred for the house, was banished to the studio. Now the finish is cracking and peeling away, damaged further by rain leaking in from the holes in the ceiling.

There is a row of galvanized buckets and a shelf of watering cans, thick gloves, rubber boots of various sizes, spades. Two shovels are lying crossed on the floor like a coat of arms. It still smells as it always did, like modeling clay and gasoline, though we never kept gas in here. Paint solvents, perhaps.

On the shelf next to the spades I find packets of seeds. The labels have faded away entirely. I pour one packet into my hand: sunflower or pumpkin, I think. The seeds in the next packet are moldy and half-eaten. The next batch, though, are tiny and brown. They'll never grow, it's been too long. Nevertheless, I pour these seeds back into their envelope and pull on some gloves. I take one of the shovels and go back to the garden. It feels good to hack at the grass as tightly woven as a burlap bag, to break the soil and flip it like a pancake, but it's hard work and my shoulders burn almost immediately. I'm gasping for breath and I know I've turned an unlovely shade of purple.

After about half an hour I've turned up seven respectable holes. Luckily they don't need to be very deep, not for these seeds, whatever they might be. I pour a few seeds in each and cover them up.

Should I water them or will that just flood them? Does the soil have enough nutrients to support them?

I lie on the grass next to my newly planted plot and breathe in the smell of the earth. If Gustav were here he would bring a blanket from the house and he would draw me as I napped. If he were here he would dig all of the holes for me and fix the sundial, and afterward we'd walk across the road and steal apples from Heitzmann's orchard. If Gustav were here I would strip off my clothes and offer myself like a salver of melon and pomegranate.

Sleeping Girl, 1889

Maria was a seventeen-year-old laundress living not far from the studio. She kept house with her father in a tiny cottage with an oilcloth tacked to the window wells and a thatched roof that never kept out the rain. The plaster was crumbling, bricks were missing. Her father was sick, a drunk; she grew what they ate and she took in laundry to pay for everything else. She attended church each day and tried to steer clear of the rough dockhands and laborers who filled the neighborhood. The city center wasn't far, but it was a long walk if you had no carriage of your own and no money for the fare. She had been only once, when she was a child, to see the Silver Jubilee procession, the celebration of the twenty-fifth wedding anniversary of the emperor and empress. She remembered carriages filled with flowers, and large, frightening people who pushed and threatened to crush her. When she thought of Vienna, she felt both in awe of its fragrance, its brilliance, and in equal measure a visceral fear of a crowded, airless space. She longed to go, to leave her father, get a job in a shop, go to hear music, but she was afraid. Such a girl, frail and credulous, could not have been prepared to meet a man like Gustav.

Maria was on her knees by the washtub when he appeared. She used the patch of dirt between her house and the one behind as her laundry area. The bodice of her dress was wet from the tub of suds in front of her. A man stood at the gate, bearded and hatless and wearing a long flowing robe. For a moment she was afraid that a messenger from God had arrived, perhaps to summon her to some special mission, and, as Maria was a girl who tried to attract as little attention as possible, she stopped scrubbing and with bowed head issued a fervent prayer that she was not chosen. She had been taught that when the angel came for you, your duty was to obey, and at the very least she hoped that if this was in fact an angel, what he asked would not be too difficult for her.

Elizabeth Hickey

"Oh, keep scrubbing," the man said. "I didn't mean to disturb you. It makes a lovely sound, doesn't it? Like a zither."

"It does," she said, surprised that an angel could speak in such a friendly, unthreatening voice.

"May I try it?" said the man, and to her dismay came and kneeled next to her, taking the washboard and laying it across his lap. "I must say that I am fascinated by gadgets like this. Did you make it yourself?"

"My father," said Maria. "He used to be a carpenter." She was aware of the smell of chemicals on the man's robe, and wondered if instead of an angel he wasn't from the asylum.

"It's the perfect object," he said, running his hand over the wooden slats so that they vibrated like bees buzzing. "Useful and beautiful." He looked at her, and she squirmed under his gaze. He smiled.

"I need a laundress," he said. "At the tailor's they told me that you might be available."

With relief, Maria realized that though the man looked like a carving of St. Peter on the front of the Church of St. Stephen Martyr, he was not going to ask her to preach to the lepers or fight the infidel.

"Yes, sir," she said.

"My name is Gustav Klimt, and I am an artist. Each week I soil a great number of rags and towels with paint, alcohol, and oil. They aren't easy to clean. What do you think the job is worth?"

"Ten rags for a shilling," she said after a moment's thought, hoping he wouldn't laugh at the extravagant price. She'd heard artists were rich, but the man in front of her obviously didn't even have the money for a suit.

The man smiled. "Don't you think you should charge more?" he asked. "I am a very well-known artist. It would look bad if anyone found out I was paying you that little."

"Five rags for a shilling?" she asked timidly.

"Agreed," he said. She watched him examine her, the untidy hair, the freckles on her chest. "In the village they said your name is Maria."

"Maria Ucicky," she said.

"Your husband is the Ucicky that sells me my firewood?"

"My uncle."

"Not married, then?" Maria shook her head. He frowned, seemingly outraged at the poor taste of the local youths.

For two months he brought her the rags each Saturday, and picked them up on Monday. Then one Saturday he asked if she could deliver them to the studio on Monday. "I'll pay extra," he said. "I have to finish this painting by Tuesday or I'll lose my commission."

"Of course," she said. On Monday she brushed her fine hair, rubbed tallow on her raw hands, and walked to the place he told her.

Maria was not foolish enough to believe that anything would come of it; she and her friends knew how such things went. A girl like her was not able to refuse a man like him, but a man like him would surely ruin her. After her visits to the studio Maria went to confession and begged forgiveness. She was frightened of hell. Her friends consoled her, but they were envious, too. He had bought her things, a hat, a shawl. They told her to model for him, make some extra money, but she was too shy, and fearful for her already endangered mortal soul. She could hardly stand the embarrassment and guilt when he touched her, how could she stand in front of him not wearing any clothes? None of her friends knew that in a few months she would bear his child. Her father hadn't guessed; she wore large aprons and avoided him whenever she could. Gustav had been kind and had not turned her away, but he hadn't said whether or not he would give her any money. She knew better than to think he would marry her. She didn't know how she would raise a child alone, or whether her father would throw her into the street.

At the studio she tended the fire, swept the floor, washed the teacups as if she were Gustav's maid and not his lover. Sometimes when he was out she waited for him there, falling asleep on the chaise with her hand under her cheek, like a child. Even as she slept she looked worried. When Gustav came in he moved quietly, so as not to wake her. He tiptoed to the easel and took down his pad of paper. Gently he moved the hand away from her face. Her blanket was peeled back and her chemise had ridden up her chest in her tossing and turning. He put them right. Her long hair tangled all around her face like seaweed, with the rhythmic *pulsing of the tide and the heartbeat. He pulled a piece of charcoal from his pocket, kneeled in front of her, and began to draw.*

When he was finished he set the drawing aside and laid his head on her belly, still flat and taut with hunger and youth. Her innocence nearly broke his heart, her rough hands, her pale, undernourished body. He was consumed with remorse. She deserved better than the life of penury and hard labor she was born to, and the life of ostracism and destitution he had given her. But it was too late; she had been too innocent to know what she had to do, and he had been too inexperienced to know he had to tell her.

For a wild moment he thought of marrying her and bringing her there to his studio to live with him. He thought of her in the garden, scrubbing away at one of his painting smocks with her wonderful washboard, of goulash and noodles on the dinner table, and children with dirty faces knocking over the easel. But that was someone else's life, not his. He woke Maria and told her she had better hurry home before her father roused from his drunken stupor and noticed she was not there.

Six

The Klimts' studio was on the fourth floor of a silver manu-
facturer's factory. To get there we caught the streetcar on
Gumpendorferstrasse, changed at the Ring, got off just on
the other side of the Donaukanal, and walked six blocks. The
money for the streetcar was Pauline's. We didn't have any money of
our own, but she had once won an essay contest. She kept her
hoard in a kerchief hidden in her underwear drawer, but of course
we knew where it was. We didn't think about what would happen
when she noticed it was missing. We left school at midday.

It was a street where goods were unloaded from ships and put
into wagons, where nets of fish were hauled into warehouses to be
gutted and salted. You could have a horse's shoe repaired, or your
own, a sail mended, or a cow butchered and divided into pieces.
The air was oppressive with the smell of things that had been rot-
ting in bins and had finally been exposed to the air.

Large families lived in the buildings surrounding the factories
and warehouses. I could see their soiled handmade curtains and
their cheaply painted oil lamps as I walked by their windows. Every
day the men went to work on the ships and the women walked to
work at milliners' and dressmaking shops in better parts of town.

In the tenement next to Gustav's building an immigrant from
Silesia and his wife had a bakery, and as we climbed the stairs the
aroma of dough and hot oil mingled with the sharp, sweet smell of
turpentine and the bitter one of iron. The stairs slanted toward the
street and a few of them gave way when you stepped on them.

The studio was cold, since the artists were consistently short of coal for the furnace, and bare, since all of the chairs were piled in the center of the room to be used in a tableau. The floor was made of cement and had cracked in places. It was filthy with charcoal dust. Some of the panes in the tall windows were broken and cardboard had been taped over them. The glass looked thin and weak, too weak to keep the cold out.

Despite this, or maybe because of it, I had never seen a more wonderful place in all my life. The artists had taped things to the walls: a color wheel, newspaper clippings about an actress named Limova from Moscow who had toured the European capitals, engravings of buildings in Rome that had obviously been ripped from books, postcards, sketches of cubes and cylinders with measurements penciled in beside them. They had a chipped enamel stove that they had salvaged from a garbage bin somewhere, and they heated water on it for coffee and chocolate. In a box next to it they kept tins of tea and coffee, cups and spoons, as well as loaves of raisin bread and paper bags of salted nuts and a nutcracker. There were shells on the floor.

There were four easels, each one with a small table next to it. Gustav was standing next to one easel, stirring something in a bowl. His table was bare except for two wooden models of the human figure, embracing.

Gustav was different here. For one thing, he was wearing a robe instead of a suit. It was like what I imagined a patient in a hospital would wear. To see a healthy grown man in it was shocking. I tried not to look at him, which was easy, since he hardly glanced in my direction. He was purposeful and completely absorbed. Every now and then he would say something to Ernst, and Ernst would laugh, but they spoke so softly that we couldn't hear them. We stood off to the side, not sure what to do. We were still in our coats, as no one had taken them. I wondered whom the other easels were for.

"Franz and Georg should be here soon," said Ernst, anticipating our question. He turned away from his table, which was much messier than Gustav's. The surface was covered with books with a forest of little pieces of paper sticking out of the side, mangled tubes, dirty bottles and cans.

We looked at each other.

"Do you ever clean up?" said Helene wonderingly.

"Why should we?" said Gustav. "This place is empty. When it gets too dirty to work in, we'll move upstairs."

The idea couldn't have been more radical to us. So much of our lives were consumed with keeping things neat. I felt like throwing my coat onto the floor. The two artists went on with what they were doing. Ernst was cleaning his brushes with a rag, one at a time, grooming them like show dogs. Gustav finished his mixing and began pouring oil onto a palette.

After what seemed like an hour Gustav went over to a trunk in the corner and pulled out some garments. He came back over to us and handed Helene a thin dress of white silk. "This is for you to wear. In the back we have a changing room." He nodded toward it.

"Where did you get this?" asked Helene, looking at the label.

"It was loaned to us by the actress Marie Geistinger." She was Helene's favorite actress.

"You know her? Will she come here? Can I meet her?"

"She only comes in the evenings," said Ernst without thinking. Then he blushed and fell silent, looking at the floor.

"She sleeps during the day and performs at night," said Gustav. "Sometimes she comes back here afterward to sit for me. That's how actresses live, you know. Like bats."

He gave me a coarse brown thing like a flour sack, and winked. "For the little girl."

"What is it?"

"It's your dress."

"Who am I to be in the tableau?"

"The servant. It's perfect, you're just the right age."

The changing room was separated from the rest of the studio by a woolen blanket tacked across the doorframe of what was once a storage closet. Nervously we pulled off our dresses and hung them on the nails that jutted from the wall. We were both self-conscious, despite the fact that without our dresses we still had on woolen underthings that covered us from wrist to ankle, and a chemise and a petticoat on top of that. I stayed as close to the closet corners as I could. Helene held her arms protectively over her chest. Awkwardly, trying not to be seen, we threw our costumes on.

I couldn't see myself, but I doubted I was much to look at. The neckline of my dress was cut straight across, what they now call a boatneck. The hems of the sleeves and skirt had been ripped out and frayed ends hung unevenly on my wrists and ankles. My broad, plump feet were bare for everyone to see.

Helene, however, was a vision, even with her chemise showing underneath the low cut dress. She was slighter than the usual Viennese girl, who tended to be plump, and the line of her neck and arms was like a dancer's.

It was a lovely, regal gown, and I could imagine Helene, her hair piled in curls, a golden band around her forehead, pointing her slender arm in the attitude of a queen.

"Do I look all right?" she asked, nervously trying to lift the neckline and fan the straps out to cover her arms.

"You'll have to take off the chemise, it looks ridiculous."

"But I can't!"

"If you go out there they'll just tell you to come back in."

"Do you really think I should? I'll be half naked."

"Try it and see." I held the dress so it wouldn't get dirty while she stripped down, then I helped her put it back on.

"I'll never be able to wear this in front of them," said Helene when she had her dress on. The sleeveless gown dipped dangerously low in the front and in the back. Large expanses of skin that no one but Pauline and I had ever seen would be on display. Helene was modest. Even in our bedroom she changed behind a sheet. That was why it was so easy to say what I did next.

"It is awfully revealing."

She put her head on my shoulder. She was shaking and her hand on my bare neck was ghostly in its chill. "I'll never be able to face them."

I tried to sound worried and sympathetic. "We could trade," I said. "I'll wear it."

"Would you? Won't you be embarrassed?"

"A little. But one of us has to do it."

We switched. I took my underthings off, Helene put hers back on. I put on the thin dress, she put on the thick one.

"Well?"

"It looks like a nightgown on you," she said. It did bag in the front where my breasts were supposed to be, and the little cord belt didn't cinch as tight as it did on Helene, but I was wearing it.

"I hope they're not angry," she said as we stepped out.

They laughed, which was not what I was hoping for.

"Baby Juno," Gustav roared. "You're a vision, really."

"I think there's been some mistake," said Ernst. He looked at Helene. "You were supposed to wear the other dress." She looked at him pleadingly. "Unless you don't want to," he said quickly. "In that case it's perfectly all right."

"We'll try it, anyway," said Gustav. "If it doesn't work we can send a note to Lotte and maybe she can come tomorrow."

"Who's Lotte?" asked Helene.

"A professional model. She works for us sometimes." It was amazing, the number of women who seemed to be in and out of the studio.

"What's wrong with me?" I wanted to know. "Why can't I do it?"

"Well, if you're going to, quit whining about it and get on the platform," said Ernst churlishly. I couldn't understand why he was so angry.

The platform was little more than a wooden box covered with a blanket. An assemblage of broken chairs, unraveling pillows, and a tatty chaise completed it. Gustav told me where to stand and positioned my arms and face. He showed Helene how to kneel so that she wouldn't get tired.

No such provision was made for me and I stood with my arm pointing toward the windows, for what seemed like hours. Helene knelt at my feet, holding a jug. Every now and then she would whisper that her neck hurt and could I see? Were they almost done? My arm ached, but they wouldn't let me rest. This is what models do, said Ernst. If you don't like it you can go home.

They were sketching my profile and so I couldn't look at what they were doing. I concentrated on counting the panes of glass and the tiles in the ceiling. The sun moved across the window. It was two, then three. My arm drooped lower and lower. At three-fifteen Gustav propped it up on a lectern that had mysteriously appeared. At three-thirty some other people came in. I couldn't see them, but the volume in the room rose drastically.

"Who're these two?" asked a man. Franz or Georg, I assumed.

"The Flöge girls, remember I told you?" said Ernst.

"Oh yes, the young ladies," sneered the other man. I heard things rattling and pages being torn. At one point it sounded like an easel fell over.

"Where've you been?" asked Gustav.

"Out late last night," said the first man.

"With Therese," snorted the second one.

"And was she good?"

The man must have gestured because all I heard was muffled laughter.

At four we took a break. My arm felt like I was wearing a fat heavy glove. Helene immediately ran into the closet to put her regular clothes back on, or to hide until the break was over, I wasn't sure which.

Gustav introduced me to his brother Georg and their friend Franz Matsch. Georg was wide and blond and was the one who had knocked over the easel. Apparently he was the reason no glass was allowed in the studio.

"He'll just break it and then a model will step on it and cut her foot and that's the last thing we need, a model with blood poisoning," explained Franz. He was blond too, but long and thin. He had a wispy mustache and red bumps on his neck. He offered me a cup of coffee.

"You were quite a trouper, staying up there so long," he said. "None of the models would have been able to hold their arm like that for that amount of time. Or willing, for that matter."

"They told me I had to." He smiled.

"If you're going to model regularly you're going to have to stand up to them. Gustav especially. He'll make you do as much as he thinks he can get away with."

"We're doing it for fun."

"So much the better. You can walk out anytime, you don't have to worry about earning enough for food or rent."

I thought about holding money in my hand, money that I had earned, and about buying as many vanilla caramels as I wanted and eating them all at once. I thought about a pair of garnet earrings and a room with a door that locked. I thought about going to the theater and sleeping until noon the next day. It sounded thrilling, but also a little bit lonely. If I ever went to live on my own Helene would have to come with me.

The rest of the afternoon passed quickly. For the next pose I had to lie on the floor as if I were dead, and I fell asleep. Every now and then a laugh or shout would jolt me awake, and I would try to hear what they were saying. They were full of secrets, full of knowledge about a darker, more muscular world than the one I lived in, and I wanted to be admitted. That was why I would do anything Gustav asked me to.

We left at five and got home before anyone missed us, since we told them our school outing to the art museum would probably run late.

Seven

One winter morning I woke up and saw that the amber sky was spitting snow. In my classroom the wind would whistle through the gaps where the windowsills had warped, and my desk was next to the window, by my own choice. From it I could watch the nuns gliding to prayers, or unlocking the big gate on their way to bring food or medicine to the poor. They weren't very interesting, but it was better than paying attention. But on that day it would be too cold to press my forehead to the glass. I would shiver through the test on French verbs and my Goethe recitation. It was a day that demanded feigned illness.

At first I just planned to stay at home in bed. It wasn't difficult to convince my mother of this plan; she believed in bed rest for everything from headaches to indigestion to skin rashes. She brought me a fat hot water bottle and a steaming drink of lemon and honey. I half-hoped she might stay with me, read something to me or play a card game, but she was going marketing. Everyone else had left already for work or school. All of a sudden the apartment was eerily quiet. Even the street noise was muffled by the snow.

Helene had recently bought a Parisian fashion paper with her birthday money. I got it and propped myself up on my pillows, intending to read, but my French wasn't good enough for it to be effortless, so I just looked at the pictures. It was a winter preview issue. There were pages of women in walking suits, tight little jackets with jabots of lace at the throat. The skirts were pleated or gathered, bustled or peplumed in back. The hats were tall and plumed. The tea dresses were filmy concoctions buried under bows and lace and ribbons. They said that blue was the color of the season: ice blue, sky blue, dove gray. The ball gowns were fantastic, silk brocade creations, with bows at the shoulders and tightly cinched belts. They were hugely crinolined. I admired the ball gowns but thought they looked uncomfortable. I liked the bicycling costume the best: velveteen bloomers and a double-breasted jacket of the same material. The girl in the drawing looked exuberant and proud.

Most of the drawings weren't very well done: cow-eyed women with extremely long torsos so out of proportion they'd never be able to stand up in real life. With my pencil I lopped off most of their bosoms, and their posture immediately improved. I raised their waists and they smiled gratefully. In the margins I drew my own ladies; their heads were the right size for their bodies, their corsets were loosened by inches and their dresses had lost most of the furbelows. It made me feel better.

I'd had a racy novel hidden under my bed for weeks, waiting for the right opportunity, so I tried that next. The wrongfully accused and fleeing marquess had been shipwrecked and was hiding in the castle of the mysterious and ill-tempered lord by the time I decided that racy novels were only amusing if Helene was there to laugh at them with me. Unfortunately she was going to her friend Amelie's after school and wouldn't be back until seven or eight o'clock. After awhile I got up and looked out, just to make sure the world hadn't disappeared.

Outside the window the street was dim and turbulent as the snow fell faster and faster. It was hypnotizing in its changing patterns. As I watched my breath fogged the window and I wiped it with my sleeve, but that made it blurry, so I leaned to the left. The few people on the streets had their shawls wrapped tightly and their hats bent to the wind. They pulled the shop doors open and the gusts of air slammed the doors shut behind them.

You'd think this sight would reinforce my desire to stay inside, but instead it made me lonely and restless. I got dressed before I had announced to myself where I was going to go, but there was never any real question. I opened Pauline's underwear drawer to fish out the fare, a by now familiar habit. In the months we'd been going to the studio, she had never counted it. At least she had never said anything. I hoped she'd win another prize before we used it all. I put on my second-best boots and tied a scarf over my head and went out the back door of the building in case any of our neighbors happened to be watching the front.

The studio would be even colder than the schoolroom, but it would be lit up and active and loud. There would be jokes, and laughter. I could walk on my hands if I felt like it, though at fifteen I was too old for gymnastics. Gustav had been known to juggle oranges when he was waiting for an answer to a problem. There would be sweets, and the earthen smells of pigments.

I passed the little park down the street from our building. Some intrepid children had convinced their governesses to take them out. The governesses stamped their feet underneath the one sheltering larch. They were young and from the country and soon they would trade in these miserable children for a lower level civil servant and a ticket to the Office of Transportation's annual Fasching ball. For now, though, they playfully warmed their noses on one another's necks and gossiped about Thilde's recent engagement.

A boy in a red coat with glinting brass buttons lay down in the snow and began flapping his arms to make a snow angel, and was promptly and roughly brought to his feet by his stout guardian and pulled away. Two little girls with golden hair streaming out of their hoods crouched and patted snowballs gently with matching green mittens. Under my clothes my skin was already pink and itching with the cold, and it made me want to fall into a snowdrift myself to cool the burning, but my new gray coat made my eyes look very blue, and my dress had real Valenciennes lace on the collar and cuffs, and I didn't want either of them to get wet or dirty. As I passed I was hit from behind by a snowball, but it was light dry snow and broke apart on impact. I turned, but the little girls were innocently patting and the boy was digging a cave with his back to me.

I packed a snowball and tossed it. It hit the park's wrought iron fence and powdery shrapnel blew into the faces of the startled governesses. I ran, gulping the icy air and watching for slick passages on the sidewalk. I got a stitch in my side from laughing and running at the same time, but I didn't care, I was so intoxicated by the freedom of being out alone.

On the streetcar to Leopoldstadt I peeked at a theatrical paper over the shoulder of a woman with waxy skin. There was a drawing of the inside of the Burgtheater that I recognized as Gustav's. He'd shown it to me months before. I wanted to tell the woman that the man who drew it was my drawing teacher, but she'd probably call the conductor, thinking me crazy. Instead I tried to read the articles and to siphon warmth from the woman's rabbit coat.

I was aware that some of the women on the streetcar were looking at me with disapproval, so I tried to look as if I were on an important errand: laudanum for my dying father, or belladonna for my brother who had whooping cough. The conductor took the ticket from my hand and looked at it closely, as if I might have cheated somehow. I waited breathlessly until he punched and went on. The circles of white confetti floated to the floor. The men on the streetcar read the papers or stared straight ahead. They seemed not to see anything that passed the windows. I wondered how they got off at the right stop. Perhaps they counted.

It was December 1889. In two years I would be out of school. Pauline had already finished and was taking a secretarial course. We weren't rich enough for her to enter society, but we were too well off for her to take most kinds of jobs. The secretarial course sounded horrible, but she didn't seem to mind it. She helped with the bills at home and had a bookkeeping ledger and a sheet of carbon paper that she carried with her all the time. In the spring Helene would be finished, but I couldn't imagine her in a secretarial course. Perhaps they would let her study music. Eventually she might be good enough to sing with the Opera.

As for me, I was an absentminded but competent student. I had no interest in science or medicine. In order to go to university in those days a woman had to be brilliant and highly motivated, and I was neither. I wasn't musical like Helene. I felt most alive in the studio, but what that meant I had no idea.

Neither my parents nor teachers had ever expressed the slightest suspicion of me or what I might be up to, which says more about the preoccupation of my parents and the innocence of my teachers than it does about my cunning. If Helene hadn't been there to anxiously watch the clock, I would have frequently been late getting home, and there would have been questions, but she was there, and we were never late. It never seemed to occur to the nuns that we might lie, and they believed our breathless stories about an illness at home with perfect faith. At home, Father attended to his business, and Mother slept and composed. As long as we didn't lose weight, cough incessantly, fail in our examinations, or get expelled, all was well as far as they were concerned.

The streetcar deposited me a few blocks from the factory building that housed the studio, and when I arrived I looked up to see if the lamps were lit. They were. I smelled challah baking as I went up the stairs. I tripped on a loose nail and fell heavily against the banister. I half expected Gustav to poke his head out and drop something on me from above. He had done that to Ernst once, with eggs. But there was no sound above me. When I got to the studio door, I paused for a moment and listened. The artists were usually so loud that the baker next door was continually opening his window to yell across, waving his rolling pin. But I didn't hear anything. Maybe someone had left the lamps lit, a fire hazard and a waste of kerosene. They would thank me when they found out that I had come by and put them out.

I pushed the door open. The floor was gritty under my feet and little sandy puddles began to form under my boots. Rivulets of water melted from my hair down my face and into my mouth. I had forgotten to wear a hat. No wonder the ladies on the streetcar had looked at me. Only a slattern went out without a hat. The melting snowflakes tasted like buttermilk soap, rich and salty. I stared silently into the studio, frozen stiff like a squirrel in the path of an oncoming cart. Gustav was alone in the studio, or rather he was the lone artist there. His hair was disheveled and he looked tense and taut, wound like a watch. He frowned with his whole face, but his eyes caught the lamplight and glowed like a cat's. I had never seen him look like that before.

The lamps were hung above the dais in the middle of the room. It was piled with blankets peaked like meringue. They looked as soft as a baby chick. On the blankets were two women I had never seen before. They moved continuously, quite unlike the way models were normally instructed to behave. They writhed and twisted and the white downy blankets twisted around their bodies. Their silk robes, Chinese red and yellow, were crumpled on the floor near the platform. They were intertwined, the two women, like serpents, a Celtic pattern of thighs and spines and necks and red and black trailing hair. Their bodies braided like silk dress trim. Woven together like warp and weft. Both were laughing as they paused at short intervals to let Gustav make a sketch. They nipped and slapped and licked. Laughing. The shadows on their bodies were smudged in the yellow light. I watched the shadows moving. It was beautiful, this shadow play. I don't know how long I stood there. Long enough for it to stop snowing and the sun to pierce the clouds painfully and to harshen the shadows and light the orange-haired woman like a sunset.

The black-haired woman looked up and saw me. Smiled. Gustav was deep in concentration and I tried to back out of the room before he noticed me, but the model said his name and flicked a shoulder in my direction. He dropped his pencil. Told the models to stop. The many-limbed creature ceased its frolicking and the disentangled pieces became two women again.

He was at my side, kissing me on the cheek. "You look frozen," he said. "I thought we said Thursday. And why aren't you in school?"

"Sick," I gasped.

"You sound terrible. Let me make you some tea." He was being gentle, pulling me into the room and out of my coat. He sat me down on the plush blankets. He did not snap at me for interrupting. That alone was enough to make my stomach knot and the nausea rise.

The models had slid into their robes and were heading toward the changing room. He called them over. The red-haired one was flushed and her chest was mottled. She was very thin but I was shocked to see the protuberance where the baby was. I hadn't noticed it before. She hunched her shoulders over her belly as if to protect it. She had blue circles under her eyes. The black-haired one looked me in the eye; I felt that she was laughing at me.

"Emilie Flöge," said Gustav, "meet Minna and Helga." They nodded; neither dared offer me her hand. I recoiled from them, barely able to mouth a greeting. They frightened me, the upthrust belly of one, the grin of the other.

"They live in Hietzing," he added, irrelevantly. I managed a nod. For a moment no one said anything. Then Helga slapped Minna on the behind.

"Get moving, you scrawny thing." They sauntered away, and once dressed, they left without saying good-bye; apparently they were regulars and knew when to return and when they would be paid.

Though they had gone, their afterimages lingered, fluttering like bats' wings at the corners of my vision. When I closed my eyes, the blocks of color floating on the inside of my eyelids were bloody and golden. I wrapped one of the blankets around myself, but it was not as soft as it had looked from afar. It made me itch. Gustav stood at the stove and watched the water boil. He was saying something about arithmetic, how I was so good at fractions and must help him with the proportions on one of his drawings. Ernst was home with a cold, he'd always been delicate, Gustav had made him promise to get some rest. Poor Emilie, she probably caught her cold from him. And Franz, he was off somewhere with one of his girlfriends, he said, and then winced. I mean, he's having lunch with his mother and his sisters, very genteel people, very correct. They didn't like his being an artist, they thought it was vulgar. He winced again. It pained me to hear him try to censor things for my benefit.

That's a beautiful dress, he said as he handed me a chipped cup of cardamom tea. The aroma of India wafted up into my face. Gustav sat down cross-legged on the floor in front of me, put his chin in his hands, and stared at me dolefully.

I didn't want to look at him. I didn't want cheap flattery. I stood up quickly and all the blood rushed to my head, momentarily filling my eye sockets with gray. When it cleared I placed my tea on the floor and went over to the easel to look at the drawing he'd been doing. My face was flushed and sweaty but I felt chilled and clammy. There they were, on the paper, Minna and Helga. I had never seen a drawing of Gustav's drawn with more passion than the two writhing bodies of these women. Every line was emphatic, every curve was suggestive. They were practically alive on the page.

I thought of a self-portrait Gustav had done as a joke. He had drawn his head, pointy beard, broad forehead, but with horns, atop a teardrop-shaped body with a deep cleft in it. He gave himself a goat's tail and hoofs. I wasn't supposed to see it, the artists had laughed over it and then Gustav had hidden it under one of his books, but I had retrieved it when no one was looking and had taken it home. Helene and I had puzzled over it. Clearly it was something illicit. It had the scent of sex on it. But we were young enough and ignorant enough not to know what it was or what it meant.

I took a deep breath. "Is it yours?" I asked. We were not allowed to discuss pregnancy or childbirth in mixed company. There were euphemisms, there were secrets. But I had to know.

"Of course not," he said.

"Whose is it, then?" I asked.

"Some tavern keeper," he said. "I go there at dinnertime. He makes a good sauerbraten."

"Will he help her?" I was relieved. He was telling me things I wasn't supposed to hear, brutal coarse things he would only tell to an equal, a friend. I felt a rush of compassion for malnourished Minna. She wasn't much older than I, after all. She could've been my sister.

"Why do you think I've kept her on?" he said. "She can't get any other work in her condition. Even other artists don't want her as a model right now."

"What will happen to her?"

"She'll be all right. She's been on her own since she was fifteen."

In an instant I felt as smart and worldly as a pet cat. I was fed, I was groomed, but the cats that ate out of garbage cans would have me for lunch. I didn't even have claws. I disgusted myself.

Gustav was standing behind me and couldn't see my tears. The thought of him pitying me, worrying about what such a sight would do to my delicate sensibilities, worrying about what I might say to my parents, as if I would tell, made me want to die.

"Look at me, Emilie," he said. Instead I gazed across the room at the pile of chairs in the corner next to the window. They were upside-down and on their sides and stacked one on top of the other, the ones near the top dangling precariously. In the gray light they cast no shadow. It was like a pile of bones from the slaughter-house. I tried to memorize the parallel lines and right angles and triangles and various tones of dark and light. Slowly the shapes sharpened into distinct pieces. I began to see each individual chair. It was a haphazard collection, begged and borrowed from friends and relatives: a stool painted white, a warped rocking chair, a tattered sofa. One I recognized from our house: the stripped frame of an old armchair, covered with a purple velvet drape. How did it get there, I wondered.

"I use models all the time," he said. "I have to, to get the muscles exactly right."

"Of course, the muscles," I said. I knew the tears he couldn't see were audible in my thick, choked voice, but there was nothing I could do about that. "Muscles are so important. Especially the movement of them." Helga's back was succulent as a piece of fruit. Minna's arms were curved like willow branches.

"How they attach to the bones and tendons," he said. "At school we studied cadavers. Peeled the skin and fat off like a winter coat. Had to have a strong stomach for that." I thought that peeling Minna would be more like blanching a peach. Her skin looked so thin, and she didn't seem to have any fat.

I clenched my fist and looked at the tendons on the inside of my wrist. They were like reeds, tied into a bundle with purple and blue string. So we were going to turn this into an anatomy lesson. "What do the muscles look like?" I asked.

"Balls of twine," he said. "Or skeins of yarn wrapped around your hands. Bundled and red, so beautiful. Doctors are lucky, to have the human body as their medium. There isn't anything more perfect in all the world. Of course I could never be one. Blood makes me queasy. And people are better when they are naked and their mouths are shut."

I began to quiver with sobs, silently at first. I knew that Gustav's mind was far away, remembering the latissimus dorsi of some long-dead indigent. He was staring absentmindedly at his painting, comparing Minna's physiognomy to others he had drawn. How her elbows were double-jointed and her torso was short. I wanted him to stay there, far away from me, but then his gaze moved from Minna's form to mine.

He grabbed my shaking shoulders and turned me around.

"What are you crying for?" he said. I couldn't answer. Now I was crying for real and couldn't be stopped, loud, wet, heartbroken, sore-throated yelps, like a puppy left alone all day. "Don't be such a baby," he said. "You're not hurt. Nothing's been done to you."

He had never spoken to me harshly before. It shocked me out of my crying. He wasn't very much taller than me and his face was very close to mine. On a cloudy day his eyes were the green of a still pond. He let his hands drop to his sides.

"I'm sorry," he said. "You're just a little girl. I should've known better than to bring you here."

"I brought myself," I said.

"I mean I should never have invited you. I'm a bad influence."

Not knowing what to say or do, I kissed him. I don't know what came over me; I suppose it was the atmosphere of the studio, charged as it was.

I had never kissed anyone not of my family before. I half-expected Gustav to pull away from me, but he didn't. His beard was very soft, which was surprising. It tickled my face. Gently he prised my lips apart and put his tongue inside. It was odd, but not unpleasant. He tasted of coffee and peppermint. I opened my eyes and looked at his eyelashes, which were long like a girl's. His arms were around me as solid as marble. I felt strangely unmoved by the event. Wasn't I supposed to swoon? Wasn't I supposed to feel something glorious?

We stopped. His eyes opened. For a moment I was afraid.

"Stop looking at me like that," he said. He traced my mouth with his finger.

"Like what?"

"Your eyes are nearly cerulean," he said, accusingly.

"I can't help that," I said.

"No, you can't." He set me aside, gently, but aside.

"Where are you going?"

"To get your coat. A sick girl like you should be at home in bed."

He held the coat open and I slipped into it. He fumbled with the bone buttons but they were too small for his fingers. He reprimanded me for not wearing a hat, said he would buy me one, a pretty one, the other day he'd seen a wine-colored one made of cashmere in a store window. He told me about the hat as if it were a soothing bedtime story.

I was humiliated. I was nothing but a little girl to him. It made me angry. I tried to think of a way to punish him.

"You've never let me draw a model," I said as we walked slowly down the stairs.

"It's not . . ." he said. "You can't." He tried to think of a reason, but there wasn't one that didn't sound bourgeois.

"Shouldn't I be able to get the muscles right, too?"

"All right then, next time you can draw one of my arms."

"I'm so lucky," I said.

We had reached the street and opened the door. Perhaps if I had had more time I would have been able to come up with something much more sarcastic and cutting to say to Gustav, but it was not to be. There on the steps, just about to enter the building, was Ernst and my sister Helene.

My sister Helene who was with her friend Amelie. My sister Helene who had never kept anything from me in her entire life.

All four of us stopped. Helene turned white and I turned pink. Her look of horror must have mirrored mine. Ernst was looking at the ground, as if we would disappear if he didn't look at us. I looked over at Gustav, who seemed very amused.

"Out for a stroll?" he asked pleasantly.

"Yes, I ran into Helene on the street and she said she'd forgotten her fur muff at the studio, so I said I'd accompany her to pick it up, then walk her home." Ernst was rattling off words as if it were a memorized speech.

"What happened to Amelie?" I said.

"What happened to being at home sick in bed?"

"It's quite a coincidence, really," said Gustav. "Emilie forgot her gloves in the studio and came to get them. I'm taking her home right now."

"Such a forgetful family," Ernst said.

"Yes, it really shows a lack of parental discipline, doesn't it?" said Gustav. He sounded as if he were about to burst into laughter.

"Shall we wait for you to fetch the muff?" said Gustav. "Then we can all walk together."

"It's all right," said Helene. She looked panic-stricken. "There's no need for you to see us home, now that we're both here. I'll get the muff another time. In this weather her cold could turn into pneumonia."

"Are you sure you're all right?" said Ernst. I noticed that his fingers were pulling on her sleeve. But she hardly looked at him.

"Yes, fine," she said brusquely. "Let's go, Emilie."

"Till next time then," Ernst said hopefully.

"Thursday," Gustav reminded us. "If Emilie's feeling better, that is."

Helene's leather glove was icy cold on my bare hand and she gripped it so tightly it began to sting. I yanked it away. We walked quickly and silently, lost in our angry thoughts. We were blocks away before she spoke.

"What were you doing there alone with him?" she hissed. I hated her accusing older sister tone. "Don't you know about him by now?"

"Know what?"

"He likes to seduce young girls. I can't believe Mama and Papa let him keep giving you lessons."

"He didn't seduce me," I said. I didn't tell her about the kiss, though a few minutes ago I had been thinking about how I would describe it to her. I wasn't sure now if I could trust her.

"Don't lie," she said. "It's too important." She yanked on my arm and turned to face me. We were the same height. Her coat was just like mine except a forest green instead of blue. Her eyes are nearly cerulean, too, I thought.

"He didn't," I said. She held my gaze to see if I would crack. Then her shoulders crumpled in relief, and she began to cry. I was alarmed. Perhaps what I'd done was even worse than I thought.

"It's all right," I said, stroking her shoulder. "I'm fine."

"It's not that," she sobbed.

"What is it then? Is it Ernst?" My first thought was that he had hurt her in some way. She never cried; but then, I remembered, neither did I until that afternoon. She nodded and mumbled something. It sounded like, "I'm in love with him," but I couldn't believe that. They didn't even know each other.

"You're in love with him?" I really looked at her then. Her face was thinner and she had circles under her eyes. Why had I not noticed it before?

"Really?" She nodded with her eyes firmly fixed on something far behind me, down and to the left.

I pulled her into the nearest café and sat her down. It was a cheap place, with sticky wooden tables and withered pastries that looked days old, but there was no way we could go home just yet.

"For how long?"

"Since the summer. July." Four months. Four months she had been keeping this secret from me.

"Why didn't you tell me?"

"I didn't want to get you in trouble if Mama and Papa found out."

I didn't understand when she could have found the time to fall in love with him, since I was almost always with her, but it turned out that it happened right under my nose. It began as furtive glances in the studio, she said. But with all of the gazing that was going on, how did she know that those looks were special and meant only for her? First it was how he adjusted her position when she was modeling. Then it was the presents he brought her: apples and pears and a jointed wooden doll he had bought from a Czech toymaker. I had never noticed him giving her these presents because he had slipped them into the pocket of her coat when no one was looking. Then came the notes. Finally, they met at the gardens at the Prater, an amusement park on the edge of town. How no one ever saw them in that popular place I'll never understand. Or how careful Helene could be so brave, and so brazen.

It had to be a secret from our parents because Helene was not yet eighteen and because Ernst was too poor to make a legitimate offer for her. Mama and Papa would undoubtedly disapprove.

"Of course I won't tell," I said. I wanted to kiss her but the man at the next table was watching us.

"I don't care if you go to the studio," she said. "I just don't want you getting into trouble." It was a measure of how much our time with the Klimts had changed us that she said it, and that I knew what she meant.

"Really, nothing happened," I said.

"All right," she said.

It was late. We knew that someone in our family must have noticed our absence by now.

"If we go in together we'll each only get half," I said. Though I wasn't aware of being cold, my teeth chattered so that I could barely speak.

"No," Helene said. I was shocked at how steely her voice was, and how much older she suddenly looked. "I'll go to the front. You wait in the alley, and when you hear the shouting slip in the back way. We'll just have to take the chance that no one has thought to check on you yet."

I was grateful, though I was terrified for her, facing all of that fury by herself. I also felt very guilty. I had been as deceptive and illicit as she.

It went exactly as Helene predicted. I lurked at the corner of the building until I heard my father's loud imprecations and my mother's wails. No one saw me come in through the kitchen. No one heard me run up the stairs. No one thought to call me for supper, or put her hand to my forehead, or see if I was sleeping. No one noticed me at all.

Eight

"She's not a Persian princess," we heard Gustav say. "You can't keep her up there forever."

Helene and I were listening through the dining room door, which even at the time I knew was a farcical thing to do, but the outcome of this meeting was too important to sit in our room and speculate about what was said.

Helene had been locked in our room for two weeks now, allowed out only to bathe. Pauline and I brought her spartan meals and sometimes managed to sneak in an apple tart or *The Decameron*. She spent the time singing mournful songs and staring out of the window. Neither of our parents would speak to her. In fact, they seldom spoke to Pauline and me either, but sat at meals exchanging dark glances and slamming down the serving dishes and glassware. Pauline and I tried to become invisible. For a change I was grateful to have school to go to. And lessons with Gustav on Saturdays, of course.

The first lesson after the kiss I almost passed out in the carriage on the way to his house, but the house was the same, the kitchen was the same, Mrs. Klimt sat there with her knitting and a plate of freshly baked chocolate tea cakes. Gustav was exactly the same. It wasn't that he was pretending that nothing happened; he seemed to have forgotten entirely. In a way I was relieved. Also disappointed.

Ernst had been trying to talk to our parents for weeks, but Mother wouldn't answer the door. Ernst stood on the step in the snow, ringing the bell again and again. Finally, Pauline had to go out and tell him to go away.

Next he tried letters, but Mother burned them in the fireplace without reading them. She wept on the sofa throughout the day, pausing periodically to practice at the piano.

Finally Gustav had gone to the pipe factory. He had offered to act as a mediator, and Father, a reasonable man, accepted readily. I doubt he would have been so agreeable had he known what I had been up to the day Helene was caught.

"We can do what we choose," Mother said. I couldn't see her but I knew her chin was jutting out from her starched collar and that wisps of dark hair were falling into her eyes. Behind her back, she was picking the trimming off of one of her sleeves. I knew because she had taught me the same trick to keep me from biting my nails. A sleeve can take punishment better, can be easily repaired. I didn't understand her attitude. Though when I was younger I hadn't tested the strict confines of our upbringing, I had always assumed that it would be our mother who would sympathize, and our father who would rage. Perhaps she was jealous that one of her daughters had attempted to escape from the prison that held her.

"What will it accomplish?" Gustav said. He sounded impatient and disrespectful. "Helene lied, she's been punished, it's time to let it go."

"I just can't understand it," said Papa. "Helene was always such a good child."

Helene gave me a guilty, haggard look. She'd hardly slept in two weeks. If possible she looked more beautiful than ever with the blue shadows under her eyes and her pale, gaunt cheeks, the dark beauty opium addicts sometimes have. She had tied her hair into an absentminded plait and golden shoots sprung in every direction.

"She's in love," Gustav said. He sounded as if he were smiling. I felt Helene blushing.

"She's only seventeen," said Papa. "What does she know about it?"

"Ernst wants to marry Helene," Gustav said. There was a silence broken only by a few sniffles from my mother. Apparently they had not been expecting it. Even though I had, it was not until that moment that I realized what it meant. She was leaving me, and I hated her for it, but mostly I hated Ernst. But then I thought, they will never allow it, and felt better.

"What does he have to offer her?" Mother said.

"She cannot marry until she is twenty," Papa said. "And she must finish school."

"All right," said Gustav. "He'll marry her when she's twenty." Helene leaned into me, trembling.

I waited for my father to shout, to say no, that Ernst wasn't good enough for Helene, that it was ridiculous even to consider it, but he didn't. There was a long silence.

"Is he a good artist?" Father asked. "Will he be able to provide for her?"

"He's much better than I am," Gustav said.

"Very well," said Father. Mother said nothing. It wasn't really her decision, it was Father's, and he had decided.

It had been much too easy as far as I was concerned.

Then, the business concluded, the transaction complete, they ate Kirsch torte and drank coffee with *Schlagobers* and talked about the opera.

A week later my father said that instead of fetching me himself, Gustav would drop me off at home on the way to his studio. They had discussed it and it was more efficient that way. My father had decided that as my future brother-in-law Gustav was now a suitable chaperone.

"I had to do it," Gustav said as I sat with him at Café Sperl. We had canceled our lesson in order to eat cake and discuss the unfolding family drama. "Ernst was making mistakes in the bookkeeping. It was getting expensive. And he burst into tears in front of Count Esterházy."

He had bought me a piece of cake frosted with marzipan, my favorite. Under Gustav's libertine tutelage I was quickly forgetting my manners. Gustav observed as I dismantled the cake, hacked off the pink and yellow rosettes of sugar and left them on the side of the plate, peeled away the icing to eat first, stabbed at the cake with my coffee spoon, pulled apart the crisp layers frosted with cocoa until finally I scraped the last few crumbs from the porcelain plate.

"You eat like a savage," he said. "And your face is covered with cake." He leaned across the table and wiped my mouth with a paint-spattered handkerchief dipped in ice water, as if I were a child in the care of a fastidious uncle. When he was finished, the corners of my mouth were red. My eyes strayed embarrassingly often to Gustav's lips, so I looked at his cake. It was chocolate with layers of raspberry jam. As he picked it apart the jelly spread across the plate like blood.

"What did the count do?" I asked, returning to the matter at hand.

"Oh, he gave him a handkerchief and his flask of schnapps, calm as could be. Later, though, he asked me if Ernst might not be better off in a sanitarium. He could arrange it, if I thought . . ."

"Poor Ernst," I said.

"Poor Ernst my . . . foot," he said. "Thanks to me he has a beautiful fiancée and a salvaged career. He's a lucky man."

"Was that the only reason, to save your business?" I couldn't help but ask.

"Well, no," he said. "The loss of our most reliable models was becoming a problem." I had been too afraid to come to the studio while the house was in such an uproar, especially alone.

"You mean your unpaid models," I said.

"Well, yes," he grinned. He seemed impervious to my serious mood. "Since you mention it, replacing you was becoming too expensive. Add that to all the bookkeeping mistakes and this affair cost the studio a month's commissions."

"What a romantic way to look at it," I said.

"Some of us just aren't romantic," he shrugged. "You, for instance. I can't imagine you crying into the curtains and singing lamentations."

"No one has ever given me reason to," I said.

"No one ever will. Those things only happen to people who seek them out," he said. "Ernst and Helene were born to have a doomed love."

I would remember our conversation years later, when Ernst was dead and my sister was drowning in the depths of grief. But at the time I thought rather bitterly that my sister had, once again, had everything turn out perfectly.

We were quiet for a while as we thought about our siblings. At least I thought about them. I don't know where Gustav's thoughts wandered but he came out in a place I wasn't expecting.

"The sexual prudery of the middle classes," he said. "I have no patience for it."

"What?" I was shocked to hear the word said out loud, but to admit that would to have been guilty of the very thing he was talking about.

"Your parents," he said. "So interesting. Enlightened and cultured in so many ways. 'Support artists!' they cry. 'But not with our daughters!' "

"They were just thinking of her future," I said, wondering why I was defending them.

"Why can't the future be different?" he said. "Why can't women and men be seen together without it ruining their reputations?"

"Why not?" I agreed. "Things can change."

"Things will change only if people like us lead the way." I wondered if he was asking me to do something. I had no desire to jeopardize my freedom anytime soon.

He painted a world without hypocrisy, where people were free to love whomever they chose regardless of age or social class or propriety, and even then I wondered if he really was interested in transforming society for everyone's benefit, or if he just wanted to do as he pleased without being criticized for it. We both pretended that the discussion was academic.

Nine

Weddings are not my favorite subject, never having had one myself. I've designed a lot of dresses for them, though. The weddings are remarkably similar to one another, whether the groom is a butcher or an aristocrat, whether the bride is pregnant already or still virginal. Somehow the sameness comforts people. The flowers will be white lilies; unless the bride's father is ill her dress will be a snowball viburnum of white; the groom will be pale and nervous and drop the ring at the front of the church; the bride will cry and Handel will be played. In my long career I hoped that just once a bride would come to the salon and ask for a dress of grass green, but it never happened.

Two years passed before Helene and Ernst married. During that time Ernst was at our house constantly. Sometimes he brought Gustav and the four of us would sing or play card games. Though we were a foursome by convenience, there was not a hint of romance between Gustav and me. After awhile even I forgot that the kiss had happened, or rather, I remembered it as something silly I had done a long time ago. Other things came to occupy me: I made a new friend at school whose mother wore clothes made in Paris and who didn't mind us pulling things out of her closet and examining them; I discovered Baudelaire and the French poets; and I fell in love.

I fell in love suddenly, as schoolgirls do, with a boy from the second floor of our building. Fritz's father had a dry goods store. We met him with his family on the street and then I saw him everywhere: on the stairs, in the Volksgarten, in my favorite bakery. He began leaving presents for me in one of the great urns that flanked the entranceway of our building: letters, bunches of violets, marzipan. I knew from the beginning that he would be going into the army in a few months' time and that only made the whole thing more romantic. When he left I cried incessantly and wrote copiously. We exchanged letters for several months and then the whole thing petered out. We had never kissed or even touched hands, but I felt that the relationship had changed me, that I was now a woman.

After the wedding ceremony we had a party for Helene and Ernst at our house. It was my designated task to shuttle from room to room, passing trays of ripe pear and pitted cherries. I didn't really mind; it gave me something to do, and I could see and talk to everyone without getting stuck with one of the aunts, who wore old-fashioned bonnets and thought the ceremony was too long and that it was a shame Helene had become a Catholic. At least now, though, their sons could get government jobs.

Pauline and I wore robin's egg blue organza dresses over constricting whalebone corsets that cost a fortune and made us hot and irritable, but there was no other way to even a twenty-two-inch waist for either of us. We were supposed to have seventeen-inch waists, but that wasn't possible. Even corsets have their limits. The dresses had bell sleeves that cascaded from a tightly cut shoulder and I worried that they would fall into the trays of food I was carrying and be soiled. Pauline gave me a tight smile each time she passed and I knew she was thinking the same thing.

Gustav was taking Helene and Ernst's photograph in front of the fireplace and people were gathered around to watch. It was a complicated enterprise involving a tripod, a black cape, and repeated explosions of flash powder. Gustav played up his role as if he were a magician. Helene was wearing my mother's lace veil, made by nuns at a convent in the Italian Alps, and a China silk gown with an organza overskirt made by a dressmaker Gustav knew. She looked like the portrait of the empress by Winterhalter, in the best sense and also in the worst. The aunts could find nothing about her appearance to criticize, which meant that her attire was sumptuously conventional. When the photography show was over everyone filled plates with roast pork and onion pudding, dumplings filled with sausage and turnovers filled with pungent cheese. The dining room table sat twenty-four, and those that couldn't find seats stood against the wall.

Pauline and I fled to the stairs, where we could unhook each other and eat in peace.

"Remember when we first moved here?" said Pauline, pressing her forehead against the polished wooden rails. "Your head fit between the bars and we played Marie Antoinette."

"You're going to get grooves on your temples," I said. "People will wonder about you."

"They already do," she said.

"I remember the three of us descending the stairs to an imaginary receiving line wearing Mama's paisley shawls," I said through a mouthful of spaetzle. "How she must have laughed!"

"And now here we are, spinsters passing trays," Pauline said.

"You're only twenty-three," I said, startled. "You're not a spinster."

"I only hope I don't have to be a nursemaid, half-masticated turnips all over my front every day."

"That will never happen," I said. "You're going to marry some distinguished lawyer. You'll pretend not to see me when we pass on the street." At least that made her smile.

"I don't look like Helene," she said.

"Think of all of the girls in your class," I said. "Not one is as beautiful as Helene, and yet they still get married." I thought she was being too hard on herself.

"Don't use that condescending tone," she said, "you're not going to marry either."

"What?" I felt as if I had been punched in the face.

"You're going to be caring for Mama and Papa and taking in sewing."

Suddenly I was shivering. "You're crazy," I said.

"Between the three of them they'll never let you meet anyone," she said. I knew who the third was without asking her but I pretended not to.

"Gustav likes having you around to flirt with. He'll crush anything before it gets started."

"What about Fritz?" I said defensively. Her laugh was ugly.

"That was like something out of a poem, and just as far removed from your real feelings. You're in love with Gustav."

"I'm not."

"You and Helene thought you were so clever, did you think I didn't know where you were going all of those months? It was my money that paid the train fare, remember?"

Of course she had known all along. Helene and I had gone on a great adventure and left her behind. We lumped her into the category of people not to be trusted. We had lied to her when we lied to our parents as if she were an old maiden aunt. We had not given her a chance to go along, to share the secret, to meet someone. And she had not said anything, had not betrayed us, and we had attributed it to our own skills at deception. No wonder she hated me.

"I'm sorry," I said. The sausages on my plate were pooled in oil and no longer looked so appetizing.

"Gustav's in love with himself. He likes to be admired. But he's not interested in anything like this." She gestured toward the garlands of narcissi draped over the banister.

"Who said I wanted to get married?"

"Don't you?"

"The institution of marriage perpetuates the subordination of women."

"Wake up, Emilie. Life perpetuates the subordination of women. That's just the way it is."

"It shouldn't be."

"What are you going to do if you don't get married? How will you live?"

"Not nursing Mama and Papa and darning other people's socks, I know that much."

"Good for you. I just hope you have a plan."

"What's yours, if we're on the subject?"

"Bookkeeper," she said. "Maybe for a druggist. Or a tailor. Some little apartment, some geraniums in the window boxes, a cat. I know what I can expect and what is out of reach. I'll be satisfied with that."

I got up, leaving my half-filled plate behind. When I was halfway down the stairs I remembered I needed to be rehooked. It was humiliating to go back but there was no one else to do it.

She was leaning over the railing looking down into the hall. Her shoulders were hunched and her dull hair was coming out of its chignon. For a moment I had a flash of her as an old woman with arthritis, a Siamese, and a parlor ivy. It made me remorseful.

"We could paint your geranium boxes," I said. "I could make stencils, of flowers and leaves, paint them pink and red, they'd look as if they'd come from a peasant village."

"Forget everything I said," she said. "This wedding has obviously sent me over the cliff. What do I know?"

Poor Pauline, she could see her own future, if not mine. But at least she kept the books at the salon instead of at some ugly, dreary man's hat shop. At least she had a room at the salon instead of at some dirty, chill rooming house. At least she was never poor. Her cats were the offspring of Gustav's tabby. She was famous for her orchids.

When I returned to my duties Gustav was settling his tottering father into a chair. Then he was turning pages for the pianist who was playing Haydn. He complimented the critical aunts and made them laugh and blush. He was everywhere, everywhere but where I was.

Suddenly, I felt ugly. My hair is too curly, I thought. Maybe I should try to flatten it with an iron. Despite my precautions, some freckles had appeared on my nose and were unwilling to leave, no matter how much lemon juice I used. My cheeks were round, and my figure was definitely not the type that Gustav preferred. I was going to be a fleshy woman, not a Rubens but definitely not a Klimt. I thought about Minna and Helga and their intertwined bodies. I was afraid of them. I was afraid to be like them.

I wanted to sit down and cry, and not the decorous kind of crying of a girl whose sister has just married or whose chevalier has taken the train to Graz. Instead I cleared plates until I heard the first notes of a Strauss waltz being played. Then I pushed through the crowd to watch Helene dance with Ernst. My sister was as pale and graceful as a porcelain figurine as Ernst whirled her around and around. He couldn't dance well, the aunts noted disapprovingly. All he seemed to be able to do was turn. Who ever heard of a groom who couldn't dance? Even ditch diggers had their own Lenten ball, where they danced like princes.

Helene's skirt beat the time like the wings of a swan. People began to clap.

My eyes met Gustav's and he gave me a little nod. He wanted to dance with me.

"Give me a kiss, little sister, we're family now," he said when we met, and brushed my hair with his lips. It was a brazen thing to do; everyone must have seen. Of course I couldn't kiss him, on the head or anywhere else. I could feel every place where our bodies touched, though: hand to hand, forearm to forearm, shoulder to shoulder. His hand on my waist was warm and I melted into it like bronze into a mold. Occasionally the front of my dress brushed his jacket.

"I never knew before how much you liked to dance," he said.

"Doesn't everyone?" I said. I could kiss him now, here, in front of everyone.

"Not Ernst," he laughed. "I tried to teach him at the studio last week. He can't count in his head. It's so humiliating for our family."

"We should cut in on them soon," I said, though it was the last thing I wanted. "I think Helene looks dizzy."

"What? Are you tired of me already?" I could feel his breath on my cheek. I could see his carotid artery pulsing beneath the skin. He'd been smoking with my father earlier; his jacket smelled of cloves and nutmeg. His lips were so close to my cheek that my breath stopped for a moment.

He pulled back a fraction of an inch. "You're right. It's either a daring rescue or smelling salts and a mild scandal." We broke apart and separated Helene and Ernst.

"I'm surprised she agreed to marry you," I said to Ernst as he flung me around the room. He was slighter than Gustav and I could barely feel his hand on my waist. His palm in mine was hot. "Unless you didn't tell her."

"Oh, I warned her," he gasped. "She said it didn't matter."

"She must love you very much then," I said, "because you're really awful."

"I know," he said. "I don't deserve this. I was just lucky. But I will take good care of her, I promise."

"You'd better," I said. "I never want to hear her sing a Bach cantata ever again."

"Now that we're safely married, maybe we can find someone for you." He was so proud of that "we," had probably been thinking for weeks about saying it.

"That's all right," I said. "I can choose for myself."

"No, no," he was excited by this idea. "Let me look around the room."

That was easy, since we made a three hundred and sixty degree turn every couple of seconds. I just hoped whomever he found wouldn't insult my opinion of myself.

"What do you think of Josef Maier?" said Ernst. "He's a decent portraitist."

"He has someone with him," I said, pointing to an auburn-haired girl in a cherry-colored dress.

"Well, there's Georg," he said. "But he'd smash all of the good china and anyway, he drinks too much."

"Not Georg, definitely," I agreed.

Then he stopped dancing abruptly.

"I know who," he said. "Wait over there, I'll be right back."

I moved to the side and looked around. Helene was dancing with Papa. I didn't see Gustav anywhere. I went into the kitchen, but everything had already been washed and put away. Pauline was turning pages for my mother, who had deposed the pianist. No one needed me for anything.

Ernst came toward me with a lanky boy, blond and pink with heat, like me. Franz, their partner in the studio. You would think that I would know him well, but he was always traveling. I had only seen him six or eight times in the past year.

"I thought you were in Greece," I said. Franz was painting Achilles for the new palace in Corfu.

"The empress has changed her mind again," said Franz. "The sketches must all be redone. I've been back at the studio nearly a week."

"You two dance," said Ernst, abruptly. "I need to find Helene."

Franz wasn't graceful, but he could keep time and talk simultaneously. "Is something wrong with Gustav?" he asked.

"Why?" I said.

He jerked his head toward a corner of the room. "Because he's over there by himself. It's not like him."

As we turned I glanced where he had indicated. Sure enough, there was Gustav, leaning forward in a chair, chin in hand, glowering.

"I have no idea," I said.

"Perhaps he wishes he were the one getting married," said Franz sardonically.

"Very funny," I said. Then, "You really think it's that unlikely?"

He pulled back a bit to look at me. "It's always the same with him. Some beautiful lady will start coming around the studio, her husband has commissioned a portrait, say. Before you know it she's dropping scented handkerchiefs and he's spending time at the Hotel Imperial. This goes on for weeks, sometimes months. And then she appears crying and makes a scene, saying her husband has left her and won't Gustav pick her up? It turns out she's been led to believe that Gustav wants to marry her, without his having said a single word that could be used as evidence in court. He's very clever that way. He never gets trapped. I'm afraid one of these days one of them is going to come around with a stiletto and finish him off."

"Someone from the opera, perhaps?" I told myself I was not surprised. I had always known that these women existed. My heart began to beat again, painfully. Almost to myself I said, "I wonder why I've never seen any of them."

"He's very careful to compartmentalize. Or usually." I wondered if Gustav had told him about me walking in on the models.

"So none of his love affairs ever last?"

"Sometimes they do, if the lady is like him. But I shouldn't be talking to you about this. Gustav would kill me."

"Because I'm like a little sister." He missed the irony entirely.

"Sisters aren't supposed to know about things like this. Don't ever tell him I told you."

Now that everyone had had a lot of wine someone called for a country dance. Franz and I were separated as we traded partners in an intricate circle dance that my mother's family used to do in Moravia.

"I have to say that you seem remarkably composed," he said when we were back together. "I thought all young ladies cried when their sisters married."

"Why should I cry?" I said.

"The empty bed, taking the leaf out of the table, packing up the rattle and baby blanket."

"You sound like a book of penny poems."

"I was trying to."

"Well, stop it, or I really will cry."

"Your sister will be fine. Ernst is the best artist of all of us."

That didn't sit well with me. "Gustav got the Imperial medal," I said.

"Don't misunderstand, Gustav's very talented. Far and away the best draftsman in the studio. But being an artist is more than skill. You have to make the patrons happy. You have to say the right things. Gustav's not like that. He's too blunt, too intent on getting his own way. People aren't happy with him. We've lost some commissions over it."

"Is that what an artist is supposed to do, try to please everyone even at the expense of beauty and taste?"

"All I mean is that he could try a little harder to be polite to important people. Humor them." We had slowed so that we were barely moving. "Maybe you could talk some sense into him."

I didn't say anything. Flattered as I was by the implication that I could influence Gustav, I was furious at the idea that anyone would try to compromise his ideals. As if I ever would!

"Are you too warm?" asked Franz, misinterpreting my flushed face. "Would you like me to get you a drink?" He seated me in a plush armchair in the corner of the room and disappeared into the crowd.

I went to Gustav's corner.

"Well?" he said. "Are you engaged yet?"

"Don't be ridiculous," I said. "We were just dancing."

"Just dancing," he said. "That's what they all say. We were just talking. We were just dancing. We were just flirting. And then I'm giving a toast at a wedding."

"Why do you care?" I said.

"Franz is a fool," he said.

"I thought he was your friend."

"All he cares about is his commission. He has no ambition. He's not interested in what the rest of Europe is doing. He's afraid to fail, afraid to displease those skeletons in the Kunstlerhaus."

One of the metal ribs in my corset had come free of its cotton wadding and was sticking into me just below my ribs.

"What has that got to do with what kind of dancer he is, or what kind of friend, or what kind of . . ." I looked for the right word but could find none.

"You know it matters," he said. "You know it matters more than anything."

I did know, but I wouldn't admit it to him.

"What I want is to make great art, art that will be remembered," he said. He rarely spoke so earnestly. "It might shock or disgust some people, but it makes visible for others what's inside my head. If you could do anything Emilie, anything in this world, what would it be?"

I could only say one of the things I thought out loud.

"I want to make beautiful things," I said. "I don't have any philosophical point to make, I just want there to be more loveliness in the world. That's all."

I looked at one sister, rubbing her back while she held a teacup for one of the aunts. I looked at the other, floating on her organza cloud.

"Maybe clothes," I said. "Like Worth."

Gustav was staring at me as if he'd never seen me before. There was a gleam in his eye, as if he'd just solved a particularly vexing problem of perspective.

"Of course you do," he said. "And you will."

"I don't see how," I said. "It's just a dream, like being an actress. I don't even know how to sew."

"You will," said Gustav.

Ten

Kammer am Attersee
December 15, 1944

O ur cottage is made of brick and roughly plastered and smells of the sea. Touch the facade and you'll scrape your hand. Once it was brilliant white but time and neglect have turned it the dingy gray of wash water. It has a steep red tile roof that is shiny when it rains. Some of the tiles are broken now and moss is growing between the cracks. We used to have impatiens around the house and geraniums in all the window boxes, but now we just have moss. Moss and lichen and mushrooms.

A covered porch faces the lake. We used to eat breakfast there. Our nearest neighbors were past shouting distance away, but we could see them from the porch. The men waved as they untied their boats in the morning.

The downstairs includes only a small kitchen and a large parlor, which was all we needed since we spent most of our time out of doors. My mother furnished them with Indian muslins and chintz and japanned furniture. Even now the Meissen plates and Steuben figurines are still on the mantel. The piano is still in the corner, the score of *Liebestraume* open on the stand.

Up the narrow, slanting staircase, the bedrooms are low-ceilinged and oddly-shaped, but there are six of them, one after the other on a long hall. I suppose the unfortunate fisherman whose only son sold it to us thought he'd have a lot more children. We needed every one of them, since we always had guests. The bedrooms are bare now, whitewashed like little convent cells, the mattresses on the brass beds broken open by mice.

Next to the garden is a stand of birches my father planted to keep the wind off of the house. It was hot that summer, even up here, and my father's face was purple and wet under his hat as he dug the holes. Some of the little saplings burned and died despite our assiduous watering, and one was struck by lightning a few years ago and had to be cut down, but a dozen are still here, thin and naked at this time of year, shedding their bark like psoriasis patients, shuddering and rattling like Gypsy carts.

I can barely remember a time when we didn't come here. Until I was thirteen we rented the house from Mrs. Thyssen, a widow in town whose husband had disappeared on the lake and was presumed drowned. When she died we bought it from her son, who lived in Salzburg and hated the place. When we were small my sister Helene and I used to walk along the shore, searching for this lost fisherman. We thought his bones might wash up on shore, or at the very least, that his ghost might rise up out of the water on some foggy day. He was like our patron saint; we feared him a little, but he was also our friend. We wrote him messages, poems, on pieces of bark. We floated them like tiny keelboats and watched them waterlog and sink, imagining them dropping fathoms and fathoms until they reached him. We didn't tell anyone about it. Papa would've thought it was morbid and frivolous and would have set us to work polishing the woodwork.

Amid the birch bark scrolls was always a good place to come and cry; the moss underneath them is dense and soft, the wind in the trees always blows a little mournfully.

The lake is long and gray like mercury spilled from a broken thermometer. It's glacier fed and breathtakingly cold, even in summer. There aren't many boats out today, only a few men fishing for carp with nets. The thin cirrus clouds are moving quickly past, toward Vienna. The dark cumulus clouds below them are moving almost as fast in the other direction. Across the lake in the village of Unterach the pastel houses are set into the hillsides like candies on gingerbread. A sound floats toward me, the sound of a finger on the rim of a glass: cowbells.

When I stand up my shoes sink into wet loam. I should have come directly from the house instead of wandering through the garden; from that direction there is a path made of broken tiles. My stockings will be stained. Even if I wash them myself Helene will shake her head and let me know that in the time I wasted ruining my stockings, I could've done five useful things. It's a strange day when the little girl whose christening dress you made starts bossing you around.

From my elevation I think that the lake with its many docks looks like an orb with many ladders leading to the center, a Hieronymus Bosch drawing of hell. All of the docks look the same: slimy and wooden and decrepit. Our dock is no different. The only way I can tell it's ours is that there is still a shred of red cloth tied to one of the posts. It's one of Gustav's kerchiefs, faded and filthy but somehow still there.

The boathouses, though, are all different. The summer people, people from the theater and the opera, have changing rooms and even kitchens for entertaining. They have little gazebos next to the water and clematis-covered pergolas. The locals have little sheds nailed together out of driftwood. We never thought of ourselves as summer people; our boathouse is as rickety as any local's, painted marine blue. Inside we keep the rowboat and oars, a canoe, and some rubber tubes for floating. It's been awhile since I've been inside, so I'm not sure if anything will still be there.

I pull the rowboat out by its stern. The white paint is curling and sticky like seaweed. There's a scrape on the port side that I can see through to the sand. I can't remember if it happened long ago and no one bothered to fix it, or whether someone has taken it out while we've been gone and torn it, but it doesn't matter.

I gather some wood and pile it up on the driest sand I can find.

The wood is damp and smokes when I light it, but it eventually ignites. The wind blows the mushroom-colored smoke right into my face. I have to pile the sand into a windbreak to keep my little blaze from sputtering out. In the boathouse is a tin can full of dried-up tar. I set it on top of the fire and hope that the tar will melt into something worth using. The boat is flipped over on the sand, awkward and helpless like a horseshoe crab on its back.

We used to have bonfires and roast sausages on sticks.

Helene appears behind me, wrapped in a gray shawl and a thick navy blue sweater that swallows her. With her pale faded skin she looks like a pen drawing, or a film. She can tell I'm scrutinizing her and wraps the shawl more tightly.

"That wood's too wet to burn properly," Helene says, shivering. "Wait until the weather clears to fix the boat."

"It's caught now," I say, poking my smoky blaze with a tree branch and trying not to cough.

"It's too cold to go out on the lake anyway."

"It'll take a while for the tar to dry," I say. Maybe by then the wind will have calmed.

"We'll get Heitzmann to do it next week," she says. She clips each word off ruthlessly, the way she does when she's irritated. It makes me more determined.

"I don't see why it matters to you if I take all afternoon," I say, knowing what her answer will be.

"There's plenty to do inside, and in the garden."

"We've got all the time in the world," I say. "If we don't weed today, we can weed tomorrow. If we don't bleach the floors today, we can bleach them tomorrow. Or the next day. Or next week. Why does it matter?"

"You're infantile," she says, disgusted, and leaves me to my smoldering fire.

Of course the tar refuses to melt into anything approaching a liquid. My patch is lumpy and uneven and Heitzmann will have to take it off and do another, but I don't care. Even the smell of burning tar is more pleasant than being stuck inside the house. I sit on the hull of the boat and watch the fire.

At half past two she comes back again with a cheese sandwich.

"You forgot lunch," she says. I'm surprisingly hungry. It must be the wind.

"A package came," she says. I don't say anything because my mouth is full and whatever it is, she can deal with it.

"I think you should come up to the house and open it," she says. Her hands are shaking. It frightens me a little. Is something wrong?

"Who is it from?" I say. I'm still poking at the fire but it's gone out for good.

"Come up," she says.

We walk single file up the path to the house, Helene in front. The lichen on the stones is slippery and a startlingly bright orange color. Crocuses, I think. In the spring we'll need crocuses. I wonder if Heitzmann's wife has any bulbs.

Helene stumbles and catches herself with her left hand.

"Let me see," I say. She shows me the scrape and I kiss it and say, "Good thing we brought the gauze bandages." Her blood is on my lip.

"Maybe Heitzmann can put in some sort of handrail for this path when he's here next," says Helene.

"Why don't you just hire him to carry us up and down?" I say, angry at her because I, too, have been thinking of all of the things I need him to do. "Doesn't the poor man have enough children?"

It turns out there isn't one package, but several collected on the sitting room floor. Helene sits me in a chair and brings them to me one by one, like it's my birthday. Then she sits on the stool in front of me, expectantly. I sever the twine and slice open the brown paper wrapping. Inside is a Chinese skirt from my textile collection. Its iridescent embroidery shimmers in the fussy room like an exotic bird.

"I thought Herta was going to sell these," I said. "We need the money."

"Who wants an antique skirt right now?" Helene says. "We'd be throwing it away."

"The damp air will rot it," I said, smoothing the skirt's pleats. Then I imagine Helene in the salon, that terrible time when we were taking everything down, pulling things out for me and keeping them hidden until I really needed them. Then the tears start to fall, my mask cracked like pottery fired too hot. I try to keep them quiet, and Helene aids me by looking out the window at the lake.

"It almost broke my heart," she says, "seeing you on the train with your one little bag. So I had Herta send them." Herta was our last head seamstress. Then, because we couldn't bear to part with her, she was our housekeeper. Now she is taking care of our apartment while we're away.

"Thank you," I say, and try to smile. "You're sweet."

There are several more boxes and we take turns opening them. There are two beaten silver boxes full of rings and necklaces; a jewel-encrusted hand mirror; four awkward looking wooden dolls carrying mesh umbrellas; the silver chalice that Josef Hoffmann made; a wooden box filled with packets of our silk dress labels. It's the dress labels that finally break Helene; they say Flöge Sisters on them.

"I know it's weak and self-indulgent to care, but I loved the salon so much," she sobs. "It was so beautiful." I try to stifle the mental image of the gray felt carpets and Wiener Werkstätte cabinets.

"Maybe we should wear them on our lapels like name tags," I say.

At the bottom of the second box is a letter from Herta. She writes that some soldiers came in a truck and took all of the paintings away. Carl Moll was with them. He told her that he was taking them to a secret warehouse for safekeeping. Our apartment building might be bombed, and they were too precious to lose. They were our national treasure, our patrimony.

"They're probably hanging in his apartment right now," Helene says.

"Then if we lose they'll get blown up," I say. "He lives across from the Hofburg."

That night we wear bonnets to bed like children playing dress-up: red, white, and gold linen, embroidered with tulips and roses. We drape our mirrors with transparent scarves. On the mantel we place two tiny pairs of brocade shoes that had belonged to a Chinese empress. It is impossible to imagine a grown woman walking in them. Perhaps she was carried everywhere. I try to imagine her: tiny, graceful, black-haired, in a silk-satin robe embroidered with lotuses and butterflies, her crippled feet ostentatiously displayed, the most beautiful part of all.

"Maybe St. Nicholas will come and fill them," says Helene.

I dream of Gustav again. He's rowing the boat in the center of the lake, swiftly, his powerful arms throwing up buckets of water with each stroke. Where am I? I'm swimming alongside. He's whistling as he rows, as he used to do, but for some reason I'm worried. Then he lets the boat ride.

"We're here," he says. Then he stands in the boat and dives off of the side. I wait for him to come up. The lake is a hundred meters deep in the middle. I think about poor Thyssen. I dive for him, but he's nowhere around me. In a panic, I dive and dive until I wake up, out of breath and clammy with sweat.

Pregnant Nude, 1890

Minna has alizarin hair in tangles to her waist. The color of it suffuses Gustav's dreams; he's never seen anything so beautiful. He uses a formula of madder root juice undoctored with sienna or ochre when painting it. Even on the street, tied back in a knot and hidden under a demure headdress, it glows like a beacon. She can't hide it, no matter how much she might want to. Such a shame that when a person dies, her hair can't be saved, but cut off from the life force it inevitably dulls. Hundreds of mouse-colored skeins in hundreds of lockets are proof enough of that.

Gustav is equally fascinated by her skeletal frame, bones jutting everywhere. The sinews that bind her hips are visible. Her cheekbones are like the spear points of some Alpine forebear. She looks older than twenty. Now that she is pregnant she is paler than before and the shadows under her eyes are blue. Her belly is already large, prominent, something from another body. She looks too weak to carry it. Gustav finds her more beautiful than before, everything about her extreme: her pallor, her growing uterus, her frailty. She is physically close to disaster. Sometimes she bleeds. She should be confined to a warm bed with a nurse to bring her soup and medicine, but it's out of the question. Her parents have thrown her out of their house and she has no income other than what he gives her. It is a quandary for him, to keep her working so he can pay her, when he knows that the work is not good for her. But she won't take charity, she says.

He is not the father. She's told him so, and she doesn't lie. A different kind of woman would have, would have multiplied the figures in her head and smiled. They understand each other, the harsh realities of where they come from. They both understand that he is leaving it behind and she never will. She doesn't begrudge him, though. It's just the way it is, so why make a fuss? He gives her work. They are pals.

Minna climbs onto the platform in the center of the room, letting her blue wrapper drop to the floor. Gustav has put a chair on the platform and she sits down. Opens her legs, closes them. Puts both on the seat of the chair and curls into a ball. Sits with one leg under her. Pose, change. She knows what kind of movements he likes, what kind of space. Other artists like things pretty and symmetrical, but he prefers awkward, even ugly. Awkward and ugly are easy when you are seven months pregnant.

"Are you all right?" he asks after a few minutes. The studio is far from warm. Occasionally she shudders. The hairs on her arms stand on end, catching the light. He doesn't want her to faint on the platform, expel the child onto the pine boards in rhythmic gushes. He doesn't think about the possibility that she might die.

"I'm fine," she says. Pose, change.

"Did you eat anything yet today?"

"Couldn't keep a thing down."

"Where are you sleeping?" She grins at him.

"Where do you think?"

"How is our friend Mr. Bachman?"

"Very disgruntled. He's afraid my condition will get around and prevent him from finding a proper wife."

Gustav tells her to take a break, get some tea, eat a roll. If he didn't tell her he needed to rest she'd keep on for hours. While she is in the kitchen he concentrates on touching up the sketches he has made, darkening, shading, erasing.

"You can let me go if you want to," she says when she comes back in, one roll in her hand, another in her mouth. "I would understand." The usual thing is to dismiss pregnant models, in a show of moral outrage or guilt or just because they are no longer useful. Their bodies cannot show up in paintings.

"Don't be stupid," he says. "I need you. Do you see anyone else here?"

She keeps her chin down and looks up at him quickly and then down again, looking momentarily like a shy child. "I look like the fat lady in the sideshow," she says.

"You might be interested to know that I have just decided to do a portrait of you. A sort of allegory of hope."

Minna looks at him in disbelief. Some of the ideas he has are beyond her. "You can't do a portrait of me. Are you crazy?"

Hope. How can she represent hope, when there is so little of it in her life? She will have this baby. She'll survive the birth, if she's lucky. Mr. Bachman won't marry her. Her parents won't take her back. Her looks will go early, a casualty of her hard life. Then what? A factory job? Prostitution? And what will happen to the child? Silently she prays for a boy.

"I'll need to do more sessions with you alone. Will you get bigger, do you think?"

"Bigger? Yeah, I'm going to be bigger." Her voice is bitter and incredulous. "Soon I'll be bigger than the studio."

Gustav brushes her arm with his hand. "Another thing. You can stay here awhile if you need to."

"I told you where I'm staying." It's not the sex that she minds, it's the suggestion of doing her a favor.

"If anything happens," he says. He pushes the robe from her shoulders. Her breasts are swollen.

"Well, I'll do the painting if you really want me to," she says. "But I don't need to stay here."

Gustav telegrams his mother that he's going to work all night. She gets anxious if he doesn't come home.

When he returns Minna is sprawled on the dias, one goose down comforter spread over the boards, another over her body. He is not sure if it's an invitation or not. When he lies down beside her she growls and turns over. When he is astride her he presses against her belly, no longer soft and pliant. The thick protective capsule under her skin guards the fetus from his weight. It excites him and makes him thrust harder. Minna winces.

"You'll kill it," she says. And then after a pause in which she takes in a few ragged breaths, "Maybe that wouldn't be such a bad thing."

Afterward he presses his ear to her belly button to hear the frothing and gurgling.

"He's all right," says Gustav. "He enjoyed the exercise."

"Pity," says Minna, rolling to her side. Soon Gustav hears her breath change; she is asleep. He puts more wood on the stove and leaves for home.

Eleven

The next year Gustav, Ernst, and Franz were being considered for the commission to paint University Hall. The theme was Philosophy, Medicine, and Jurisprudence. They moved to a new studio, in Josefstadt, where they had a garden and more room to work. They began making sketches for presentation to the Arts Committee of the Ministry of Education. It was an important commission and all three wanted it desperately. Ernst, in particular, drove himself hard. Helene had just had a baby, a girl also named Helene, and he keenly felt this new responsibility.

Then he got sick. He continued to work for as long as he could, but after several weeks he stopped going to his studio altogether. I watched him grow even thinner than he had been before. When I played cards with Helene at night, the wracking coughs that came from the upstairs bedroom were unnerving. Helene and I both cringed at each attack. He would not let Helene call the doctor, though the baby, not six months old, came to stay at our apartment so she would be safe.

He said he was not concerned. If the baby had been sick, that would have been something to worry about. But he had been sick many times; as a child he had had pneumonia three times, and whooping cough twice. He always got well, he said.

When the doctor finally came he said that Ernst had scarlet fever. He was worried Helene would catch it, too, but she refused to leave him. As it turned out, he left her.

It was December and dark at three o'clock in the afternoon. The gravediggers used pick-axes to break the ground in the cemetery. Gustav stood between his mother and Helene, but as to who was holding up whom, I couldn't be sure. I was on Helene's other side, and she stood up straight, holding the baby, without any help from me. She wouldn't look at me and none of us said a word.

Both of the gaunt haunted shells next to me were, I knew, wracked with guilt about something they should have done. Gustav had not gone to visit Ernst on the last day; he had actually seemed better. Helene thought that if she had called the doctor sooner, something might have been devised to save him. There was no way to tell either of them that they had done all they could. They wanted to blame themselves, which was easier than blaming God.

The priest was young and it was his first funeral. His cassock billowed around his thin legs and he kept his eyes in his book of prayers, where he had placed a piece of loose paper filled with tiny script. He attempted consolation, saying that there was a reason for Ernst's death, that God must have wanted him for Himself, but he didn't seem to believe this anymore than we did. Then he implored us to be hopeful, forgiving, and mindful of God's grace. Gustav spat on the ground when he said that, and the poor priest leaped backward as if he'd been attacked.

Gustav stepped forward to give his eulogy. He had a crumpled piece of paper in his hand but he never looked at it or at any of the mourners. Instead he looked into the horizon as if it were a gem he was examining for flaws.

"My brother," he said, "was a fool. An idealistic, optimistic, smile-happy fool."

Here Helene looked over at me in terror and the other mourners shifted in their shoes as if they were suddenly too tight, but none of us made a move to stop him from talking.

"He grew up poor," Gustav went on, "but never let it make him bitter. He was often ill as a child but was seldom petulant. He made many friends in art school, and never became competitive or backbiting or gossipy. He actually helped others with their work on his own time, even though he knew that raising their marks would work against him. He shared his supplies even when he could not afford to buy his own.

"He was the same way in the Kunstlerhaus and in the studio we shared. He was an excellent draftsman, better than I. The clients liked him, and he knew how to talk to them. He knew how to say what they wanted to hear. He knew how to listen to them and repeat back what they'd said with some artist jargon thrown in to make them feel intelligent. And with touching obedience he'd give them exactly what they wanted, even if they wanted something gauche or gaudy or stupid.

"Not that his work was bad, not at all. It was conservative, but it was good. He could not draw an ugly line, he could not mix an ugly color. He had a gift for the figure, and an attention to detail that bordered on obsession.

"As a man he was honest and decent and kind. While other artists were off with actresses and dancers, he married a lovely girl and had a child." Here I lifted my eyes from the spot on the ground and glanced over at the clump of artists to my left. Franz caught my glance and gave me the smallest smile.

"He did everything right," said Gustav, "and look what it got him."

There was excruciating silence as we waited for him to say more, hoping fervently that he wouldn't, even though it was a nihilistic place to end. The poor young priest jumped in front of Gustav at the first moment that it was clear he was finished and read a passage from First Corinthians in a hoarse voice.

When it was over Helene dropped a box of pencils onto the casket. Gustav would not watch them shovel the dirt on. He walked away. I watched him recede into the distance, wondering where he was going, if he was all right, but I didn't follow. The Klimts' house, where the wake was to be, was not far away. Perhaps, I thought, he would walk there, though the blowing ice pierced like needles.

The wake was a sad mirror of the wedding we had hosted less than two years before. My mother was rocking the baby and singing to her. Pauline tried to get Helene to eat a roll with apple butter. My father listened attentively to the wails of Mrs. Klimt. Gustav had not come back.

The artists milled around the staircase, looking awkward in their best suits and trying not to talk about their latest commissions and their difficulties of space and perspective. I went toward them, meaning to ask if any of them had seen Gustav, but when Franz saw me coming he detached himself from them and made for me. He had been away from Vienna for some time. He looked plump and rested, but that may have been because everyone around me was so hollow-eyed with worry and sleepless nights. He smiled another timid smile, the broadest one propriety allowed. His very health made me despise him suddenly.

"I was in Budapest when I got the news," he said. He had not dared to ask Gustav anything, and he wanted to know: How long had Ernst been ill? Had he been bled? What medicines had they used? Was he delirious, and had he said anything? I tried to listen and to answer his questions, but as he talked I scanned the room. When I next looked back at Franz he was waiting for a reply to some query I had missed entirely.

"Gustav's run off," I said.

"He probably needs to be alone," Franz said. He touched my hand. "It's the best thing for him, really. But you, you look as if you need something hot to drink. Even your bones are cold."

"I'm fine," I said, brushing him off. "It's Gustav I'm worried about."

"That eulogy was a little . . . unhinged. But he'll be all right."

I allowed Franz to fetch a cup of hot cider for me, but as I drank it I thought of Gustav. I knew where he was, of course. Was it true; was it better for him to be alone? My instinct told me it was not, but I wasn't sure I was the person who should go to him. But who else was there? I got my coat and slipped out the door. There were carriages waiting outside and I commandeered one of them. It was a lengthy drive. I shivered into the cheap silk lining of the carriage, wishing I had remembered my gloves.

The studio gate was open and the cats were huddled together on the steps. I picked them both up and carried them under my arms like loaves of bread.

It was gloomy and dark in the entrance hall. The shades were shut and none of the lamps were lit. I released the cats and they scuttled away. In the studio there was no fire and it was nearly as cold inside as out. Gustav was hunched over a stool, staring at the easel. He had thrown off his suit and put on his painting smock. Socks and spats and collar littered the floor as if a passionate affair were in progress, but he was alone. If I hadn't seen him in the smock every day for years I would have thought he had escaped from a sanitarium. The gown was made of rough cotton and couldn't possibly keep him warm. He'd even taken off his shoes. The painting was a portrait of Helene in a white dress on a couch of Mediterranean blue.

"Such a good painting to go unfinished," said Gustav, not looking up. I went no closer.

"You could finish it," I said.

"That would be like making love to someone else's mistress," he said. I saw that he was holding an artist's knife in his hand. "Like making love to the mistress on the day of the funeral."

"Why don't you put your clothes back on and come back to the house?" I said slowly and carefully, as if talking to a child.

"Shut up," he said. "I'm listening to the painting."

"Do you want me to go?" I asked.

"I don't care," he said, not taking his eyes from the canvas. I took that as a positive sign. I walked over and stood behind him to look at Ernst's painting. Helene looked very soft and serene. She stared straight out of the canvas. She was stretched out on the sofa à la Madame Recamier, but everything was slightly blurred, as if in candlelight. Behind her was a black-and-gray Chinese screen.

"I didn't know he liked Whistler," I said.

"He hated Whistler," Gustav said. "It was for your bitch of a mother. Look how disgustingly hopeful the damn thing is despite that."

"He didn't know he was going to die," I said.

"We're all going to die," he said. "What right do any of us have to be hopeful? What right did he have to paint this?"

"He had to paint something," I said.

"No he didn't," he said. "He could have gone to work in a bank and lived a long and healthy life."

"He could just have easily died young working in a bank," I said. "It wasn't art that killed him."

"It was me," he said. "He only went to the Academy because I did."

"He stayed because he wanted to. And how did the Academy give him scarlet fever?"

"Long hours standing in those unheated rooms. He didn't have the constitution for it."

"Your mother's been asking for you," I said. "I didn't know what to tell her." I was eager to shift the conversation in a more reasonable direction, but I wondered why. Why should he censor his thoughts to make me comfortable? And what was so terrifying about his grief that I wanted him to suppress it?

"I wish she had died, the whore," he said. "He got his weak constitution from her. From her and from living in rat-infested hovels as a child. And never having enough to eat." He put his face in his hands.

Quietly and gently I stretched out my arms to touch his shoulders. I put my hands on them lightly, as if he were a precious piece of sculpture. I tried to breathe my sympathy and my love into the touch, but I must not have done a very good job, because he threw off my hands, drew his arm back and in one angry and assured movement he sliced the canvas from one wooden stretcher to the other, diagonally, left to right.

It was as if the air went out of the room. I gasped for breath. If Gustav would destroy a piece of art, any piece of art, much less Ernst's, then he would do anything. He would kill himself, or me, or anyone. I felt sick at the thought. Sick, and weak, too weak to fight him, but I had to.

I grabbed his arm and pried the knife from his hands. If he had resisted I would never have succeeded, and we would have both been sliced open like melons, but he didn't fight me. When I had it I threw it as far as I could. It landed near the fireplace.

Helene's face was ripped apart. I almost expected to see blood coming from it. The unpainted portion of the canvas waved loosely and forlornly, but the other side curled stiffly, defiantly upward. We stood and looked at the mutilated painting.

"We can probably repair it," I said after a while.

"Get it out of here," he said. "I can't look at it anymore." As I took it off of the easel I glanced quickly at his face, painfully contorted but dry of tears. I propped the ruined canvas against the wall, facing inward, like a child being punished.

I went back to Gustav.

"Burn it," he said. "Some day when I'm not around."

He had nothing to look at now except for me, and I had nothing to look at except for him. I was afraid to get too close to him, for many reasons. I was acutely aware that he was naked underneath his smock.

"At least put your shoes on," I said.

He lunged for me and grabbed me around the waist. Instinctively I pulled away. Then he fell to his knees and sobbed into my dress. I was no longer frightened. It was like soothing the baby, or my sister; it required the same caresses, the same gentle sounds.

"It's all right," I said. "It's all right." He had some freckles on the crown where the hair was thinning. I stroked the back of his neck.

"Why didn't I get scarlet fever?" he said. His voice was hoarse and thick. "Why couldn't I have died?"

What could I say? Should I take the tone of a minister and tell him that God's mercy is great but inscrutable? Or that of an intellectual and tell him that God is dead?

"I don't know," I said, "but thank heaven you didn't. I would have had to go after you." I couldn't say this as fervently as I felt it, so I spoke lightly, as if making a joke.

His eyes were those of an icon, wide and opaque. There was no spark of mischief or vigor or curiosity.

"You would come after me?"

"Like Orpheus going to Hades to rescue Eurydice," I said.

"Hades," he said sadly. "I guess that is where I'm going, if there is a God. And if there isn't I'm going to the same eternal nothingness we're all going to, which isn't really that much better."

"You're not going anywhere," I said. "I need you."

He stood up. I wasn't sure whether he was going to strike me or bite my cheek, it really could have been anything, that day, but he kissed me, awkwardly, pressing his closed lips into mine as if they were a piece of overripe fruit I wasn't sure wasn't rotten. I didn't know what to do, what he needed from me. I kissed him back, but gently, as I would my niece, or a kitten I found in an alley. His face was salty.

"No," he said, "not like that." He seemed angry at my mistake and grabbed me by the shoulders. The flesh of my upper arms ached with the pressure of his fingers. I would have bruises, thumbprints dark as plums. When he kissed me he breathed into me his desperation and his despair.

"Gustav," I said, trying to push him back. "You don't want to do this."

"I've always wanted to do this. And what has stopped me? Propriety? Respect, restraint, honor? She's just a little girl, I said to myself, I know her parents, I can't betray their trust. Then, when you were no longer a little girl, I told myself, she's not of my class, she's meant to marry someone else and I can't ruin her future. But what does any of that matter to me now? What does it matter to you?"

I wasn't sure what mattered to me. Sometimes I still thought I would make a good marriage, have children, do all of the expected things. But home, family, marriage, all of that disappeared from my mind when he touched me.

There wasn't anything else to say. He backed me toward the modeling platform, yanking off my coat and hat and dropping them to the floor. I thought briefly about dust and pencil shavings, then forgot about them because he was unbuttoning my jacket and pulling at my blouse.

I had thought about this moment a hundred times. It had taken place in the old studio, in his mother's house, in my house, in a gondola in Venice, and on the back of an elephant in the Belgian Congo. In my imagination all of our lovemaking was characterized by exquisite choreography and calm, deliberate words. It was something like a Bernini sculpture I had seen at the Kunsthistorisches: smooth and cool as marble, soft and gentle, limbs perfectly placed. I had not thought it would be so ugly, so tangled, that his elbow would smash my fingers, that my hair would become caught in one of my fasteners; that it would be more like a disease, dark and insatiable, than a sculpture or a play.

I thought he would be disappointed when he saw me. He had looked at the bodies of so many women who were engaged professionally in the task of being beautiful. I was fatter and softer than Minna, more freckled than Helga. I had a yellow bruise on my thigh from bumping into a table and a mole on my left nipple. With someone else they might not be really looking, really noticing every imperfection, but of course he was, even in the dim light. He wouldn't miss anything, and so I closed my eyes as he looked at me, not wanting to see his expression.

He moved quickly, smoothing me as if making a bed. His hands were on my cheeks and then around my neck and then pressing into my breasts. I thought I would stop breathing, but he stayed there just a moment before sliding down to my waist and belly. Then his hand was inside of me and I cried out when he stopped, but he rolled me over and examined the back of me, too, running his fingers down my spine. Then his hands were gone and I heard him pulling his smock over his head.

Then it began, and I couldn't see, only feel, his feverish skin, his weight, a deep pain and tearing and then the rhythmic pounding of my forehead knocking into the floor. I put a hand there to pad it but he took it and slid it underneath me.

"Touch yourself," he said. "Where I was touching you. It will feel good." Of course to touch yourself is a terrible sin, but no more terrible than what I was already doing, so it seemed pointless to refuse. He was right. Immediately I felt as if my lower body was paralyzed. All went numb, but at the same time there was an electric charge, like being hit by lightning. And then with a final thrust that I thought would break my insides, his whole body tightened and shook and then he was slumped over me.

I felt that I should cry, it was the thing to do in all of the novels, but my eyes were as dry as bone. I felt scooped out, gutted as a trout. My skin burned where his beard had rubbed into it. I looked over at the ruined canvas. One of the torn flaps lay face up on the floor, and one of my sister's cobalt eyes stared across the room at me. Gustav slid from inside of me and rolled onto his back.

I must have slept because when I opened my eyes there was a blanket on me and Gustav was sitting cross-legged next to me, stroking my arm.

"Are you all right?" he said.

"I'm not sick," I said, though I was beginning to be. The enormity of what I'd done was sinking in.

"You do know what to do?" he said. I knew what he meant and I turned away from him, ashamed.

"To prevent pregnancy," he said. He was going to teach me the trick that whores knew.

"This is very important. When you get home, you must fill a bottle with vinegar and douse yourself inside. Do it again tomorrow. Do you understand?" I moved my head up and down, and he patted me on the back, through the blanket, as though we were talking about a telegram I must send to Franz or a cake I must order from the bakery.

"I'll light the fire and we can sit awhile before we dress." He got up and walked naked to the fireplace. I couldn't help watching him; after all, he had studied me but I had not had as much as a glimpse of him. He was beginning to be heavy in the middle, not fat or misshapen, but solid, like the chief of a tribe who gets the choicest parts of the kill. There were gray hairs mixed with the dark ones on his chest. His penis dangled between his thighs, small and tender-looking now, pink and innocent as a newborn puppy.

He came back to the platform and sat down with his back to me. I was afraid to touch it.

"I'm sorry," he said. "It was insanity, what I did. Please forgive me."

"It was grief," I said. "But don't be sorry."

"It won't change anything," he said. I wasn't sure if he meant it as a consolation or a warning.

"No," I said.

Twelve

How could we go on with the drawing lessons after that, as if nothing had happened? We could not. I had finished school, and Gustav was extremely busy. I was far enough along in my training that I could sketch on my own. But it was equally unthinkable that we should not see each other, and together we found a solution: we would take French lessons together. Gustav was worried that his bad French would make his travels more difficult, his correspondence with French artists more awkward, and compromise his work in Belgium. My French was competent, but I was unhappy with my pronunciation. And so we went weekly to Madame Czerny on Karntnerstrasse. Afterward we always went to a café for a couple of hours, and Gustav talked about his work.

He pretended that nothing had happened, and returned to his old ways, brother to my sister, uncle to my niece, teacher to my pupil, and I tried to pretend that it was what I wanted, too. It was as if the grief were an opiate and now that it had worn off a little he wanted to believe that it had been the drug and not himself that was to blame.

I was going to say that it was easy, effortless, but of course that is a lie. I'm forgetting how he came to me in my dreams, night after night, real as life: red smock, thick fingers, an inexplicable daub of titanium white on the back of his neck. Night after night he came. He was painting in the studio with his back to me. I talked to him and he didn't answer. He just kept painting. Or, I was at the window of the apartment, waiting for him. He was late. Anxiously I watched the street below. I contemplated sending a telegram. It was not like him not to let me know if his plans changed. And then I saw him, parading below with a circus menagerie of models and prostitutes and washerwomen around him. They were dressed in every conceivable color and style of costume, flounces, ruffles, trains, leg-o'-mutton sleeves, batwing sleeves, petticoats, every possible embellishment and waste of fabric. They held his hand, tugged at his coat, hung on his shoulder. They laughed with painted lips. I called down to him. For a moment he looked up and saw me. He waved. And then he walked on. Over and over I dreamed about him rejecting me in a hundred different ways. Each time I would wake up terrified, the tears I refused to shed while I was awake leaking onto my pillow in sleep.

I really should have guarded my propriety even more carefully than ever after what had happened, but the hypocrisy of it all exhausted me. If people were whispering they were only saying what was true, so why try to pretend?

After Ernst's death Gustav became even more impatient with the politics of being a successful academic painter, and bored with what was expected of him. He seemed almost reckless in his disregard for his more conventional clients, including the Ministry of Education. At the same time, he had not fully shaken the desire to be liked, and the desire to be lauded and praised. He worried that the committee the ministry had picked would dislike his sketches. My usual role was to listen and try to reassure him.

"They picked you, didn't they?" I said one day as we sat in the Café Sperl. I put a piece of marzipan on my tongue and let it slowly dissolve.

"Jodl mentioned the School of Athens as a model," Gustav groaned. "He'll be the worst." We wrote down the names of the committee members on a damp paper napkin. We were in the process of ranking them, from most supportive to most contentious, when the door to the café opened and a blast of cold air carried in a thin man with a stiff, pointed mustache. He glanced about the café and when he saw Gustav, gave a little bow and headed toward our table.

"Well, Herr Klimt," said the man. He waved the *Neue Freie Presse* at us as if nothing more needed to be said.

"Herr Hoffmann, Emilie Flöge, a friend of the family. Emilie, may I present Josef Hoffmann, architect," said Gustav. "He works with Otto Wagner."

"The great Otto Wagner," corrected Hoffmann, "and I only work for him, though one day I do hope to be able to say that I work with him. I'm sorry to say that the day does not appear to be imminent. May I sit down?" Without waiting for an answer he slid into one of the wrought iron chairs and hailed a waiter. "Mocha," he said. "With three sugars and extra whipped cream. And a piece of this torte the young lady has. I have the constitution of a hummingbird," he explained to us. "I have to eat continually just keep the flesh on my bones. Now. What I wanted to discuss. This last meeting we had, when the officers rejected the idea of bringing some of the work of the Nabis here." He paused for breath. "What did you think?"

"I thought it was even worse that they refused to sponsor a show of younger artists," said Gustav. "Vienna is already backward, now it is getting a reputation as being hostile to artists."

"Exactly," said Hoffmann. "The last thing we want; all the talent will leave, go to Paris or Berlin. The Kunstlerhaus is completely moribund, and why not? The same white-haired men have been running it for fifty years! The last French painting they looked at was a Bouguereau. They still think of themselves as young artists!" His mocha and cake arrived, and he began to take large bites and wash them down with long slurps.

For some time Gustav had treated me as an intellectual equal and so I was not afraid to speak my mind. "Why don't you over-throw them, the old men?" I asked.

"It's not that simple," said Hoffmann, with a surprised look at Gustav. "They've been elected to their positions. The next election is two years away."

"With enough supporters you could stage a coup," I said. Both men stared at me with bemusement, and, was it admiration? "Why not?" I said.

"You didn't tell me your young friend was a revolutionary," said Hoffmann, laughing. "She has the right spirit."

"Some of us have been meeting separately," said Gustav. "Me, Moll, a few others. You should join us."

"You're a step ahead of me," said Hoffmann. "I was going to ask if you wanted to get some people together. I'd be happy to join you, and I'll ask Olbrich to come, too. I think he'll have some good ideas."

His plate as empty as mine, he drained his coffee and stood up. "I have to meet with a construction crew for an apartment building over by the Naschmarkt. What a bore, they always tell me what I want can't be done." He waved his hand and was gone. We sat for a minute and caught our breath.

"Well done, Emilie," Gustav said. "I've never seen Hoffmann look so flabbergasted. You've become quite the provocateur."

I asked if I could come to the meeting, but Gustav said he was afraid to bring me, for fear I'd be running the group by the end of the evening. It was an affectionate joke, and I smiled. But what he meant was that I was a girl and not an artist, not a real artist. I was a dilettante who made pretty sketches. As such, I was not invited.

It took a week and two pieces of caramel cake for me to forgive Gustav. It shames me now that I was so cheaply bought. Gustav knew that downcast eyes, sorrowful mea culpas, and an artful application of cocoa and sugar could not fail to melt my heart. Then he left on a trip to Italy. He was gone for several months, but he wrote me postcards constantly, sometimes five or six in a day. The weather in Italy was terrible: infernally hot and dry. It irritated his lungs. The bread was excellent but the sweets left a lot to be desired. He did not like ricotta cheese. The art was fine, but he couldn't wait to return to Vienna, he said.

The day after he got back we meant to go to the opera. He had very good seats and it was *La Traviata,* one of my favorites, but that afternoon a card came from the studio, saying that it was going well and he had to stay there. It was typical of him, and though I was disappointed, I was not surprised. I went instead with Pauline and two of her friends.

Though I didn't play or sing especially well I was a typical Viennese: passionate about the opera. The opera house was brand-new and bright with gilt. The carvings were so intricate that each time I came I chose a column or a ceiling panel to study at intermission. The opera was an event and I enjoyed every part of it: my hand running along the cool yellow marble of the grand staircase; opening the red velvet door to our box and hanging my cloak in the vestibule; looking out across the crowd at faces familiar from newspapers; looking out at the city from the balcony and in at the crowd through my mother-of-pearl opera glasses, a gift from my parents on my last birthday.

Once settled in my seat I scanned my program excitedly to see who was playing. Then Katharina, to my left, whispered in my ear.

"Isn't that Klimt over there?" she hissed. I turned my opera glass in the direction she had pointed. Gustav was in a box with a young woman in a very large, very ugly green tulle hat. She lifted her chin and laughed at something Gustav said. The light reflecting off her bright hair made her gleam like a Christmas tree ornament. Her lacy dress was very snug. She lifted her eyes and stopped as if she recognized me. I was temporarily blinded by a piercing ray of malice.

"Who's he with?" someone asked me. "She's stunning."

"I don't know," I said, not hearing myself speak.

"It's Alma Schindler," Katharina said.

"You know her?"

"Not personally, but she's the talk of the town these days."

"What has she done?" asked Pauline, knowing that I could not ask.

"It's mostly what Klimt did. You don't know about it? I thought you would since you're such friends of his."

"Perhaps he was embarrassed to tell us," said Pauline. "It sounds scandalous."

"I should say it is," said Katharina, obviously enjoying her role as storyteller. "He followed her to Italy against the wishes of her family and declared his love on the steps of some church or other and would have run off with her if her stepfather hadn't put a stop to it. They are forbidden to see each other. Isn't that romantic?"

Mahler had entered and everyone was applauding. I felt my sister take my hand.

"I heard they were engaged," said the girl on my right. "Maybe they'll have to elope. Maybe the scandal will drive them to leave Vienna and live abroad."

I hardly noticed the music during the first act. I unpicked all of the trimming on the left sleeve of my dress, until there was a ball of blue silk floss in my lap. I told myself that Gustav was free to fall in love, and with whomever he chose. What had happened between us was a mistake, an aberration, a dream. The opera was a kaleidoscope, indistinct shards of color. My eyes returned again and again to the box on the other side of the theater. Alma Schindler. I began on the other sleeve.

At the intermission I led Pauline out to the balcony for fresh air. I had been going to look at one of the frescoes in the drawing room, but now I couldn't. I couldn't even breathe properly. Across the Ring I could see the lights of our district. I looked in the direction of home, trying to pick out which was ours. More than anything I wanted to jump off of the balcony and fly there. Pauline must have sensed what I was thinking because she was holding my wrist so tightly she stung the skin.

On the stairs we ran into Gustav. He was getting a drink for his companion, who was waiting in the box.

"Miss Schindler is writing an opera based on Nietzsche's writings," he said, smiling nervously. "She wants me to design the sets and costumes."

"So this is research," said Pauline.

"Yes," he said neutrally.

"Well then, we won't keep you." Pauline bowed and led me out onto the terrace.

"What do you want to do?" she asked. "Do you want to leave?" I could only nod. She left me there and went back to our box to collect our coats. She told her friends that I was ill, and if they exchanged knowing glances among themselves she didn't mention it. We waited on the terrace until the house lights went down and then slipped through the empty lobby and away. On the carriage ride home I stared unseeing out of the window, lost in my thoughts.

So Pauline had been right after all. I was in love with him. I didn't want to be; I wanted to be in love with someone my own age, someone shy and earnest who would send me flowers or try to ingratiate himself with my father, not someone old and libertine, someone who would never marry me, someone who would doom me to a childless life of spinsterhood. Hadn't Gustav said that I was too sensible for that?

Pauline, to her credit, didn't gloat, but led me up the stairs and put me in bed. She rubbed my back until I fell asleep, and in the morning got up early to make cinnamon bread for me. She brought me magazines and chocolate-covered cherries and a bouquet of irises, as if I were an invalid.

Thirteen

I avoided Gustav for a while. I had to; it hurt too much to be near him. But he wouldn't accept it. He wrote me wheedling notes, apologizing for lying. He groveled. When I did see him he always had a present for me, a Moravian doll in folk costume, a box of truffles, a silver bracelet. The more disgusted I looked, the harder he tried.

He never apologized for Alma, though.

Slowly, I thawed. I couldn't seem to help myself. I found his antics charming, his beseeching smile adorable. And without him my days were a tedious and empty round of marketing and dusting. In the evenings I studied French or sketched my parents as they read. Forgiving him meant a return to cafés, to parties, to discussions with artists and long strolls in the Volksgarten. Is it any wonder I gave in?

The next spring Gustav announced to the Kunstlerhaus that he had formed a new group of artists, dedicated to raising the level of art in Austria. The older members of the Kunstlerhaus didn't take very kindly to this news. During a contentious meeting, Gustav walked out, and his supporters followed him. Several days later he resigned from the Kunstlerhaus altogether. He called his new group the Secession and was elected president of it. They modeled themselves after other rebellious art movements like the Pre-Raphaelites. They decided that they would publish a journal, called *Ver Sacrum*, and that they would have a gallery to show their own art and also to host traveling shows. Gustav began making draw-ings for the Secession building.

Berta Zuckerkandl had a party to celebrate the founding of the Secession and he asked me to go with him. Though I was dying to go, it was more nerve-wracking than being presented at court would have been.

Among the musicians, writers, and especially artists of Vienna, Berta Zuckerkandl's Sunday night gatherings were famous. If you were young and struggling, an invitation often meant your first major commission, if you spoke well and didn't look too seedy. The apartment was sumptuous enough to intimidate the daughter of a factory owner. In it one could forget sordid things like bills and groceries existed. The drawing room walls were crowded with art-work; a portrait by Whistler, two dark and bright Dutch flower paintings, a cartoon by Rubens, drawings by Ingres and Delacroix. Later I found out that this was just a fraction of what she owned; her drawing room was a rotating exhibition that changed with her mood. Brocade chairs and sofas were arranged in corners. An intri-cate parquet floor spiraled dizzyingly from underneath the enor-mous chandelier. When the heavy drapes were tied back you could look across the Ring to the Rathaus, gleaming as if with phospho-rescence. Lights from people's homes were strewn like glitter.

Berta Zuckerkandl was a large woman of indeterminate middle age, strong-boned, with a stern mouth and a regal bearing. In fact, the night I met her she was wearing plum-colored velvet and a copious amount of diamonds. She kissed Gustav and then fixed her eyes on me.

"Who is this little girl?" I didn't like the way she looked at me, as if I were too insignificant to waste her precious sight on. To her, a woman was worthless until proven otherwise.

"Emilie Flöge, a friend of mine."

Berta Zuckerkandl looked surprised. "I didn't know you had time for friends, Gustav. I thought you were too busy revolutioniz-ing art."

"I can't work all the time, you know." He grinned at her.

"Of course not." Her eyes drifted to me. "You are a secretive man, aren't you?" She squeezed his hand. "I'll speak with you later." And we were away from her, swimming through the crowd.

Carl Moll was upon us before we had gone very far. He wanted to talk about an artist's meeting they had called for the following week. I hardly listened; I was too busy looking around. There were flowers everywhere, blindingly white: the elegant flutes of calla lilies in every window, a thick rope of peonies and stock on every mantel. Light reflected off of every crystal in the chandelier and every jewel in the ladies' hair. I knew few people there, but I recognized Josef Hoffmann from the café. Mahler was there with his arm wrapped in the velvet curtain, gazing out over the city. Several people came over to talk to him, but he waved them away.

Then my eyes met those of a woman across the room. She stood alone, gazing impassively into the crowd, a still point among rustling skirts and passing waiters. Tall, gaunt, and awkward, her body was twisted as if the owner were attempting to make herself invisible. In contrast to the fantastically ornamented women around her, she was wearing a slim and unadorned white silk dress. She held her hands in front of her in a little knot, a pose I was to learn was characteristic. Her head was supported by an impossibly long neck, which seemed to be reinforced by an elaborate choker of pearls and diamonds. There were dark shadows below her heavy-lidded eyes and thick brows above. She was not beautiful, and yet she was compelling. For a long time I watched her. No one came to talk to her; I wondered if she had come alone.

Gustav saw her, too; he broke off his conversation with Moll and we watched in silence as Gustav maneuvered his way toward the woman in the white silk dress. When she saw him she smiled slightly and untangled her hands to offer him one, which he kissed.

"You must meet my stepdaughter," Moll said, while I tried to look at him and not at Gustav and the strange woman. "She's here tonight. I think you'll like her, she's just your age."

"I'm sure I will," I said politely.

Hoffmann appeared with crumbs in his mustache and a drink in each hand. "I don't know how this happened," he said. "Here, you take one." I sipped it gratefully; it gave me something to do with my hands.

"If you'll excuse me a moment, I'll fetch her," said Moll. My eyes returned to Gustav and the woman in white. I had not seen him with a woman since that night at the opera, and I had never seen him with someone like her. She leaned against his shoulder. He took her by the wrist and held her bracelet to the light. They laughed.

"Who is that?" I asked Hoffmann when Moll was gone.

"Adele Bloch-Bauer. Wife of the sugar magnate. Extremely rich, extremely unhappy." He looked at me intently. "The classic Viennese type. Schnitzler could write a novel about her. In fact, he probably has."

"How do she and Gustav know each other?" I asked despite myself.

"I believe her husband has commissioned Gustav to paint her portrait."

"Where is he?"

"Oh, he never comes to parties. He thinks they are a waste of time. Adele loves them, though, he can't stop her from coming."

"Sounds like a terrible marriage."

"Oh, it is. But she likes it that way."

Moll was back. "My stepdaughter," he said, "Alma Schindler."

Alma had luxuriant auburn hair piled on top of her head in the latest style and large green eyes. She was small and voluptuous. Her dress was as revealing as the one she had worn to the opera, and her emeralds were ostentatious. She was not pretty, but she managed to convince many people that she was a great beauty by the sheer force of her will. I looked over at Gustav, pleading with my eyes for him to come rescue me, but he did not look up. Why hadn't he told me that Alma was Moll's stepdaughter? Why hadn't he warned me that she would be there? As Moll ticked off her accomplishments like so many circus tricks, Alma appraised me unsmiling. Then Moll and Hoffmann left us alone to become friends.

"I've seen you before," she said. "At the opera."

"Yes," I said.

"How old are you?" she said.

"Twenty-two."

"Then we're not the same age, I'm eighteen. Gustav said you draw. Who are your favorite artists?"

I always hated that question, as I liked different qualities in different people, but had few that I admired unreservedly. Still, I named Manet and Ingres, the great French master of draftsmanship.

"That's so art school of you," she said. She laughed. "Everyone in Paris is talking about Cézanne these days. Also someone called Braque. What do you think of him?"

I had to admit I hadn't seen any of his work.

"Well, staying here you'll never see anything. You have to travel. I've just been to Italy. Have you ever been there?"

I hadn't. Did I know Italian, Greek, Latin, or English? No, I did not.

"This is tedious," she said. "We have nothing in common at all."

"Perhaps Mr. Moll thought we shared an interest in art," I said, but she missed the allusion.

"You're nothing but a dilettante, while I am going to be world-famous."

I was so shocked I couldn't say anything. She waited for a moment and then changed course. "You've known Gustav quite a long time, haven't you?" she said.

"Since I was a child," I said. "Our families . . ."

"Yes, I know," she said impatiently. "He's told me all about you." I pondered what it could mean that she knew all about me and I knew nothing about her. "So it's only natural that he would feel a fondness for you, and keep you around to do odd jobs, and take you to parties as a special treat, but it would be a shame if you were to think it was anything but that." Her keen eyes took me in from the cut of my dress to my embroidered shawl. "Though I must say you're not irredeemably ugly. And that's a nice dress. Well, good-bye."

I stood alone in the crowd as she slid away, noticing for the first time that a chamber ensemble was playing Schubert. Heavy skirts brushed mine, the plumes of hats touched my cheek, the laughter of couples and patches of conversation filtered in. "The tonal shifts represent the phases of beingness," "Did she really have an affair with the archduke?" I suddenly understood what the woman in white had felt as I watched. I saw Gustav coming toward me holding two glasses. And the woman called Adele swept by like a white moth circling a lamp.

At dinner I was seated between Josef Hoffmann and another architect, Koloman Moser. Gustav was across from me, next to Alma, where I could watch them. She played with her emerald necklace, drawing his eyes to her bosom. She laughed hoarsely, and leaned in very close to whisper something in his ear.

I wished I could wear a blindfold, like a horse being led from a burning barn. Instead I focused on my dinner companions. I liked Hoffmann, thin and beaky and full of boundless energy, his eyes alight with ideas. Moser was quieter and somewhat preoccupied with drinking, but when he saw me glancing at him shyly, he pulled a piece of paper out of his pocket and unfolded it on his plate.

"It's my final design for the Secession building," he said. He pushed his plate toward me so I could examine it.

"It's like a Greek temple," I said.

"Of course," he said. "We need an antidote to all of those overwrought buildings on the Ring, don't you think?" Hoffmann grabbed the drawing from me and stuck it close to his face.

"I like it," he said. "Much better than Gustav's, with the pediment. Though are you really sure about the gilded laurel dome? It's so . . . round."

"Everyone knows of your fetish for the square, Hoffmann," said Gustav. "It may shock you that some people think the circle is the most perfect of all shapes. The Alpha and the Omega."

Hoffmann tossed the drawing back to Moser. "Curving shapes make me nauseated. And you know very well that I'm an atheist."

"Will you build it, despite its blasphemous dome?" asked Moser.

"Of course," said Hoffmann. "It will still be the most beautiful building in Vienna, even with a big head of gold cabbage on top of it."

We were eating Camembert and figs when Alma spoke to me.

"Do you plan to be involved in the Secession, Miss Flöge? As a secretary, perhaps? You could stamp envelopes."

The sound of people lifting their glasses and setting them back down was suddenly the loudest in the room. No one had ever spoken to me in such a way, and in front of so many people. I glanced at Gustav, and felt dizzy with anger; was he not going to come to my aid?

"I'm sure we'd be honored to have Miss Flöge's help in whatever capacity she wishes," said Hoffman kindly.

"Thank you very much," I said, "but I'm working on something of my own."

"Working?" said Alma, snickering. "What could you be working on?" The table was silent as they waited for my answer.

"I'm planning to open a fashion salon," I said. The idea had come to me suddenly, in the midst of my nearly paralyzing fear, but as I said it I knew that it was true.

"That's so feminine of you," said Alma. "But then it's clear you are a clotheshorse."

"Clothing design is no less important than architecture," said Hoffmann. "In fact, it's architecture for the body. What would I do without my bespoke suits?"

"What would Alma do without her corsets?" said Berta, winking at me. I was grateful to her, and proud of myself; I had won her over.

Alma narrowed her eyes at Berta. I had to admire her fearlessness. "Gustav, was this your idea?" she asked. I watched her squeeze his arm high up, on the bicep.

"This is the first I've heard of it," he said. Perhaps he hoped that this would convince her that I was independent, but to me it made me seem like a dilettante, just as Alma had said.

Someone changed the subject to the date of the first exhibition. Alma and I both sulked.

"I wasn't really serious," I said to Gustav the next day at the café. "I had to say something so as not to be completely humiliated." I was still angry with him for smiling blandly as Alma attacked me. And I was terrified. A fashion salon: What had I been thinking? The hothouse atmosphere at Berta's had clearly intoxicated me.

"Don't let Alma bother you," he said. "She's harmless." I said that I doubted it, but he just laughed. "You can handle Alma," he said. "And I think a fashion salon is a wonderful idea." He leaned across the table and took both of my hands. "You must do it."

So, although I was convinced that it was impossible, I began to investigate how one goes about opening a fashion salon. Gustav and I made appointments at several of the best salons in Vienna and had fun pretending to be a rich married couple. He bought me several very expensive dresses so I could be measured and go to the fittings. At the end, when we had the dresses, we took them apart to see how they were constructed.

When I told my father what I was thinking about, he made calls to many of his business associates and made appointments for me to visit the best suppliers. Sometimes he missed whole days at his factory to accompany me to some far-flung corner of the city to look at brocade. Perhaps because he didn't have a son, he was glad to do these things for me. Perhaps he was secretly proud that I would be in business, like him.

I had never seen anything so wonderful as row after row of fabric bolts, stacked five and six and seven high, arranged by color so that I traipsed from white to cream, through taupe and brown, yellow and gold and orange, pink and red and wine and violet and blue and black. Then there were the textures: sheer muslins, stiff organzas, sturdy cottons, wools nubby and fine, silks slick and thick, heavy jacquards. There were florals large and small, and stripes and plaids and toiles, paisleys and geometrics. There were showrooms entirely of net and tulle. There were bins full of passementerie. There were bead men and button men and lace men and ribbon men, there were workshops where girls ruined their eyes on painstakingly delicate embroidery, there were factories that made thread and factories that dyed it.

Perhaps my father was glad to have something to talk about with me. Living with so many women, he never was able to talk about the things that interested him. Or, rather, he talked at us and we pretended to listen while our minds were far away, thinking of theater schedules or grocery lists or the Van Dyck altarpiece. While he and I toured the wholesalers we talked about cost per unit and profit margins and delivery charges.

I don't really know what he thought of my plan. He never expressed an opinion one way or the other, never said it was reasonable and practical or outrageous and unfeminine and would ruin my marriage chances, but he got us our first commission, before the salon opened, to make aprons for a cooking school. Someone he knew in the government knew someone whose cooking school it was. He thought perhaps if they liked our work, we might be employed by the government to make nurse's uniforms or railway porter's jackets.

To my great sorrow, he never got to see the ladies at the Opera, descending the great staircase in dresses I had made. He never got to see the success the salon became.

Fourteen

It took a full year of work before the Secession was able to hold their first exhibition. For one thing, it had been difficult to find a place to hold it. The artists were precluded from using the Kunstlerhaus, of course, and many places were too expensive, or too dark, or too inconvenient, or too ugly. Finally they decided on the Horticultural Society. It had a glass atrium for the plants and was full of light, even in March. They had an indulgent board, chaired by Berta Zuckerkandl's uncle. Most important of all, they agreed to be paid in artwork.

The paintings arrived in crates on ships, hand-delivered by the artists themselves, or, in one instance, wrapped in paper and lashed to the back of a mule. There were forms to be filled out, and frequent trips to the customs office at the port. There were couriers, often young artists, who needed to be paid and fed and housed until the show ended and they took the paintings home. Everything—the paintings, the programs, the invitations, the bills, the government officials, the artists—all accumulated in Gustav's studio until it was difficult to find space to walk in, much less paint. Gustav swore that the day the show ended, anyone still lingering on the property would be shot.

Not that he had much time anyway. He had to make sure all of the work arrived and then hang the show. It was his idea to hang the paintings singly at eye level and not stacked floor to ceiling. It seems obvious now, but at the time it was considered radical. There would be so much empty space, the thinking went, people would complain they weren't getting their money's worth. Gustav countered that the exhibition would draw crowds precisely because it was unusual and scandalous.

Others besides Gustav had more practical worries. The entrance fees were a major part of the Secession's budget for the following year. If people stayed away the Secession might not make enough money to continue.

Finally, everything had been done. Every statue was placed, every flower arranged, every ego soothed. There was nothing left except to dress and appear at the opening and see what people thought.

The day of the exhibition Gustav arrived at the Horticultural Society early in the morning and spent the hours before the opening moving paintings around and pacing and counting the bottles of champagne. I stayed away, knowing there was nothing I could do and that I would feel self-conscious just standing around.

I was anxious for him, though. Many newspapermen would be there, like Adolf Loos, who was vitriolic toward everyone but seemed to particularly dislike Gustav. He would write something scathing, and Gustav would be laughed at, because like it or not he personally had come to be the spokesperson and symbol of the group. None of the others would feel it like Gustav. It was also possible that the police would shut the show down, if they found something particularly vulgar at the exhibition, or pretended that they did. And, worst of all, what if no one came?

I wore a slim and sleeveless dress of Aegean blue jersey, with a neckline that draped like a Greek chiton, and a long silver chain set with peridots. Gold really looked better on me, but silver, declared Hoffmann, was the ideal material for a craftsman, so silver it was. With my satin opera coat in a slightly paler blue, I felt that I could defend Gustav against any onslaught, by the sheer force of my gorgeous outfit.

Helene and I arrived early, arm in arm, just as we had done for Gustav's exhibition years before. This time the heavy brass doors did not intimidate us and we pushed them open with authority. Frigid air blew in behind us, and then we were inside.

Vienna is cold in the winter, and the typical Viennese apartment was drafty and poorly heated. That's why everyone went to cafés, to get warm enough to think, to talk, to work. Even the cafés were only warm relative to the apartments. In the summer Vienna was conversely terribly hot, but of course everyone went away.

That is to explain why I was unprepared for the tropical air inside the conservatory. Only a few paying visitors had arrived, and were sweating their way around the room, handkerchiefs out. In contrast to the people, the palms and orchids looked ecstatic. I couldn't imagine how stifling it would be when the place was full. Hadn't anyone noticed it before?

Helene and I shrugged out of our coats as quickly as we could and left them with a young man who looked despondent to be stuck in the lobby with the minks and sables. Helene, ever sympathetic, gave him a large tip and told him to go buy himself some cadmium red. Then she turned to me with a worried look.

"Leave it to Gustav to forget something as trivial as physical comfort. Why don't you tell the ticket-taker to prop the doors open for a little while?"

"We have to do something," I agreed, "but I should ask Gustav first." I didn't want to presume an authority I didn't have. I scanned the room for him.

The reporters had come early, too, to get drunk. They were congregated around the bar, hoping for a riot or a brawl, anything but a common art show. The artists were hard at work at the fruit and cheese, gathering it up like squirrels. The waiters passing canapés of herring and cod tried to steer clear of them but occasionally one would get caught and lose his entire tray.

The middle of the room was clear except for a powerfully built man and a tall, frail woman who were huddled around a square piece of sculpture.

Adele was wearing a dress the color of the flushed faces of the reporters. They were not touching, they were not even looking at one another; Gustav was explaining the sculpture to her, why it was so important, something about the movement, the roughness, as if the sculpture had burst out of the stone. No one had done that since Michelangelo. He could have been teaching a class at the museum. Yet I was afraid to approach. I felt rather than saw what was between them.

Adele saw me coming but did not show any expression. I touched Gustav's arm and he jumped as if I had shocked him.

We had never been introduced, Adele and I. Since that night at Berta Zuckerkandl's I had heard her talked about, variously, as "beautiful and charming" and "cruel and insane." She had floated past me at several parties, but Gustav had never mentioned her. I found this ominous.

I had imagined a personality for her based on these brief glimpses and tidbits. I thought she would be snobbish, looking down her nose at me, the daughter of a factory owner. Not that she would say anything overtly rude. No, she would be exquisitely polite, quiet, and seeming a little shy. Every now and then, though, she would stick the stiletto to me. Unlike Alma, who preferred a club. I assumed she was quite intelligent in a devious, vicious way. I would have to be very careful with her. Compounding my difficulties, it would be a great coup if I could eventually secure her as a client. It would not do to offend her.

Gustav introduced her to me as his patroness. I was just Miss Flöge. I would have grasped her hand but she kept hers securely behind her back, a boyish gesture inappropriate for a formal evening. Was she snubbing me? Her face was blank, her heavy lids fluttering down over her enormous green eyes, obscuring her thoughts. She was my age, but she seemed years older, world-weary. Her shoulders stooped under the weight of some invisible burden.

"I came to ask if it would be all right to prop open the front doors. People are broiling."

Gustav looked surprised, even though his face was red and wet.

"Are you warm?" he asked Adele.

"I never am," she said, and it was true she didn't look it. She was as pale as the marble in front of her. I must have raised an eyebrow, so she went on. "My husband is always complaining about how much it costs to keep our house warm enough for me. Of course I always keep the dining room as hot as I possibly can. He suffers terribly."

I wondered if I had misheard her. "Where is your husband tonight?" I asked. "I'd like to meet him."

"No you wouldn't," she said flatly. "He despises art. He only cares about money. If there were art made of money, he would like that. Gustav, darling, you must make a painting of money. A still life. Or a sculpture made of it, like papier-mâché. Wouldn't that be something? And then I could buy it and put it on our mantel."

I was too embarrassed to say anything else. I turned to Gustav. "What do you think?"

"About what?"

"Opening the doors."

He shrugged, as if Adele's answer had settled the question. Adele was not warm, therefore there could be no problem. I gritted my teeth.

She looked at my dress. "Who made this?" she asked. I told her about Jaeger and about his movement to reform women's dress. It had been made using one of his patterns.

"I've never seen a material like that before," she said. "May I touch it?" I nodded and she reached out to touch my shoulder with her gloved fingers. I saw now why she had kept them hidden behind her back. They were twisted and stiff, as if she'd been struck by an attack of arthritis while playing a difficult passage on the violin.

"What's it made of?" she asked.

"Cotton," I said. "It's knitted, not woven."

"Interesting. Is it comfortable?"

"Very," I said. "It stretches when you move."

"Well, that would be a relief. But don't you feel a little like you're wearing a nightgown in public?"

"All the avant-garde women of Berlin are wearing similar designs," I said. "Not to mention Paris."

"You've sold me now, Miss Flöge," she said. "Both my husband and my mother hate the avant-garde. It's one of two things they agree on, the other one being that I am stark raving mad. Can you blame them, though? That blue is all wrong for me. Does it come in other colors?"

"I saw a blood red fabric in a catalog that would be stunning on you."

"Oh, I hate red," she said. "It's so obvious. My mother made me wear a red hat every winter for years. Every year in October I got a new one. When I was small it was a little felt tam-o'-shanter. I used to lose it on purpose in the park, but it was always replaced. Just last year she gave me a scarlet cloche for my birthday. I was going to give it to my dressing maid, but I didn't ever want to run into her out on the street in it, it would have made me sick. So I burned it."

Despite myself, I was beginning to like her, her wildness, her sense of humor. If she was joking.

"Not red then," I said.

"Not red," she said. "I like pale colors."

"Miss Flöge is going to open a fashion salon, you know," said Gustav. "Then she can make all of your clothes." I blushed.

"Someday," I said.

"Well, sign me up," said Adele enthusiastically. She liked her dressmaker well enough, she had plenty of things, but on the other hand, a cotton jersey dress would be novel, and she wanted to please Gustav and displease her husband. And it was not as though she had to worry about money.

That settled, I returned to the problem of the heat. I went to talk to Moll. Yes, he agreed, it was too warm. Yes, we should open the doors, that was what they had been doing in the weeks of preparation, but someone feared it would be too drafty for the opening.

He would do it himself, but he had just spied some very important patrons and needed to talk to them right away. Could I do it?

Yes, I could. The doors were heavy; the brass umbrella stands wouldn't hold them, but several bags of potting soil I located in a back room did the trick. It was a horticultural society, after all. I received a few strange looks as I made my several trips through the party lugging heavy burlap sacks, but it worked.

I went to the powder room to wash the dirt off of my hands. As I opened the door I saw Alma, in voluminous red, seated on a chaise.

"Did you fall into a potted fern?" she asked, "or is this the new fashion you're debuting tonight?"

I didn't answer. I went to the basin and cleaned myself off as best I could. When I sat down on the chaise next to her the comparison was discouraging. Though free of dirt, my face was flushed and shiny with sweat. The hothouse atmosphere had curled my hair into a frizzy halo. I had a smudge on the bodice of my dress that I couldn't brush off. I tried to comb my hair with my fingers but it only made the problem worse. Next to me, Alma was immaculate and composed. Her hair was tied into an intricate knot at the back of her neck that was perfectly smooth.

"Pomade?" she said, holding it out to me, in such a way that her diamond rings caught the light. "You could really use it." I took the tin with as much appreciation as I could gather and rubbed some of the sweet-smelling grease between my fingers.

"I'm actually glad you came in," said Alma, watching me try to make myself presentable, "because there is something I want to say to you."

I waited.

"He's asked me to marry him," she said. "I thought you should know."

I couldn't believe it. I tried to keep my face composed, my heart beating at its usual rhythm. Mechanically I smoothed my hair.

"Have you accepted?" I asked.

"Theoretically," she said. "It's a little complicated because my mother doesn't exactly approve. He's so much older, and has a bit of a reputation. But you know all about that. So for now it's a secret engagement."

My mind was remarkably calm. I thought to myself that if he truly was engaged to Alma, he would not be out in the gallery with Adele. Perhaps the engagement was a way of appeasing her, of assuaging her jealousy.

"Well, congratulations," I said. She seemed disappointed at my muted reaction.

"I'll invite you to the wedding, of course. Maybe you could even make the dress. Gustav says you're training to be a designer."

I had to get out of there. I snapped the pomade tin shut.

"You really ought to get married," she said. "I could find someone for you. I know lots of people."

"I don't need your help," I said, standing up and taking a final glance in the mirror. I tried not to look at the condescending little smile on Alma's rouged lips.

I went back out to the exhibition. The temperature in the hall had dropped several degrees. The rooms were now filled to the point of immobility. Scanning the crowd, I saw my sister and began weaving my way toward her.

The next day I took all of the papers so I could read the reviews. The *Times* said the exhibition was an intellectually muddled collection of the ugly, the degenerate, and the merely stupid. The *Neue Freie Presse* said it was a welcome display of contemporary artistic talent and wished the Secession much success.

The gallery was packed with people for the two months the exhibition ran. Even the emperor arranged to have a private viewing. The art sold well. Adele bought a Puvis de Chavannes. Alma's mother bought two Meuniers.

Fifteen

Then my father died, suddenly, of a heart attack. He was at the factory, as usual, examining some equipment, when he collapsed. There was nothing to be done for him; he was dead before the doctor arrived. Though his hair and beard had been white for years, I did not think of him as old; in fact he was fifty-nine. I had depended on his experience and his business sense to guide me through the opening of the salon. I had imagined a grand opening party at which he served as master of ceremonies. His ruddy face would beam with pride as he toasted his talented daughter. Now that could never be.

We planned to go to Attersee as usual that summer, but it would not be the same. Who would show me the hawks hidden in the trees around our house? Who would take us to church in the village and tend the vegetable garden and fall asleep in a chaise on the terrace as soon as luncheon was over?

We invited Gustav to come. He had been asked for years, but something had always kept him away: traveling, too much work, some woman or other. Each time he complained that Vienna was warm and uncomfortable and boring. Everyone else was away. Each time he wrote to me and begged me to come home. This year, though, I made it clear that I could not do without him. Knowing how fragile I was, how heartsick, he disentangled himself from his obligations and we spent two months together.

Not together, of course. My mother was there, and my sisters, and my niece. Gustav had a bedroom down the hall from mine, but he hardly ever used it; he preferred the camp bed he had set up in the greenhouse, which he used as a studio. He said he was up so early that it would disturb us to hear him clomping around, especially since he was prone to losing his shoes and turned everything upside down when he was looking for them.

In the morning he took bracing swims while everyone else slept, and joined the rest of us for breakfast on the terrace just as the sun cleared the mountain peaks. Most days he and I would row out on the lake; or rather, Gustav rowed, an oar in each hand, furiously, to work his muscles, while I sat back and enjoyed the breeze. When we reached the middle and had anchored, Gustav would plunge into the water, thrashing in the icy cold, and strike out for the pier on the opposite shore. On the return trip he would roll onto his back and spit water into the air like a whale. Climbing back into the boat, where I lay soaking up the sun, he would push me in and make an elaborate play of rescuing me, though I was the stronger swimmer. I wore a hat to protect my skin, and to prevent a headache from reading in the hot sun, but he grew tan and weathered from the sun, wind, and water.

Often he took his easel out in the boat and did paintings of the mountains and the town of Unterach, houses piled on top of one another like children's blocks, or a clump of birches on the shore. My job was to steady the boat and row just enough to keep us from drifting with the current. Or we would hike into the hills and he would paint the fields and the alpine wildflowers en plein air.

When we were completely worn out we would go back to the house and eat sandwiches and lie in the sun. Gustav took his work back to the greenhouse studio and refined it. He had sworn to forget his portrait commissions and the University Hall paintings for the summer.

The greenhouse looked much different then, with all of the glass side panels open on a sunny day, the floor neatly swept, and everything in its proper place. There was an old chaise I called my own, and while Gustav worked in the afternoons I liked to study

French fashion magazines and Arts and Crafts journals and make sketches.

One day, when I was deep into drawing a print of Japanese umbrellas, which I hoped could be produced, Gustav asked me to look at the new sketches for *Medicine,* the first of the University Hall paintings. His resolve to forget them had lasted all of a week.

He seldom asked me what I thought at this stage, but earlier in the year the committee had criticized his sketches and asked for changes. He had considered resigning, but in the end Franz talked him out of it and they signed the contract just before he came to Attersee. Now he had to figure out how to incorporate the changes in a way he could stomach.

I knew that there were general objections to the supposed indecency of the sketches. I knew they thought the girl that represented suffering mankind was obscene, and wanted a youth in her place, but having never seen the sketches I wasn't sure what that meant. I just assumed that the committee members were a bunch of repressed idiots who knew nothing about art. I wasn't prepared for what Gustav showed me.

Ten or twelve large sheets of paper were tacked together to the wall to form one enormous mural. It had to be large, of course, because it was to be mounted on the ceiling of the Great Hall, and no one would be able to see it if it wasn't. Its size was breathtaking, but that was the least of it.

I don't know how I had imagined Medicine should be portrayed: Hippocrates under an olive tree, teaching a group of eager, chiton-clad youths, or men in modern dress bending over the beds of the ill in some spotless infirmary.

In Gustav's allegory of medicine, Hygeia, the goddess of health, was in the foreground, looking like an avenging angel, dark, mysterious. I could not help thinking that she was an Adele Bloch-Bauer type. Had he been thinking of her? Hygeia was hardly compassionate-looking, holding her snake and her cup. You could not be sure whether she was coming to heal you, or kill you.

Alone on the left side was a nude woman, arms outstretched, who floated in space, held aloft by a watery substance, like amniotic fluid. Here was the obscene girl. Her pelvis was tilted forward in a suggestive way. All of the figures seemed to be suspended in the same viscous liquid. They were clumped on the left side of the painting like a pile of corpses. Some were in fact skeletons, shrouded in the long hair of others. Pregnant women, old men; all of humanity was included, suffering, tormented, dying.

It was a nightmarish painting.

"It seems . . . very personal," I said. I hated myself for sounding like a tactful, disapproving patron.

"Not at all," he said, already defensive. "It's a philosophical work. Why would you think it was personal?"

He rarely said Ernst's name. He paid Helene a generous sum every month and was a conscientious godfather to his niece. But he never talked about him. The day after the funeral he cleared out Ernst's studio and hauled everything to the dump. The only thing he kept was a ratty wool pullover that Ernst wore when the studio was cold. Gustav didn't wear it; he hung it on a chair. When he moved his studio the sweater came with him. It looked like Ernst had gone for a walk and would be right back.

"When I look at it I can't help thinking about Papa. All the doctor could do for him was close his eyes. And Ernst, the insanity of a twenty-eight-year-old dying of pneumonia, with all the best doctors in Vienna listening to his heart, and telling us to rub his chest with camphor, and none of it doing any good, and watching him slowly choke to death."

"That might be what you think about, I can't control your thoughts. I'm sorry about your father, but he was the last thing on my mind."

"And Ernst?" I said.

"I don't think about him," Gustav said. "What good would it do?"

"I don't believe you," I said.

"I can't listen to this," he said. "What are you trying to do to me?" He seemed to be in physical pain.

"In eight years have you ever talked about him?" I said.

"I am talking about him," he said, gesturing toward the painting. "Didn't you just say so? Do I have to cry, and tear my hair, and put on sackcloth and ashes? Would that satisfy you? If I acted like the wife of some Bedouin herdsman?"

I tried to interrupt him but he went on furiously. "This isn't about Ernst, it's about what happened after his funeral. You want me to talk about that, don't you? You probably want me to tell you that I love you, that I've been in a fog of grief, but now I'm ready to come out and marry you. Is that want you want?"

It was cruel and unfair, and all I could do was stand before him with tears slipping down my face. I had never mentioned it, never thrown it in his face. I had silently endured months of torture about Alma, waiting for him to tell me they were engaged. And now, this.

I left the studio without answering him and walked to a poppy field about a mile from where we lived. I lay down in the red and orange flowers that rustled like paper when the wind blew. It was hot in the sun.

Gustav and I rarely fought, so neither of us knew how to make up. When I came back to the studio he was standing in front of the painting. He looked at me penitently.

"Something isn't right about Hygeia's crown," I said. "And she's too fuzzy. She looks too much like your dying shades."

He nodded.

I pointed to a figure on the far right. "She unbalances the whole thing. I think she'd be better an inch toward the center."

"You're right," he said. He went on drawing.

Everyone else was playing charades that evening, but neither of us felt like it. We decided to sit out in the garden and listen to the crickets.

We walked down the brick path, away from the greenhouse, toward the other side of the garden. The stone bench at the very edge of our property was the destination. We wouldn't be able to hear any laughter from the house, or see the lights in the parlor. When it was dark enough we wouldn't be able to see the house at all.

Our garden was in the English style, weedy and disordered. Climbing roses and lilacs and wisteria grew over a row of trellises. The stone bench was cold underneath my hand. The roses were about ready to bloom; I counted a dozen hard green buds on each bush.

He took my arm and, pushing the sleeve up to my shoulder, drew on my skin with a charcoal pencil he pulled from his pocket.

I drew back, confused.

"I've had an idea," he said, "and I don't seem to have any paper handy."

"So I am to be your canvas?" I said.

"Why not?" he said. "You're washable."

It was a new headdress for Hygeia. What had been a crown of leaves in a corona around her head was replaced by a pattern of circles and crosshatchings, more like a snood than a crown. That was what he was drawing onto me.

I shuddered with a sudden chill as he varied the pressure from the gentlest tickle to a bruising press into the flesh for a darker, more adamant design. The light was almost gone, grainy, like in a photograph, and I wondered that he could see to draw.

"Haven't you drawn enough today?" I asked. The charcoal crumbled in his hands and he pressed his hands to my face and covered it with shadows.

"You look like a little girl I used to give drawing lessons to," he said.

"Or a widow," I said and winced at my mistake.

"Do you remember when we first met?" he said. "I hated you that day. With your expensive blouse and your soft little hands and your self-satisfied smirk. I hated your father and his expensive tobacco and your mother and her tacky French combs. I wanted to gnaw you all to pieces and spit your carcasses into the gutter."

"What stopped you?" I said.

"I didn't only hate you," he said. "I wanted you, too. I wanted to possess you and I wanted to be you in all your robust health and full stomach and comfortable innocence. I wanted to corrupt you and I wanted to protect you."

"You've done neither," I said. To myself I added, So he has always wanted me.

"You see," he said, "I always fail at everything."

I pressed my lips to his shoulder.

"At the studio . . ." he said. I waited. "It wasn't just Ernst, you know."

"It's all right," I said.

"You know," he said and paused. We were getting very close to something, and I felt as weightless as the woman in the drawing of Medicine. Any moment now I would float away, or dissolve into the bench like a dead thing into the earth.

"What is it?" I said.

"I want to paint a portrait of you," he said.

"Aren't you sick of portraits?" I asked.

"I've never done one of you," he said. "What a disgrace! You should design a dress and I'll paint you in it."

I took the pencil. "Hold out your hand." I held his hand in my lap and wrote on his palm, as a teacher might do for a blind person. I wrote my name into his skin. Then I smeared it until it was illegible.

"What did it say?" he asked.

"Nothing," I said. "Turn your hand over." The skin on the other side was drier and took the pencil more easily. I began to draw a school of fish that swam upward toward his elbow. He shook with silent laughter as the pencil tickled, then took it back and began to trace the bones in my hand.

"You have a hand like the wing of a bird," he said. "Your bones must be hollow."

The moment hovered there, wrapped in gauze, and his beard was soft against my face, nuzzling my cheek. I love you, I thought, but did not say.

"Dear Emilie," he said, and kissed me. It felt like diving into the sea from a granite promontory: I closed my eyes, put aside my fears, and leaped. For a moment there was no sight, only taste and touch and smell.

He stopped.

"What is it?" I said.

He stood up. "I'm tired," he said. "Today has kicked the stuffing out of me." He began walking toward the greenhouse. I followed.

"Do you want me to come?"

"If you want to," he said. "I have to get up early."

We slept on the floor of the greenhouse, entwined innocently, like retrievers worn out from a day of hunting. It was only as I was drifting to sleep that I realized that I hadn't said "I love you" out loud.

In the morning an errant ray of sun pierced a cloud and woke me up. Next to me, Gustav made a sound like a zipper closing. I put my share of the blanket over him and sneaked back to my room.

Everyone else was still asleep, apparently. I slid under my down comforter, to make my bed look as if it had been slept in and to warm my stiff joints. Though the bed was soft and I was tired from a night of fitful rolling on the hard greenhouse floor, I couldn't quiet my mind enough to drift off.

I remembered the time in the café, when I was a little girl still and he rubbed my face with a handkerchief dipped in ice water. The water stung my chapped cheeks and made them even redder, and he said something about them, how they wouldn't be out of place in a Watteau. I asked what a Watteau was and he paid the bill and took me straight to the museum, where they had a Watteau, the doll-like figures of a girl and boy having a picnic. I didn't like them, insipidly drawn and precious, and said so. Gustav agreed but then pointed out to me the delicate, almost invisible brushstrokes and the infinitesimal variations of color in patches I thought were just pink or just blue. I could learn more from the things I didn't like than from the things I did, he said. He wanted to know what I thought of others, of Brueghel and Bosch and a strange man who painted portraits of the seasons shaped out of vegetables. He laughed delightedly at some of the things I said and argued with me about others, but always took what I said seriously. I had an interesting mind, he said. But now I was no longer a little girl.

In the fall, Gustav moved his studio to Hietzing. He and Franz Matsch had been sharing a studio but little else for several years. The partnership was now dissolved, though they still shared in the work for University Hall.

The studio was just beyond the southern wall of Schönbrunn Palace. It was a short walk past the stonemason's workshop from the train station to the studio. The houses in the neighborhood, Gustav's included, were painted a cheerful, dairy yellow, like the inside of a buttercream chocolate, which contrasted attractively with their red tile roofs and black or dark green shutters. Gustav's bungalow was just off the main street and hidden behind a stone wall and a deep copse of lindens and alders and pear trees. A wrought iron gate opened onto a brick path that led to the house. Behind the house an overgrown garden of impatiens and ivy was usually inhabited by several cats, which hunted birds and sunned themselves on the wall and the paths. Beyond the garden, alfalfa fields of artificial-looking luxuriance stretched for acres. The front door of the studio opened onto the room where Gustav slept when he stayed at the studio. A long narrow hallway led past the tiny kitchen to the large room with windows that opened onto the back garden.

This is where Gustav was working when the controversy over his painting of Philosophy, one of the University Hall paintings, broke. *Philosophy* was, if anything, more disturbing than *Medicine*. Near the center an amorphous face emerged from the ether: was it God? Wisdom? To the side a column of naked, sinewy figures embraced and clutched their heads in despair or agony. And below them, nearly cut off at the bottom of the canvas, a clear-eyed, sinister woman stared directly at the viewer. Who was she? What did she represent?

The university professors were horrified. There was a meeting. Eighty-seven of them had signed a petition demanding that *Philosophy* not be hung in the Great Hall. They considered it an affront to reason and learning. The papers all carried accounts of the scandal, with various interpretations depending on their political slant. All of the critics weighed in, some very cruelly.

He was disheveled and angry when I arrived at the studio.

"I knew this would happen," he said. "The academics. They think art is like science, or should be. They want a nice equation, x plus y equals z. But it's impossible. And even if it were possible, it wouldn't be art."

"I know," I said. The only thing to do in these situations was to listen sympathetically until the rant had run its course. Then, when you had reached the end of that, insulting the critics usually worked.

"Jodl called my paintings ugly. Ugly! Can you believe that? Of all the things you could call them, I never thought anyone would call them ugly."

"I've never seen anything so lovely," I said. "Disturbing and frightening and terrifying, but lovely."

"Well, you're supposed to be disturbed and terrified. Anyone who isn't is in denial of what life is."

"I know," I said.

"Kraus said my paintings showed that I was ignorant of philosophy and that stupid people shouldn't be allowed access to brushes and paint."

"You know that's not true," I said. "Even stupid people should be allowed access to brushes and paint."

Gustav smiled, but only briefly. "Of course you know you're not stupid," I said. "Kraus just said that because he has a talent for sticking the knife in just the right spot."

"He's brilliant, though," said Gustav.

"Not when it comes to art," I said.

"Then after Jodl finished calling my paintings ugly, he said my symbolism was dark and obscure and incomprehensible."

"So?" I said. "Does that invalidate it, that few can comprehend it? Are you required to make paintings that the masses will enjoy? It's to hang in the university, not in the train station."

"True," said Gustav.

"Someone must have had something good to say," I said.

"Wickhoff did. He said it was courageous and original. But that doesn't mean he liked it."

"What are you going to do?" I asked.

"I've been working too long to give up now. I'll finish *Medicine* and *Jurisprudence* and hopefully the committee will reconsider or someone else will step forward. They're too big for a private individual, is the problem. I may have to keep them. It'll cost me. Others might cancel, too, because of bad publicity."

"Don't worry," I said. "You might not know that I am going to run a very profitable fashion salon. You'll be taken care of."

"You'd support a poor broken-down artist in his old age?" he said. He took my hand and squeezed it.

That night I lay awake for a long time, my body aching for him. I wanted to dress and go to the studio, where he was no doubt awake, working or sitting watch with his painting. I was afraid that I would meet Alma there, or Adele, or worse, someone else. Instead I held him in my mind's eye and gave myself what pleasure I could.

When things calmed a bit I went to sit for Gustav as he made the sketches for the portrait of me. It took time for us to design a dress, and for me to have it made up. I decided to make a dress like the one I wore to the first Secession exhibition. I took the ideas I had gleaned from Jaeger—the lack of a corset, the jersey fabric, the simple shape—and added some ornamentation of my own.

Designing clothes is all about proportion, the ratio between the neck and waist and the waist and ankle, the length of a sleeve, the height of a collar, or depth of a neckline. I'd always hated mathematics and I was attracted, magpie-like, to things shiny and glittery, but I tried my best. I bought beautiful fabrics that it seemed impossible could make ugly pieces of clothing. I was, of course, wrong. Theoretical designs were all very well, I discovered, but on a human body they were completely transformed. My prototype designs taught me more than any school could have. They were uniformly horrible, and I struggled to understand why. Even Gustav couldn't really help me. He knew when something looked wrong, and if it were a drawing he would know how to fix it, but he was at a loss to understand needle and thread, seams and placement of armholes.

Little by little I learned to balance top and bottom, front and back. I internalized the mathematical equations that dictated that something was right. I created each piece in my mind, on my own body, backlit so that the silhouette was all I could see. Or I took a piece of fabric and a dressmaker's dummy and started pinning and unpinning and repinning. The floor of my room was covered with pins, and Pauline would forget and puncture her feet on them. The macabre dummy, headless and stitched up the front and back like a wounded soldier, repeatedly frightened us when we came into the room at night.

After a dozen discarded attempts the dress was finally ready. It was aubergine jersey and skimmed straight and narrow down the body. I made a bolero jacket with blousy sleeves to match. With the dress complete, Gustav had to make room in his schedule for a portrait that wasn't for a wealthy client. When at last the schedule was cleared, I took the train to Hietzing, stopping in the stores to pick up milk for the cats and chocolates for myself.

While he worked we talked about the workshop he and his friends were putting together. It had all begun because Berta Zuckerkandl had complained to Gustav one night at dinner that her table did not match the art on her walls or reflect her taste. All of her silver was French, ostentatious, and embellished with roses and vines. She swore that if one of her artist friends could make her a very simple silver service, she would pay him handsomely and throw all of her French silver away. Hoffmann replied that while she was at it, she should have some china made as well so she could be rid of her gaudy Sevres plates. From there, helped along by carafes of dry Riesling, they discarded her glassware, her table and chairs, her sideboard, her wallpaper, her rug, her jewelry, and her clothes. They created the Wiener Werkstätte, modeled on the Scottish architect Charles Rennie Mackintosh's Glasgow School. They imagined a pottery studio, a glassworks, a metalworks, a woodworking studio, and a textiles department. Gustav said that since I was already far ahead of them in the fashion department I should work with the artists in charge of it. Perhaps my salon could make up their designs.

Gustav believed, much more than I did, that I would have a salon. It was one thing to look at fabrics with my father, and make myself a dress or two, it was another to rent the space and hire the workers and find the money to do it. He said it would all be easy, and had procured leasing agreements from several sewing machine companies to compare. He had called on three linen mills with me and they had given us their bids. In truth, it would have been difficult to do without him. People were always so much nicer to me when he was along, even if they did not recognize him. They thought he was the money behind the operation, which I suppose he was. He had offered to give me an interest-free loan to start. We were going to try to use local materials and local labor as much as possible. That meant no French silk, but our quality had to be at least as high, or our customers would think our clothes inferior and turn up their noses at them. We were trying for an avant-garde clientele, so it was all right, even preferable, to alienate conventional people. But not so many that we couldn't turn a profit.

We had lunch in the garden. The cats ate off of our plates and we took turns tossing them away. The cats, of course, not the plates.

"Today we are using the first Hoffmann prototypes," he said. "What do you think?"

The coffee was in a hammered silver tin that looked less hammered than dented. The pewter receptacles that held butter, cream, and sugar were better; they'd been done in molds. I rearranged the bread and pastry in a careful square on the checkerboarded lacquer tray.

"It's better this way," I said. "When do we start designing square food? Can fruits and vegetables be grown square?"

"Brat," he said. He handed me a cup and saucer of black porcelain rimmed with red squares. "Hoffmann hasn't slept in about two weeks, painting this china by hand."

"It's Greek-like," I said. "Greekish. Grecian."

"You sound like you're conjugating French verbs. Do you like it?"

"I think it's perfect."

"Tell him that and he won't believe you, but he might agree to design your salon," he said.

At two we went back to work. I had been posing for a half hour or so, and I was daydreaming about another dress I was going to make for myself, out of a gorgeous green peau de soie from Bianchini. I had seen it at a warehouse and immediately coveted it. It was very expensive, but I thought perhaps Gustav might buy the fabric for me for my birthday.

"Did Berta really say she'd let me make her a dress?" I asked. I knew she didn't care a thing about clothes.

"Not without some persuasion. She said if I designed the print and you made her look twenty pounds lighter, she would wear it to the Opera."

My sewing wasn't good enough yet for me to know how to make someone look twenty pounds lighter, but I was sure it could be done. There were a million tricks of drape and cut.

My dress would be a sheath, that would not be too difficult for me. It would have floss of the same color embroidered onto it in a pattern of vines, and then I would have crystals the color of seafoam and aquamarine sewn onto the vines. Maybe someone in the fashion department of the Wiener Werkstätte would know how to make me a pair of matching shoes.

Just then there was a determined rapping at the front door. Gustav frowned with annoyance.

"Ignore it," he said. "Farmer Naumann has lost his dog again, the third time this week. On Tuesday I lost two hours and sprained my ankle looking for it." The knocking continued for some minutes, then stopped.

"The red pointer?" I asked. "It's just a puppy."

"Maybe it was hit by a cart."

"Gustav, how can you say that?" I knew he wasn't serious.

"I'll send Tristan out after him next time. That cat could make mincemeat of any dog."

Then we heard the sound of someone forcing the door.

"What the hell?" said Gustav. I dropped my pose and turned toward the hallway to wait for whoever it was to appear: the police, the farmer with the missing dog, a model, a burglar. But it was not any of these. It was Alma.

"I suppose you thought I would just go away if you cowered in here," she said. I had never seen her hair loose and she looked much younger that way, a child. She waved her cloak, with its scarlet silk lining, like a matador. "I suppose you thought you could stop answering my letters and I would just disappear." She turned to the platform where I was still standing, ludicrously, as if I could make myself invisible. "And I suppose this is somehow your doing," she said, "though I can't imagine what you could have done or said that would make him come back to you."

"Alma," Gustav said in what he must have supposed was a soothing tone, "leave Emilie alone." He said that they should go out and have a talk in the garden, that she should take a few deep breaths.

"You think I can breathe in this dress? I wore it especially for you."

"Alma," said Gustav, then stopped.

She was working herself up to a dramatic act of violence, but I couldn't tell whether she was going to fling herself at Gustav or rip his favorite dress to shreds in front of his eyes. Finally she removed her glove and swept the contents of Gustav's worktable to the floor. The three of us listened to the glass smash and the metal containers roll with a sound like spinning tops until at last they came to rest and it was silent again.

"Emilie, make Alma some tea," Gustav said. He had decided that something stronger than appeasement was required. He took Alma by the shoulders and pushed her to the platform. She collapsed onto it.

I was glad to leave them. I was afraid she might throw something at me. There was already hot water on the stove. I rinsed one of Josef's new cups and poured Alma's tea into it. Some of the glaze appeared to be dissolving into the liquid, turning it rusty red. When I returned to the studio with it Gustav was kneeling beside her, stroking her hand. I held out the cup and she took it without looking at me.

"You play with people's feelings, you know," she said to Gustav. "You seem to think you live in a painting, or an opera, where there are no consequences. Have you ever thought of another person other than yourself?"

It dawned on me that she was enjoying herself. I am swooning on my lover's settee, she was thinking to herself. Our love is tempestuous and passionate. He will see the tears glittering like diamonds in the corners of my eyes and will not be able to resist me. I knew she was going to write it all down when she got home. Her breath rose and fell quickly. His favorite dress was moss-colored and showed plenty of décolleté, of course.

I was not sure what Gustav would do. It was an affecting performance. Would he send me away? I didn't think I could bear to be exiled, not in front of Alma. I got the broom and dustpan and began sweeping up the shards of glass. I tried to make it look as if I wasn't listening.

"Mahler wants to marry me, you know," she said.

"Of course he does," he said. "Who wouldn't?"

"You don't."

"I'm a fool," he said. "I'm a second-rate, broken-down paint dauber. I'm old and ugly. I don't deserve you."

"I don't care."

"But I do. I'm thinking of you, Alma. How long would you be happy with someone like me? You wouldn't be able to be the queen of society married to me. I stay at home and work. I don't go out, I don't really fit in society. You'd be embarrassed by me. You'd be unhappy and have affairs, like Adele Bloch-Bauer."

"You're not thinking of me, you're thinking that Carl will have you shot."

"You really think Moll would shoot me? I'm not afraid of him."

"I love you," she said.

"You're twenty-three," he said. "You have many loves ahead of you. You'll look back one day and laugh that you ever thought of me."

"You're in love with her," she said accusingly. He looked up at me, still sweeping aimlessly, and lowered his voice. I couldn't hear what he said to her, so I watched her face. It did not turn pale and shocked, or satisfied and mocking. She drooped a little, but smiled at the same time.

After that he got her back into her cape and led her to her carriage. I watched him get into it with her and ride away. Since there was nothing else to do, I locked up the studio and went home. I didn't cry, that would have been weak. I would've had to admit to myself how relieved I had been not to see or hear about Alma, how horrified I'd been to have her reappear, how crushed I had been to see Gustav leave with her without a backward glance. Brutally repressed tears are the most painful kind: boiling hot and choking, as if someone had covered your head with a pillowcase. Afterward, a vile headache and a contorted crimson face. Better to let them out, I learned many years later. They're cooling, they effect a calm. Afterward, you can think.

* * *

I came to the studio the next day to sit and to see what he would say, but I could not ask what had happened with Alma. I could not ask him what he had said about me. He seemed unusually cheerful, even singing as he prepared for the day's work in a hoarse, off-key tenor. He looked as if he would burst out laughing at any moment.

"Is something funny?" I couldn't resist saying.

"Everything," he said. "Everything is funny." I couldn't tell whether that boded well for me, or ill.

In a few weeks he was ready to begin painting. Our routine changed, became more serious. Gustav did not like to waste time and had no patience with mistakes.

He had often described his daily ritual to me: he arrived early and pulled up all the shades, lit a fire, and put water in the kettle. Then he roamed the studio, picking things up, putting them down. He didn't look at whatever he was working on, not yet. Sometimes he looked at the background that was set up on the model's platform, or he examined a sitter's clothing as it hung on hooks in the hallway.

He took time preparing his materials. No one else was as reverent. People who didn't know him imagined a careless, messy studio, but they were wrong. Now that he worked alone everything was clean and precise. His linseed oil was so pure you could cook with it. He liked to rub it into his hands, which were often chapped. He cleaned his brushes with flannel rags and soft soap. He sorted his rags. The stiff ones were sent to the laundry. He liked to breathe in the smell of the turpentine, and joked that it had made him crazy.

By the time I arrived the studio was warm. The oil that had been as thick as corn syrup when Gustav arrived in the chill room now had the consistency of vinegar. It was time to mix the paints. He poured the pigments onto the palette, umber and sienna and ocher and amaranth. They smelled like chalk and dirt and limestone dust. With a palette knife he layered oil into the powders. The wax paper became gray and saturated.

Gustav turned his palette knife in a puddle of oil and pigment. He touched everything on his table in a sort of talismanic ritual. He cleaned every brush on the hem of his smock. He stirred the mud-brown turpentine, half-filled with sediment, like the Danube in the spring. He dumped his knives and sponges out of the bags in which he kept them. Finally, for at least ten minutes he stood before the painting and studied it to discern the plan for the day.

While I waited for him to look at me I did jumping jacks and toe touches and jogged in place. It was the only way I could tire myself out enough to stand still for so long and keep from twitching. Gustav liked the color it brought to my skin. When I knew he was ready I got into position, knowing he would come over and adjust it. He liked to ask me to do impossible things, like put my foot behind my ear. I would ask him to show me, and he would spend several minutes in painful contortions before he said "Enough!"

I tried to relax my face into a pleasant expression, and arrange my body exactly as it had been the last time. If I slipped by the tiniest fraction he would notice, and reprove me. I couldn't see the painting while I modeled, and Gustav covered it with a sheet during breaks.

Not being able to see the portrait he was making of me drove me crazy. I could not ask him about Alma but I thought the painting might tell me something he would not. I tried asking him in a general way how the work was going, but he was on to me; he refused to tell me a thing. He just shook a brush at me and said, "No questions until it's finished!" While I was at the studio he never left me alone; he knew temptation might get the better of me, that I might run over and lift the sheet if he went to the kitchen or signed for a telegram.

I had to do something. I could've come to the studio at night, or when I thought Gustav would be gone, but he kept such odd hours that I was afraid I would be caught. So I went to my sister.

After Ernst's death Helene brought her daughter back to live with us. They shared a room that was meant for a maid's room, but she didn't seem to mind. She took over most of the housekeeping and never complained at the sad turn her life had taken. She was still the most beautiful widow in Vienna. That day she wore a pink silk scarf tied around her head and tiny tourmaline earrings. She looked like a girl in a Dutch painting. Helene, now nine years old, lay on the rug reading an illustrated Hans Christian Andersen while I told my sister what I needed her to do.

"Just pull the sheet off and look at it," she said. "Why all the cloak and dagger?"

"He won't let me see it until it's finished."

"He won't let me. You act like you're about eight years old. Actually, I take that back. At eight you would've yanked that sheet off right in front of him."

"Will you go tonight?" I gave her my studio key. "Gustav and I are going to the Opera, but he'll probably go back to the studio afterward."

"And what is it that I'm supposed to look for? Some psychological insight? Something about his feelings?" It sounded stupid when she said it out loud.

"Something like that."

I don't remember what we saw that night, I was too anxious. I thought that he could see through me and know what I was up to, but he must have decided it was what had happened with Alma and the fear of seeing her in public that made me so nervous. His way of making it up to me was to bound around me like a puppy, beseeching me with his innocent eyes and charming me with his boyish high spirits.

I kept him out late afterward, pretending to be hungry. Then I went home.

When I saw Helene the next afternoon she did not bring up the painting right away. She had been put in charge of finding a location for the salon and had visited several buildings in Mariahilf, where we lived. She wanted to tell me about square footage and the terms of the various leases and the pros and cons of each of the spaces, but it was the last thing on my mind at that moment.

"Well?" I said when I couldn't wait any longer. She knew what I meant.

"It's nearly finished," she said. "Another week or two, I imagine."

"What does it look like?"

"It's good," she said unhelpfully. She wasn't looking at me and trying to cover it up by pretending to help Helene with the little piece of embroidery she was working on. Maybe she thought the tableau was so pretty I'd get distracted.

"You mean a good likeness?" Her vagueness irritated me.

"Some people might think so."

"But not you?"

"In the painting you're . . ." she tried to think of the right word, "slinky. Or snaky. You're like one of the water sprites. Which would be fine except that it is you, it's uncannily like you, and yet it's not."

"What about it is like me?"

"It's hard to describe. You really have to see it." I wanted to scream at her in frustration.

"Helene, you have to tell me something more."

"It's blue and purple and gold and silver."

"Thanks, that helps."

"I'm trying, Emilie, I really am."

"Do you think he loves me?"

"From looking at the painting or from everything else?"

"Either one," I said.

"You know I don't know the answer to that."

"But what do you think?"

"Maybe. I don't know."

"When you looked at the painting, did you think, 'He is in love with this woman'?"

"I thought, 'He wants her to be someone else.' "

When the painting was finished, Gustav at last asked me to look at it with him. I was glad that Helene's surreptitious examination of it had prepared me. We stood in front of it silently for a few minutes, and he poked at a corner with a sponge and touched some spots with flecks of titanium white. It was always hard to get him to declare that there was nothing more to do.

On the canvas, the dress I had made was unrecognizable to me. It was a royal purple and moved toward the floor like a river; aquamarine blue fish with golden eyes swam lazily down it while the silver beetles on the jacket pilled tightly. The attenuated figure inside the dress had fabric wrapped tightly around her slender neck. She had a bare décolleté and long slender fingers wrapped around her jutting hip. Her dress tapered off into the bottom of the picture, leaving her footless and bound. The face was mine, but it was blurry and indistinct, the cloud of hair like my own on a rainy day.

Helene was beautiful. Everyone knew that. My own case was trickier. Some days and from some angles I thought I was pretty, but a change in the light or a shift in perspective, and I was quite plain. In the sixteen years since Gustav made the pastel drawing of me I had still not reconciled myself to my strong jaw, but I now wore my hair in a way that minimized its severity. I looked good in hats. Profile was my best angle. My face looked too wide straight on. My forehead was a little low, and my neck was a little short. Occasionally I was forced to admit that my complexion was good, or that my eyes were a lovely shade of blue, but most often when I looked at myself in the mirror I saw only the structural imperfections.

The woman in the new portrait was stunning and—I blushed at the thought—sexy. She had challenging eyes. Her expression was powerful and just a bit sinister and it spoke of an inner life entirely different than the one I thought of myself as having. Was there any of her in me? Did I not know myself?

According to Helene, who knew me better than anyone, my assessment of myself was accurate and it was Gustav who did not know me. But I wondered if Helene had been looking at me too long to see me clearly. Maybe I was more like the woman in the portrait than I could admit.

"What do you think?" he said. He had been up all night with the painting; he danced in front of it with the wild energy of an exhausted man. I hesitated. It was an unfair question, like trying to assess your own intelligence. It was a gorgeous, swirling, painterly masterpiece, but because it was of me, it was impossible to be objective.

"Is this really what you see when you look at me?" said the self-absorbed girl, while the artist remained silent. Gustav sighed, but he seemed more amused than offended.

"Once you said that a drawing I did of you made you look like a child. Now you think I've made you look—what? Too womanly? You must admit you are inconsistent and hard to please."

"Why am I stretched?"

"I thought you'd complain I'd made you look like Berta," he said.

"I just wonder if you really see me at all," I said, echoing Helene, "or whether you've created someone you want me to be."

"I'm a portraitist, not an anatomist. Of course my view is subjective."

"I think I look . . ." All I could think of were Helene's adjectives. "Snaky."

"Does it frighten you?" He was serious now. We didn't look at one another, but only at the painting. I felt exposed, naked.

"Yes," I said.

He was silent for several minutes and I listened to his thoughts pass through the air like clouds.

"It frightens me, too," he finally said. "That's why I had to paint you this way. Painting you any other way would have been the easy way out. There's nothing more despicable than a cowardly painter."

The idea that Gustav could be frightened of me, of some aspect of me, was ludicrous. I might frighten myself, but that was different.

"It's like *Philosophy*," he said. "It would be easy to represent it as rational and orderly, like the School of Athens, but that would be dishonest. It's completely terrifying to make visible the chaos of human existence, to admit the darkness of the human mind, but once you've done it you can see that there is light there."

"The light shines in the darkness, and the darkness has not overcome it," I said.

"Yes," he said. "If you want to put that interpretation on it."

"Do you wish I was more like her?" I shrugged toward the painting.

"But you are," he said. "You just don't realize it."

The woman in the portrait would have worn something erotic that day, something like the emerald Alma always had cradled in her bosom. She would have put soot on her lashes and rouge on her cheeks and brushed up against Gustav as he spoke and given him come-hither looks. But I would have felt ridiculous.

I love you, I didn't say. Instead I suggested we have lunch. I had brought smoked mackerel and rye bread.

Gustav gave the portrait to my mother, but she disliked it. She kept the painting in a closet and refused to display it anywhere in the house, even when visitors asked to see it. After a few years Gustav asked for it back, and sold it to the Historisches Museum der Stadt Wien in 1908. The tourists come and peer at me and check their guidebooks and stare some more. I'm so real they think they can smell it on me.

Sixteen

Kammer am Attersee
January 8, 1945

W e spent the day sewing blackout curtains. Among the packages Herta sent, among the antique textiles and glittering jewelry, was a soft parcel tied in brown paper: thirty yards of unglamorous black cotton, stiff and waxy. Its only redeeming feature is that it is woven extremely fine so that it is completely opaque. If you fell from the sky next to the house in the middle of the night you wouldn't be able to tell that anything was there. If you were flying above you would think you were over water, not a quilt of farms and towns and castles. You'd become disoriented, not believe your instruments were right. Maybe you'd crash into the mountains and die in fire and ice. That, they tell us, is the idea.

Soon after we arrived the local magistrate had sent us a notice: all houses were to conform to the regulations within thirty days. There followed, in typical Austrian style, a precise description of what cloth was and was not acceptable, detailed measurements and instructions for making the curtains, hours during which the curtains must be in place, and the penalties to be imposed for those who failed to abide by the rules. There will be a surprise inspection.

Other people had known for weeks that this was coming. The only stores that still had the right cloth in stock were charging five times its value. I could have paid the outrageous markup, but it might have killed me. Instead I went to see Heitzmann, but he had none to spare. In a last-ditch effort before admitting defeat and giving the profiteers their reward, I wrote to Herta in Vienna, without much hope that she would be able to find the stuff, or that she could get it to us in time. But she and the mail service are as reliable as ever.

My fingers are stiff and I can hardly see what I'm doing; I prick myself every few minutes. The material is ugly and you would never want to make clothes out of it. I try to imagine a suit, say on Adele Bloch-Bauer, and the idea makes me shudder. It might work for a coat with a small round collar and shiny plastic buttons, something to wear in the rain, in the country. Something to wear when you are old and no one cares how you look, least of all yourself.

The sewing, though, is strangely satisfying. I haven't sewn in a long time. I pinned, and I draped, I measured, I drew, but other people did the sewing, women with graying hair pinned up to expose their bent necks, clenched and screaming in pain. I told them what to do and they did it on machines. Unless they did the beading or finishing work, in which case the work was even more arduous. A girl didn't last very many years at beadwork.

When I lift up the cloth and hold it to the light, I note with satisfaction that the stitches are tiny, precise, and even. The hem is as straight as the edge of a table and the thread shines on the dull cloth like tarnished silver. These stitches wouldn't be out of place on a ball gown.

When we received our first commission Helene, Pauline, and I sewed two hundred and fifty aprons, by hand, in the parlor, since we had neither a seamstress nor a sewing machine, not yet. They were made of coarse, unbleached cotton the color of oatmeal. They were unadorned, unlined, and one size. The pattern was given to us to copy. There was little more to do than cut out a shape, hem it, and attach ribbons at the neck and waist. It seemed there was no way to impose any of my personality. To me then, longing to play with yellow silk and beaded net, they were mind-numbingly dull, but in the end it was good for me. It taught me that the expensive fabric and the gaudy trim are the rosettes and not the cake itself.

Somewhere along the way I thought to add pockets to the front of the apron. I thought a cook might want to put a thermometer in there, or a whisk, or a pair of shears. The owner of the cooking school raved about them, those pockets. It made me realize how little, and how much, it takes to please people. All you have to do is give them exactly what they asked for with some addition that they didn't even know they needed until you showed them.

Neither Helene nor Pauline seemed to mind that I had essentially drafted them. Both of them needed something to take their minds off of the knowledge that they were alone. So did I.

It was a start. We were being paid.

I told Helene of those times as we sat in the matching pink chintz chairs in the parlor of the lake house sewing widow's weeds. She's heard the stories a thousand times before, but she never shuts me up. The drab fabric in our hands stood out oddly in the colorful room, like a dead flower in a beautiful arrangement. The rain poured like a waterfall from the gutters and the fireplace smoked and made us smell like sausages. I wished I could go out for a walk, but there was a curfew now. And I can't say that the chilly rain was very appealing. If only I had a coat made of black oilcloth, something to make me invisible in the night, then I could go.

"When I first began I was always afraid of making a mistake," Helene said, "cutting something wrong and wasting good fabric, or sewing a pocket on crooked. I was afraid you'd be disappointed in me. Now I can drop a stitch and no one will care."

"Maybe the inspectors will," I said. "Maybe they're sticklers for good sewing." She said she doubted it, seeing some of the things the women in the village wore, and I had to agree.

Then a menial job could seem like a once-in-a-lifetime chance, a few shillings could seem like a fortune. We had everything ahead of us: riches, fame, success.

Helene reminds me how hard that time was for her mother. You had everything ahead of you. She was a twenty-three-year-old widow with a two-year-old child. All she had ahead was grief and drudgery, dependence and loneliness.

Do you think it was so terrible? I wanted to know. Was she miserable?

No, she said. I don't think so. But I would never want to be where she was.

The moment was becoming too painful for both of us, and with relief we turned to a discussion of aircraft, a convenient topic because neither of us knew the first thing about them. We tried to imagine how they navigated, what kind of instruments they might have, what kinds of engines. Did they use the same kind of fuel as my little yellow roadster, long since commandeered?

"I don't think we can stop them," Helene said, "we can just make it harder. It's really Vienna we're protecting, you know. Nobody cares about us out here."

"And they shouldn't," I said. "We're nothing. It's the Secession they should be protecting, and the Kunsthistorisches."

I tried to imagine Poiret, slender and modish, perhaps in a specially designed aviator's cap and goggles, firing down on me. The image was ridiculous, but comforting somehow, like poking out the eyes on a photograph of an unfaithful lover.

It was already twilight at four o'clock when we hung the curtains, nine sets of them, in the kitchen, the parlor, the six bedrooms. and the bathroom. The house shrunk to half its former size. I had forgotten how much space windows create, even on a moonless night, or a cloudy, starless one. I felt claustrophobic, the scope of my world reduced to this tiny unprotected box. If anything came at you, you wouldn't be able to see it until it was too late.

I cut the sprouting eyes from our potatoes and put them in a paper bag. Later we'll plant them. Boiled in salty water, eaten with stewed greens from Heitzmann's garden and fresh bacon, they didn't make a bad meal. After that there was nothing to do but go to bed.

STUDY FOR *ADELE BLOCH-BAUER,* 1903

It is well known among certain people that Adele Bloch-Bauer takes lovers. Publicly, many are disapproving of a married woman carrying on that way. At the very least she could be more discreet about it. In private, among the women, especially, the tone is somewhat different. Her husband, it's said, beat her unconscious when he found out she couldn't have children. He keeps another family in the provinces somewhere. Poor Adele, the lament goes. She's so unhappy, so lonely. Let her find her consolation where she can. Women feel protective of Adele, her physical frailty and her self-destructive recklessness touch their hearts. It's unlikely she'll live long, they think, between her abusive husband, her melancholy, and her fragile health. A cold could send her off, but it's just as likely to be a bottle of pills. Only her family thinks to themselves that Klimt is the one to be concerned about, not Adele.

For the gossip is that her current lover is Gustav Klimt, the painter. Of course he denies it. Frau Bloch-Bauer is a lovely woman, he always says. She is a joy to paint. The subtext is clear to all: he would not presume to conduct an affair with a client, a wealthy woman of society. He is graceful in his denials, practiced and smooth. Of course no one is fooled for a minute, nor does he expect them to be.

For her part, Adele has many acquaintances but few, if any, friends, so no one is sure just what is happening. She glides alone through the parties she attends, seemingly everywhere, but afterward no one remembers having talked to her. And when her husband is in town, Adele gives parties where butterflies are released in the conservatory and ice sculpture towers over the guests in the drawing room. She enjoys the theater of it, enjoys the stage managing and the set design. She invites people known to be sworn enemies and places them next to each other at dinner. Yet people still come, because of her husband. And because one week it will be spider monkeys shipped from Madagascar and the next it will be red velvet drapes and dancers from the Bolshoi.

There has never been consensus concerning Adele's beauty. She is the kind of beautiful woman who is most admired by men, leaving the women in her circle slightly bewildered but not threatened. The men are bamboozled, the women decide together. They feel for her, of course, but they are as brutally honest in discussing her looks as they are in discussing each other's when the person in question has stepped away. Adele's face is long and bony, her body gaunt, her hair too dark, her eyebrows too thick, like a Gypsy's, her features rather thin. Her eyes are lovely, it is true, green in some lights and gray in others, but they are heavy-lidded, reptilian. Her teeth are too prominent. Adele is striking, in her way, but that's not the same as beauty. At dinner the women argue with their husbands. They never see what the men do, the abandon hidden below the quiet exterior, the sexual energy, the capacity for violence. After sex with Adele Bloch-Bauer, a lover might be advised not to fall asleep. Eventually the men are beaten down. Perhaps the wives are right, they say. Perhaps it isn't beauty at all. But each one is wondering when Adele will be through with Klimt and if she might be persuaded to look his way.

Adele and her husband are giving an engagement party for Gustav Mahler and Alma Schindler. It is a rare event; Mahler hates parties, especially ones in his honor, and only agreed to this one because Alma cried and threw things. They stand on the parquet in the entrance hall, Mahler and Alma, one gray and uncomfortable, one foot planted toward the door as if he could escape, the other, lit up like the Ringstrasse at night.

Gustav Klimt enters the room, greeting the groom and kissing the bride, who holds the kiss just slightly longer than etiquette proscribes; has she forgiven him? he wonders. They have barely spoken since the day at the studio, when was it, two years ago. He's had several angry letters from her since then, which he has not answered. By answering he would have to concede that there was something between them, and he prefers to believe that these grievances of Alma's are delusions.

Gustav dislikes parties almost as much as Mahler does—the mindless chatter, the late hours, the distraction from his work, the chance of an uncomfortable encounter with an old lover or ideological foe, the chance of making a slip in etiquette or revealing some ignorance that twenty years of polishing hasn't managed to cover—yet he goes to every party where he knows Adele will be. Not because he desperately wants to see her, though he does, but because he enjoys watching her from across a room while thinking graphically of what is under her dress. The thrill of the charade. Will he go too far? Will she give him away? The threat of being unmasked, the danger of a loss of self-control arouse him the minute he sees her.

"You are looking lovely," he says to her, leaving Alma's confining embrace and brushing Adele's hand with his lips. He thinks of the crippled fingers underneath the gloves and what they are capable of. Of her painted lips and where he would like them to be.

"How very kind of you," she says, looking over his shoulder in a vague way. It is a trick she has that he cannot stand. Is he boring her? Is she thinking of him at all? It is intolerable and in order to master the situation he leaves to greet other friends. He feels her eyes follow him. He will not return to her for the rest of the night, he vows. To see how she will respond. To see what her next move will be. Before long, though, the anticipation has become unbearable and he feels compelled to force Adele's hand. When he sees her watching he slips into the library and pretends to examine a very bad oil painting. There is a man in the library reading the titles of books, but when he sees Gustav he looks ashamed of this display of social awkwardness and disappears. Gustav is alone in the library. Soon he feels her breath on his neck.

"You always ignore me," she says.

"Quite the opposite," he says. "I am never more acutely conscious of you than when we are not together."

She has a high-pitched, barking laugh, tinged, he thinks, with hysteria. She produces the sound a few seconds longer than seems appropriate. Others may fall for your facile lines, her laugh says, but you have met your match in me. I have no illusions left to shatter. Ironically, what he

has just said is true. When she is near him she is a woman. He is famil-
iar with the parts, the limbs, the sexual machinery. He is expert at say-
ing the things that will induce a woman to spend the night with him.
He knows what will make her look upon him with passion, with affec-
tion, and, when the time is right, with hurt or annoyance or anger. It is
only when she is standing across the room, when she is talking to some-
one else, pretending not to look at him but tracking his movements with
her peripheral vision; it is only from this distance that he knows her
fully. There is no sense in insisting. Instead he places his hand on her
waist. His thumb presses against her ribs. Sometimes he thinks some-
thing inside of her will snap.

"I saw your little friend downstairs," says Adele. "I'm afraid I may
have slipped up. It's so hard for me to be dishonest, you see." Gustav's
sudden anger is a surprise to him. He feels that the moment is absurdly
melodramatic, like something from a novel; he thinks that he might
strike Adele, who has moved away from him as if anticipating this and
stands with her back to the painting, eyes veiled under those hooded lids.

"She will never find out," he says. "If you tell her I will kill you."

"My husband threatens to kill me all the time, and if he hasn't, you
won't," she says.

"I'm not joking, Adele. She must never know."

"It's charming the way you protect her. Fatherly, almost. And yet isn't
it rather insulting, too? She's very intelligent. Don't you think she
knows already?"

He has no response. I am not a subject he ever discusses, not with
Hoffmann, not with his mother, not with anyone. I am in his life and he
does not want to know why, or in what way. It repulses him that the
woman standing before him is discussing me as if I were some guest at
the party about whom some especially fascinating gossip is known.
There she is, poor thing. Doesn't know. Maybe one of us should tell her. I
heard she does know. After she greeted Adele I saw her take a glass of
champagne and down it in one gulp. I saw you do the same thing, that
doesn't mean anything. But I think she knows. Look at the set of her
mouth. Not many women of her age have a mouth like that.

"She's not to know, she's not to be hurt," is all that Gustav can say. He knows that on Tuesday he will return to Adele's house and for the sitting she will wear something I have made; though the salon is months from opening I have taken to making things for a few select people, for publicity. I had made some scarves and shawls and Adele had insisted she must have one of each. He will sketch her in this apparel as the tension grows unbearable. They will not speak, waiting to see which one of them will break first. Finally he will have to put his pencil down and at least stand and stretch his shoulders. When she sees him move Adele will walk out of the room without a word. She won't go to her adjoining bedroom, but to a guest room down the hall. When he gets there she will already be draped across the bed, limp and pale. She'll show no excitement or enthusiasm as Gustav undresses her; she wants him to think she doesn't desire him. When he's reached the final layer, when he's discarded corset and petticoat and chemise, she will tell him that she wants to wear the scarf or the shawl while they make love, and he will press his flesh against Adele's with this square of fabric entangled between them.

Seventeen

ustav and I went together to Adele's party for Alma and Mahler. I was beside him when he kissed Alma. I kissed her, too; her cheek was warm and smelled of powder. I felt sorry for Mahler, he looked as if his suit was two sizes too small. I kissed Adele; she smelled of jasmine. White flowers were her favorite.

"I'm so glad you could come," she said. "You've never seen my house. When I have a moment, I'll give you a tour. It will take hours, thank God. I'm dying to get away from all of these people."

"When is Klimt going to finish that damn painting?" asked her husband when we were introduced. "I pay him enough for five or six paintings. You see that space at the top of the stairwell? That's where it's going when he's finished."

The stairs were marble, smooth and cascading like Michelangelo's at the Laurentian library. The chandelier thirty feet above our heads glinted with hundreds of crystals. "Eight hundred and twelve," said Herr Bloch-Bauer when I complimented it. It weighed four hundred pounds, he said, and was brought in pieces from Prague. I imagined it falling on him.

The apartment was much gaudier than Berta Zuckerkandl's. Every room was done in red and white and gold, like the imperial palace. I understood now why Adele hated red, and why Gustav said she often threatened to tear the place down to the ground and start over.

Gustav disappeared soon after we arrived. I could manage very well without him by this time. I sat on a yellow silk chaise with Berta and drank. By now she was my friend and no longer frightened me. She had helped me to find investors for the salon and, despite her innate skepticism of fashion, had promised to come and be measured and then to be extremely stylish and extravagant in the coming years.

At parties like this Berta didn't mingle; she sat in a corner and waited for people to pay their respects, and then gossiped about them after they left. It was an entertaining way to pass an evening. The waiters kept coming with their trays and I kept putting empty champagne flutes on them and taking full ones away. Adele must have had thousands of such glasses. I wondered who washed them.

During a lull Berta asked about the preparations for the salon. Moll and Moser, Hoffmann and Mahler, all had come and gone. She wanted to know if Adele was on the list of those who would be given the first appointments when we began taking measurements and making personalized dummies for top clients. I said Adele had not asked to be, though she had already bought a few small things, and I could not bring myself to ask her.

"She will ask you," said Berta. "She wants to get a good look at you, I imagine. In private, I mean." I did not pretend that I didn't know what she was talking about, because you couldn't pretend with Berta. She knew everything that went on. And despite the fact that she was Gustav's friend, I knew that she sympathized with me, and that I could trust her.

"She'll be disappointed, then," I said. "I don't present much competition."

Berta looked as if she wanted to shake me; in fact she put down her glass and pinched my arm.

"I doubt that's what she thought," she said. "If it was . . ."

I knew what she was going to say. If she had thought me harmless, she wouldn't have disappeared with Gustav. She wouldn't have felt it necessary. The next sitting would have been good enough.

"It's not like it was with Alma," I said. "I like Adele, despite everything. I could stand for them to be together. If he'd married Alma I would've jumped off of a bridge."

"You're a fool, Emilie," said Berta. Her voice was harsh and angry, like my father's when I forgot to do something.

"I know," I replied dismally. "Everyone tells me that: my sisters, Alma . . ."

"You don't understand me," Berta said. "You're a fool for thinking that Alma or Adele are any stronger than you are."

"Aren't they?"

"You could have Gustav, even have him all to yourself if you really wanted him. But you have to decide if that's what you really want."

I thought she was crazy and I told her so. But she only smiled and flagged down another waiter.

Bloch-Bauer appeared beside me. "Where is Adele?" he hissed. Berta said that we had been sitting in the same spot for the last hour and had not seen her.

"She's disappeared," he said. "At her own party, goddamn it!" When I said I would look for her Berta sighed theatrically and stood up to leave. I'll leave you to your martyrdom, her expression said.

"Look for Klimt while you're at it," Bloch-Bauer said. "But make sure you make a lot of noise, to give them plenty of time to dress."

I got the tour of the house that Adele had promised, wandering the rooms looking for the two of them. They were not in the ballroom or the many sitting rooms around it, where guests who were tired of dancing could sit. They were not in the card room, or the billiard room, or the library. They were not out in the gardens.

Eventually I found Gustav in the conservatory, a small, oddly shaped room with yellow silk walls and plenty of claw-footed mahogany chairs. He was alone. He sat on the stool of the piano, his elbows on the keys. As I came in he sat up to a jangle of notes and began to turn the pages of sheet music on the rack.

"Where's Adele?" I said. He tried to look surprised at the question.

"I haven't seen her since we came in," he said.

"What have you been doing all this time?" I said, trying to sound curious and not accusing.

"Sitting here. I didn't much feel like a party."

"We could have gone."

"It would have seemed rude."

"Herr Bloch-Bauer sent me to find Adele. She's wanted back at the party."

He finally admitted that he and Adele had had an argument "about the painting." I did not challenge him, only asked him where he thought she was likely to be. He said that he had left her in the library.

I said that she was not there now. He thought she might have gone upstairs to her bedroom. I asked him to lead me there since presumably he knew the house well. I got a strange look for that, but he took me up the back stairs past several maids' rooms, onto a hall with a feminine sitting room, a dressing room, and then, at last, the bedroom. He did not follow me inside.

She was sitting in the window seat, surrounded by wine-colored velvet cushions, watching the sash of her white dress flutter out of the open casement. There was a halo of smoke over her head and a smell of tallow. As I got closer I saw that she had a candle in her hand, and was applying the flame to the inside of her forearm. When she felt that I was there she put the candle on the windowsill but kept her back to me. I could see her skin through her thin dress. She was shaking. I closed the window and snuffed the candle with my fingers.

"Are you all right?" I asked.

"Are you?" Adele said. I ignored her.

"Your husband's been looking for you," I said. "The guests are wondering where you are."

"They don't really care, and neither does he, except that it makes him look bad. As long as they have their food and their music, and pretty things to look at, it doesn't matter." She turned to look at me. "I don't know why you came looking for me. I would think you'd be happy to have me disappear."

"Of course that's not true," I said. I touched her hand and turned her arm over to look at it. "How badly is it burned?"

She laughed and I could see the redness and the pearl strand of blisters running from wrist to elbow. "I suppose I'll need to wear long sleeves for a while," she said, " but you can arrange that, can't you? For now I think my shawl will cover it, if held just right."

"I think we should put something on it," I said. "We should ring your maid for some salve."

"Don't bother," she said. "I like the throbbing, it makes me feel alive. What I would really like is a moment alone with Gustav. Could you ring for that instead?"

We were silent. She was looking at me with eyes like cinders; black on the surface, lit from within with some kind of fire.

"Of course," I said. "I'll fetch him." As I left the room I heard her stand up to open the window again.

"She's in there burning herself with a candle," I said.

"What can I do?" he said with a shrug. "Shouldn't we go get Bloch-Bauer?"

"You're the one who's upset her, you'll have to make it up." I pushed him through the door. "I'll wait for you here," I said.

"It might take awhile," he said. "Adele's so nervous and excitable."

That seemed rather an understatement, but I restrained myself from making any sarcastic comments. "I'll wait for you here," I repeated.

The doors were made of heavy oak, and I could neither see nor hear anything. I could imagine it quite well, though, his pleadings and jokes and caresses and her slow thaw. I traced the designs on the intricately carved doors with a finger. There were glossy landscapes painted in the coffers of the ceiling and I amused myself with them for several minutes. I counted the tiles on the floor.

"Adele needs some air," he said when he came out. "She's quite ill. We're going to take her carriage for a turn around the Ring."

"Didn't she get enough air from sitting into the wind for God knows how long? Wouldn't it be better to put her to bed?"

"You know no one can tell Adele anything. She wants to go. I'll take care of her. Tell him it's all right."

"If anyone sees you . . ."

"I'll be back before you know it."

I went back downstairs to find Bloch-Bauer, to make up a story to soothe him before he went looking for Adele. There he was in the drawing room, by the fireplace, telling bawdy jokes with two other businessmen. He was laughing, not thinking about Adele at all, but of course when he saw me his rage returned. I told him that Adele's maid had taken her out for fresh air, but he knew what I meant, and his face swelled like a balloon. He put his face so close to mine that I could smell the brandy. That smell always reminded me of my grandparents, who drank it by the quart, as a tonic.

"Tell me what they're up to. You know, I know you do."

I demurred.

"Are you some sort of procuress, then, setting up his little trysts?"

This was so insulting that I could not answer, but he went on without waiting for a response. "Surely not. Surely you're in love with him. You don't want to see him with Adele any more than I do. Tell me what you know and I can catch them and put a stop to it."

All I knew, I said, was that Adele was ill and had gone out for fresh air.

Then where was Gustav, he wanted to know. He had already gone home, I said. Sometimes an idea would strike him, wherever he was, and he would have to leave immediately for the studio.

"Is that what he tells you?" he said. "I don't know much about artists, but I do know men. I'd advise you to get away from him before he does you some real damage."

"I don't need advice," I said.

"If I had the chance to do it over I'd let Adele rot. I only married her because her father offered me some generous terms to take her off his hands, but it wasn't worth it. I've earned that money, many times over. Adele pretends to be fragile but really she's tough as bear hide. Well, she can do whatever she wants, except make a fool of me. I won't allow that." I thought about asking how he proposed to stop her, but I didn't want to know.

"Adele is lonely," I said. "She craves friendship. Is it any surprise that having failed to find that in you she would look for it in a sympathetic artist?"

For a moment I thought he might strike me, but then he laughed. "You're a wonderful girl," he said. "Loyal to a fault. I should have married someone like you."

"Maybe I'm not as nice as you think," I said.

I left the party and went home. Instead of going to bed I went to the sewing room. That was where we stored all of our supplies until we found a space to rent. It was where I kept the beautiful green dress I had made. I lit a lamp and there it was. I had not known until that moment that it was meant to be my wedding dress. Seeing it there, limp and bedraggled, was like glimpsing an actor backstage while a play is being performed. It still needed to be hemmed and all the loose threads pulled in. A few of the satin-covered buttons were missing. I had begun embroidering the skirt but not the sleeves, and the crystals were still in their boxes. I wouldn't be able to use them after all, sewing them on by hand would take months. I slipped out of my clothes and pulled the dress over my head. It was difficult to slide into with no one to help me, but at last it was in place, and I held the bodice closed with my hand.

Of course it fit like a coat of varnish on a table; you couldn't slide a piece of paper between my waist and the bodice. I turned in front of the mirror, noticing how the soft color made my hair look redder and how flattering the elongated silhouette was, but only for a moment, because I had a lot of work to do. It was fortunate, I thought, that Adele was thinner than I, because it is much easier to take in than to let out. I took the dress off and hung it back in the closet until I had carefully wiped the table. When I had thrown on a colorful printed dressing gown (it happened to be one I was making for Berta, but she would never know she wasn't the first to wear it) I laid out the dress and began ripping.

As satisfying as it is to take pieces of cloth and bind them together, there is something in some ways more fulfilling about pulling them apart. It makes a wonderful sound, the snapping of the threads. I had to guess at Adele's measurements but I thought I could get pretty close. She was much narrower in the shoulders and her arms were like twigs, so the sleeves had to be removed from the bodice and the bodice from the skirt. I knew that the color of the dress would make her look sallow, even ghoulish, but that seemed fitting. I happily abandoned myself to destruction. Tearing the fabric makes a beautiful sound, too, a metallic sound, but this fabric was heavy and didn't tear easily; I had to make a cut with the scissors to start it and even then my hands were sore with the effort. I had managed to rip the skirt from hem to waist before I remembered I couldn't ruin the dress, I was only supposed to be altering it. The skirt would have to be remade. The bodice had to be lengthened and tightened. I worked all night, finally falling asleep at the table. When Helene found me there, she didn't say anything, except to offer to make me breakfast. In the afternoon I hand-finished the embroidery on the skirt. I put it in a dress box, carefully layered in tissue paper, and had it sent to Adele.

Eighteen

I was almost thirty and except for one brief flirtation as a girl I had never thought of anyone but Gustav. But I was coming to realize that there would always be another Alma, another Adele. If they married, or moved to Paris, or died, it wouldn't make any difference. I needed to make a decision. I could continue on this way with Gustav, knowing that he would never marry me, or I could look for someone else.

I told myself that getting over a broken heart and finding another love was easy; didn't people do it all the time? I went to Secession parties and tried to flirt. But what Pauline had said years ago turned out to be true: everyone knew of my association with Gustav and no one dared to offend him by approaching me, especially when it was clear that my heart wasn't in it. There was an unbreachable wall around me, it seemed. So I decided to focus my energies in another direction: the salon. I decided that after years of preparation it was time for Schwestern Flöge to come into being.

My sisters and I rented two floors in the Casa Piccola on Mariahilferstrasse. It was not far from the Kunsthistorisches Museum. Of course it would have been more fashionable if we had been able to locate inside the Ring instead of just outside it, but we couldn't afford it. Our mother, faced with the prospect of living alone in the apartment where we had grown up, decided to sell it and move in with us. All she asked, she said, was for her own rooms with a separate entrance and kitchen, so that she could be entirely independent. We enlisted Josef Hoffmann and Koloman Moser to design the apartment and the salon. They worked quickly and efficiently, and soon we prepared to move from one side of Mariahilf to the other. While I wrapped lamps in tissue and packed boxes full of blouses and blankets, I worried about the salon and the risks I was taking. Years of planning had gone into it, months of construction, hours of taxing figures and standing in lines at government offices and filling out paperwork. Days of anxiety when we thought we wouldn't have enough money to finish, or a bolt of fabric arrived wet and ruined. Now everything was in place. The seamstresses sat at the machines, already at work on preopening orders by Berta and others. The cutting tables already had shreds of fabric and spilled pins on them. Pauline's head already hurt from squinting at narrow columns of figures, and Helene already felt cranky from waiting in the sitting room for someone to come so she could be charming and agreeable to them.

Every detail of the rooms was as perfect as Josef Hoffmann could make it, which was saying a lot. The salon was serene and spacious. The walls were white, the furniture black, the carpet gray. From the sofa in the receiving room I could look across through the large windows that looked west, to the Kunsthistorisches. The panes were among the largest yet made, and Hoffmann had insisted that no fussy draperies mar the view of them or of the city beyond. At first, Helene said, it was like going to the opera and seeing the soprano naked onstage, but she soon got used to it. For Pauline the room was a cell for the criminally insane, bare and clinical, and nothing I said could change her mind.

Yes, it was all perfect, but I was worried sick. What if the clothes I made fell apart after one wearing? What if they were considered tasteless or vulgar or ugly? What if no one bought them? What if too many people bought them and I couldn't accommodate the demand? What if we couldn't pay our seamstresses? What if everyone laughed at me, at my amateurish efforts to run a business? It seemed that there were endless ways to fail. The possibility of success, on the other hand, seemed wildly improbable. How could the thing coalesce?

When I unlocked the doors that day in September I felt as if every lady who passed the building was looking at me critically, evaluating my outfit and the sign on the door and judging it worthless. Why else would they walk by without stopping? It didn't matter that none of them had appointments, and that the lady who did, Margaret Stonborough-Wittgenstein, was peering in the window, pacing impatiently in small circles before the door. I took her wrap and held it across my chest as we ascended the stairs. I didn't want her to see how I was shaking.

Margaret wanted a white velvet dress with an embroidered skirt. Gustav had told her what to order, she said. He was going to paint her in it. How wonderful, I said. It was a good advertisement for the salon, our clothes in a portrait by a famous artist. She had wanted Poiret, she said, but Gustav had talked her out of it. She was black-haired and long-necked; soft-spoken and shy. She was very young. I talked about the painting and about Gustav and at the end of an hour she decided to order a coat and a blouse as well. She liked my patterns, she said. I was so lucky to have Klimt to do the artistic things for me. And to pay the bills. I wanted to tell her that I had drawn those patterns myself, that Gustav held a promissory note with my signature on it for the full amount he had invested, but I knew it wouldn't do any good. There was nothing to do about the gossip but ignore it.

Though I have to admit I dawdled a bit on making Margaret's coat, and padded the bill just a little.

Telegrams kept the door opening and closing all day. Every time I heard the bell my heart began to beat faster. Would someone walk in without an appointment? Would someone come early? And most of all, would Gustav come by during the day to see how things were going? As each appointment ended, I tidied up the changing rooms, and another customer arrived, in one-hour intervals, all day, only stacking up in the sitting room to eye each other aggressively when Berta stayed too long at her appointment, unable to stop talking about the party she'd been to the night before. Eight hours, seven appointments. It was hard to know if that was a success or not. An established house could see dozens more. After each customer left Pauline quickly tabulated the charge for their order, subtracted the projected cost of labor and materials, and added that number to the day's column, but I didn't want to know. The running total made me too anxious. Instead I supervised the progress of the seamstresses when I wasn't with a customer. At the end of the day Pauline showed me the day's final number. It was enough to make the payroll for the month. We had priced the clothes well. They were expensive enough to compensate for the small volume, but no one had blanched at their bill. At least for one day, we were a success. But Gustav had not come.

The next day all our appointment times were full, but on Wednesday we had several hours free. So I was surprised when the bell rang in the middle of the morning. It was not the kind of place to get walk-in business. I left the cutting room and walked down the hall to open the salon's brass door.

Adele was climbing the stairs behind two men who worked in an accounting office on the fourth floor. In the strong daylight she looked frailer than she usually did. When she reached the landing where I stood she seemed out of breath. Searching for a pleasantry, she admired the marble turning staircase, praising it as if I had carved it myself. She thought the words Schwestern Flöge, pressed into the door in a typeface Moser had come up with, was a wonderful idea, and the fanciful watercolors he had done for the hall were charming. I wondered if this was the startling, bitter woman I knew. I offered to take her coat, cutting her off before she started in on the color of the walls, or, God forbid, me. The last thing I wanted was personal praise from her, whether she meant it or not. She slipped off her voluminous mink and handed it to me. I nearly buckled under its weight, and wondered idly how much it had cost.

"My husband told me to be on my best behavior," she confessed as we headed toward the sitting room. "He said he didn't want any scenes like that night at the party. He was quite menacing."

"Don't worry," I said. "You can be yourself."

"Thank God," she said. "I was tired already, complimenting that ridiculous staircase not fit for a place of business, trying to think of something nice to say about you and not being able to think of anything."

The sitting room was elegant, white and black like the rest of the salon. The built-in cabinets were painted with a stylized floral motif, and were so unobtrusive most people thought the walls were paneled. Here and there floor-to-ceiling mirrors made the room look twice as large as it was. Hoffmann's furniture, a simple sofa, a couple of ebony chairs, several tray tables, and a vitrine, managed to be both delicate and substantial. I was proud of the room, as I was of all the others. There was not one extraneous feature. I knew that it might look odd to someone used to so much more opulence and ostentation. I almost hoped she'd be shocked, or horrified. Instead she looked delighted. She almost smiled.

"I wish you'd let me copy this room at my house," she said as she slid onto the white divan and lay across it as if she were going to take a nap. "I've been dying for an excuse to throw all of my furniture away. It's so heavy and those carved armchairs with their horrible lion's feet make me want to scream. Well, you've seen it, you know. My husband loves it, of course, the way he loves all those mounted heads in the library. He loves to shoot things. That's why I never go into that room, they all stare at me so reproachfully for letting him kill them. But of course I can't stop him. I imagine that if I stood in between him and a mountain goat he wanted to shoot, he'd shoot me to clear me out of the way."

"Here are the books," I said. As she made no move to open them, I sat down beside her and turned the pages for her. I couldn't decide whether she was used to being waited upon, she wanted to humiliate me, or she was embarrassed to show her hands.

"He's painting my portrait, you know," she said.

"Yes," I said.

"I don't like the sketches. They make me look too pretty. I think I need something new to wear." I waited for her to say something about the dress I had sent her, but it seemed that she was going to pretend it had never happened.

"Something to make you look ugly?" I almost laughed. "I'm so pleased you thought of me."

"Something to make me look interesting," she said. "Something new, something different."

As I turned the pages for her I marked the designs she liked with little pieces of paper. After a while she brought her hands to her lap, though she kept the tips of her fingers curled under. Coral bracelets carved to look like snakes twisted up both arms.

"It would help me help you if you'd tell me about yourself, what you're looking for, what you need."

"I have no needs," she said with a perfectly straight face, "only unfulfilled desires." She stared off toward the window while I tried to think of a way to talk to her. She was unlike anyone I'd ever met, and I was new to the business of selling things to people. I hadn't known how complicated it could be.

The nervous tapping of my foot finally broke her concentration and she turned to me, brusque now. "What can I tell you that you haven't already read in some gossip column or been told by some chatty dinner partner? My husband is president of a sugar company. He is frequently away on business, as they say. I am in poor health and cannot have children. I rarely engage in outdoor activities. I read too much Heine and Goethe, I entertain, I make everyone around me as miserable as I can. Is that the proper kind of information?"

"Well, I won't be measuring you for a riding habit, for a start," I said.

"Of course," she said, mollified. "Of course you would need to know these kinds of things."

Over the course of the afternoon I learned that Hoffmann had just agreed to redecorate her entire house, they hadn't signed the papers yet, but it was all settled. She had known Gustav for eight years. The night they met he had told her she looked like a biblical heroine. He had asked her to pose for him as Judith holding the head of Holofernes. She had been intrigued and flattered by the comparison, and had agreed. I was taking her measurements as she told me this. She stood there in her corset, as uncomfortable and helpless as a snail pulled from its shell, and I took perverse pleasure in her discomfort. She flinched when I touched her with the measuring tapes. She seemed unable to stand up straight. I resisted the temptation to stick her with pins.

At the end of the first week we had a small party at the salon, to celebrate the opening. Moser designed the invitation, of course, an etching of a young woman in front of a mirror, printed on handmade paper from the Wiener Werkstätte. It was sent to all in the Secession and Wiener Werkstätte, and a few others. Moser came early, bringing with him a gift, a bronze vase he had made. He carried it around the room with him, looking for the perfect place for it. He often collided with Hoffmann, who was acting as set designer, covering all of the sconces with blue wax paper until the salon looked submerged, an Atlantis. There was not a flower in sight; he wouldn't let one in the door. Instead there were lacquered boxes and empty vases on the tables. They were as proud of the place as if it had been their own child.

When Hoffman arrived he had handed me a heavy object wrapped in tissue paper; it was a silver chalice he had cast, decorated with scrolls of vines and leaves. It was breathtaking and my sincere comments embarrassed him. Unlike Moser, he was unwilling to express an opinion on where to put it. The others helped me decide. On the mantel, said Moser, where everyone could enjoy it. In my bedroom, said Helene, it was too beautiful to share. But when Hoffmann said that every object he made was meant to be useful, not decorative, I knew where it should go. I put it on the cutting table to hold my pins. The customers might never see it, but the seamstresses would, I would; it would serve a purpose. It served it well; it stayed in that same spot for thirty-four years.

Our mother was there, minding young Helene and critiquing the looks of the bohemian types that filled the strange rooms. Berta came and brought her cook to make the short ribs and spaetzle and beet salad and orange cream cake. Once the room had been decorated and the vase placed and the cook set to work, the six of us, Hoffmann, Moser, Berta, Helene, Pauline, and I began to get very drunk on light and fizzy new wine.

Adele brought me a calla lily that Hoffmann promptly banished to the stairway. I promised her that after he left I would bring it back. Moll's wife brought roses and told me that Alma was far too busy to come, now that she had married Mahler. What a shame, I said, as I put her flowers on the stair with Adele's. More and more people streamed in, each with a token and some kind word. As I spoke to everyone and thanked them and pointed them in the direction of the wine and the food, I was waiting for Gustav. He still had not come.

In the weeks before the salon opened, Gustav had been strangely absent. Helene and Pauline had worked as hard as I and we had the unstinting support of Hoffmann and Moser, but when there was a crisis or a sudden decision, I had no one to turn to for advice. The weight of the venture was on my shoulders, and where was Gustav? I suspect that he did not want to take the attention away from me, did not want other people to think that this was a vanity project that he had underwritten. I didn't care. Gustav should have been with me in the front of the room, at my side, accepting congratulations alongside me. He was the only one who could make me laugh and release all of the anxiety I was feeling. He knew all of the right things to say to me. Even Helene, who had known me longer than anyone and knew how nervous I was, had already sent me into a panic by matter-of-factly telling the daughter of the master painter Rudolf Von Alt that we really knew very little about sewing.

Moll was making a toast, saying something about a creative alliance and supporting each other, when Gustav slipped in. There were lots of cheers; Moll was a good speaker and the wine had been flowing very freely. But I had stopped listening when I saw Gustav.

I hated myself for it, but the first thing I noticed was that he was empty-handed. If Alma's mother could bring something, why couldn't he? The second thing I noticed was how tired he looked. Lots of people turned to greet him, but he stayed in the doorway instead of pressing through to the center of the room, where I was. He caught my eye and I was surprised to see a wistfulness in his, grief almost.

When Moll finished speaking there was a lull as everyone waited for Gustav to give a toast. He pretended not to notice, and after a moment someone else got up to say something. Then when he was done everyone looked at Gustav again, but he just smiled and shook his head. Even the jeers of his friends in the Secession couldn't rouse him. When everyone had spoken and people began drifting toward the door, I was finally able to reach Gustav.

"It's wonderful, Emilie," he said. I couldn't tell whether he meant the party or the design of the room or the venture itself, or some combination of all three. He sounded vague and distant, as if he were surrounded by glass. He could have been talking to a visiting dignitary from Spain.

"Thank you," I said, formally, and then, "It's yours, too, you know. You can take some credit for its success."

He shook his head. "It's yours." He seemed to be trying to rouse himself from his mood. "Yesterday Hermine Gallia asked if I could help her get an appointment with you. Usually people are asking other people to help them get appointments with me."

The guests had all gone and Helene and Pauline were collecting glasses and putting them on a tray. The lights of the Ringstrasse were as starry as they were at Berta Zuckerkandl's.

* * *

The salon was an immediate success. In the months before the salon opened my friends and I had managed to generate great excitement among a certain small circle of the very rich and the avant-garde. Schwestern Flöge quickly became their salon. Our clothes were very expensive; a skirt could cost as much as a seamstress might make in a year. No one seemed to mind. I soon discovered, however, that ignoring Paris altogether would quickly result in insolvency. We couldn't survive on Reform dress alone. So I compromised. We made progressive clothes for those who wanted them and more conventional, stylish clothes for everyone else.

Gisele Koehler and her mother, who paid me a visit in the month after we opened, were typical. Gisele was a large blond girl, and her mother was a moonfaced woman who stood behind me and criticized every move I made. Hadn't I better put the silk camellia at the bosom? It looked strange on the left shoulder, unbalanced. Gisele was lopsided, you know. Her right shoulder was higher than the left. It wasn't usually noticeable, but to put the camellia on one of them would call attention to it. The last thing a bosomy girl like Gisele needed was more bulk at the décolletage, but I didn't say anything. Poor Gisele was already blushing at her mother's matter-of-fact recitation of her faults. In a few years her blond hair would turn ashy and she would be elephantine. I hoped she'd be married by then. I vowed to banish the camellia entirely. Already the dress was a shiny pink nightmare. That was the drawback of trying to make money. Sometimes you had to sacrifice taste altogether.

"I have a lovely black silk with an embroidered camellia pattern," I said. "Why don't we try the dress in that instead?"

"Black? On such a young girl? Are you crazy?" said the mother. "No one's died. And Gisele looks wonderful in pink." I sighed.

"Gustav's here," said Helene, quietly, from the doorway.

"Klimt is here?" said Frau Koehler. "I must speak with him. I want him to do a portrait of Gisele."

Helene gave me a look that said, Lucky Gustav. "He's in the sitting room," she said to Frau Koehler. "Come down and I'll bring you some coffee."

Frau Koehler looked from Gisele to me and then back again, hesitant to leave her precious daughter alone with me. She'd heard stories. She narrowed her eyes at me and then said, "All right, but I'll only be a minute."

When Frau Koehler was gone, I grimly kept pinning. Grimly was the only way to pin, otherwise the pins would fall out of my mouth. I slipped my hand into the silver chalice as if I was pulling a carp out of a pond. Pins briefly stuck to my hand and then dropped to the floor.

"This dress is a disaster, isn't it?" said Gisele from the dais. Her voice was surprisingly soft and melodious. I wondered if she sang.

"It'll be fine," I said.

"You know it's a disaster," she said. "Mother wants this pink satin and it's all wrong for me. She wants tight sleeves and a high waist and that's all wrong for me, too." I stopped pinning and looked up at her.

"What would you like?" I asked.

"I saw a dress in the book I liked," she said shyly. I went over to the table and picked up the pattern book. "Show me," I said.

The pattern she liked was a more modern style, looser and much more forgiving. "This is the dress for you," I said. "Forget the other dress. I'll tell your mother I lost it or something." That made her laugh.

"She'll kill us both," she said. "But she'll let me keep the dress so she can say she got it here."

"Do you want to look in the fabric books for a material?" I asked her. "I can cut a piece off a roll in the back and bring it to you if you like."

Gisele didn't want to look at the fabric books. She wanted to come with me and see the fabric room. I never took customers there, but something about the way her eyelids drooped at the corners touched me. She was as innocent and helpless as a baby seal.

"Come," I said. I gave her a robe and some slippers to wear.

The fabric room had previously been a workshop that made wooden toys. There were no windows, which was good for the fabric. It was dim and cool. It was the closest thing to a fashion designer's paradise. Roll after roll of fabric, satins and velvets and brocades and lace, organza, chiffon and wool. They were arranged by color, all the whites together segueing into the creams and the yellows and the peach and orange and scarlet and violet and indigo and green. I could wander the aisles for hours. "How about dark blue?" I said.

On the way to blue we passed a bolt of green peau de soie and without thinking I reached out and ran a hand over it.

"That's so pretty," Gisele said.

"Yes, I know," I said. "I once made a dress for myself with it. But then I gave it away." I don't know why I told her, except that she had sympathetic eyes.

"Such a beautiful color," she said politely, not understanding. "So bright."

"Maybe we'll use it to make you a dress someday," I said. "For your engagement party, perhaps." I pulled her on.

"If Mama ever lets me out of her sight long enough to find a beau," she said. "And if he doesn't mind that I'm so plain."

"What do you think of this?" I asked, pulling out a softer, less starchy silk than the peau de soie, and in a deep ocean blue.

"Nice," she said.

"We can do a chiffon overlay if you like, perhaps a lighter blue, or a net. I think we have some embroidered nets that would look incredible." I pulled the bolt out of its place and carried it to the section where the nets were. We found a robin's-egg blue one, embroidered with silver chrysanthemums. When I had noted the fabrics on her order form I took Gisele back to the fitting room to pin a muslin prototype on her. The new dress was of a style that was very easy to pin, and it took only a few minutes. I was thankful, because despite my sympathy I was growing weary of Gisele. So she was plain and her mother was a tyrant. She was nineteen years old and she would marry and have fat homely children and be perfectly unhappy like everyone else. It was no tragedy.

When we were finished I waited for Gisele to dress and brought her down to the sitting room. Gustav was standing by the window looking down at the patrons of the Casa Piccola restaurant while Frau talked loudly at him from the white sofa.

"I'm so sorry," said Frau Koehler, "I lost track of time. This is my daughter, Mr. Klimt. Won't she make a lovely portrait?"

I waited to see what he would answer. But he had been flattering people like Frau Koehler for many years now, and there was no hesitation or falsity in his voice when he told her how Rubenesque Gisele was, how charming, how beautiful. She lapped it up.

"I trust that everything is all settled with the dress?" she said to me, several degrees more coldly. Now it was my turn, and it was hard to keep a straight face with Gustav looking at me with mock solemnity.

"I think you'll be very pleased," I said.

"What did you decide about the camellia?" she asked. "Because I really feel . . ."

"Gisele wants to surprise you," I said. "But trust me, you'll love it."

"Well, I don't like to pay for things I haven't seen, but I came here on the advice of Frau Moll, you know, her first husband was my husband's first cousin, and I always trust her taste."

"I'll need to see Gisele in two weeks," I said. "Helene can make an appointment for you in the office."

Gustav promised to appear at their apartment the following Thursday, and somehow the two of us managed to bundle them out of the room and shut the door.

I sat down where Frau Koehler had been and took a piece of pastry off of the tray Helene had brought down for her. I put it on a little plate, but after a bite I decided I wasn't hungry and began to tear it into little pieces instead of eating it.

"Look at you," Gustav said. "Hermann Koehler's daughter." He pushed his chair backward against the wall like a schoolboy.

"Hoffmann would kill you if he saw that," I said.

"Koehler's in thick with the emperor," he said, balancing his weight so that the chair hung between the wall and the floor before slamming down. It made me wince.

I shrugged. "She thinks I'm a harlot. She only comes here looking for scandalous gossip."

"So what if people talk?" he said. "People have been talking about me for fifteen years at least, and there's no sign of it letting up."

"I can't do the things you do," I said. "I'd be stoned to death."

"You're incredibly popular," he said, ignoring my bitter tone. "I read an article about you in the *Times*. And Helene told me you were written up in *Mode*."

"It won't last," I said. I wasn't feeling very celebratory. "How are things at the studio?" I asked. "How is Miss Wittgenstein?"

"She's delightful," he said. "I can't understand a word she says, but she is lovely to look at."

"Have you started the painting, or are you still sketching?"

"I think I finally captured the right pose today. She's interesting, so it's easy. The hardest part, you know, is always creating character for a face that is lacking it. I don't have that problem with her. And her dress is going to be a dream to paint."

"You're welcome," I said. "I thought you'd like it."

"I'm doing too many portraits," he said. "I'm booked all the way through April. I'll be glad when summer comes and no one can bother me. I think I'm going to paint the field of poppies this year, or perhaps the orchard. Or we can hike up to the castle."

"That's a long time from now," I said. "A lot can change between now and then."

"What, you're not going to invite me?" He was grinning; the possibility had never crossed his mind.

"We'll see," I said.

He didn't hear me. An idea had come to him. He felt in the pocket of his coat for a pencil and pulled out a box. He looked at it in surprise, as if he had forgotten it was there.

"I have something for you," he said. "A present."

"My birthday was months ago," I said. "And you got me something, the Charles Rennie Mackintosh book."

"It's your belated salon opening gift," he said. He handed me a marbled paper box tied with a black grosgrain ribbon. I could tell that Hoffmann had made it; it was a work of art in itself. I shook it because I thought Gustav would enjoy the suspense. It rattled loudly and something slid from one side of the box to the other. It was too big for a ring and too small for a book. Unless the size of the box was a ruse. Gustav would do something like that. I contemplated the box for a long time, until Gustav got impatient and started whistling. I untied the ribbon.

At the bottom of the box, wrapped in tissue paper, was a large silver pendant, shaped like a cat's face, on a short chain. Across the pendant was a chevron pattern of lapis and carnelian.

"Hoffmann made it," he said. "Do you like it?"

I fumbled with the clasp, hoping he wouldn't see my fingers trembling. "It's wonderful," I said. "Did you design it?"

"Of course. Do you think I'd trust Hoffmann with something like this? Turn around and let me put it on you." I gave him the pendant and lifted up my hair.

"Forgive me," he said, and paused. I couldn't see his face, but he sounded very serious. I waited. "It was supposed to be ready the day of the grand opening, but the gems got held up in Antwerp or something. That's why it's so late."

"Since I had no idea it was coming, it's not late to me," I said, looking out of the window. I could see the crowds of people walking in the Volksgarten.

"You can put it on a longer chain if you want," he said. "Are you sure you like it?"

I wanted to turn around and kiss him, but I did not. "Of course I like it," I said. "I'm going to have some coffee. Do you want some?" I went into the kitchen to brew it so he wouldn't see me cry.

When it was ready I brought everything on a tray and set it on the table. When I sat down to pour myself some I noticed that there were sketches strewn across the floor.

"I got bored sitting here, waiting for you before," he said, when he saw that I'd noticed the drawings. "Frau Koehler went on and on, it was really terrible. I didn't like to look at her, she has that hairy mole on the left side of her chin and she insisted on staying turned that way through the entire conversation."

"How trying," I said. "Of course I'm the one who's going to have to see her undressed." I picked a cup and filled it for him, over-flowing into the saucer with whipped cream. That was the way he liked it.

"You'd better hope she drops you then," he said. "Or that her husband the colonel suffers a reversal of fortune." He opened the window and looked down on the people sitting on the terrace of the Casa Piccola restaurant. "Poor souls," he said. "That place has terrible coffee."

"And worse sandwiches," I said. "No meat at all." I went to the window and looked out. Despite the coffee and the sandwiches, the tables on the street were crowded. A man with a bright green feather in his hat looked into his cup as he stirred, while his com-panion pulled her roll apart and looked at the street. At another table a thin young man stood up suddenly and knocked over a wrought iron chair. Gustav came and stood beside me, holding one of the sketches he'd made earlier, now folded into a shape resem-bling a crane. I took it from his hand and flicked the paper out of the window. For a moment it rose on an air current, then fell lazily down, landing on the table of the man with the green feather in his hat. The man reached for the paper, unfolded it, and looked up, puzzled. I ducked back inside.

"My precious drawing!" said Gustav in mock agony. "How could you?"

"You have so many," I said, pointing to the carpet. "If we run out you can make more."

"You show so little respect for my work," he said. "Everyone else is so careful with it, holds it by the corners, sprays it with fixative, puts it behind glass, even the most careless scribbles. I think of everyone you are the only one to catch on to how worthless it all really is."

"Of course I don't think it's worthless," I said, feeling guilty now.

"I'm teasing you, silly," he said. "Of course I don't care. Throw it out the window, set it on fire, wipe your ass with it, it's all the same to me. It's just thinking out loud. It doesn't mean anything. If it were a painting you were chucking onto poor innocent people that would be different, but . . ." I had to smile in spite of myself.

"Go on," he said. "Do the next one." It landed on one of the umbrellas, but a student who had seen what happened to the green feather man stood on a chair and retrieved it. By now many people were looking up at our window and waving. Some of the waiters were scowling. The drawings rained down on the café patrons like so many cherry blossoms in the spring, but it didn't take long to exhaust our supply.

"Last one," said Gustav, handing me a drawing folded in the shape of a leaf, which upon unwrapping proved to be a sketch of my own face. I tore it into bits and dropped the pieces from the windowsill. It landed on the tulle hat of a woman sitting alone. She shook her head and brushed at it with her gloved hand. She had large dark eyes and she looked sadly at me, wanting to know why the others had been so much luckier than she. I closed the sash.

Nineteen

I have six drawings of Adele, all very similar. She is wearing a voluminous striped dress. The folds of the skirt cascade down the page and spill off of it. The pencil drawings contain only shades of gray, but I know that the dress she wore was pink, the pink of a blush wine, or of inflamed skin. In most of them she has no eyes and only the barest outline of nose and mouth, but her twisted hands and her thick bow-shaped lips give her away. There is one, though, in which he has drawn in her eyes, and it stares out at me with shocking likeness. When I look at it I can smell her jasmine perfume and the cherry pastries that were her favorite. I keep that one near the bottom of the pile. It's too unnerving.

Tonight, after Helene had gone to sleep, I pulled the drawing out of the portfolio. Then I locked my bedroom door, though I knew that was silly, like a grown woman hiding candy under her bed. From whom was I trying to hide? Gustav? Adele?

My room was stifling and smelled of the emergency gasoline I'd paid a small fortune for in the village and spilled on my clothes walking home. The blackout curtains made the room feel like a cave. I blew out the lamp and then rolled up the curtain and opened the window. Let the Russians find us. They're going to anyway, no matter what we do. The coolness of the dark night air dried the tears on my face.

I made that dress, the one she wore in those drawings, hating it, hating the sickly pink color, the soggy thin silk, the prim stripes. The way she smiled at me when she chose the fabric I knew she'd hated it, too. Something had happened since I had last seen her to make her change her mind completely. I'd tried to talk her out of the style she'd picked, it was from another dressmaker's book, something from some long-ago season, tight-waisted, full-skirted, a whalebone bodice. I reminded her that she'd wanted something radical. Nothing I could say would convince her. She'd had it made to get back at Gustav, to flaunt her respectability in his face, to torment him, to hide herself. He drew it over and over, but the face never seemed to belong with the body, so when it came time to do the portrait he made an outline and filled it in with something that suited her better.

I left the drawings on the table by the window, underneath the lamp so they wouldn't blow away, and stumbled to the mantel to fetch the matchbox. I had been thinking about what I was going to do for a long time. I stood there at the window, thinking about them, then I struck a match. The flame was the only light for miles and miles. For a moment I only watched the blue flame and inhaled the sulfur. I let the first match burn down to my fingers. Then I sifted through the pile and pulled out the drawing near the bottom, the one with the eyes. I held the next burning wisp of wood to it and it ignited so fast that it was gone, blown out of the window in a shower of ash, before I had time to register what I'd done. I lit the next one, a larger drawing. The heavier paper took longer to burn, the pieces were larger and glowed red as they fell. Tiny bits of ash floated and drifted and finally settled on the windowsill.

Then one by one until they were all gone, lost.

He had made two portraits of Adele. She had modeled for the first in the pink dress, but when it was done there was nothing of the pink dress in it. Instead she was wearing a dress of gold, Byzantine in its intricacy, patterned with triangles and eyes and peacock tails. Above this stylized mosaic her face was as stark and real as a photograph. Some critics said that he didn't care about his sitters, he was only interested in the thickets of design he built up around them, but that was not true. That portrait said what was important to say about Adele.

It said plenty about him, too; he was in love with her when he painted it, of that I feel sure.

The second portrait, done years later, is chalky, pastel. He was in a different phase, using a different style. And the affair was over. He was playing with a Chinese motif in the background, warriors on horseback. Adele stood under a dark cloud of a hat, in the same pearl choker she wore in the first, middle-aged now, not quite the mysterious sexual being she had been.

Sometimes I think about destroying the paintings. If I set them on fire the canvas would scorch before it finally caught. There would be a smell of burned hair and gasoline. The pigments would turn the flame many different colors. Sparks would fly off the paintings, and I'd have to chase them down and stamp them out. The paintings would fight against extinction, crackling with tiny explosions. I'd burn my hands. Adele's face would melt like wax and disappear. Her hands would be the last thing to go, withering in a cloud of acrid smoke.

Moll has those paintings now; perhaps he has burned them. The thought wakes me from my stupor, and I'm consumed with guilt. What kind of curator destroys the work she is charged with protecting? How could I do it?

I can't stay in my room with the evidence and so I dress and walk out to the lake. Perhaps I'll stumble, hit my head, then I won't have to think all of these tormenting thoughts.

But of course I don't. I've been hiking all of my life, and I'm still surefooted. Every so often the moon comes out from behind the clouds and I am able to orient myself. By the time morning comes, I have arrived in Unterach, on the other side of the lake. In the gray dawn I sit in the church until it is a reasonable hour to appear at the door of friends we have there. They give me breakfast and dry my shoes, and then row me back across the lake.

FEMALE NUDE, 1907

It is only June but it is already unbearably hot in the apartment in Josef-stadt. How three people can live in such a small room is a mystery, even if two of them are children. The room is on the fifth floor with no ladder. If there were a fire they would all perish. It happens all the time in Vienna. The windows are clean on the inside but so coated with grime on the outside that very little light gets in. The room smells like a cham-ber pot. When Gustav comes to visit he complains that the place isn't fit for human habitation, and he's right. He wonders aloud what foul mess her downstairs neighbors could be cooking to create such a stench. They're from Bucharest, Mizzi says shortly. He goes to the window, already open as wide as it will go, and pushes on it. Why do I come here, he moans out of the window. Mizzi slaps him, hard, on the back and then both of them sneak a look at the boy.

The boy has alert hazel eyes and a wide nose like a saddle. He sits cross-legged on the floor, ignoring both of them, absorbed in the top Gus-tav has brought him. He spins it again and again. The sound has already begun to grate on Mizzi's nerves. Go outside with that, she snaps. The boy obediently leaves the apartment without a backward look. "Outside," for him, is the dingy hallway. The tenement they live in is on a crowded street of buildings just like it. There is no place to play.

You've got to get out of here, Gustav says. With what money, Mizzi almost says, then doesn't. You should be here in August, she says instead. Of course Gustav is not there in August. He is in the lake district with his wealthy, successful mistress. My being here wouldn't make it cooler, Gustav says, selfishly ignoring the fact that it is because of him that they are there at all. Why doesn't he make life easier for her, when he could obviously afford it? Yet he comes to visit her at least once a month, some-times more, and brings things for the boy, oranges and pencils and pic-ture postcards. Mizzi wants to tell him not to bother with that trash, will he just give her the money for good shoes and hearty, meat-filled stews in the winter? Will he pay for a proper school? She writes him long pleading letters and he writes back that her letters upset him and that she should be more cheerful. While she reads she screams in rage and her neighbors pound on the walls to shut her up.

Let me draw you, he says. He pushes her gently toward the mattress on the other side of the room.

For three crowns, she says, pretending to be joking. That's more than the daily wage for a seamstress.

Two, he says.

How do you want me, she says, resigned. She strips off her dingy skirt, her chemise. She's bonier in the chest than she used to be. Having the last one, the baby in the cradle in the corner, has shriveled her breasts, and going without so the boy has enough to eat has wasted her figure.

Leave your boots on, he says. He places her face down on the bed. Her ass is the best part of her. He has often said that its countenance is more beautiful and noble than many a face. He arranges the bedclothes around her into a disheveled pile, as if something illicit had just happened. Nothing will, though. He is tired of her. Her looks are gone; all she is to him is a whining shrew who threatens to expose him to his family. It's the only power she has left.

Mizzi falls asleep while he works. Modeling always bored her, but the money was too good to turn down. When she was younger she would daydream about dresses she would buy when she was married to Gustav, the house she would live in, the people she would meet. She was a fool, that girl, her younger self. She had all of the arrogance of youth and beauty. Now her thoughts are painful to her and she blots them out with brandy whenever possible.

In the hallway the boy is bored with the top. He wants to go back into the apartment and eat a piece of the cake he knows Papa has brought. The door won't open, though. It's a situation he's used to. Instead he kicks the new top down the hallway as if it were a ball. It hurts his foot a little when he kicks it and makes a horrible clatter as it bounces past door after door. Mrs. Koppelmann is sure to come out and smack him with a broom, like she did the time he hurled the heavy, fat oranges at her door again and again until they broke open and bled their sticky juice everywhere. He can still feel the pull of it at his shoes as he runs past. He grabs the top and hides in the stairwell.

Twenty

In 1905 Gustav admitted defeat and gave up the University Hall ceiling panels. The continuing controversy—the endlessly critical newspaper editorials, the contentious meetings with the committee—was wearing on his health and affecting his other work. He returned the commission and advised the committee that since he had given back the money the paintings belonged to him. They didn't see it that way, and sent some men out to his studio to collect the paintings. Gustav held them at bay with a shotgun, an incident that only deepened his reputation as a renegade. In the end they sorted it out. Gustav got to keep the paintings and eventually sold them.

That year he also left the Secession. Some of the other members felt that Carl Moll's association with the Gallery Miethke violated the tenets of the Secession, that it made him too commercial. Gustav defended him, but when they put it to a vote, Moll and his friends lost. Moll would have to cut his ties with the Gallery Miethke or leave the Secession. So he and his friends left.

The salon was wildly successful. I dressed everyone: Fritza Riedler, Mäda Primavesi, Elisabeth Bachofen-Echt, Berta Zuckerkandl and her daughter Amalie, Johanna Staude. I dressed them, and Gustav painted them. At the opera people nudged each other when I passed, and not because I was a famous concubine. I worked very hard. I got rich, not Adele Bloch-Bauer rich, but enough to pay Gustav back and support my mother, and my sisters and my niece. I could hire a cook, and then a chambermaid and a chauffeur.

Attersee became even more of a refuge, now that I was so busy and had so many responsibilities. The month I spent there was blissfully free of bills of sale and fittings and demanding customers. Gustav met me there every year, no matter what he was working on or where he had been traveling. It was the one time in the year when we were not separated, living in different houses, working long hours, traveling to different places. When I woke up and came down the stairs I knew he would be on the terrace, waiting for me. I knew that we would spend the afternoon hiking, or swimming, and the evening playing games. I knew that there wouldn't be anyone else in his studio, no models, no society ladies, no friends. I had him all to myself.

We were at breakfast, in August 1905. The mail was delivered and Gustav received two letters. When I handed them to him I noticed that they were from Tigergasse, in Josefstadt. Helene raised an eyebrow at me, but I pretended I didn't see.

"Who's this assiduous correspondent, Gustav?" she asked, not very subtly.

"Aren't you nosy," said Gustav, and put his letter under his plate with a wink.

"Of course. What did you expect?" But all she could get from him was that they were from "a friend."

The clouds toward Mondsee looked threatening, so Gustav and I decided to take our usual swim in the morning instead of the afternoon. Mother was taking Helene, Pauline, and little Helene shopping in the village. They were to have lunch at a restaurant and would be gone most of the day.

As Gustav pushed away from shore with one of the oars, we floated through the lily pads in a congenial misty rain. I rowed us to a spot a few hundred yards from shore while Gustav set up his easel and began daubing at a small canvas, trying to capture the wisps of fog floating near the bank before the weather forced us in again. I took a stroke now and then and tried to think of a way to find out who the letters were from without sounding like a shrew. Josefstadt was a slum, but a young artist could be writing him from there, or an aspiring journalist. I thought about Minna and Herta and hated the poisonous ideas I was having.

"Do you have a secret admirer?" I finally asked, trying for a jesting tone. I spoke to his back, as we both faced the shore.

He didn't answer at first.

"I don't have any secrets," he finally said. His hand continued to move, washing the canvas with the gray of a female bluebird. "I always tell the truth, you just have to ask me straight out instead of trying to tease things out of me."

"Who were your letters from, then?"

"Adele," he said.

"From Josefstadt?" I was incredulous.

"She keeps an apartment there."

Now I understood where they went the night of the engagement party. It filled me with rage that I had defended him. Now I wanted to know it all, before I lost my nerve and settled back into an anxious, hopeful state of denial.

"Is there anything else I should know?" I asked. "As long as we are being honest?" He didn't answer me. I would have to ask yes or no questions, as if we were at a trial.

"Are you secretly married?" I asked.

"No," he said.

"Do you have children?" He nodded and it took my breath away. Every time I thought I knew all there was to know, he surprised me.

"How many?" I asked.

"I'm not sure," he said. "Three that I know of." I wanted to jump out of the boat and swim to shore. And he kept painting.

"Who's the mother?" I asked next.

"Mothers, plural," he corrected. "Mizzi Zimmerman and Maria Ucicky."

"Are they models?"

"No," he said. "Well, Mizzi used to be."

"Prostitutes?"

"Now Mizzi is a seamstress," he said. "Maria is a laundress."

I trailed my hands in the water, and without me to steady it the boat began to drift and turn. At last Gustav was forced to stop painting. He grabbed the idle oars and, turning to face me, rowed furiously toward the middle of the lake. Perhaps he knew that I was contemplating abandoning ship.

"Stop," I said. "I want to go back." I expected the pleading expression, the wheedling, little boy grin he used so effectively when he was in trouble, but the soft hazel eyes were hard and dark.

"No," he said. "You have to understand, Emilie, it's not . . ." he struggled to find the words to explain. "It isn't . . . these things, they happen, you know . . . they're not . . . I don't."

Words were not his medium. His floundering made me sick, and I cut him off.

"The children?"

"Three boys," he said. "Ten, seven, and three years old."

"Are you still with them?"

"Maria I have not seen in many years." A pause. "Mizzi . . . sometimes."

We were well past the swimming float and almost to the point where the lake's depth drops suddenly from nine to a hundred feet, when the light mist that had been falling suddenly became a full-fledged downpour. Gustav began covering the paintings and supplies with a blanket to keep off the worst of the rain. The storm was nearly upon us and the thunder sounded like heavy trucks crossing a rickety bridge though we could not see the lightning bolts, only the clouds turning on and off like lightbulbs. "Hadn't you better row?" I said.

"I'm spent," he said. "We can watch the storm from here." I reached back to grab the oars but he pulled them away from me.

"Give me the oars," I said. "I'd rather not die out here with you."

He smiled and let them slip from his hands into the water, where they drifted cheerfully away. I watched for a moment in shock. Without the oars we'd be floating in the lake until someone came along and rescued us. We'd be helpless.

"Christ!" was all I had time to say before I dove in after them. It was glacially cold. For a moment I couldn't breathe. My lungs seemed to have contracted, receded like mollusks into protective shells. The cotton robe I wore to boat in was now as heavy as iron, pulling me under. I managed to untangle myself from it. Now I was in only my chemise and it was much easier to move. I surfaced. The small stinging drops warmed the surface, at least relative to the depths. I couldn't touch bottom so I tread water and scanned for the oars. In a minute I located them several feet from the boat, the cherry-red stripes on the handles bobbing in the whitecaps. I swam over to them and grabbed them. They were fairly heavy and it was hard to swim with them. I held on to the side of the boat and threw them over one at a time. I was about to climb back in when the rage hit. He was just sitting there, in the boat, watching me.

I dove under the boat and capsized it.

The canvases, Gustav's paint box, Gustav himself, the oars again, everything crashed into the water. The boat floated upside down like a turtle shell. I reached for it and turned it over. Gustav was nowhere to be seen. For the moment I didn't care; I found my robe and threw it into the boat, I found the oars again and tossed them in.

Gustav still hadn't appeared. I saw a couple of paint tubes floating in the water and grabbed them. Now I was starting to worry. I had no idea how long it had been since the boat had capsized. Two minutes? Three? It was a long time to hold one's breath. Instead of getting back into the righted boat I decided to swim around it and look for him. I called his name, but all I could hear was the wind. I dove and felt around in the water; the rain had made it too cloudy to see clearly. Panic was setting in. What if I'd killed him?

Then from behind me something grabbed me around the waist and threw me up into the air and down into the water. When I came up he was laughing. Lightning cracked like a whip as it struck a tree across the lake. I watched it catch fire.

"You thought I had drowned," said Gustav with glee. "You were beside yourself." He squirted me in the face with water he had cupped in his hands.

My legs were weak with relief, but I didn't want him to know that, so I floated on my back and looked at the clouds. "I was worried about the canvas," I said. "The water will ruin it."

"Who cares?" he said. "I hadn't really begun yet."

We began diving to recover his paintbox and his favorite brushes, which floated on the surface like needlefish. We even found the painting, though it was ruined with mud. We tossed everything back in the boat and hauled ourselves over the side. On the way back we each took an oar, with the wind, straight into the fog that had now completely enveloped the land. We couldn't see where we were going, but we could hear the wind chimes on the front porch and steered toward them. Gustav whistled as he rowed, and every now and then he would grin at me.

When I could see the shore was only twenty yards away, I let the oars rest on the water and coasted, catching my breath. The boat slid into the space next to the dock like a hand in a glove. Gustav tied a hasty knot to secure it, and I handed him all of the things in the boat.

Gustav had twigs in his hair and mud on his face. His shirt was torn and smeared with blood from where he had caught himself on the side of the boat when he fell in. Puddles of muddy water formed around him on the dock.

I ran to the bank and collapsed on it. Raindrops fell into my eyes and into my mouth. The sky was the color of an old dingy chemise. I couldn't breathe properly and I wanted to cry, but then I was laughing silently, racked with it, there on the bank, in the mud. The whole thing was so ridiculous. Gustav must've thought I was having a seizure. He came and sat down next to me, though the bank was rocky and cold. We watched the leaves blowing off of the trees.

He rolled onto me, not kissing me, just looking at me, pulling the leaves out of my hair, wringing out the curls and watching the rainwater drip onto my soaked shift. The pressure of his body was warm but I began to shiver uncontrollably.

Then as if someone had blown a whistle, we stood up and ran for the house. Our wet clothes made a sucking sound as they were pulled apart.

We left everything we had so carefully rescued from the lake to blow right back in again. I left the robe I had embroidered by hand with designs I had found in a book of eighteenth-century Czech patterns.

We untangled ourselves from our wet clothes in front of the fire, still giggling like children. When we were naked and more or less dry, there was nothing to do but run up the stairs and hop into my bed under my thick comforter. Gustav couldn't very well go back out to the damp and drafty greenhouse.

It was like the time of Ernst's funeral in the sense that one emotion transmogrified into another. This time, it was rage that had become lust. My skin was warm and damp and cherry pink. My limbs were sleepy with warmth and rest. I felt a little drunk as I reached between his legs. I wasn't virginal and innocent this time, though. It was I who seduced him. It was I who made him cry out.

He fell asleep but I could not. I propped my head on my arm and watched him.

If he and I stayed together, I realized with a shudder, every day would be like today. I would carry my suspicion in my heart like a tumor, and it would grow and grow and eat me from the inside. I would worry about who else he was with and how many times and was he in love with her. I would begin to read his mail and open his journal when he was out. I would cry every day. Soon I'd be throwing tantrums like Alma and slicing at the skin on my arm with a kitchen knife. I would be as crazy as Alma and Adele put together and Gustav would come to hate me. Perhaps one day I would turn the boat over and not look back to see if Gustav was all right. Perhaps one day I would get in the boat alone and row away. Perhaps I would swim to the middle and drown and neither of our bodies would ever be found.

I thought about what Berta had said, that I could have him all to myself if that was what I really wanted. But under what terms? At what cost to him, and to me?

Gustav and I could be coconspirators and like minds, but we could not be lovers. The fact that I had come to this realization all on my own was of no comfort whatsoever.

Twenty-One

Gustav and I returned to Vienna a few weeks later, but almost immediately I made plans to leave again, to go to the fall couture in Paris. I had talked about going for several years but I had never felt that I could leave the salon for such an extended length of time. Now the salon was running smoothly. Pauline handled the books, ordered supplies, and paid the bills. Helene kept the appointment book, received the clients, and kept them happy. I was in charge of design. The cutting and sewing rooms were my domain. Still, any one of the three of us could fill in for the others, at least for a little while. I could be away and feel confident that when I returned the salon would still be there. There would be no shoddy dress that fell apart, no mix-up with the orders, no mistake on the bills. No catastrophe would occur to ruin my reputation. And I needed to get away.

It was my first trip to Paris, my first time abroad, and I was alone. I expected to feel blue about it but I wasn't. I stayed at a small hotel in the fashion district. My room was small but the walls were covered in wine-colored silk damask that matched the bed hangings. The restaurant downstairs served a lovely sole meunière. The hotel was filled with dressmakers like me, from Berlin and London and Prague, and I quickly made friends. Our days were filled with tours of the fabric houses, Rodier and Lesure and Bianchini. We took the train to their factories outside of Paris and learned how the fabrics were made. We learned what innovations they were working on: stronger silk, synthetics, knits. I ordered all kinds of things. I attended mannequin shows put on by the couture houses, Worth and Poiret. Afterward I had appointments at each of them and bought their patterns for the spring season.

That was how we made most of our money, making up dresses with the Parisian patterns and altering them to suit our clients. As everyone says, the Parisian and the Viennese lady are differently shaped. Many of our clients were plump. Even a svelte Viennese lady had a bigger frame, more solid bones, and considerably larger bosom than the average Parisian. When I took the patterns home I adjusted them. It's much harder than it sounds. You can't just make everything a little bigger. It's like building a sand castle: if you change one thing, even the slightest bit, everything else collapses and has to be reconfigured. Some people have a talent for it, can do it by feel, and I'm one of them. The proof was the popularity of the salon, not just when it was a novelty, but year after year.

It pained me a little bit that we couldn't make a profit on Reform dress, but it was a limited market. We still made those styles, and some clients bought them, but not like they bought the latest from Paris.

Gustav sent me a postcard every day, sometimes several in a day, but I did not reply. I tried to put him out of my mind.

When I wasn't working I went to the Louvre and walked the streets near my hotel. At night the other dressmakers and I went to dinner and to the theater and the opera. I went to the outdoor markets and found antique pasteboard jewelry and Moroccan blankets. One day we chartered an omnibus and toured Versailles.

The postcards from Gustav became more and more wheedling, more desperate. Where was I? What was I doing? Was I having so much fun that I couldn't write? Was everything so tedious that I couldn't write? Was the weather inclement? Was I sick? Sometimes I would write a postcard to him, a maddeningly short one, like: "Weather is cool and drizzly," or, "Went to Rodin's studio today." And I would get a frantic missive back, anxious that I was dressing warmly and carrying my umbrella, or full of questions about Rodin that I would never answer. I must admit I enjoyed his obvious torment.

I stayed six weeks. I returned on a Friday and Gustav made me promise to come to the studio on Saturday. I spent the morning at the salon, catching up on what I'd missed. Pauline went over the new orders with me, and the seamstresses showed me what they were working on. My niece Helene was making up her first blouse and I gave her some advice on her basting technique. I pinned a skirt for Berta Zuckerkandl's daughter Amalie. I was very happy to be back in my workshop, to dip my hand into the silver goblet and pull out a handful of straight pins. I relished the feel of the felt carpet under my feet, the clatter of the sewing machines, the rumble of the laundry trucks on the street below. I showed Helene the catalogs I had brought back and we went through them, trying to guess which would be our biggest sellers. They were baking cakes downstairs at the Café Piccola and Helene had made pecan shortbread cookies and hot chocolate especially for me. She was full of stories and gossip from the weeks I had been gone. I hated to leave, but I had promised, so at one o'clock I took the train to Hietzing.

When I arrived at the studio there was a boy lying on the grass in front of the house. With the overcast skies and cold wind the morning frost had not melted. I thought the boy must be dead, to lie there on the frozen ground. He lay face down and very still. He didn't hear me until I was practically stepping on him. The portfolio next to him on the grass told me that he was one of the many students who were always accosting Gustav, begging him for his help. The better ones knew to write a letter and ask for an appointment. They arrived neatly groomed and on time and Gustav was invariably kind to them, even though most of them were hopelessly bad. This boy's pants were three sizes too big and held up with a pair of hand-crocheted suspenders. His cuffs were unbut-toned and his dirty sleeves fanned out around his wrists. He was the worst-dressed artist I'd seen since the day I met Gustav.

He heard my footsteps and rolled over to face me. I saw a homely face, with a bent nose and wild hair and ears that stuck out absurdly. He was very young.

"He's not home," he said. "I rang the bell a half hour ago."

That was very unlike Gustav, whose habits were extremely regu-lar and who never ate lunch. I wondered if he might be sick. Or per-haps he was not answering the door in an effort to avoid the boy, who looked at me as if he expected me to join him on the grass.

"I have a key," I said.

"Are you his wife?" he asked. I winced.

"No," I said. He rolled to his side and propped his head on his hand.

"Are you his lover?"

"What a question!" I said. He shrugged.

"I guess that's a yes."

"What's your name?" I asked. I thought it would be better if I got rid of him. Gustav could never deliberately hurt anyone's feel-ings, especially not a fledgling artist, but I had no such qualms.

"Egon Schiele," he said.

"Those are your drawings?" I said. "Would you mind if I looked at them?"

"Go ahead," he said. "But even if you dislike them I'm not leav-ing until Klimt comes."

I picked the portfolio up off of the grass and carried it to the front steps. Egon Schiele followed me and sat down next to me. I opened the portfolio.

I could see immediately that he was an excellent draftsman. There wasn't a misplaced line to be seen. They only lacked some spark of interest or life to make them art.

"You're at the Academy of Fine Art?" I asked. He nodded. "They make us do these ridiculous exercises there. You know, pro-

file facing left, profile facing right, the bust of Voltaire. But near
the back are some things of my own."

These things of his own were drawings of a little girl, and they
were like nothing I'd seen before. She was naked in a way that
Gustav's nudes were not. The young man used none of the formal
devices others did to soften the angles, the protruding bones and
awkward rolls of flesh. In the first one her hands were crossed in
front of her and she leaned her weight on one hip. In the next she
put her hands on her hips. Her gaze was matter-of-fact.

"My sister Gertie," he said. Some of the drawings were colored
in with chalk. I shivered as I looked at them. They were ugly, repul-
sive. His sister looked sick and deformed. Did he hate her, to draw
her that way? More than ever I wanted him gone, but I had spent
enough time around artists to recognize genius, and this warped
boy had it. I sighed.

"Are you hungry?"

I let him in and made him a ham sandwich. He ate it ravenously.
He told me that he'd been born in Tulln, that his father had died
two years before, that he disliked the uncle who was now his
guardian, and that he was never going to marry, he was going to
live with his sister until he died. After he had eaten he wandered
slowly around the studio as if it were a shrine. African sculpture,
Noh masks, Japanese armor—Gustav had collected all kinds of art
objects, which he displayed around the studio. Schiele examined
everything carefully. He touched the half-finished canvas in the
center of the room as if it were the Virgin's foot.

When Gustav came back he explained that he had developed a
craving for sausages and mustard that had to be satisfied. Instead of
a sentimental reunion after weeks apart, we talked about bratwurst
and I introduced him to the boy. Gustav looked slightly annoyed
by the unexpected company but took the proffered portfolio and
sat down on the chaise. I watched as Gustav flipped through the
drawings, and knowing him as I did I saw the surprise and joy of
discovery in his face. The boy, without such knowledge, fidgeted

and pretended to examine a book of Japanese woodblock prints. Every few seconds he would sneak a glance at Gustav's expression.

Still Gustav said nothing. He just kept looking. He was looking at the last drawing of Gertie and seemed unwilling to tear himself away from it. The boy's careless ease was entirely gone. He was gnawing at his thumb.

"Put the boy out of his misery, Gustav," I finally said. "He's in agony over here."

"Do you think I have talent?" the boy asked. It took Gustav a moment to answer, he was far away, in deep conversation with the boy's drawing. There was a sickening pause. Then he roared with laughter. "Yes!" he said. "Much too much!" The worry left the boy's face and he even smiled. Gustav clapped him on the back and nearly knocked him over. Then they talked art. Gustav quizzed him about his classes, what exercises he did, who his teachers were. When Gustav understood how poor the boy was he bought two of his drawings and invited him to dinner the following night.

At last he left and Gustav and I were alone.

"You see the winter came while you were away," Gustav said.

"It would have come regardless," I said. I wasn't feeling sentimental. I walked around and looked at the canvases he was working on, as the boy had done. They looked much the same as when I left.

"I'm working on something new," he said. "It's taking up a lot of my time, doing the prepatory sketches." He showed me a drawing of two lovers embracing.

The motif was not new; he had used it in the *Beethoven Frieze* he had done for the Secession exhibition of 1902. That was called *Here's a Kiss to the Whole World!* He had done a similar cartoon for the mosaic frieze for the Palais Stoclet and had called it *Fulfill-ment*. But he had never executed the idea in an oil painting. He had never shown the image in isolation, only as one of a series of images.

"I think the idea can work by itself, don't you? It's so simple, yet so weighted with symbolism and emotion."

"Like a Byzantine icon," I said. He was using a lot of gold leaf and pattern in his work at that time. It all fit together.

Compositionally it was a tricky problem. In the *Beethoven Frieze* the figures had been nude and the man's figure had completely covered and dwarfed the woman. That wouldn't work for the painting. At least the woman's face should be visible. Perhaps they should be in profile. None of the drawings he had done so far had really worked. He showed them to me, and we dismissed each one. He pulled out his sketchbook and we huddled over the page as he scribbled ideas. We tried out some possible poses, like actors blocking a scene.

"Suzanne is a fine model, but she doesn't understand what I'm trying to do. And her body type is all wrong for this. I need someone else," he said.

"What about Lise?" I said.

"Would you do it?" he said.

I thought he was joking. I hadn't modeled since he painted my portrait. And I already had an occupation, and plenty to do.

"Who is going to model for the man?" I said. "You?"

"I don't need a model for him," he said. "He's not important."

Gustav hated to draw himself. In fact, in his thirty-year artistic career he put himself into a painting exactly once: *The Globe Theater*, one of the Burgtheater paintings. The only reason he painted himself in was because he needed a male figure and could not afford to hire a model and he had already put in Ernst, Georg, and Franz Matsch. He obscured his face with an enormous Elizabethan ruff and a well-placed shadow. From then on he made sure his own face and figure were never required for a painting. It helped that as he moved away from history painting he painted men less and less.

Maybe it was because he was ashamed of his physical imperfections. He was short, shorter than I was though neither of us mentioned it. Only vigorous exercise with dumbbells and long daily walks kept him from running to fat. He had lost most of his hair. So it may be vanity that kept him from self-portraiture, or its opposite. They are so hard to tell apart sometimes. I am not interested in painting myself, he said if a journalist asked him about it. Why would anyone want to look at a picture of me? I am interested in other people. I am interested in women particularly. He disliked interviews and rarely gave them. If you want to know about me and what I want, look at my paintings, he said to them.

We took Egon Schiele to the Cabaret Fledermaus, which the Wiener Werkstätte had conceived and designed as a sort of clubhouse for the Viennese avant-garde. It had only been open a few weeks and it was impossible to get a table, but Gustav had a standing reservation.

The cabaret was a Josef Hoffmann masterpiece. The walls of the bar were covered with brightly colored and individually decorated ceramic tiles; some people thought they looked like the work of a mental patient. The tiles clashed crazily with the black and white floor tiles. Those same critics who didn't like the wall tiles said the overall effect was of the world's fanciest lavatory; but then, there were still a lot of people in Vienna at that time who clung to the heavy drapery school of design. Some people were scandalized that food was served on white tables without tablecloths. Hoffmann loved the scandal and the notoriety; it was great for business.

It was hard to tell what Egon Schiele thought. When he came in the door, half an hour late and with his hair still wet from his bath, though there was a biting wind, he stopped and stared for a moment, then, catching sight of us, proceeded toward us. He said little but drank glass after glass of gin as a band played the latest popular songs. It seemed everyone we knew was there that night: August and Serena Lederer, Fritz Waerndorfer, Berta, Moll, Moser, Alfred Roller, Hoffman; and Gustav made sure that Schiele was introduced to them all as his new protégé. When Moll heard that Gustav had bought two of his drawings, he tried to sign the boy to Gallery Miethke without so much as a peek at his work. The boy said he would think about it. Moll convinced him to come to the gallery with his portfolio the next day. It struck me that the boy was not nearly as grateful or as eager as someone else might have been. It was as if he already knew that the power was all on his side, even though he was a poor drawing student. The sight of Moll, fat and prosperous in an expensive suit, cajoling the skinny boy in a filthy jacket, was quite amusing to me.

Berta appraised the boy and found him arrogant. She bet Hoffmann a set of teaspoons that he would disappear from our world within six months. Moser spoke to him about designing some postcards for the Wiener Werkstätte and he seemed interested in the idea. We ate pumpkin bisque and roasted capon with truffles. When we reached the brandy-soaked apples with ice cream, Gustav asked him what he thought of it all.

"It's utterly decadent," said Schiele. I couldn't tell whether he meant it as a compliment or not.

"Well, that's Vienna for you," said Gustav cheerfully. "We're not Puritans." He winked at me. "At least not most of us."

"Lutherans aren't Puritans and you know it," I said.

"Of course not," he said. "Remind me again of the church of your childhood, that lovely empty box."

"Hoffmann would have loved it," I said. "Come to think of it, he should design a church."

"The Palais Stoclet is his church," said Gustav. "It's going to cost more money than any church ever has, at least."

"I'm not sure I'm cut out for it," said Schiele. "Maybe I'd be better off somewhere in the country, in a little cottage, with plenty of time and space."

"Don't be an idiot," said Gustav. "Everyone who can help you is here. I want you to submit some work to the show we're having next year. As many things as you like. Just don't run away now that we've found you."

What boy, what young, untested artist could resist Gustav's flattery and charm? Schiele blushed into his drink and promised he would work very hard over the next six months to pull together some work to show.

"I've been thinking," I said. "About Reform dress. It's just not selling as well as it should. What if a prominent artist were to design some dresses? Don't you think more people would buy them?"

"It depends on who the artist is," said Gustav. "Our friend here might do something really sensational that every lady in Vienna might want to buy."

"I don't like clothes," said Schiele. "I don't like to look at them, I don't like to draw them. It's only when you get someone out of their clothes that you really get something interesting."

"Well said," laughed Gustav.

"You could sketch the designs and we could decide together what materials to use. They could be made up at the salon and we could get a mannequin to wear them. Maybe we could have a show."

"You should make them up for yourself," Gustav said.

"Are you trying to make me into a model?" I asked. "Why not Elisabeth?" She was our house model. "She'd be a much better advertisement than I would."

"Not true," said Gustav. "A designer wearing her own clothes is always the best model."

"Your clothes," I said.

"Our clothes," he said.

After dinner the resident acting company performed satire of current political events. After that, a woman with a rich, darkly colored alto voice sang sad songs until closing time, when Egon Schiele stumbled drunkenly back to his studio and stayed up all night drawing tableaus of the night from memory.

After I had convinced Gustav to put himself into the new painting of the couple embracing, he spent the next few weeks trying to get out of it. He said he could not draw himself.

"You have mirrors," I said. "Lots of artists use mirrors. Or I could photograph you. Or someone could photograph the two of us and you could paint from the photograph."

"No," he said.

"Then I won't do it," I said. He pouted. He said he would get his new favorite model, Anna, to do it. He told me how lovely she was, how compliant.

"Fine," I said. "It's fine with me if you don't want me to do it. You asked me, remember?" But after a week or so of this he capitulated.

"Only for you, dear silly," he said. Dear silly was what he often called me. "Only for you would I subject myself to this torture."

We worked on putting the pose together. We couldn't both stand because I was too tall. He had me kneel in profile and then turn my head to face him. I angled my chin up as far as I could and brought my hands to my face. I closed my eyes. He made several days' worth of sketches of me like that until I started to get impatient and reminded him of his promise.

"Just for a minute," he said, "just to see what it looks like." I could hear him setting up the mirrors, one against the wall behind me and one propped up on the easel. Then I felt a hand at the back of my neck and another on my chin. I felt lips on my cheek. Put your hand on mine, he said as he pushed my dress down, off of my shoulder. I opened my eyes and stole a glance in the mirror. I felt oddly detached, as if I were watching strangers courting in the park. I hardly recognized myself in the mirror. It was a calculated pose, a facsimile of love. Gustav wasn't thinking of love at all when he created the painting. He thought about space and weight, a thousand elements of composition so familiar to him he only registered what was right and what was not.

"Why did you want me to model?" I asked him one day.

He shrugged. "Because it is perfect for you."

"But why?" I asked. He thought for a moment.

"I wanted someone authentic, he said. "Not too perfect, not too practiced."

"Thanks," I say. "You wanted someone graceless and bovine and all your models are far too beautiful and perfect to work."

He wadded up a piece of drawing paper and tossed it at me. It floated briefly before falling to the floor far short of where I was kneeling and thinking about massaging the awful crick in my neck. "Don't be difficult," he said. "You know exactly what I mean."

And I did.

Gustav usually worked very slowly; some of his paintings took five years to finish, but this one was completed quickly because he wanted to exhibit it in the Vienna Art Show alongside the portrait of Adele Bloch-Bauer. They were a pair, he said, because of the gold, because of the pattern, because of their Byzantine antecedents. I couldn't help but think, though, that he was working quickly because this painting meant something more to him than the others, that it had personal significance. He wouldn't let me see it, of course. He said I would have to wait for opening night of the art show like everyone else. Impatiently I waited for the day when I could see what he'd made of us, not just of these awkward modeling sessions, but of all the years that came before.

Twenty-Two

For the first time in a week, it is not raining when I wake up. Helene and I decide to pack a picnic and walk to Schloss Kammer, the nearby castle. Schloss Kammer is a red-roofed stucco villa in the hills above the town, surrounded by trees and carefully tended gardens. Gustav and I used to go there all the time, to paint or sketch. If we were lucky and the tourists stayed away, we could pretend that we were the lord and lady of the castle, inspecting our gardens, admiring our view, and lounging about our grounds. Gustav thought that people and the natural world were both endlessly fascinating, but that they did not belong on the same canvas, so when the tourists were there, we usually turned around and went home. There will be no one else there today, I feel sure. Helene and I will be mistresses of the castle. Though on summer days Gustav and I did not have to contend, as we do now, with the mud.

Helene throws together some bread and cheese sandwiches and we put on our sturdy boots and set off. Our trees have timidly begun to send out the first pale green shoots. The effect is a blurring, as if the bare tree had moved slightly while its photograph was taken. The air smells of manure and new grass. The earthworms have come up and I try not to step on any of them.

We meet no one on the road, and suddenly I realize that it is Sunday. We are the only ones not at church, praying for victory.

After a mile we turn onto the path that takes us up the hill to the castle. It's a little bit slippery and I'm glad I've brought the oak walking stick I found in the greenhouse. Now I have to watch out for slugs. I have no qualms about killing them but I hate the feeling of them under my shoes. There are some limbs down along the path and patches of snow that have refused to melt. After a few minutes I turn around to look at the panoramic view of the mountains, circling Lake Attersee like the jaws of a trap. The clouds press in on the jagged peaks, smooth and white with snow. When it melts in a month or two the meadows will be carpeted with avalanche lilies and gentians, phlox and lady's slipper.

When we step onto the allée of trees that lead to the entrance I shiver a little, though I'm warm from the climb. The rows of trees on either side of the road create a geometric exercise in perspective and frame the stucco and glass and red tile just beyond like a viewfinder. With each step I see a new picture. This was a favorite spot of Gustav's. He painted the castle several times from this vantage point, and I can't be there without seeing his paintings. The real trees are not quite as forbidding as the painted trees. They are spindly, and need pruning. No one is living at the castle now. It was built for a prince in the eighteenth century, and the prince's descendants are riding out the war in Madagascar. The castle was once scrubbed creamy white, though in Gustav's paintings it was often golden yellow. Now instead of glowing and beckoning magically it looks sad and ordinary, streaked with grime, the windows shuttered.

We find a spot on the muddy lawn. The grass is matted and yellow. Helene, ever handy, rolls out the canvas tarpaulin she brought.

"I wish we had the roadster," I say. "The roads are desolate. We could easily reach top speed. We'd never have to brake."

"What would we do for gasoline?" Helene says. "Even if the car hadn't been requisitioned?"

"Details, details," I say.

"We'd get stuck and there'd be no one to push," Helene says. "That car weighed, what, two tons? We'd never get it out ourselves."

That's the difference between Helene and me. She seems content with what the days bring her, while I'm the one who is always wishing for something else, something I can't have, something there's no point in missing. She doesn't remember her father but she looks like him, or what I imagine he might have looked like if he'd been allowed to reach the age of fifty. Her expression is intense and her salt and pepper hair is sliding out of its knot. I take her hand and feel its warmth, its strength.

We sit quietly for a few moments contemplating our little valley. A pair of goats wanders onto the lawn, nosing at the ground, searching for new grass. On the other side of the lake, in Unterach, church is letting out and they are ringing the bell. The tune is Stuttgart. From here the houses look like pastel candies. Everything, the lake, the sky, the air, is a tone of grayish blue. If I were a painter I would use Prussian blue, titanium white, burnt umber. Unlike Gustav I would paint the whole enormous sky, with its distant, icy clouds and its low, wide, blanketing ones. I would paint the reflection of the sky and clouds in the water. But I would include the people in my paintings. There would be a boat in the lake, or more than one. There would be girls bathing on the shore, and families out for a stroll in the town, wearing their Sunday best. The lake wouldn't fight the people for the viewer's attention, and the people wouldn't distort the sky's cold perfection with their worn shoes and tanned faces.

"Remember the motorboat?" Helene says. "Uncle Gust was so proud of it. The first motorboat in all of Austria!"

"I remember when he almost ran over Heitzmann's mother with it," I say. "And when he ran out of gas near St. Wolfgang and had to leave the boat and swim home."

"How did you get it back?" Helene says, though she knows the story very well.

"I rowed him over," I say. "He had told me that very morning that we should get rid of the rowboat, that it was obsolete and taking up space in the boathouse. But after that I never heard another word about it."

Helene pulls out the sandwiches, some apples, and a few squares of chocolate wrapped in foil. God knows where she's been hiding those. While we eat she asks me for more stories about Gustav, about her mother, about Ernst, and to oblige her I talk and talk until the afternoon is gone.

THE KISS, 1907

Alone in the studio, Gustav stands before his new painting. He arrived at the studio breathless after his long morning walk, full of anticipation. Today is the day he really begins. He has the design, his canvas is prepared, he has blocked in the figures, he is ready to begin. Yet he cannot. For over an hour he has been looking at it, but he is no closer to putting brush to canvas than when he first arrived.

He paces the room, he opens and then closes the window. He picks up one of the cats and rubs its belly until it growls and scratches his face. He makes himself a pot of coffee and drinks it in front of the canvas, trying to understand why he is having so much trouble. A painting is like a game of chess; you have to plan your moves. When he left the studio the night before he thought he knew how to attack it, but sometime in the night it had changed on him.

It's not so different from other paintings I have done, he thinks. Although making an allegorical painting about love is about the most arrogant thing one can do. What the hell do I know about love? Compared to this, an allegorical painting about medicine or philosophy is a modest undertaking.

There they are, gray and shadowy, his penciled-in figures, waiting to be brought to life by paint. On the left, a man. Not himself. He never seriously considered making the man a self-portrait, of course. He just said that to appease Emilie, who was being strange and unreasonable about it. She should know that he will never do a self-portrait, not for anyone, not even for her.

And on the right, this girl. Who is she?

Well, it's Emilie, of course. A little bit attenuated, a little bit stylized, but recognizably Emilie. She has Emilie's mouth and Emilie's hair and Emilie's hands. And that is the problem, he realizes. He has always said, if you want to know about me and what I want, look at my paintings.

He knows that if he paints a likeness of Emilie Flöge in an embrace with a robed man, even if the man is indistinct, everyone will know. There will be gossip about it, and speculation. And he had asked her to model for the painting with exactly that outcome in mind. He wants to do something, make some declaration. He has felt her slipping away lately, so busy with her own work, her traveling. He wants to pull her back toward him. But now that he is here with the painting he realizes that he can't do it. It can't be Emilie, not, at least, in any obvious way.

It takes a few hours to alter her outline. The shape of her face has changed. Her hands belong to a different woman. Emilie will be disappointed, he thinks. She's been waiting for me to do a decent portrait of her for how long? He chuckles a little ruefully. Most of her life. He's never really understood why she didn't like the portrait of her. What was all that nonsense about him not knowing who she really is? He knows her better than anyone does, better than Helene, better than Pauline, better than her mother. He decides not to tell her yet. When she asks how the painting is going he can just say that he had to make some changes to the figures. That will be all she will need to hear to understand. It's the reason she is the only person he feels entirely comfortable with: he doesn't have to talk a lot, doesn't have to go to elaborate lengths to explain himself. He tries not to think about the look on her face when she sees the finished painting.

Is it artistic considerations or personal ones that are pressing him to change the painting into something less specific, more universal? It's hard to be that self-conscious. It's hard to look that closely at one's own psyche. All he really knows is that when he thinks about the girl as a portrait of Emilie he can't pick up a brush. He is paralyzed. When he thinks, she is just a girl, any girl, he can mix his paint and he can lay down an undercoat of burnt umber and he can start to build up the painting with ocher and raw sienna. And it is the difference between going out of his mind and being, at least for the hours he is working, at peace.

Twenty-Three

Gustav made fifty drawings of dress designs. Some were too fanciful to actually be made, and others had to be modified in the interest of cost or durability or practicality. We had long discussions about fabric and embellishment, and he described to me exactly how he wanted each one to look, what kind of impression he wanted each one to give, how he wanted it to hang on the body. Eventually we narrowed the group down to thirty-two looks. I translated his drawings into patterns, and took the patterns to the salon to make them up to my own measurements. First we made prototypes out of muslin, to make sure I had transposed the ideas correctly and that they fit the way they were intended to. Then, when they had been draped and pinned to satisfaction, we brought out the rich materials that Gustav had spent a small fortune on. It was odd and a little embarrassing to have so many clothes for myself in production; I felt like the Empress Elisabeth.

When the dresses were ready Gustav and I met for a photography session at the studio. I hung them all in the hall, which made it look odd, like the prop room at the Opera, with all of these clothes crowding out the woodcuts and sculpture. We took the photographs in the garden, and in between I would go inside and change into the next one.

First I modeled a straight, narrow column of a tea gown, in a carnival print, with three-tiered, cascading bell sleeves.

"Turn and look toward the door," he said. "Think of marzipan torte."

"Don't talk about food," I said, "I want to be able to fit into these dresses when we are done photographing them. Tell me how the painting of the embrace is going."

"Frustratingly," he said as I stood still for the lengthy exposure.

"Is that even a word?" I said.

"You moved your mouth," he said. "Now it will be blurry."

"It might be a nice effect," I said.

"You just want to keep talking," he accused. "Be quiet and let me complain about how badly my painting is going." He told me that the figures were still not right but he had decided just to paint them as they were. He told me about laying the background too thick, and of having to wipe it clean, and how many hours of labor he had lost. He told me that the price of gold leaf was ridiculously high. I listened as I modeled a pale pink wool jersey party dress with white chiffon sleeves. I modeled a black evening dress with a black-and-white checkerboard collar and yoke while he told me about a new artist the Wiener Werkstätte had discovered, a young man named Oskar Kokoschka.

"He's well-grounded in drawing, a student at the School of Arts and Crafts. Not that you'd know it to look at his work. He's a wild man, but very promising."

"Wilder than Schiele? More promising?"

"Hard to say," Gustav said. "At least as crazy, but in a different way."

"When do I meet this newest prodigy?" I said.

"Soon," he said. "Turn your head a little more to the left. We should have a dinner party for him." What he meant was that there should be a dinner at my place, with him as nominal host. But I was used to that.

"All right," I said. "Just give me a few days' notice." I went inside and changed into a summer dress with a black-and-white pattern of triangles on the yoke that were straight out of the Stoclet frieze.

The photographs appeared in the *Journal of Arts and Crafts*. In the photographs I am laughing, my hair up in most of them so that the necklines are visible. Gustav usually shot me in profile, which was always my best angle. I wore the necklace Gustav had given me. Gustav is outside the frame but he is everywhere in the photographs, in the clothes, and in my smile. If you blew the photographs up you would see him reflected in the iris of my eye.

The Kiss was exhibited at the Art Show, Vienna, in 1908. All of the former members of the Secession, who had not had a show since they left that group three years before, took part in the exhibition. The city lent them an empty lot where a concert hall was to be built, and Hoffmann created a fifty-four-room exhibition complex with terraces, gardens, courtyards, an outdoor theater, and a tearoom. The show was timed to coincide with the celebration of the sixtieth anniversary of Emperor Franz Josef's accession. All of the art was Austrian. Gustav had a room to himself, and exhibited sixteen paintings.

I was too busy to help with the preparations, and Gustav would not let me see *The Kiss* until opening night, so I saw the painting for the first time when I arrived at the reception. It was very crowded and of course the thickest throng was in Gustav's room, and around his new painting. As I mingled in the crowd people kept coming up to me and telling me how much they loved it, and didn't I love it, too? Yes, I said, it was wonderful, and I stationed myself against the wall opposite the painting so that when the crowd cleared I could get a good view.

I was standing there looking at the backs of people's heads when Gustav brought over a tall, thin man with round, owlish, heavy-lidded eyes. He had a worried, drawn forehead and a long face, most of which was chin. He looked like the kind of man who might become more handsome as he got older, but now, at twenty-two, he was quite plain.

"Emilie Flöge, Oskar Kokoschka."

"Delighted," I said. I told him how much I admired the poster he had done for the show, the one with the young girl. "It reminds me of folk art," I said.

"It came to me in a dream," he said. "All of my best ideas come to me in dreams. But I like the other poster I did a little better."

"I hope that one did not come out of a dream," I said.

"No, I modeled that one after Goya, *Saturn Devouring His Children,* do you know it?"

I said I did, though I had never been to Spain to see it. He explained to me the title of the poster was *Tragedy of Man,* and that death of course was the first tragedy of man, and that was how it connected to Goya, though the pose of his figure was not really the same, nor was the painting method. Goya, he said, understood death better than any artist who ever lived. He spoke hurriedly, as if he might be carted away before he was finished. He turned often to Gustav to make sure he understood. I thought that the boy might have been suffering from insomnia, or malnutrition, or both, and invited him to dinner right away. Then Gustav led him away and I stood waiting. It was close to the end of the evening when I finally got to see *The Kiss.*

I realized immediately that he had cheated me. Gustav was not in the painting anymore. He had thrown out the drawings of himself and painted in a cartoon man. His face was almost completely obscured, and the little bit of cheekbone and brow that did show looked nothing like Gustav. The man's swarthy complexion was nothing like Gustav's. His hair was too plentiful, too dark. Something was odd about his neck, something wasn't right anatomically, which, considering how many figures Gustav had drawn with ease, didn't make any sense. The man's body was swathed in a caftan of the kind Gustav wore when he painted, but this robe was a disguise, it hid everything, it made him just a shape, a block of gold.

He had painted me out, too. The girl in the painting had a sweet, generic face. In vain I looked for my cheekbones, my strong jaw, my thin, wide mouth. But they were altered, smoothed, rounded. I noted with dismay that the girl had Adele Bloch-Bauer's hands.

This girl, whoever she was, was balanced on a precipice. Her toes gripped the edge—was that sexual ecstasy or desperation? Her feet were wrapped or tied with golden vines. The man, whoever he was, seemed better off. He was on the safe side of the cliff. Somewhere under that robe he had feet, unbound feet that could carry him away. He was guarding his expression, his feelings, by turning his face away. In a moment he might tire of the girl and push her off of the cliff. He might leave her in despair, with no choice in her agonized mind but to fling herself over. Her blissful face betrayed her ignorance of the darkness all around her. Her face was the center, the heart of the painting. Suddenly I was furious with her, with her open face and heart, her innocence and youth. Didn't she know the danger she was in? How was she going to get out of this? I wanted to smack her, to wake her from her trance. But she smiled on and on.

Of course the painting was an icon. It was an allegory, not a portrait, and was never meant to be anything but that. Did I hate it for what it was or for what it wasn't?

If he knew what I thought it would break his heart, and as many times as my own heart had been broken I wanted to spare him that, so I searched for something, anything about the painting that I could honestly say I loved. I said the wildflowers reminded me of those at Attersee. I said I loved her dress. I wondered aloud if the dress could be reproduced, how expensive that much golden thread would be, and how heavy. I praised the use of gold, the texture of the background. Gustav didn't seem to notice anything amiss. And when he dropped me off at home I went into my room and thrashed at my pillow until I was exhausted and able to sleep.

The painting sold to the Austrian Gallery for a ridiculous amount of money. It was a sensation, but Gustav was most excited about Kokoschka and his children's fairy tale, *The Dreaming Youths,* which he had dedicated to Gustav. Gustav thought it was the best thing in the show, though the reviewers, predictably, were outraged at his bold, primitive designs and bright, flat colors. Gustav told Kokoschka that he should measure his success by the amount of vitriol he incited, and that he should be very pleased with the outcome of the Kunstschau.

* * *

In 1911 I was the one hosting an event, for a change. Poiret came to Vienna with his mannequins on his tour of the European capitals. With the help of the Wiener Werkstätte I organized a reception for him, in the gardens of the Prater, an amusement park on the edge of town.

It was late summer, the air hot and still. We covered the tables in white linen and arranged white ceramic pots of delicate cyclamen in the center of each one. The tables flanked a long runway where the mannequins would walk when they modeled Poiret's newest collection. The gazebo where they would change costume was screened with white cotton shades. The invitation specified that the guests should wear only white. The women, of course, wore their best white Poirets, in honor of him.

Adele wore a gold necklace set with enormous opals that would not have been out of place on Cleopatra. She waylaid me to tell me all of the details of Friedericke Beer's latest affair. Schiele brought his girlfriend, a beautiful coltish girl in a cheap cotton dress. Hoffmann carried an alabaster cane and went around to all of the tables and recentered the centerpieces. Alma came, but she could not wear white. Mahler had died three months before, and she was still in mourning. She stood out dramatically among the other, pale figures in her conservatively cut black crepe dress. I thought she must be fainting in the heat, and when I saw her sitting alone, fanning herself ineffectually with a napkin, I felt sorry for her. I sent Kokoschka over to her with a glass of ice water, so perhaps I should be blamed for all that happened afterward.

After I had greeted everyone I stood a little apart, watching to make sure everyone seemed happy and that no detail had been forgotten. I wore my own dress, a simple shape but embroidered in pale ecru with fanciful flowers and birds. Around my neck I had draped a magenta Wiener Werkstätte scarf. It was cheating, but I wanted people to be able to find me in the crowd.

Gustav appeared at my side, looking very tan in his pale suit. "Is our guest enjoying himself?" he asked.

"He's talking to Moll," I said. "What do you think?"

"I think he is being bored to death with the minute details of running a gallery," Gustav said. "Do you think Moll would try to get money from the poor man?"

"I think we should rescue him before there is an international incident," I said. I took Gustav to Poiret and introduced them. They spent the first few minutes politely praising each other's work. Then Gustav asked him how he liked Vienna.

He loved the charming people, he said. He loved the garden at the Prater, despite the bees. He loved the way the women walked, so different from Parisian women, more natural, less studied. He loved the kirsch he drank, and the pork-filled turnovers dusted with powdered sugar that he ate.

"Ah, Vienna!" said Gustav, as if that said it all.

"Your scarf," Poiret said. "I love your scarf." He pulled at one end until it came free. He held it in both hands and examined it as if it were an ancient artifact.

"Silk voile," he announced. "From Bianchini. But I never saw this color."

"It was dyed exclusively for the Wiener Werkstätte," I said.

"The embroidery is very well done," he said. "Will you let me keep it?"

"Why not?" I said. "I have many others."

"All the same color?" he asked. I told him that one style was acid green and the other was a melon color.

"I think I can incorporate something like this into my next collection. It's inspired by the Orient and is very silky and flowing, lots of movement and many thin layers. I think this will work very nicely."

"Does Emilie get a percentage of the profits?" Gustav asked. Poiret laughed. "No, but I promise I will send her my very best ensemble as a present."

When he had gone Gustav wiped his brow in mock relief. "I was afraid that if he stayed he would take all of your clothes and you would be left standing naked."

"Like a very bad dream."

"Or a very good one for someone else."

Elsewhere at the party, a momentous love affair was beginning. Alma and Kokoschka had not met before, since Alma had been in New York when Kokoschka had begun to work for the Wiener Werkstätte. When she returned she had nursed Mahler through his last illness, and though she was already having an affair with the architect Walter Gropius, she was by all accounts genuinely distraught. For weeks afterward she did not go out. In fact, this was her first public appearance since her husband's funeral. Alma and Kokoschka had not been properly introduced, but I forgot about that when I sent him over to her. In our circle things like that didn't matter quite as much anyway.

I don't know what he said to her; if I had considered it at all I would have said that he was too unpolished for her, too odd. He was certainly much too young. But when I glanced at them again I saw that they were engaged in a conversation of great intensity. Kokoschka had grabbed her hand in the midst of some earnest declamation, and she allowed him to keep it.

We were only talking about art, she said later. He didn't even try to kiss me until weeks later. But from that afternoon until he was called into the army they were never separated. He painted her in 1914, a painting called *The Tempest*. The background is a blue-black ocean and in the center, two lovers recline. The man is cadaverous, the woman suffused with white light. Their relationship was like a great dark storm that consumed them both and left them damaged afterward.

Twenty-Four

The next year Schiele was arrested and put on trial for obscenity. Gustav had known for some time that Schiele was drawing children, and, though he did not see the harm, had warned Schiele of how other people might interpret what he was doing. The trial was in Neulengbach, a half hour from Vienna by train. Gustav was terribly worried about him and went to the courthouse the day the verdict was read: his drawings would be burned. It was a terrible moment and seemed to presage what was to come.

War had been on the horizon for some time, but I had been trying not to think about it. I was of two minds about it all. On the one hand, what use are lovely gowns or fashion photographs or even paintings in times like these? But on the other hand, in ugly times the world needs beauty more than ever. Eventually Gustav and I decided that we must carry on with our work, though the assassinations in Sarajevo horrified us, the death of the emperor saddened us, news of the war depressed us. What else could we do? I could train as a nurse, or join a relief committee, neither of which held much appeal for me. Gustav was too old to be a soldier, even if he had wanted to be, and not glib enough to be a statesman. He did not want to write articles for the newspapers, or give speeches. He only wanted to paint.

It was difficult for me to continue making clothes of the quality I had before, as the ports were blocked, and goods were impossible to get or insanely expensive. We made do without French fabric,

French patterns, French magazines. I tried to compensate with even more stringent standards of workmanship, though the silk was cheap and flawed. My customers were appreciative and loyal.

Life was not easy during those years, certainly. Things were rationed: flour, meat, fuel. But you could still get them if you knew the right people and had enough money, and I did. Most of the time I tried to pretend that nothing had changed. Gustav and I still went to Attersee in the summers, and he was painting furiously, turning out canvases faster than he ever had before.

Then, in the fall of 1917, Pauline contracted pneumonia and died after several weeks of illness. I thought it was the worst thing that could happen to me, to lose my sister. My sister, who had tied my hair ribbons and lent me money and supported me all of my life with her solidity and practicality. For months I was in a sort of daze, until something much worse happened.

I was reading in the sitting room. Even in times of sorrow there was always an intense feeling of satisfaction in the back of my mind that the felt carpet beneath me was dense and soft, that the spindle-backed chair underneath me was lacquered ebony, that the tea tray in front of me was hammered silver and perfectly square. For years I would take a few moments in each busy day to admire my walls or my cabinets and door hinges. If it still existed I might do it yet.

I was looking through an old *Journal of Arts and Crafts*. I had remembered there had once been an article about Romanian folk dress, and after going through several boxes of back issues I had at last found it. The article was accompanied by several photographs and even more drawings. As ideas came to me for new designs I scribbled notes in the margins.

It was January 11, 1918. The bread ration had just been reduced and there would be food riots and massive worker strikes in the suburb of Wiener Neustadt in just a few days, but by then I wouldn't even read the papers, much less care what was in them.

It was bitter cold that day. Gustav had icicles in his beard as he walked to the studio and an awful headache, but the cold can give you a headache, especially if you are balding and have forgotten to wear your hat.

Johanna Staude was coming to sit for him. He made his usual preparations, stopping once to lie down in front of the fire. He couldn't seem to get warm. Later I found the bottle of aspirin on the floor, the pills scattered everywhere. He must have left it open on the sink, and the cats had batted it to the floor.

He was fifty-six, not old at all. Still very strong. No arthritis in his hands, still rowing across the lake, still painting through the night, still juggling countless lovers. There were six canvases in his studio in various stages of completion: *The Bride, Amalie Zuckerkandl, Portrait of a Lady, Portrait of a Lady in White, Full-face Portrait of a Lady,* and *Johanna Staude.*

Johanna had severe bone structure, a square face. Gustav put a feather boa around her neck for softness. Then he threw some extra kindling on the stove. They told me later he wouldn't have felt very bad, just a little nauseated. He didn't even mention it to Johanna. While he was mixing his paints Johanna dragged the boa along the floor for the cat, which stalked and pounced tirelessly. She told Gustav that her son had just said his first word: sugar. Gustav, to tease her, told her it was not a good sign at all. He drew a pig with a curling tail on a piece of scrap paper to remind him to send her some little pink sugar pigs from Demel's.

She was light-eyed, warm, full of laughter. I always liked her; I was sorry she had to be there. It must have been horrifying for her. But for Gustav's sake I was glad that she was there, and not some flighty young girl who might faint or run from the studio in a panic. I think about it all of the time, even now; what could have been done differently, how it could have been stopped. But it happened.

Finally Gustav was ready and Johanna draped the feathers over her shoulder again and only her hands moved, fiddling with the boa's ends.

"Stop that," Gustav said reprovingly. "You drop your chin when you do that." Gustav was hard at work on the highlights of her face. They were a lurid orange and blue. The background was still completely unworked, stark white, like an unmade bed.

Then he felt a sudden vertigo. A rush, as if the air were being sucked from the room. Then a sharp pain. It was everywhere, all over. His body hitting the floor sounded like a sack being loaded onto a freight car.

Everything happened very slowly. He was conscious at first. On the ground but still dizzy. The air was filled with paint. Johanna kneeled beside Gustav and touched his face. Her hands were cool; her voice was deep and soothing. She said something to him, but he couldn't understand the words. The cat brushed his back against Gustav's calves. Like a sick horse he tried to stand, Johanna said, but he only managed to lift his head a few inches. Then he said one thing.

"Send for Emilie."

Johanna ran from the room and found our friend Naumann, with the recalcitrant dog. He went for the doctor.

I was in the sitting room reading when the telegram came. I didn't even take a coat. I ran down the stairs and out into the street. Once inside the cab I realized that I was still holding the *Journal of Arts and Crafts* in my hand. I opened the window and threw it out into the ruts of ice the wheels of the cars made.

When I got to the studio the doctor was there. He had a white beard and a black medical bag. He asked me if I was Gustav's wife. I said I was. He said that Gustav had had a stroke. He looked sorry when he told me there was nothing he could do. He might recover on his own; sometimes if the damage was not too severe the brain could heal itself. The only thing to do was to take him home and wait.

He lay on the sofa with a blanket thrown over him. Johanna kneeled beside him, trying to spoon some water into his mouth. The water ran out of the right side of his mouth and onto the floor.

His left eye was completely open, the right a gruesome half-open, like a corpse. His face was lifeless, slack. His fingers were stiff and curled, like Adele's.

I took him to the salon. All I could think was that I wanted to be with him every minute, as long as I could. I put him in my own bed. I didn't consider the symbolism until much later. Day became night and then day again. The doctor came and performed his examinations. He left behind medicines, which I administered. I bathed him and changed the soiled linens and turned him so that he didn't develop bedsores. I spooned consommé and oatmeal and pureed vegetables into his mouth as if he were a baby. When I was too exhausted to go on, Helene relieved me and I collapsed into her bed. Visitors came, with their pots of amaryllis and their nervous, uncomfortable smiles. I wished they wouldn't bother.

Slowly, Gustav emerged from his stupor. After a few days he could sit but he still could not speak. His eyes rolled aimlessly around the room and his mouth was set in a grim snarl. I looked for the Gustav I had known and couldn't find him. Still, I knew that I would be grateful for any bit of him that remained, even if it was this pale husk of the man I had known.

A week passed, and then two. I thought that he was well enough to be given a sketch pad and a pencil. I thought it might cheer him. And the doctor said the mental stimulation might speed his recovery. I wrapped his fist tightly around the pencil and gave him what I hoped was an encouraging smile. On the first attempt he pressed the pencil too hard against the paper and it sprung from his hand and hit me in the chest. I put it back in his hand. The second time, trying to be more gentle, he let go of the pencil, and it rolled off of the bed and into the corner. I fetched it and brought it back to him. The third time he managed to hold onto it, and I left him alone to draw what he pleased.

When I returned a few minutes later with his dinner, he was still working. I set down my tray and looked over his shoulder. In twenty minutes he had drawn a circle the size of a pea. The next day he spent an hour on a wobbly triangle. The next day he worked the entire afternoon to create a V with lines that did not intersect.

The next day I found the broken pencil underneath the bed.

When Gustav discovered that he couldn't draw, all of the life went out of him. He stopped eating. I pleaded with him, I told him that with time he would be as he was before, that he was getting better, that he shouldn't give up, but I don't know how much he heard or understood. I told him I needed him to live, but perhaps that wasn't a good enough reason.

He died of pneumonia on February 6, 1918.

The last word he said was my name.

Twenty-Five

The nurses had shaved his beard in the last days and he looked nothing like himself. Schiele drew a death portrait of him, but I could not bring myself to look at it, then or ever. Sometimes it is reproduced in books and I always quickly turn the page. The papers were full of the peace negotiations with Ukraine and Russia, and the speculation that the war might soon be over. There was only the smallest notice of Gustav's death. Some city officials offered to have a special burial, erect a monument, have a ceremony. I said no. After what had happened with the University Hall paintings, after he had been turned down countless times for a professorship, after he had been excoriated in the press, to receive acceptance posthumously—it was galling. Schiele thought that his studio should be kept as it was, turned into a museum for future generations. I thought the idea was a good one, but Gustav didn't leave much money when he died, and his sisters, who had always depended on him for support, needed the money that the things in the studio would bring.

As executor, it was left to me to go through everything. One day in the studio I happened to see a sketch on his worktable. It was a sketch of *The Kiss*, in a pile of things he'd done the year before he died. I didn't know why he would make a sketch of a painting long finished, but then I was arrested by the letters running up the side of the drawing: EMILIE.

Why had we never spoken about the painting? Now it was too

late, and I was left with this drawing and so many unanswered questions. I put my head down on the table and wept.

When Gustav died I was only forty-four, but it seemed as if the best of life was past. I was not the only one who thought so. When Gustav died, and then Schiele, and Moser, and the war ended with the dismantling of the empire, everyone felt that the light had gone out of our lives. There were still parties, so there were still dresses to be made, but fewer and fewer of my customers bought the Reform dresses anymore. The daughters of my original clients thought my prints were quaint and my embroidered coats extravagant and outrageous. They asked me for ordinary things, things anyone could make. With no one to design for I felt that I was only a dressmaker, not a designer any longer.

Berta still had parties, and so did Adele, and artists still flocked to them, but the art world had passed us by, gone to the Bauhaus, and we all knew it. Alma married the architect Walter Gropius and moved to Berlin. Kokoschka had gone to Dresden. With each departure there were fewer of us to carry on.

Without Pauline, without Gustav, Helene and I clung to one another, and depended more and more on my niece Helene. We still went to the Opera and to the theater, but more often we stayed at home. Helene played the piano and sang, or we played cards. We often invited Hoffmann or Alfred Roller over to fill out our table, and I enjoyed their companionship, their friendship, but that was all.

There could be no one else. I knew some people thought that was silly, that I was making a martyr of myself, but Helene understood. Alma could have a torturous, tangled love life, married to Mahler while having affairs with Gropius and Kokoschka, married to Gropius while bearing children by Franz Werfel, but that life was not for me.

It was almost imperceptible at first, the way my customers drifted away. One immigrated to England, another to America. In 1920 my mother died in her sleep. In 1925, when she was still quite young, Adele died of meningitis. Another died of cancer. Some switched their loyalties to new houses, new designers. I let some of the seamstresses go.

In 1936 my sister Helene died. It was a terrible blow. We had been constant companions for more than sixty years, business partners, friends. I wasn't sure I could survive without her, and sometimes I still have my doubts.

By then the political situation had become very bad for the Jews of Vienna. New restrictions were announced every day: those on the university faculty were fired, then the students were expelled. Men lost their businesses. I had never been interested in politics, only in art, and though I was appalled I am ashamed to say I paid little attention. I had no idea where it would lead.

As things got worse more and more people left, sometimes with the police on their heels: Alma left early in 1938, bound for France; Ferdinand Bloch-Bauer escaped to Zurich but had to leave everything behind, including the portraits of Adele.

When the Germans came into Vienna, those of my customers who hadn't already fled were sent away. We were told they were being relocated, and I watched as their houses and paintings and furniture were confiscated. I wept to see them go, but I fully expected that when the political situation changed, they would return. Now I am not so sure.

The salon, too, was doomed. Cut off from our suppliers in France, our clientele dwindling, even a sentimental person could see there was no saving it.

It was November when we dismantled the salon, a nasty time of year. The wind blew needles of sleet into your face when you went out. Upon returning, you shook a lake of half-frozen water out of your coat onto the floor. It kept Helene busy wiping the stairs with a cloth so no one would slip. The trees melted and dripped and refroze like candlesticks. The summer flowers lay collapsed in stiff brown heaps like fallen soldiers.

We had been preparing for months, letting one seamstress go

and then another, until only Herta was left. Then there came the day when I saw the last customer and she placed the last order. I've forgotten, probably on purpose, just who it was. I remember what she ordered, though: a suit, something practical and dreary in dark blue wool. It seemed fitting.

The very last day the salon was open to the public I watched from my window as a group of soldiers supervised three old women as they scrubbed the street. The women wore woolen scarves on their heads. A crowd was watching. Two of the women were crying, but one was not. Her mouth was clamped shut like a change purse; she did not seem afraid. Finally the women were allowed to go. The crowd dispersed, the women stumbled to gather their belongings, which were strewn along the street.

We sold what we could: sewing machines and bolts of fabric and light fixtures. We had a fire sale and it was humiliating to watch shabby businessmen picking disdainfully over the things Gustav had so carefully designed and Josef Hoffmann had so carefully executed. Some of them didn't even know who Hoffmann or Klimt was.

Then came the men with their trucks to haul the refuse away: the naked dressmaker's dummies, good only for kindling, and broken tables and chairs.

Helene sorted through the papers. There were still bills to be collected and paid, tax forms to submit, balance sheets to be completed. It would take several months to see it through, even though we would no longer be open for business.

After the trash men had gone with the load of large things Herta went through the piles of what was left. One heap of things was to be discarded, the other to be kept. The discard pile was three times the size of the other. There were treadles and spindles; unsold hats and scarves and skirts; spools of lilac and umber and turquoise thread; packages of needles; trimmings of all kinds: fur, embroidery, lace, ribbons. There were tiny onyx beads like apple seeds, opalescent sequins, dyed-pink ostrich feathers, intricately carved wooden combs.

Then it was over. Everything was sold, the papers filed away, the money in the bank. We were left in the ugly cramped apartment. We volunteered to sew uniforms. At least it kept us busy.

I lived simply with Helene in a small fourth-floor walk-up apartment on the Mariahilferstrasse and tried not to think about the past. Until Carl Moll came to visit.

Twenty-Six

C arl had just been appointed Minister of Culture, a very important position. I had read about it in the papers. I never expected to see him again; it had been years. But there he was, in the vestibule of our shabby apartment.

It was a hideous place. The walls, a humorless gray, were peeling. The floors were uneven and the windows filthy. With the Wiener Werkstätte furniture we couldn't bear to part with all jumbled together, it was embarrassingly cramped. There were tables stacked under the piano and books piled on the vitrine. Instead of being plucky and tying cords around ourselves and hanging out of the window with a bucket and a rag, or being enterprising and hanging tapestries over the walls to cover up the water stains and throwing rugs over the floors to cover up the knots, we cried for a while for our lost salon, our gray felt carpets and silk wall coverings, and then we gave up altogether the idea of living in beauty as we once had.

To make matters worse, all I had in the house was a teaspoon of coffee and some digestive biscuits that were still in the cabinet only because neither of us liked them. Helene, in a whispered conference in the doorway, said she would make scones if I could keep him talking for a few minutes. Keeping Moll talking had never been difficult.

His once blond hair was nearly white now, but he still filled the room with his size and his expansive personality. He threw open his arms as he talked as if to embrace me.

"Emilie," he said. "It's been too long. Old friends such as we are should not let so many years pass."

I wondered why he had come. I had only seen him a few times in the last twenty years, the last several years before when I went to his gallery to see the paintings of a young artist I liked.

"We have a sandwich in a café nearly every night," I said by way of an apology when Helene brought the weak coffee, no cream, no sugar. "Two old ladies with no one to look after tend to get lazy about cooking."

"Nonsense. Your hospitality is always excellent." He took a letter from his pocket. "I have something to read to you. From Alma."

Alma had fled Austria to California with her third husband, a playwright who was writing screenplays now in Hollywood. Carl and I were both a bit fuzzy about what a screenplay involved, but it was clear Franz was quite successful.

"She asks about you," he said, skimming the lines. "Here it is, she asks if you have been able to keep your business going, and whether you and your dresses are as beautiful as they once were."

"She must be terribly homesick," I said, "to write such nice things about me."

"Now, now," Moll laughed gently. "Alma adores you."

"What does she say about California?" I said to Moll, wondering why she was writing to her stepfather. There was little love lost between them, especially now. Still, I hoped he would read more of the letter. He flipped through the pages. "The light here is extraordinary, it seems to come from everywhere at once, what a joy for a painter! Unfortunately I am not one, and neither is Franz, but we think often of our artist friends and how much they would enjoy it. We live in a yellow stucco bungalow that reminds me a little of some of the cottages in the suburbs, but of course none of the cottages had a swimming pool and a dozen orange and avocado trees."

"Alma always was one to gloat," I said. It was strange, how much I wanted to talk about Alma when once I would have been perfectly happy if she had fallen into some mountain crevasse and disappeared forever. But Moll put the letter away.

"Alma knows she will never return to Austria," he said. "She is thinking of the future. She's always been less of a romantic than you."

"Why are you here, Carl?"

"To ask you to join in building the new Vienna. A Vienna that will be the most prosperous and beautiful of the capitals of Europe." I laughed bitterly, the only way I seem to laugh now.

"I liked the old Vienna. I had a fashion salon."

"You built your success on false foundations. It was no wonder it couldn't survive. I'm asking you to begin again. Properly, this time. The government is willing to underwrite you."

I tried to understand what he was saying. "Be the official couturier of the new government?" It sounded absurd. "But how can my clothing be used as propaganda?" He looked irritated for the first time.

"This word, propaganda. It sounds like you've been listening to British radio. All I'm asking is for you to reopen. Under our auspices."

"Who would my new clients be? All my old ones are dead or in exile."

"No one is dead, Emilie," said Moll soothingly. "Your fickle clients have all abandoned you for Horst Gernbach, that's all." He patted my hand sympathetically. "We'll help you. You can dress the wives of everyone in government."

It was a horrifying thought. I had seen some of these men in government. Everything about them was ugly, from their eyes to the set of their lips to the way they walked. Their uniforms were drab, their insignia stark. I did not want to imagine what their wives might look like. To shut Carl up I said I would think about it. But he was not finished. There was one more thing. He was taking some of the paintings in my possession for Hitler to view. Not my paintings. The "paintings in my possession." As if I were merely looking after them while their real owner was away. Moll was mounting a large exhibition of Germanic arts, and the Führer apparently had long been interested in Gustav's work.

"The Führer is a great patron of the arts," Moll said. "You know that he once thought he would be an artist himself. Fortunately for us, he took a different path, but his artistic sensibility is still strong."

"Gustav's art isn't political," I said. "You of all people should know that."

"All art is political. You of all people should know that."

"Gustav's work belongs with me."

"Aren't you being a little selfish, Emilie? Of course I understand why, understand perfectly. . . ." He paused as Helene came in with the scones. She hadn't sifted the flour and there was just the tiniest bit of jam in the bottom of the jar, but Moll didn't seem to notice these inadequacies. He put four scones on his plate and dug out all the jam he could with his coffee spoon.

"But people deserve to see Gustav's work."

"What about the museums? Borrow from them."

He leaned forward in his chair and his curatorial greed began to show. "But to have privately owned, little-seen works! How much more significant, how much more interesting."

Though Moll knew he didn't have to ask my permission to take the paintings, and he knew that I knew, he was still trying to persuade me. Hadn't we sat in cafés and dreamed up the Secession together?

"Gustav would want you to give them to me for the exhibition, Emilie," Moll said. "It's important for his artistic reputation that the paintings be seen in this show. You don't want him to be forgotten."

"Gustav will not be forgotten," I said. "I will never allow it to happen."

"It's not up to you," he said. "If I want to I can seize all of his work and have it destroyed."

There it was. We sat silently and he watched my face as this information sank in. "If I remember Gustav correctly, and not through a haze of sentiment, he was an artist and he wanted his work to be seen. He didn't care where, or why."

Moll was powerful. I was no one. I had not known until that moment how precarious my position was. Anyone who had something they wanted was in danger. I just hadn't counted on being someone who did.

Then, suddenly, I had a strong desire to laugh, and wished Gustav was there to share the joke. In his lifetime his work had been condemned as ugly and dangerous, and now it was to be celebrated as a great achievement of his nation.

At first I hadn't hung any artwork in the apartment. Somehow it seemed insulting to the work. I kept it all wrapped and stored in closets and some big paintings were leaning up against the walls in my bedroom. But then I had relented and hung one landscape painting opposite the bed, where I could look at it often. It was of a poppy field at Attersee and spoke to me of sunny afternoons and giddy walks in the country. I led Moll to it and watched him appraising it. I pulled everything out of the closet and sat on the bed while he unwrapped each item and wrote the titles down in a leather notebook. There were four more paintings of the countryside near Attersee. There was the portrait of my niece when she was a little girl. The pastel of me when I was twelve. The paintings called *Hope I* and *Hope II*. Cartoons for the Stoclet frieze. Cartoons for the University ceiling panels.

"Someone will be by tomorrow to pick them up," he said when he was finished.

"Will I ever see any of it again?" I asked.

"You can come to the show," he said.

"Then what?"

"We'll see."

I discussed this with Helene. We tried to think of anyone we still knew in the government to whom we could appeal. But everyone had left.

"What has happened to Moll?" Helene wondered. "When he first opened the gallery he tried to show controversial work and he hardly charged anything so that everyone could see it."

"Everyone will be able to see this show," I said. "It's just that the meaning of everyone has changed."

The soldiers came as Moll promised, and took everything away. How could I have let them? They had guns, but they wouldn't have killed me. I let them do it. Some great curator, defender. For a week I stared out of the window. Then one day I saw a military truck pull up and Moll got out.

"He's changed his mind about the exhibition," he said from the doorway, as soldiers brought the paintings back into the apartment. They carried them carelessly, knocking things over, and dropped them to the floor like sacks of grain. "Or, not the exhibition, but he no longer wants to include Klimt's work." He made it sound as if Gustav were someone from an art history text, like Dürer or David, someone dead a long time, not someone he had known.

I stared at him. "We . . . ah . . . collected some Klimts from some other people," he said. "There were a lot of portraits. He of course wanted to know who the people in the portraits were."

Then I understood. Amalie Zuckerkandl. Margaret Stonborough-Wittgenstein. Serena Lederer, Adele Bloch-Bauer, Hermine Gallia.

"Even though your paintings weren't . . . controversial, he didn't want them. For a moment I thought he was going to order me to burn them all."

"What happened to the other paintings?"

"Don't worry about them, worry about yourself. You're now being investigated. All of your financial papers from the salon are liable to be seized."

"For what? What are the charges?"

"You could be arrested at any time. It doesn't matter what I say. If you have you taken any steps toward emigration I would push them forward." He was trying to be kind. But I was not grateful.

"Vienna is my home."

"Not if you want to stay out of jail."

The only question was where to go. Helene wanted Paris, but to live abroad as an exile, to never see Austria again, to leave Gustav behind, it was unthinkable to me. Then I thought of Attersee. The area is rural and sparsely populated. But was it far enough away? We wrote some letters to our neighbors and they let us know that the town was quiet.

And so we came. There is firewood stacked shoulder high in the shed, and down comforters by the dozen in the closets. We have a well and tinned food and a very generous neighbor. We could bunker here forever.

When I was in Vienna in my dim and ugly apartment, I used to stare at the painting of the poppy field, memorizing each crimson daub, remembering how happy I had been when Gustav painted it. Sometimes I would nearly cry of homesickness for him and for Attersee. Ironically, now that I am here, so close that I can walk not fifteen minutes and stand in the spot where Gustav stood, those times are further away than ever. The field is wet and beaten down. It is not the time of year for poppies.

Twenty-Seven

Kammer am Attersee
April 6, 1945

Yesterday the Russians captured Baden.

I heard the planes in the night, buzzing like malignant insects. I wrapped my quilt around me and went to the window. It was a clear night and the moon lit them. Intermittently they would appear, very low, so low I could make out the Cyrillic letters on the sides. Of course I couldn't read them. I went down the hall to wake Helene. She was lying on her back with her eyes wide open.

"Let's go to the potato cellar," I said, pulling at her arm. She said that if they meant to bomb us no potato cellar would do any good, and if they didn't, we might as well stay in bed and be warm. Still, she allowed me to drag her from the bed, trailing her blanket across the floor like a bride.

The planes were deafening when right overhead, but they were not meant for us. They were flying east. In a few minutes they were gone, and we returned to our beds and what was left of a sleepless night.

In the morning we turned on the radio, but could get no reception, so we read on the terrace, or pretended to, waiting. It was chilly in the shade and we were both wrapped in afghans, cocoon-like.

One of Heitzmann's boys has been bringing our letters from town, the youngest, Peter is his name I think, a gangly freckled child of eight or nine, always with some straw or leaf in his hair and crumbs at the corners of his mouth. Ordinarily the boy would stand quietly on the steps until we looked up before he announced himself, but this time we heard his shouting before he appeared from between the trees. He was running in his coltish way and his hands were pumping at his sides, empty. He shouted, almost triumphantly, that Vienna was on fire.

He's never been there, of course. He's not seeing familiar faces, familiar streets. He's thinking of the planes, and the explosions, and maybe the chance of seeing a Russian soldier. Maybe one parachuting out of a crashing plane. He and his brothers play at battle in and around the barns, and don't understand why their mother punishes them when she finds them at it.

He'd heard about the bombing on his shortwave radio, from a station in Switzerland. There are whole neighborhoods in flames, but he couldn't remember which ones, no matter how eagerly we prodded him, afghans flung aside, veiny hands grasping for his collar. He backed away from us, a little frightened. The eastern ones, maybe, he said, trying to appease us, or the ones to the south. The opera house, though, he knew was rubble. At that Helene fell back into her chair. And the Danube. The Danube is burning, he said.

I imagined a glowing skin of airplane fuel over the water. It must be beautiful, this liquid fire. I wished I were there to see it.

Helene gave the boy his usual wage, though she forgot to give him his gingerbread cookie, made with the last of our sugar. When he had gone we went inside and huddled by our own radio, but the station from Vienna had been knocked out, apparently, and no one else seemed to know any more than we did. We left it on anyway, and waited. It sounded bad for us, the opera house was so close to our apartment, not more than half a mile. We talked about Herta and the apartment and I thought about the paintings. I wondered about the art museum—was it awash in flames, were the frescoes Gustav had painted early in his career turned to ash? I thought that Gustav's studio would be all right, it was so far out of the way, but what about Casa Piccola, so close to the city center? Though the salon was long-gone I couldn't bear to see the building destroyed. But then I felt that I couldn't stand to see any part of Vienna damaged, and my feelings wouldn't make one bit of difference. The bombs would fall anyway.

It is several days before a letter comes. There is a long story to tell about how it managed to find us, with the postal system suspended and the city in chaos, but I stand there next to the vegetable garden while Heitzmann's boy tells me about the man who walked and rode a horse and was almost run over by a battalion of soldiers going in the other direction and all I can think about is what information the envelope might contain.

The paper inside the envelope is warped by rain and the ink has run. Herta's handwriting is shaky even at the best of times, but I can make out what I need to know.

The apartment is gone. The building was hit directly by a bomb, she says. The bombing was fierce and the firefighting crews were not able to enter the area in time to keep it from burning to the ground. She went there the morning after, when the rubble was still hot, and burned her hands looking for things of ours, but all she managed to find was some flatware and the shards of one of our lamps. She does not mention the paintings.

So the worst has come to pass. There is a certain relief in it. There is no sense in worrying anymore; I can focus on realities instead of contingencies. I can realign myself to exist in a world without certain works of art. I try to imagine tiny Herta picking through smoking rubble trying to rescue our spoons. I don't want the boy, still waiting patiently for his coins, to see me sobbing like a child. I hand the paper to Helene without speaking. I can't say the words out loud.

"It's a miracle she wasn't killed," says Helene, finally. Her voice has a catch in it but she pulls herself up and reads me the part that describes the fate of our neighbors. Professor Weigel and his wife, next door, were killed. Frau Schatz escaped by jumping from a fourth-floor window and has a broken pelvis and leg.

The Casa Piccola was not hit. The Great Hall of the University is completely destroyed, and the back half of the Secession building is blown off. The dome is still there, though.

"The great head of cabbage!" says Helene. Now she is crying. I reach into my pocket and hand the boy the first thing I pull out, a ten-shilling note. He runs, thinking I'm going to realize my mistake and call him back. They are just names to him.

The Great Hall. Where *Medicine* and *Philosophy* and *Jurisprudence* were to hang.

"What else?" I say to Helene.

"Carl Moll came to the apartment two weeks ago and removed all of the paintings to an underground storage facility."

We walk back to the house and sit on the porch, where we can look at the lake and not talk. In the western corner, up in the eaves, a pair of sparrows are building a nest. They travel fearlessly from the birch trees to the house and back again, paying no attention to us at all.

I look in the other direction, toward Vienna. Of course all you can see from my vantage point is mountains and atmospheric haze. It is a jarringly warm day for April. The air smells of hay, and the idea of a war raging a hundred miles away seems absurd. There are sheep walking in the road.

Maybe Herta's reports are not true. Maybe she got them secondhand. Haven't the police cordoned off large areas of the city and instituted a strict curfew? Maybe it's only a rumor about the Great Hall, and the opera house.

I pull the letter out of my pocket and read it again, but she does not say she heard that the opera house was destroyed, as I had hoped. She does not say that someone told her the Great Hall is rubble.

If I was there, I could protect it, I think, though I know that's absurd. It was cowardly to leave the city at the last moment, leaving it at its most vulnerable moment, just before the onslaught, and I'm not a coward. I would risk being shot or strafed or starved.

I could go back. I could row the little boat all the way back and tie up in a canal. I could catch a ride on an army truck carrying a bunch of farm boys to prisoner of war camps.

But I am a coward. I am not ready for the accounting, not yet, the tally of buildings lost and buildings saved, paintings burned and paintings not. In my mind Vienna is still whole, I can see it. When I am stronger I can go back and face the losses. When the war ends I will go back.

Until then I need rest.

I'm dreaming: I'm making a painting of Gustav. My canvas is life-size and unwieldy. It dwarfs the room. Once I lose my balance and fall into the canvas and knock it over.

I've drawn him in red conté crayon, in the middle of the canvas and full-face, like a child's line drawing. It could be the work of a mental patient. Yet the eyes are well done; they belong on a different drawing, the cross-hatchings somehow imbuing life. The eyes look down and left, into the picture instead of out toward the world. Beside Gustav I've drawn a caricature of him as a goat, his head supported by a round body consisting of two sacs. The background is covered with filthy words written in calligraphic script.

I don't remember writing those words, but there it is in front of me. Gustav must have done it, I think. It must be covered up. I begin painting over everything with bright, thick strokes of black and yellow. All the time I know that this is naïve, that artists build up their canvases layer by layer, starting with thin washes and working their way to the vivid colors, to the flecks of white and silver. You don't just swathe a blank canvas with bright paint. I'm going to ruin it. I'll have to start over. Still, the urge to hide what's underneath is too strong.

Gustav's figure is distorted, his hands too large, his forehead two-thirds of his face and exaggeratedly furrowed, his whole face wavering like the surface of water. He's wearing a sack suit covered with peacocks and his feet are tied with a woman's yellow hair. In the background are stars and spots and poppies and samurai warriors and, inexplicably, the face of the Virgin from a painting by Dante Gabriel Rossetti. I've painted another woman in as well, tiny and almost invisible in the carnival pattern. It is myself, of course. All this frenetic work is very tiring, and when the canvas is saturated and nothing of the under layer is showing, it's a great relief.

Then the man in the portrait turns his head and looks at me. "Let me out," he says. I find this unsurprising. I slash the hair binding his feet and cut him away from the background with a palette knife and he steps into the room dripping paint all over the floor. He sits down on the arm of the sofa and soaks it with paint, which begins to seep onto the tables and chairs and is soon climbing the walls like crimson and purple vines. Soon I can't see anything amid all the violent color except my own hands, but I can still hear Gustav's voice.

"Emilie," he says.

THE
PAINTED KISS

Elizabeth Hickey

A Readers Club Guide

About This Guide

The suggested questions are intended to help your reading group find new and interesting angles and topics for discussion of Elizabeth Hickey's *The Painted Kiss*. We hope that these ideas will enrich your conversation and increase your enjoyment of the book.

Many fine books from Washington Square Press feature Readers Club Guides. For a complete listing, or to read the guides online, visit www.BookClubReader.com.

Discussion Questions for *The Painted Kiss*

1. Discuss the experience of reading a novel that explores the lives of historical persons. In what way is it different from reading a wholly fictional story? What, if anything, did you know of the artist Gustav Klimt before reading this book? Did the story contradict or expand on anything you knew? Did the character you grew to know in this story surprise you?

2. This story is told during two different periods of time in Emilie Flöge's life: the late 1800s and the mid-1900s. Why do you think the author chose to tell it in this way? What kind of perspective do we gain from the older, wiser Emilie, who is portrayed against the backdrop of World War II? How might this novel have been different had it unfolded in a more linear fashion?

3. Emilie has been raised in a world where outward appearance means everything. Taught from an early age that women, especially, should be more concerned with how they present themselves than with how they feel or what they think, her relationship with Gustav is iconoclastic for her. Not only is he interested in her innermost thoughts and feelings, but he shows little interest in the world of polite society. Talk about what Gustav symbolizes for the young girl. In what ways does he challenge the reigning views of this particular time in history? How does his role as artist allow him to do so?

4. Gustav and Emilie share similar artistic temperaments. While Emilie's salon, even very early on, is a raging success, she struggles to maintain artistic integrity, despite the fact that her customers, more often than not, are less interested in art. As she points out, "That was the drawback of trying to make money. Sometimes you had to sacrifice taste altogether" (198). We see this over and over again with Gustav's art as well—artistic vision

often clashes with the bottom line. Discuss the way this concept is explored in this novel. Is there any solution for artists, a way for them to remain true to their ideals without starving? Talk about the ways this debate continues in today's world.

5. At one point, Gustav paints a picture of Emilie in a dress that she has made. Emilie is somewhat frightened by the outcome, asking, "Is this really what you see when you look at me?" Klimt's response is more about the nature of art than the particular painting, as he explains: "It would be easy to represent it as rational and orderly, like the School of Athens, but that would be dishonest. It's completely terrifying to make visible the chaos of human existence, to admit the darkness of the human mind, but once you've done it you can see there is light there" (170). What significance does this idea have in terms of the larger story? How do artists like Klimt show the dark side of life while also giving hope? Is there hope to be found in this story?

6. Late in the novel, Emilie explains how Gustav keeps their relationship private: "I am not a subject he [Gustav] ever discusses, not with Hoffman, not with his mother, not with anyone. I am in his life and he does not want to know why, or in what way" (179). Does this quotation illuminate the nature of their relationship? Why is it so important to Gustav that Emilie not be discussed by other women?

7. Along the same lines, why does Gustav feel the need to compartmentalize the women in his life? While he treats Emilie as a companion and a kindred spirit of sorts, one who (except for rare occasions) is not to be sullied by physical passion, he has seemingly little trouble bedding and carrying on with other women. As long as these two worlds do not meet, he seems somewhat satisfied. What might this say about his personality? Why does he place Emilie on a pedestal, while every other woman is fair game? Is it hypocritical, or does it betray the countercultural ideals that he espouses, that he wishes to keep Emilie pure?

8. What about Emilie's part in this relationship? Why, at the sake of her own happiness, does she spend her youth in a perpetual state of limbo with a man she knows will never marry her? Does Emilie have a self-destructive side, which allows her to fritter away her time (as some might describe it) with Gustav, or do you think she really believed that one day he would be hers? Is it possible that Emilie is drawn to Gustav precisely because she cannot have him? What do you think the author would say?

9. Adele, perhaps one of Gustav's most interesting mistresses and one of his most well-known subjects, is a difficult character to unpack, both for our protagonist and for the reader. Pampered though she is, she exudes melancholy to the point of being tragic. At one point, as she talks with Emilie about what kind of new dress she would like, she states, "I have no needs, only unfulfilled desires" (194). Discuss the nature of desire as it is presented by Adele in the novel. What distinction is there between a need and a desire, and why does Adele feel the need to call attention to it? In what ways might Adele be representative of women in her social class? Why is she so unhappy, so filled with ennui, despite the advantages that she has as a woman of wealth?

10. Ruminating on Gustav and his relationship to his work, Emilie thinks, "Some critics said that he didn't care about his sitters, he was only interested in the thickets of design he built up around them, but that was not true. The portrait said what was important to say about Adele. It said plenty about him, too; he was in love with her when he painted it, of that I feel sure" (207). Klimt is a somewhat elusive character in this story, as he is only presented through the eyes of Emilie. Her viewpoint is not only subjective in the way that all viewpoints are, but also because she's in love with the man and perhaps sees a side of him that others may not. To what extent should we trust our protagonist? Is her view a wholly reliable one? Do you agree with her assessment of Klimt, or do you think that she might be blinded by her feelings?

11. Late in the novel, as Emilie observes some paintings of Adele, famous paintings that she has been "charged with protecting," she fantasizes about destroying them. What makes her want to do damage to Klimt's work, and why does she ultimately refrain? How does this moment represent the complicated relationship between Emilie and Gustav?

12. To the Gustav Klimt of this novel, *The Kiss* seems to be one of his crowning achievements. Although he begs Emilie to model for the painting, he feels compelled to change her figure later on, so that it looks less like Emilie and "more universal." In your opinion, is it Klimt the artist, or Klimt the man who decides to change the painting in such a way? Although he wants this painting to "make some declaration" about himself and Emilie, in the end he can't quite bring himself to do it. Why is this?

13. Why do you think *The Kiss*, an allegorical painting about love, is so meaningful for Gustav? What is love to a man like Klimt, a man who refused to support any of the illegitimate children he fathered, yet who genuinely seemed to care for the people in his life?

A Discussion with Elizabeth Hickey

Q: Can you share with us some of the details about your journey to becoming a published author?

A: I was born and raised in Louisville, Kentucky. My father is a retired lawyer, my mother a Presbyterian minister. I always knew that I wanted to be a writer, and I used to give my mother stories I had written as Christmas presents, but during childhood and adolescence I was more interested in becoming an Olympic swimmer. Unfortunately, I was stymied by a lack of athletic talent. In high school my art teacher had us paint copies of famous paintings. I attempted to replicate a painting by Vuillard that I found in the Armand Hammer exhibition catalog, and I wrote an essay about the artist's life. That was my first real introduction to art.

I went to Williams College in Williamstown, Massachusetts, where I majored in art history. I knew before I got there that the class I most wanted to take was a writing workshop with Jim Shepard, but I was very intimidated. I applied as a freshman and didn't get in (few freshmen did) and then waited until I was a senior to reapply. Jim turned out to be an amazing teacher and mentor, and once I became serious about writing there was no going back.

After graduation I went back to Louisville and worked at a publishing company and an independent bookstore while I prepared my graduate school applications. I was rejected by many writing programs and was wait-listed at both Indiana University and Columbia. I was considering moving to England and other radical life changes when I got the call from Columbia in August 1995. I was, I swear, the last person they took off of the waiting list. I had about two weeks to pack myself up and get to New York. While at Columbia I was able to regularly visit the Metropolitan Museum of Art, the Frick Collection, the Museum of Modern Art—all of the great museums in New York.

I received my degree from Columbia in 1999 and moved to Portland, Oregon, where I worked as a secretary at a law firm. After a year, I quit and lived off of my savings while I worked on *The Painted Kiss*.

Q: What research did you do for *The Painted Kiss*?

A: Early in the writing of *The Painted Kiss* I spent many hours doing research in Avery Library at Columbia. I read books on Klimt, on Schiele and Kokoschka, the Secession, the Wiener Werkstätte, anything pertaining to the period. I took a lot of notes and wrote a lot of pages, many of which did not stay in the book but which helped me work out what story I wanted to tell. In 1998, my husband and I traveled to Austria and Central Europe so I could continue my work on *The Painted Kiss*. This research was less formal and involved visiting the sites where Klimt and Emilie lived and worked. I was surprised, for instance, when visiting Klimt's last studio in Hietzing, to discover that it was not a dull gray stucco building, as it had appeared in the black and white photographs I had seen, but was in fact a bright, buttery yellow. That is the kind of detail that library research cannot provide! I visited the Secession building, where the *Beethoven Frieze* is located, and the Belvedere museum, home to many of Klimt's paintings. Interestingly, there was a show on Carl Moll's landscapes there when I visited, which mentioned that he had committed suicide when the Russians arrived in Vienna, but neglected to mention his collaboration with the Nazis. I drove around Lake Attersee to see what the countryside there was like. And I tried to absorb as much of the feeling of Austria as I possibly could with my limited German.

Q: Tell us about the book's main character, Emilie Flöge.

A: Emilie Flöge was a young middle-class Viennese girl when she met the painter Gustav Klimt and was drawn into his world of artist's models and rich patrons, sex, and freedom. Emilie became Klimt's pupil, his friend, his lover, and his companion. Along the way she struggled to find a place and creative outlet for herself. Eventually she opened a fashion salon and became nearly as successful in that world as he was in his.

Q: What made you want to write this book?

A: I have always been fascinated with art. I would have liked, perhaps, to have been an artist myself. I've taken drawing and painting classes, but I just don't have the skill. In college I tried to write papers that combined my interest in art and in literature, but that was a miserable failure, as my GPA attests. In 1993, when I was working in the sales department of a publishing house, I received a card from a sales rep that had a picture of Klimt's painting *Hope I* on it, but slightly altered. The caption read: "Mrs. Klimt Sews a Patchwork Quilt." It made me wonder about Mrs. Klimt. My next job was at a bookstore and I was able to borrow a biography of Klimt. I learned there was no Mrs. Klimt, but there was an Emilie Flöge. The idea for the book then germinated for four years, until I was in my second year at Columbia. I was floundering for a subject and a style. My short stories were not working and my teachers were questioning my ability. I was beginning to question my ability. I began writing impressionistic pages on Emilie for joy and respite, and I realized they were better than anything else I was doing. I then worked on *The Painted Kiss* off and on for the next seven years.

Q: One of Klimt's paintings is the subject of a Supreme Court case. Does this tie in with the book in any way?

A: The issue of repatriation of art taken by the Nazis is very much at the fore-front in the international art world these days. Marie Altmann, a niece of Adele Bloch-Bauer—one of Kilmt's models who appears as a character in the book—went to the Supreme Court recently to try to get Klimt's por-trait of Adele back from the Austrian government. I touch on the subject of Nazi looting near the end of the book, when many of Emilie's clients are stripped of their assets or forced to flee and leave everything behind, and when Emilie herself has her collection of Klimt artwork forcibly removed from her possession.

Q: What is it about Gustav Klimt's art that has given it such timeless appeal?

A: I'm not sure any art is timeless. I think different styles go in and out of fashion, and right now seems to be a Klimt moment. Maybe the paintings' sexual charge appeals to our highly sexualized culture. At the same time they are suffused with a kind of existential doubt and a paradoxical hope that maybe we can understand. More generally, I think as human beings we are fascinated by portraiture. That may be why portraiture is making such a comeback in contemporary art. Abstraction was the thing for so long, but regular people were alienated by that. We like to look at other people. I think also the modern world has done a grave disservice to our everyday environment, and most of us are faced daily with a lot of ugliness. Klimt's paintings are an antidote to that. They are like jewels—beautifully colored and patterned.

Author's Note

The act of writing historical fiction is inherently a compromise. The *literal* truth, as opposed to the *artistic* truth, of characters' lives rarely (if ever) allows for the successful plotting of a novel. In attempting to solve this dilemma, instead of altering the facts to fit a dramatic narrative, or dramatically changing my narrative to fit the facts, I chose to focus *The Painted Kiss* on the aspects of a life that are omitted from the historical record or which pass into obscurity with the death of the subject and her contemporaries. How Emilie Flöge met Gustav Klimt, what they talked of while they boated on Lake Attersee, what she thought and felt about him, what he thought and felt about her—these are things that history cannot tell us, though the frustration of not knowing is compensated by the opportunity to imagine.

In trying to hew as closely as possible to the facts of Emilie Flöge's life, I have relied on Susanna Partsch's *Klimt, Life and Work* (Munich 1993), Wolfgang Georg Fischer's *Gustav Klimt and Emilie Flöge* (Vienna 1987), Angelica Bäumer's *Gustav Klimt: Women* (trans. Ewald Osers, London 1986), and *Klimt* by Frank Whitford (London 1990). Because Emilie Flöge was not a famous artist or political figure, her mention in the historical record is a bare outline that begins and ends with her salon and with varying interpretations of her connection to Klimt.

Occasionally I have intentionally diverged from what I know to be the literal truth. People and events were omitted from the novel for purposes of simplification (for instance, Emilie had a brother who does not appear in the story), or dates were changed for dramatic effect. In the novel Klimt makes the pastel drawing of Emilie when she is twelve, but the real drawing I am referring to was done when she was seventeen, and there is no evidence that he drew either of her sisters. Klimt would have sketched the pregnant model Herta for the painting that became *Hope I* within a year or two of its 1902 completion date, but I have him drawing her in 1890. The character of Gerta who appears briefly at the beginning of the novel could be any number of women who were in and out of Klimt's studio during those years, but all of the other women in the italicized passages did exist, and more or less in the situations in which I chose to show them.

Many historical figures appear in the novel—Carl Moll, Adele Bloch-Bauer, Alma Schindler. I cannot claim to have captured their essences accurately. Carl Moll did in fact become Minister of Culture under the Nazis, but the episode in which he appropriates Emilie's art collection is entirely fictional. The portrayals of Alma and Adele are necessarily colored by the views of a biased narrator, and in the interest of telling a good story. Alma reported in her memoirs that Klimt broke her heart. Adele wrote no such book, and the nature of their relationship is pure speculation on my part. The aim of historical fiction is not to render the past exactly as it happened—an impossible task—but to imagine it as it might have been.